EUROPA

GREIG BECK

SEVEREDPRESS

EUROPA

WWW.SEVEREDPRESS.COM

ISBN: 978-1-923165-51-9

We thought we were going there to look for life.
But the life there was actually looking for us."
Greg Morgan, NASA.

Europa is a Galilean moon orbiting Jupiter. It has an atmosphere, thin, but composed primarily of oxygen. At a bitter -220°F to -260°F degrees, the moon's surface is inimical to human life. But below that icy shell is a relatively warm, salty ocean that has about twice as much water as all of Earth's oceans combined.

Europa could conceivably harbor extraterrestrial entities, and this has led to a call for missions to explore these vast oceans for life that could be as small as a single floating diatom, or as large as a pod of blue whales.

It wasn't until 2020 that the first remote piloted craft landed on Europa and an underwater drone was launched into the moon's icy depths. The returned images were unbelievable, disturbing, and were never released to the public lest they cause confusion. Or panic.

However, what it did do was raise the temperature on the burning question: is there *other* life in our solar system? And within five years, NASA launched The Traveler Mission.
Afterward, nothing was ever the same again.

PROLOGUE

Today – Perry's Mountain, Maplesville, Alabama
NASA lead scientist, Greg Morgan, and three of his mission astrophysicists were in the first helicopter as it sped across the night landscape just outside of Maplesville, Alabama. All were mired in their own uneasy thoughts.

The last Europa mission communication before going transmission dark had been confusing, and frankly, frightening – the crew had sounded scared to death – in fact, out of their minds with fear. Just remembering that audio made Greg feel sick in his stomach.

Greg had a personal stake in the mission – his brother Brad was on it. He was the captain. And now, somehow, someone had made it home – made it home, but not in an American pod.

"Coming up on crash site, now," the pilot intoned.

The group turned to look out of their small porthole windows. In amongst the pitch black of the heavily wooded forest the glow from the burning embers was like a fifty-foot wide landing strip to hell. At its end was a cup-shaped depression and the blackened soil was piled up around it like an old rug. In its center sat an escape pod.

The pilot slowed, switched on the huge undercarriage lights, and they illuminated the entire hill side.

"*There! There!*" Andrea almost shouted.

Greg stared down at the scar in the landscape and saw what had excited his colleague – slumped with his back to the pod was a lone figure in a spacesuit.

"Unbelievable," he whispered without turning. "Can we set down here?"

"No, not here," the pilot replied and began to circle the site. "Maybe further up."

"Please hurry." Greg sat back staring at nothing as his mind whirled. The first manned mission to Europa, the smallest of the four Galilean moons orbiting Jupiter, had ended in all communications being cut after a seriously frightening last transmission. There was a dismal expectation that it was a multi-billion-dollar failure with the loss of the entire crew: his younger brother, as well as eight other brilliant young men and women, all gone.

And just when all had seemed at its lowest point, NASA detected the escape pod re-entering the Earth's atmosphere. Computer scans said there was a single unidentified occupant inside. Identification unknown. And now they were down and out of the capsule.

Please, please, he wished.

Greg shut his eyes and rested his head against the cabin wall, feeling the rotor vibrations through the skin of the craft tickle the inside of his ears. Without even thinking about it he lifted his thumb to his mouth and chewed on the nail's corner, something he hadn't done for decades.

"Found a spot. Setting her down." The pilot slowed in the air.

It was Greg Morgan's forty-fifth birthday today, and this is how he was going to spend it. But right now, he wouldn't want to be anywhere else. Because more than anything, they needed to know what happened. To his brother, to the mission, and to the rest of the crew. Like, yesterday.

He'd been with NASA going on twenty-three years and had never felt more like a nervous kid in his life.

As he stared out of the small window he couldn't help his vision turning inwards and taking him back to when the Europa mission started.

He remembered his younger brother, Brad, pestering him to find out what the latest news from NASA was, and telling him that one day he was going to fly a spaceship.

They hovered for a moment, and then the helicopter slowly dropped toward the ground.

Greg smiled wistfully – he remembered everything – and it all began with an angel in the darkness.

PART 01

THE ANGEL IN THE DARKNESS

If you stare into the darkness at nothing, eventually, there will be, something.

CHAPTER 01

June, 2000 – NASA Mission Control Center (MCC), Houston, USA
"He-eey, wait a minute," a young Greg Morgan whispered to himself as he leaned closer to his screen. *"Did I just see that?"*

Greg's eyes were unblinking as he watched the bluish-white surface, striated by light tan cracks, sworls, and streaks.

The unmanned probe had touched down hours ago, settling onto the icy surface of Europa, the smallest of the four Galilean moons orbiting Jupiter. The tiny moon was four-billion years old and was primarily a ball of water covered in a thick layer of ice.

They knew now that the hypothesis that there was a liquid ocean existing beneath the surface was proven true. Their modelling had also suggested that heat from tidal flexing caused the ocean to not only remain liquid but be surprisingly warm. In fact, it was also expected that the ice moved similarly to Earthly plate tectonics, and the massive grinding had released minerals to create a salt water environment which might be very similar to Earth's oceans.

Europa had all the elements for life, and now they were there, human beings, or at least their electronic eyes were, looking for extraterrestrials via an unmanned probe.

Greg snorted softly. Not extraterrestrials, rather they were looking for terrestrial life, as right now, they were the extraterrestrials.

Greg and twenty other technicians with varying banks of screens collecting probe telemetry, as well as visual, chemical, light spectrum, and environmental data, were reviewing the information package collected from the last data squirt from the probe.

While the teams waited for the aquatic probe technology to be readied, many of the technicians watched the moon's surface, checking for anomalies, or just anything interesting.

The Europa frozen skin was deadly cold, and bleak, but not featureless as there were plains, valleys, towering ice crystals, and even mountains, all made of ice. But thankfully, there were no storms, and in fact, not even the breath of a breeze. Unlike its mother planet, Jupiter, that experiences auroras, ferocious windstorms that could grow to thousands of miles wide in a few hours, and lightning streaks that bolt horizontally for miles in weather patterns so extreme that they can be seen from space.

The other feature of Europa's surface was that from time to time a water geyser would erupt, spewing vapor hundreds of feet into the air, where it would fall back as ice crystals, sometimes staining the surface. And other than an occasional falling meteorite, for the most part the moon was as silent as the grave.

But the surface wasn't their objective because Greg and the other scientists knew that all the action, if there was to be any, was going to be below the surface.

He leaned closer to his monitor, his eyes narrowing. He focused in on one specific area, and then what he thought he might have only imagined, happened again.

Greg jumped to his feet. "*It moved. It moved.*"

***

Dan Domich, the control center's lead supervisor, and every other technician in the room turned to him, and some leapt up to rush over and peer over Greg's shoulder.

On his screen they saw that Greg's camera perspective was pointed at a smoother section of ice and snow.

"What did you see?" Domich asked, after muscling in to his desk and leaning forward on his knuckles.

Dan was tall, dark, and shiny-headed bald. He had never joked or even been seen smiling, and right now his thick brows were creased into a single dark, bushy line over his eyes, as he looked from Greg to the screen, and back again.

"I saw it – something moved." Greg slowly sat and pointed; he knew at nothing now but white on white. "Wait, wait for it. Hold on." He backed up the tape and reran it.

Dan, Greg, and the other techs watched his screen with unblinking eyes.

After several minutes Domich straightened and placed his hands in his pockets.

"No wait. Here it comes," Greg said, pointing at a spot on the screen.

After another moment, there was a speck of light, and then a tiny hill of ice crystals toppled over.

The group watched for a moment more.

"*Hmm-hm.* Reflection." Domich turned to him. "That's it?"

Greg nodded.

"Okay, good job, Greg." Domich patted his shoulder. "Keep watching, son."

The other technicians drifted back to their desks.

"It looked...like a hair, or something." Greg sighed as he felt himself mentally and physically deflating. "Yeah, fine."

"Probe is ready." The remote team had finally maneuvered the robotic arm to extend outwards from the lander holding the three-foot probe. It was basically shaped like a long bullet, with a rotating screw head that would be heated. It was based on the design tested down at the Antarctic and used to drill down through the ice cap to reach the buried lakes, and once there, swim around and collect data. In fact, the Antarctic buried lake was almost the perfect test run for Europa's oceans.

Dan Domich closely watched the aquatic drone preparation. "Here goes twenty million bucks of tech. Hold onto your asses, everyone." He folded his arms. "*Engage.*"

The team turned back to their respective screens to monitor environmental conditions, the lander's technical health, and importantly, the robotic arm as it extended the probe over a selected area of ice. They had little to do, as everything now was preprogramed into millions of lines of code that were written months if not years ago. They would or could only intervene if there was a significant anomalous event.

"Countdown. On my mark," the technician said, his fingers lightly resting on the controls. "In three, two, one, *mark*. Initiating burn."

The probe's tip glowed and began to turn, screw-like, as it was slowly lowered. It touched the ice and went straight through it, creating a pool of liquid around the nose cone.

"Releasing... now."

The robotic arm's clamps opened, the probe was released, and it continued its solo journey. Water immediately gushed upwards due to displacement, but it soon stopped, then turned white as it refroze, creating a smooth mound like an ice scab over a wound.

"And. Here. We. Go." Domich knew that the launch, the 390-million miles of travel, and the gentle touchdown were to be applauded. And they were. But this was where the rubber hit the road – if the probe failed, it was all over. Everything had to work, first time. There was no workshop, spare parts, or do-overs.

The laboratory simulations via computer models, and the proof of concept testing down at the Antarctic lakes had shown them that the probe tech was sound. And should work. But he knew that if anything was going to go wrong, it would do so in one of the most remote and harshest environments they had ever encountered. Compared to this, the moon landing was a seaside holiday in Bermuda.

Domich's jaw clenched so hard it began to ache. After another five minutes his eyes slid to the wall clock. *Come on*, he breathed. *You can do it.*

He paced along the line of technicians and stopped behind Eric Leung who was monitoring a sonar image of the aquatic probe as it melted and drilled its way through the ice. The man was totally absorbed in his work.

"Eric, talk to me," Domich said softly.

Leung spoke without taking his eyes from the screen. "No debris, no hard objects, no voids, on schedule and all proceeding as planned."

"Good, good." Domich knew the ice layer over Europa's seas was between ten and twenty-five miles thick. However, there were 'oases' areas, where the ice was extremely thin at only two miles, and they had touched down at one of the thinner areas to pierce. But even with this thinner area, melting through over ten thousand-feet of ice was still going to take many hours to reach the sea below.

"Time to emergence?" he asked.

Leung didn't hesitate a second. "Three hours, forty-eight minutes, and counting down," he replied. "Ice is medium density and conforms to our projections. Emergence still expected to be on schedule."

Domich nodded and went and grabbed himself another coffee. He stopped to look up towards the large screen on the far wall – once the probe broke through and was swimming it would display the images from the nose cone cameras.

There was a lot riding on this, on him, and his team. The lander and the probe would keep gathering and transmitting data for as long as their batteries held out. But if the probe failed before it had a chance to send data and images, well, even though they would have plenty of information gathered by the lander that would keep them busy for years, the project would be a multi-billion-dollar disgrace at a time when scrutiny over NASA spending was at an all-time high. That could kill the space program for decades, or maybe even for good.

Domich drew in a breath. "Come on, Nemo," he whispered the nickname they'd given to the small swimming probe named after the tiny big-hearted fish in the animated movie.

He paced, waited, got coffee, waited some more, and also went to his office to try and do some administrative work as the probe continued to burrow down. He even loosened his tie and lay on the couch for an hour, but couldn't relax enough to sleep.

Eventually he returned, and soon after there was a growing level of activity amongst the team.

"Coming up to end of ice layer," Eric Leung announced monotonously. "Trajectory and rate of burn is still good."

Domich felt a flutter of nerves in his stomach, and he put his fifth coffee down and approached to stand behind the man. He folded his arms.

Leung was deadpan. "Breaching in five, four, three, two…and…*through*." The small probe suddenly accelerated but was immediately brought to a stop by the technicians.

Hands flew over controls as the device was prepared for the new aquatic environment – the drill cone was ejected, revealing a clear dome nose cone packed with sensors, cameras, and a powerful light. The rear of the tiny craft slowly extended stabilizing fins and then silent propulsion jets also came to life.

"Up on screen." Domich turned to look at the far wall as the camera feeds were engaged. They waited, but there was nothing on screen but fragmented fizzing and white noise.

Domich could feel his heart beating hard in his chest. *Come on, little guy, give us something, please*, he prayed. *Show us what you can see.*

The screen remained a fizz of white wavy lines. He lowered his head and began to pace with his hands on his hips. Every so often he stopped to look up hopefully, and then sigh.

He knew that the lag in data transference meant the information received was not instantaneous, but they had positional satellites to catch and onsend the data packets that contained the data and cut the hours-long information delivery time down to mere minutes.

He glanced at the digital wall clock that had numbers counting down the hours, minutes, seconds, and fractions of seconds.

Be cool, he tried to tell himself, *we're still within the expected delivery window*. He lifted his coffee to his lips, and felt its slimy coldness, winced, and put it back down.

No, he argued back, *it's taking too long. Something has failed.*

He turned to look along the line of now silent, and expectant faces of the technicians.

"Communication handshake," Leung suddenly announced. "Coming online."

Domich's head snapped around. "Put it up, put it up."

The huge wall screen of the data center lit up as the aquatic drone's feed was transferred from Leung's computer. The white screen suddenly went from white fizz to black, totally black.

"Lights up," Domich said.

The blackness was immediately cut by a pipe of white light that extended out into the blackness to be swallowed by the nothingness.

The darkness was absolute, and they could have been drifting in the void of space except small, white dust-like flakes floated through the light beam.

Already Nemo was capturing the environmental debris, tasting and analyzing it, and returning its judgment.

Eric Leung looked up. "Not krill, not algae, or any type of biological fragment," he said. "Ice crystals, calcium fragments, mixed with silica flake. Mostly like what they found beneath the Antarctic where the hard packed ice ground up against the bedrock."

Leung kept his eyes on the screen. "All clear on all quadrants. Ready to follow predetermined route." He turned.

Domich nodded. "Proceed."

His command brought a flurry of activity amongst the other technicians. Dozens of men and women were monitoring, analyzing, and recording a hundred other aspects of the submerged world.

Leung turned back, his face calm and eyes half lidded. "Accelerating to five knots."

The craft zoomed ahead in the darkness.

"Ocean depth?" Domich asked.

This time, senior technician Lisa Duke answered. She was mid-thirties, owner of an infectious laugh, and had a desk littered with small Disney figurines collected from years of Happy Meal enjoyment.

"We are currently in the Copernicus Sea, one of the shallower areas," Lisa said through her grin. "A mere forty-two miles deep."

Domich whistled, but he already knew that. To put it in perspective, the deepest place in our oceans on Earth was the Mariana Trench that dropped down to around seven miles. But on Europa, the ocean covered the planet and ranged from forty miles to one hundred miles deep.

Another fact that had to be taken into consideration was that the bottom of the Mariana Trench, seven miles, exerts eight tons of pressure per square inch, which was the equivalent of having one hundred adult elephants standing on your head. But at forty miles the pressure would crush the probe down to a ball of metal the size of your fist. And at a hundred miles, well, Nemo had a specially hardened casing, but its maximum dive depth was potentially ten miles – *potentially*, because they could only test it to seven miles.

Domich knew it wasn't an ideal sample as they'd literally be skimming the surface and had no idea what would be down on that impenetrably dark abyss.

This time around they would remain a mystery. But that didn't matter to Domich and his team, as they waited patiently, all still glued to their screens in the darkened room, as they were ever hopeful that they had found life. After all, the water was saline, relatively warm, and the density was good, at least in the upper layers.

Domich half smiled; they'd had evolutionary theorists make suggestions of what forms of life might exist on the watery world and based on their understanding of deep-sea creatures on Earth, if anything did, or could, live in those Europan depths, it would be near totally boneless, perhaps like the deep ocean, jelly-like blobfish. Or it would be armor plated as all hell, like some sort of trench living isopod that were mini tanks. Interestingly, the thing about isopods was that the deeper you went in the ocean, the bigger the isopods got.

Frankly, he'd settle for any form of life, as that would be the impetus for more funding and perhaps the next step – a manned mission. But that all depended on what happened here and now.

Almost trance-like he watched the dark screen as the small drone followed the pathway of light generated by its powerful forward light. He knew how important it was for their scientists to find some evidence of life, but he was primarily the nuts and bolts guy, and for him, as long as the probe operated to specifics, and nothing went wrong, his job was done.

Their expectations were high – there might be evidence of things like ancient stromatolites that were found in Earth's Antarctic lake. They were microbial mats that were some of the oldest life forms on Earth at around 3.5 billion years. Maybe the same thing could exist within Europa's icy oceans. Or maybe there was something more. Something bigger and more complex.

Here's hoping, Domich wished.

Minutes ticked by, then hours, as the small machine sailed through the cold dark waters of Jupiter's frozen moon. He had just come back from a break, and checking his watch noted that he'd be handing shift over soon as his day was nearly done.

The hours of a totally black screen and the knowledge there'd be days more of it as they followed their predetermined route, meant it was hard to maintain a high level of enthusiasm. For him, the touchdown, the launch of Nemo, and the satisfactory operational performance, should already be a win.

"*There*," Greg Morgan said over the top of the background noise of the control room.

Domich's head snapped around. "What've you got?" he asked, closing in on the young man and his screen. When he saw who it was, he remembered Greg's previous alarm over a toppling hill of snow and ice, and his excitement was tempered just a little.

But the young man's eyes went from the large wall monitor relaying the probe's view and then dropped down to his own screen. "Rewinding."

Domich stood behind him, waiting, again.

"Replaying," Greg said and initiated the playback.

He had selected a small window of image data and replayed it. When it ended he half turned, his eyes almost feverish. "Did you see it?"

"Again. Slow it down." Domich frowned, still not seeing anything.

Greg replayed it, this time slowed down by fifty percent. He lifted a hand, index finger extended, as he pointed at the top-right corner of the dark void of water.

"Wait for it. Wa-*aaaait*, a-aaand, *there*," he stabbed his finger.

This time Domich saw it. Or saw something. It was a pinprick flash of light.

"Could have been our own lights bouncing off some floating ice." Domich straightened. "Frame by frame this time."

Greg did as asked.

"Here we go..." he said as it approached the flash moment. "*Now.*" He stopped the film.

By this time there was a small crowd gathered around behind them. People whistled, swore, or *oohh* and *ahhd* softly.

Domich inhaled deeply through his nose and let it out through his pressed lips. It wasn't just a single dot of light, but two dots. Close together.

Like eyes, his mind whispered.

"Ice reflection," someone said from behind them. "Has to be."

"Or, eyeshine from a *Tapetum lucidum*," Greg said, and half turned. "It's the tiny mirror-like structure in the back of dark-adapted animals' eyeballs. It helps them see in the dark." He shrugged. "And the two spots can't be our reflection. Because we only have a single light beam."

Domich grunted, not willing to call it just yet. "Improve resolution."

Greg nodded and had the AI program make adjustments to the film to improve its clarity. After a moment, they saw something else.

"*Okay,*" Domich whispered.

"There's more than two." Greg Morgan's eyes blazed. "A cluster. A cluster of eyes."

***

Domich paced for a moment, thinking about what they had seen as Nemo continued on its lightless direction. He needed a good reason to deviate from their route. But they might travel for hundreds, or thousands, of miles and see nothing but black water.

He stopped and turned. "Anything on scanners?"

"All clear, all gradients, all quadrants," came the reply.

He decided. "Bring Nemo back around. Let's follow those lights and see if what we have is a reflection or..."

"Eyeshine," Greg finished for him.

Domich half turned, "...or at least something more interesting than a reflection."

"On it." Eric Leung took control of Nemo from its auto pilot program and turned the small probe around. "Heading is now forty-two degrees north-east. Propulsion down to investigation speed of three knots."

The small craft glided through the inky water, a tiny steel fish with a bright cyclopean eye in an ocean that seemed bottomless and endless. And in a way it was, because if they circumnavigated the tiny globe, they would eventually return to their starting position without ever striking land.

"Coming up on where we saw the lights," Leung said softly.

Domich now watched the big screen with the intensity of a hawk. But there was nothing in the light beam.

"Anything?" he asked.

"Still all clear," Greg replied.

Domich drew in a deep breath and let it out slowly. All clear on sensors basically meant all clear for a few miles in all directions. But there was no way they could know what was going on outside of the range of their equipment.

It might have been nothing. Or it might have been, something. And right now they were like a tiny mouse trying to find a single cookie crumb on a football field. In the dark. And already they were about to pass out of the sighting zone.

"All stop, remain in hover mode," he said.

Domich's eyes narrowed as he stared out into the void of dark water.

"Rotate three-sixty degrees." He folded his arms.

Eric Leung pivoted the craft, but it was hard to tell if they were even moving without any landmarks or perspective. There was just a pipe of light that was swallowed up after a few hundred yards.

Suddenly, Domich saw something that actually made him feel like he got a physical jolt. "*Stop!*" he yelled.

He craned forward and pointed. "There. There they are."

The lights out in the darkness were just pinpricks. But they were there.

"Anything on sonar, or long-range scanners?" he asked.

"There wasn't just a few seconds ago. But there is now," Greg Morgan replied. "We have a mass out there at the far range of our instruments. Size is indeterminate."

"Wait. There's more," Domich whispered.

More lights came on and created a long image. They flickered, moving along a line, or pulsed. Different colors played over the thing.

Then they went out.

"What's it doing?" Domich asked.

"I think, it's a bioluminescent display," Lisa Duke, their borrowed marine biologist, replied softly as she watched the large screen. "Some deep-sea creatures do this to signal to their own species, and sometimes to attract a mate." She straightened. "Or to draw in their prey."

"Or maybe it's a warning display. Territorial," Greg added.

The lights came on again and played even more frantically along whatever the thing was. They came on in a straight line, then branched out in a flower shape, then like a mass of waving threads.

"This thing is big," Greg said. "Those long tendril things are several hundred feet in length."

And then it reorganized itself again. The final display looked like a figure with huge wings.

Greg snorted softly. "An angel."

"No angel I've ever seen," Domich said. "Take us closer."

Leung engaged the propulsion system and the small craft glided forward.

The angel shape vanished and then the lights out in the darkness suddenly flared, all of them, and for one brief second they might have glimpsed the real shape of the thing.

"Holy shit," Lisa said. "It looks like…"

It suddenly began to speed toward them.

"Here it comes," Greg said excitedly. "If it was a warning, we just ignored it. So now it's going to…"

"*Back up, back up!*" Domich yelled.

The technicians' hands flew over their keyboards and control panels.

"Can't outrun it; coming too fast," Eric Leung breathed. "It's big. Bigger than we thought."

Domich craned forward. "*Evasive actio…*"

It was too late. The small craft was enveloped and the only sign of that was the pipe of light on their screen was shut off as something totally covered it.

"We're going down," Leung said.

"Sinking?" Domich asked.

Greg shook his head. "Nope, too fast for that." He worked his keys for a moment. "Putting up metrics."

A depth counter appeared on the wall screen and its numbers raced higher as in seconds Nemo plummeted from a depth of several hundred feet to several thousand. And then kept going without a sign of stopping or even slowing.

"Engage full thrusters," Domich urged.

Once again hands flew over keyboards as the group tried to adjust fins, foils, and thruster jets. But there was no change.

"Four thousand three hundred and twenty-two feet," Leung said as his eyes remained fixed on his small screen.

Domich folded his arms tight, and his jaws clenched for a moment. They were approaching crush depths, and he had no way to stop it.

"Depth speed increasing. No response to commands," Diego said. "Capsule is being compromised."

Domich half turned. "By the water pressure, or…?"

"Unknown. But we haven't reached crush depths, yet," Eric Leung replied. "I have no control over Nemo anymore." He looked up. "However, Nemo's tag is still transmitting."

"We could try rerouting the electrical system for a short, sharp charge over the skin," Greg suggested. "It might frighten whatever that thing is away."

"No." Domich shook his head. "We're the aliens here. We might end up damaging or killing it, and that would not be a great first contact scenario." He sighed. "All we can do is stand by and witness Nemo's demise," he said ruefully.

They watched the counter as the small pulse signal continued down into the lightless depths, with the numbers flickering ever faster: seven-thousand feet, eight, nine, and it was accelerating.

"How deep is it there?" Domich asked.

Lisa didn't need to check. "This is the Copernicus Sea, one of the shallowest, but still forty-two point six miles deep."

Domich half smiled. He knew it was nearly four times beyond what they could get down to. He exhaled. "Goodbye Nemo."

The small pulse winked out when it hit twelve thousand feet.

The mission team leader on duty looked up. "And that's that."

Their mission was over almost before it started. But in fact it was a resounding success. They had just proven beyond doubt, that life existed in their solar system. And they had recorded it.

Domich's lips curved into a half smile. "Hope to see you again one day, angel in the darkness. Who, or whatever you are." He headed back to his office, still with a fluttery feeling in his stomach.

He had a lot of calls to make.

CHAPTER 02

Three years ago – Wyoming, USA, The Morgan Ranch
Brad Morgan and his father, Clay, stopped on the hill looking down over the ranch's outer fields. There were a herd of three hundred Hereford cattle all being herded into massive pens all around the ranch.

The work had been done quickly because they used drones now to scout for the loose remnants of broken herds, and he and his dad only rode out to bring in the stragglers that had been hiding in the brush.

The drones saved them days of work and plenty of money, and at first his dad was hesitant, calling Brad's drones *flying eggbeaters* and a waste of time.

But after getting him to agree to a demo, he grunted once, which was about as much of an approval he was ever going to give, and he then agreed to a muster test. In their first run, the drone cameras allowed them to pinpoint the herds in hours instead of days. Plus they saved on fuel, and cowhand wages. Technology won this round.

Brad noticed the good size of some of their animals. They'd all bounced back from a severe parasitic infection of a few years back – when you heard the word 'tapeworm' most people thought it was something that just gave you an itchy asshole. But in cattle, if left untreated, it can end up so much worse.

Ben's herd had become infected by eating contaminated grass, maybe from wolf or coyote droppings. By the time the problem had been detected, many had *Cysticercosis*, a parasitic tissue infection caused by larval cysts of the tapeworm. These larval cysts had moved from the gut to infect internal organs, muscles, and then even onto the brain. The flukes curled up in their heads in little pockets they made for themselves in the brain tissue and fed on the soft and warm, protein-rich medium, and in turn secreted a substance that kept the cattle's immune system from detecting them.

The cattle suffered from confusion and undoubtedly severe headaches, and in the worst cases, total behavioral changes – some went from their usual docile selves to aggressive animals that attacked the other cattle, and in extreme cases, even taking bites out of them.

His dad had said at the time that things can go bad real quick. And he had been right. He also said that some of the cattle were so overrun on the inside they were more worm than they were cattle. A sickening concept, Brad thought.

A single dose of *Albendazole* had sorted most of them out. But by then up to a hundred cattle had to be put down as their brains and flesh were overrun by the worms. Just like his dad had said.

But that was then.

"Nice'n fat this year. That's a lot of money on the hoof." Brad turned to his dad.

"Yep, been a good year," Clay replied. "Nothing like rain, sunshine, and hard work to make for good quality beef." He turned to his son. "Would have been a lot quicker if that damned older brother of yours was here to help."

Brad wiped his brow and turned to his father. "Dad, you know Greg would if he could. He's got important work to do; big NASA space mission coming up."

He continued to look at his dad for a moment more. The man looked tired. He was just seventy-three but working the land, the sun, hardship, and everything else had taken their toll on his face and body. And then on top of that, Jill, his wife of thirty-five years passed away. It took his dad nearly a year to get over it. If he ever did.

Brad took time out from the Airforce, and Greg from NASA, and both had come straight back to the farm to help out, and for the first few weeks, his dad would barely even get out of bed.

Three years later and he had recovered. Mostly. He still had his quiet moments, but at least he had found his passion again. And was laughing more.

"Well, be a big cookout tonight, and your brother is going to miss out," Clay announced. "Least you're here; you up for it?"

"Will there be beer?" Brad grinned.

Clay laughed. "Hell yeah, and by the barrel."

Brad slapped his thigh. "Then I'm in."

It was good to see his dad happy. His brother, Greg, had worked for NASA for decades, and Brad had joined the Airforce. With the work Greg was now doing, he was going to be tied up for months, years. And now Brad was too.

It was time to tell his dad that he had been chosen for a space flight – the Traveler Mission – he was to be the first commander of a manned visit to the moon of Europa. And he would be gone for years. At least the Morgan brothers would be sort of working together, he thought.

Brad sighed. He'd been putting it off for weeks but would tell his father tonight.

After the cookout.

PART 02
THE TRAVELER COMES HOME

CHAPTER 03

Today – Mt Sinai General Hospital, Special Emergency & Quarantine Center

"Turning left." The clump of doctors and nurses swung the gurney hard left into the next stark, white-tiled corridor without slowing a beat. They surrounded the large Perspex coffin-like box that Commander Brad Morgan was encased within, and some reached in via attached plastic gauntlets to fix or check monitors to his neck and try and take assessments of his physical status while still in his environmental suit.

They were in a special emergency section of the hospital that dealt with level-5 biohazard infections, or in rare and exceptional cases like this, returning astronauts.

Following close behind the group was Greg Morgan, with two of his senior NASA astrophysicists, Jenny Alvarez, and Caroline Jenner. They were the only ones not wearing full contamination suits, and Greg knew that was going to limit his access to his younger brother very soon.

Brad would be housed in an area of the hospital that was hermetically sealed off, and he would stay there until he was examined externally and internally for contaminants, biohazards, or anything else he might have inadvertently brought back from an icy moon over three hundred and ninety million miles away.

The gurney turned again, and Greg had to jog to keep up as they wheeled his brother at breakneck speed, and at the same time tried to cut him out of his environmental suit that was tougher than leather and was resisting even the sharpest of their shears.

Morgan sighed – he had so many questions he needed answers to. Brad had been the Traveler Mission leader and was the only occupant of the escape capsule that had crash landed in the Alabama forest. And so far he seemed to be the only survivor of the entire mission.

His eyes were closed, and his mouth hung open behind the oxygen mask. Blood and something that looked like dark-green petroleum jelly streaked his face and matted his hair.

Greg sped up. "I want to know the moment he wakes up." He moved in closer. "And is able to talk."

"Let us work here," the chief medical specialist said over his shoulder, as the nurses and doctors pumped oxygen into his lungs.

Greg saw they finally managed to get the environmental suit open, and it exposed his LCV, his Liquid Cooling and Ventilation Garment, that was a tight-fitting item covered in sewn-in pipes for distribution of a liquid that was used for cooling and warming the body. But this too was smeared with the green-tinged goo.

"What is that?" Greg asked, not really expecting an answer.

"LCV leakage?" Jenny Alvarez suggested from behind his left shoulder.

"Some sort of lubricant from the Russian capsule?" Caroline Jenner said from over his right shoulder.

The underlying suit was sliced open and pulled back. They wiped the mucous from his torso and attached electrode pads to several places on his chest and side. Immediately other machines sprang to life.

"Erratic heartbeat," a nurse said. "Temperature is way too high. He'll fry his brain." She lifted her head. "I want cooling pads, now."

Greg tried to force himself closer again, and one of the doctors glared. Greg glared back. "There are eight other members of his mission team that are still missing. We need to…"

"We understand." One of the nurses firmly took hold of Greg's arm. "We'll let you know, as soon as he's out of danger." The group headed into a quarantine room and the door swung shut behind them.

She stood in front of Greg looking up into his face. "Just let them do their work, Mr. Morgan, and hopefully you can talk to your brother when we clean him up and make sure he's out of danger." She smiled up at him. "I promise."

"I…" Greg began and looked down at her, ready to fight on, but was disarmed by her calm demeanor and pleasant face. He nodded. "Okay."

Thank you, she mouthed and began to turn away.

"One thing…" He reached out to her, and she stopped. "I need the recorder from his suit. It's important."

She nodded and then turned to also vanish into the room.

Greg Morgan and his small team was left standing there watching the closed door with a large yellow biohazard warning symbol on it for a few moments.

"He'll be fine," Caroline said and placed a hand on his shoulder.

"I know, I know. He was always the tough one," Greg said.

"So, what now, boss?" Jenny Alvarez asked.

"Now?" Greg finally turned away from the sealed operating theatre. "Now, we wait to get the mission recorder from his suit and interrogate its contents. They were designed to upload all the mission data from the voyage, as well as the collective logbooks – all the crew members were required to spend time creating daily updates into their online diaries. Provided nothing was somehow destroyed, then most of what we need to know should be stored there."

He checked his wristwatch. "In fact, the pod should have been transported back to our labs by now. That's something else we need to look over before the Russians find out we have it and demand it back."

"Sounds like a plan," Caroline Jenner said. "As long as the team were still creating the logs, even when things were going, *ah*, wrong."

"Yeah, let's hope." Greg headed back down the stark and now empty corridor, followed by the two young scientists.

CHAPTER 04

Greg Morgan stood with hands on hips from the first-floor gangway looking down into the aircraft hangar-sized area in the NASA labs where the Russian escape pod sat on a raised platform. Scientists scurried over, in, and all around it, looking like white carrion beetles working over the corpse of a dead animal.

First thing Morgan saw was that it was larger than normal, and it made him think it might be the entire command section of the Russian spacecraft that he had read could be jettisoned in times of emergency.

There was room for several passengers. *So where were the rest?* he wondered. The last communication received from The Traveler Mission was sent by astronaut Heather Winterson, their biochemist. Greg remembered that she had sounded scared out of her mind.

He drew in a deep lung filling breath and let it out slowly. There were too many questions to count right now. And far too few answers.

He looked back at the pod and saw that the heat resistant tiles covering the pod were scorched down to a greyish black of its base metal by the heat of reentry. But obviously the inside had done what it was designed to do and preserved the life of the sole occupant, and by luck or the grace of God, it was his brother.

The pod itself was primarily a forty-foot slightly flattened globe covered in armor plated heat shielding, some basic thrusters, and a huge parachute. It was self-programmed to return to Earth, and land. And that was it.

It was large enough to fit three people. Four if pushed. Everything was automated and once inside the escape pod the only task for the occupants was to enter the cryo-pods, and then the intelligent systems would basically put them to sleep and then watch over them in their hibernating state for the voyage home. It was similar to the American design but seemed a little more rudimentary.

Greg flipped through the preliminary report that told him that Commander Brad Morgan had managed to make it inside, and launch. It also told him that his brother had brought with him quite a stockpile of dehydrated foodstuffs and water which he shouldn't have needed – maybe he was just bringing them as a safety net as he distrusted the Russian craft's cryo-tubes to work for the entire return voyage home.

The other strange thing was that he had also dragged in spare spacesuits belonging to three of his colleagues – Nina Barker, the second in command, Hiroyuki Nakagawa, the biologist, and also Angie Sommers, their bio-linguist. They were arranged into the shape of people next to himself in the other pods.

Did he do this for comfort, peace of mind, or as a form of company?

Another mystery was that the spare suits were also smeared with the green-tinged goo that Brad Morgan was covered in. Samples of which were also being analyzed. He guessed it didn't matter. The upside was he got to interrogate all the suit's recorded data.

Greg sighed audibly and it turned into a groan. He had so many questions that it was tearing at his mind, and he hoped Brad woke up soon. Their analysis of the craft would be illuminating, but by no means exhaustive, and it could never substitute for an interview with a living subject.

Greg came down the metal stairs to the hangar floor to watch the work being undertaken. While his brother was still in a deep coma, the pod would be vacuumed and analyzed for debris down to the most microscopic speck of Europan dust.

His phone pinged with an update from the tech analysis of the suit's computers, and he felt a little of the load lightening when he read it.

"Thank god," he whispered and closed his eyes for a moment.

The data files were all intact in the memory banks. Terabytes of images, voice records, and environmental analysis – each crewmember was automatically recorded in the form of a diary entry every day, and it only switched off when it detected a slowing of the heartbeat during sleep.

The Traveler team of nine astronauts was to be split into two groups – an external group taking an overland rover to explore the surface of the moon. And then also a deep dive team that would pilot a submersible that would firstly burrow below the ice and then embark on a predetermined path to explore the dark depths. A little like Nemo from twenty years ago, but this time carrying a human crew.

The intelligent systems would organize the data chronologically, and Greg Morgan prayed it would shed light on what happened to the Traveler Mission, its crew, and the work they were doing on and below the Europan moon.

According to his preliminary report the diaries were being uploaded and processed now, and he expected to be one of the first to get access to the data.

Greg quickly headed back up to his office, and once there sat back heavily into his chair. He couldn't focus on anything else while he waited for the mission data to be presented to him, so he sat staring at nothing as he allowed his mind to wander back to the day just over twenty years ago when they, *he*, spotted the eyes in the black void of the massive ocean, that became known as the 'angel' in the darkness.

There had been something down there in those inky depths. And he had been waiting over two decades to find out exactly what it was.

And he bet his brother knew.

***

It wasn't until 10pm when Greg Morgan's computer pinged with an incoming message making him rise from his trance-like fugue and lean forward to open it. He saw it was a report on the strange mucous-like substance covering his brother and the pod's interior, and also a link to the mission data folders organized by date. These folders were then categorized by individual crewmember.

He was eager to read the mission files, but the weird slime intrigued him as there was nothing stored on the craft that might have produced it. He opened the report link and scanned through it.

Morgan's brows came together. '*No conclusive identification.*' Not unexpected, he thought. But the theoretical biologists had then made some best guesses. '*Degraded microbial matter. Similar to stromatolites.*'

"*Stromatolites*… kinda makes sense." Morgan sat back.

He knew that stromatolites were extremely primitive life forms from a period called the Archean era at Earth's dawn. They tended to clump together to form long structures that looked like slime mats. They were some of the first life on Earth some 4.5 billion years ago, and the only remnants were now found near deep ocean vents at the bottom of ocean trenches.

Though this explanation wasn't unexpected coming from a water world. What wasn't expected was how the hell did Brad get covered in it?

Greg knew his brother was leading the aquatic team, but he didn't think that entailed any external work.

He sat thinking for several minutes. Could they have exited the submersible? Who knows what they found down there.

There was really only one way to find out.

Greg then followed the mission diary link, and a notation told him the opening entries were from Commander Brad Morgan himself as they were preparing for touchdown on Europa.

It was late, but all desire for sleep had vanished and Greg refilled his coffee cup and settled in for however long it took to get some preliminary answers. He opened the first file and went to the voice-data recording.

Greg had a pen and paper for note taking and played the first entry and his brother's deep and confident voice drifted from the speaker. His first sensation on hearing his brother speak was of how much he missed him. Then he felt immense pride at what he had achieved, and he wished he could speak to him directly.

When he wakes, he thought.

Greg knew the recording software would take all of the crew's voice data and combine it into a coherent string, but for now, Brad Morgan took the lead.

Greg sat like stone as the senior astronaut, his brother, began to speak to him and took him along on his fantastic mission journey.

PART 03
FOR SOMETHING THAT HAS ONLY KNOWN DARKNESS, LIGHT IS AN ABOMINATION

CHAPTER 05

Commander Brad Morgan blinked open gluey eyes, and groaned, feeling like he had a vodka hangover from hell.

He had been in cryo-sleep before but never for this long. He, along with his crew, had been asleep for just on two years, one month, and thirteen days – a relatively fast trip because they had chosen the launch time to coincide with the preferential elliptical orbits of both Earth and Jupiter, and therefore its moon, Europa, that basically put them at their closest points to each other. If they hadn't, the travel time would have been more than double that.

Even now they still had another few weeks to go before they arrived at their destination orbit around the ice shelled moon.

He groaned again and then coughed. His lips, mouth, and throat were sticky and dry, but he wasn't thirsty, more like he was a machine in desperate need of lubrication.

He blinked some more, his vision cleared, and he wiggled his fingers and toes. There was no suspended animation like in the movies, instead they were sedated, meaning they slept the entire trip. Attached electrodes massaged and exercised their bodies so they wouldn't lose muscle mass, and they were kept hydrated and fed through multiple tubes and waste eliminated by catheters.

His body felt okay, but still, when he sat up, he grimaced as his spine had lengthened and that, along with his other joints, ached like a bitch. But he knew that would pass after he had been on his feet a few days.

Morgan rubbed his face and was thankful that they had been given hair and nail growth retardants otherwise he'd be contending with a two foot beard and hairdo.

He stretched and grimaced as the catheters were withdrawn. "I'll never get used to that," he muttered and looked around.

The other Traveler Mission members were rousing themselves, coughing, mumbling curses, or chuckling.

"Ouch." He half grimaced as Angie Sommers pulled off the adhesive plugs that held her heart monitors in place and winced as a little skin came away from her ribs after being glued to her side for so long.

"I hate that," she complained, and dabbed at the raw spot.

People reached for water tubes, some made fists and curled toes to test muscles, and some slung legs over the side of their capsules to hold their heads in their hands. He knew they'd be feeling like him – dizzy, slightly nauseous, headache, and weak muscled.

They had three weeks before they actually arrived at Europa, and they had a lot to do. One of the main things was to get back in top shape for a potentially arduous mission – the mental and physical demands would be unlike anything any of them had ever experienced. In fact, unlike *anyone, anywhere* had ever experienced.

Unless you counted the Russian mission. The Gorbachev II, long range Soyuz space ship had launched long before they left. It had successfully made orbit around Jupiter, and then negotiated a landing site on Europa. But then all updates about the mission craft and its crew ceased.

Roscosmos, the Russian space coordination facility, had stopped putting out information. Reading between the very large lines meant that the worst case scenario had probably occurred, and they either crashed on landing attempt or had a technical failure and simply drifted off into space.

Here's hoping we have better luck, he thought.

Brad Morgan looked along the faces of his team; there were nine of them including himself as the mission commander. Next to him was Angie Sommers, bio-linguist. She spoke over fifty languages, and had written papers on animal expression systems, such as bee and octopus communications. If they encountered anything that resembled intelligence, it was up to her to get in the first word.

Heather Winterson threw her legs over the side of her capsule and one foot tapped spasmodically to some beat only she could hear – she worked her jaw and mouth muscles making silent *oooo-eeee-ooo* expressions. She was their biochemist, but online gaming was her first love.

Next up was Hiroyuki 'Hiro' Nakagawa, their evolutionary biologist. He was charged with obtaining visual, and hopefully physical, evidence of anything living. Their objective was to describe how it evolved on Europa's icy surface or in its stygian ocean depths.

The mission also had three engineers who would keep things running and trouble-shoot on the go – Eddy Bourke, Jake Wesley, and their second in command team leader, Nina Barker. All were already up and on the go.

Next to last was Benito 'Benny' Giordano, their communications expert, and then finally their quant, Oliver 'Ollie' Masters, their all-round geek who was a mathematician and theoretical physicist.

Morgan thought it was a good team, and he sat staring at nothing for a moment as his mind organized his tasks into categories of near term, medium, and long term. Then he ran over the tasks his team would be doing – there was a hellova lot to do, and even though they had several days until they landed, he knew it would seem not nearly enough time.

He trusted his team, but it was the technology he believed was the risk – everything had been tested a hundred times, in computer simulations, and also in massive icy flotation tanks at their Neil Armstrong Test Facility in Sandusky, Ohio. And once more up at a frozen Arctic base to test run the land-based rover vehicle.

But now it was time for the rubber to really hit the road, so everything had to work first time, and perfectly, and their lives would depend on it.

Their engineers could do basic repair and updates to the equipment, but there was no machine shop and spare parts would be nearly four hundred million miles away.

Morgan tilted his head back on his neck and shut his eyes. They'd be on and under the Europa moon's surface for just five days, less than a week.

One team would be deployed on a surface mission to the Plain of Circes where discolored streaks hinted at either mineral deposits from geyser eruptions, or perhaps some sort of biological growth. That team would be led by his second-in-command, Nina Barker.

Then, team two, led by himself, would take charge of the large subsurface probe that would melt and drill its way down to the ocean and take a tour of the depths. The special submersible was basically a water-going tank and had the ability to dive down to ten thousand feet while still maintaining good speed and maneuverability.

They would be following the path of a small probe named Nemo, that disappeared twenty years ago.

Nemo had seen something in the Europa ocean depths before it mysteriously vanished. It was that footage that lit the fuse on their expedition. Whatever was down there had potentially indicated a form of communication, and now it was the Traveler Mission's task to investigate. To find it. And maybe even communicate with it.

Brad smiled, remembering his older brother Greg telling him about it. Brad had still been at high school then, but his brother's explosive enthusiasm had ignited a fire within his own breast, and twenty years later, here he was about to find answers to his brother's questions about what that glowing 'angel in the darkness' really was. The concept alone nearly blew his mind.

Brad got to his feet; he needed the AI systems to run a quick integrity and equipment check, and then he needed to organize the crew. And his body told him he needed to hit the gym.

***

Their few weeks orbiting Europa went by quickly and soon the icy moon loomed large in their view screens as the time ticked down to landing. The group crowded around and looked at the near glowing blue ball.

The tiny moon had a slightly pastel blue appearance as its surface was composed of almost pure water ice that generated some solar reflection. However, in addition, there were various salty compounds below that ice that reacted to the astral radiation of space and emitted its unique glimmer.

Seeing it up closer they also saw there were blemishes and brown streaks that looked like surface veins and bruises which were expected to have been created when the water pressure below the ice punched through in massive geysers reaching miles into the thin atmosphere, and when it dropped back and dried and refroze, it left behind a mineral residue.

"Duck egg blue," Morgan whispered at the glowing ball.

He knew up close it wouldn't be so smooth, as there were valleys, mountains, and plains all made of ice and snow. Even though on paper the aquatic, below-ice mission was the most dangerous, once they melted their way down, for the most part their going would be literally flying unimpeded through open water. But the MGV – Mobile Ground Vehicle – or Rover, would need to navigate a path through some dangerous ice terrain that would throw shade on the most arduous places in the Antarctic.

There were many large and smooth areas on the surface that would have been potential landing sites, such as the 'Pwyll' impact crater named after a character from Welsh legend. Or there was another like the huge 'Tyre', which drew its name from the mythical mermaid, Tyros, which was a remnant of a large impact that was characterized by a set of concentric circular fractures more than sixty-miles across. All of them would have made for easy going for the lander.

But it was decided the touchdown area was to be one of several 'dark spots' on the surface. Areas that looked like blemishes on the surrounding icy crust of Europa. These features were first seen by the 1979 Voyager mission and had diffuse outer margins and little topography.

The theories were that they could be minerals from ejaculate from the planet's oceans after an impact. Or they could have been some sort of growth – algae, fungal, or something else entirely. And it was this that made the area attractive to the scientists planning the mission.

Morgan turned to watch his crew smoothly and efficiently going about their routines. He saw Jake Wesley taking Heather Winterson a coffee, and he caught the look they shared with each other.

He knew that there was a hint of romance blooming there but hoped they kept everything professional. After all, they had all made a pact, knowing this was a mission where they could suffer injuries, or even in a worst case, fatalities, and if that happened they agreed they would continue with the mission and not pull out. To do that might mean the end of the space program for decades. Or even for good.

He scoffed softly and turned to see Nina Barker looking at him. She half smiled and nodded. He returned the gesture.

They both came out of the same astronaut training sessions and had immediately hit it off. They were both single, and he knew that Jake and Heather weren't the only ones that might have something to follow up when they got home.

But right now – *focus* – they still had a lot of work to do.

Their craft, the Traveler, wasn't a dispatch craft or just a drop ship, it was a lander. It was designed to get down on the surface and deploy the two vehicles – the over-the-surface rover, and the submersible, Bruce, a little play on the upgraded and much larger version of Nemo.

Then when the mission was completed, the Traveler was designed to launch from the surface. Both the rover and Bruce were staying behind and coupled with lighter atmosphere and reduced payload, meant they would burn minimal fuel when taking off in exactly five days' time.

This time stamp was chosen because the elliptical orbits of Jupiter and the Earth would be once again close, shortening their trip back. It was not to be missed, or they would need to wait for another complementary orbit – another five days – not too much. And that was their fallback. But the delay heightened the risk to the mission and meant dwindling resources. And if for whatever reason they missed that second one, then the Earth would have moved out of its close orbit, and then that was it; the next orbital handshake was over twelve months away, and long after they ran out of supplies. And as far as Morgan was concerned, that was never going to happen on his watch.

Morgan checked his combination data unit on his wrist and checked the timer. He drew in a deep breath and let it out.

"Go time."

He rose to his feet and headed back to check each team member's preparations. Every minute of the time on Europa's surface was valuable, exciting, and history making, and no one wanted to waste a moment. And frankly, everything was planned to the second so there was no time to spare. They needed to arrive on the Europa surface ready to go.

It was his job to pilot them in, land, and within one hour deploy both craft. The only team member remaining onboard with the Traveler was Benny Giordano, who would be in contact with both teams, and also home base.

Though the man was disappointed not to be going on one of the surface or subsurface missions, his job was the most important of all – without him, they had no eyes and ears with each other, and no connection to back home. However, if there *was* a problem with Bruce when they were below the surface, everyone knew, there would be no one to come get them.

Morgan half smiled; he knew that it got worse because if there was a problem with the lander, there would be no rescue mission from Earth. At least none that could be mounted and arrive within five years.

Their one life-line was the life rafts; escape pods built into the ceiling of the Traveler – two of them – each able to take four comfortably, and five if they crowded. Space onboard was not a problem, especially if they were sedated.

Morgan sat a moment with Angie Sommers, their linguist.

"Boss." She grinned up at him.

"So, do you think you can do it?" he asked.

"Talk to them?" She shrugged. "If there's something down there to talk to. And they feel like talking. And we arrive at the right place." She sat back.

"The right place? *This* is the right place," he replied.

"I hope so." She fully turned around in her chair. "But imagine if an alien species arrived on Earth, and they landed, say, in the center of the Sahara Desert. Or the Antarctic, or the Amazon jungle. They might conclude after trying to talk to the lemurs, or penguins, snakes, or jaguars, that there is no intelligent life."

"I get it." He nodded. "I think we are. In the right place. We'll follow Nemo's path from twenty years ago, where they encountered the, *ah*, resident."

"The resident?" She nodded. "I like that." Angie tilted her head to him. "Just remember, we're the aliens."

"Got everything you need?" he asked as he rose to his feet.

"Well, it's too late to go back if I've forgotten anything." She grinned. "But yeah, I'm ready to roll. And excited as hell."

"That makes two of us." He gave her a small salute and did the rounds of the other Travelers, as they called themselves. They'd trained years for this, and now they were about to leave their footprints in the history books – as an astronaut who set foot on an astral body nearly four hundred million miles from Earth. Who could ask for more?

He saw all were in final stages of their prep, and even though none had really slept all that well after coming out of hibernation, they all looked fit, alert, and impatient.

In six more hours they were coming up on the Europa touchdown target and had a last crew meal together where they splurged on the best of the rehydrated foods that included everything from salmon and butter sauce, turkey and cranberry, and fried steak – all ground down to mush with vitamins and minerals added. But at least the nutritionists and chemists who had created them had kept their eye on the actual taste so what they got was both healthy and nearly delicious.

"Carry on," Morgan said as he sat down with his tray amongst the group. He had a bag over his shoulder.

The group had silenced for a moment in the presence of authority, but then Nina Barker pointed to Angie.

"We were just throwing ideas out about what a Europa inhabitant might potentially look like." She grinned. "So far we have mermen and mermaids, giant blob creatures, and intelligent whales."

"What are the defining characteristics?" Morgan asked and sipped his coffee.

"Deep oceans, so maybe no hard framework – bonelessness," Hiroyuki suggested. "And intelligence." He grinned. "Europa's ocean have been here for four billion years. Long enough for evolution to have sparked an intellect."

"And physically robust. The ability to withstand cold and crushing depths," Nina added and then turned. "What about you, Captain? What do you think?"

"Maybe like a jellyfish." Morgan put his cup down. "Sure, why not? They can withstand cold, and pressure."

"Intelligence?" Nina raised her eyebrows.

"Okay, then, how about, an octopus – boneless while being extremely strong and dexterous. And they're smart."

Angie Sommers bobbed her head. "Yeah, or something like them."

"No, maybe exactly like them. I'm serious," Morgan replied. "Anyone ever heard of *panspermia*? It's the theory that some or all of life on Earth started somewhere else and was seeded to our planet. Maybe from a falling asteroid." He nodded slowly. "There's even been papers written by scientists that suggest octopus really *are* aliens." He lifted his cup again and toasted the crew. "So, my money is on something like that."

"*Panspermia*. I like your thinking." Nina lifted her mug and toasted him back. "Life arriving from somewhere else in the cosmos."

"One more question," Morgan said. "We've all seen the footage of Nemo's disappearance. The size of the, *ah*, indigenous anomaly, that was either a single large entity, or maybe multiple things operating in a coordinated school formation. So, would anyone like to take a guess at what the real size of the entity is we may encounter – big or lots of little ones in a school?"

"Deep sea gigantism," Angie offered. "The deeper you go, the bigger things grow."

"I agree. Such a big ocean, plenty of room," Heather said, and Jake nodded vigorously.

"The square-cube law." Ollie Masters had his hand raised.

Everyone else just looked confused.

"Ollie, are you making up weird shit again?" Jake scoffed.

Ollie grinned back but shook his head. "Nope. It's a mathematical principle that describes the relationship between the volume and the surface. Basically, this principle states that as a shape grows in size, its volume grows faster than its surface area. It has serious implications for biomechanics. As a physical mass increases so does gravity's effect on the respiratory system, musculoskeletal system, and locomotion. Eventually the creature can't cool itself down or support its own weight."

"I've heard of that. But does it apply here?" Angie turned. "Hiro, you're our evolutionary biologist. What do you think?"

Hiroyuki nodded. "Good science. But you already answered why it does not apply here. We all know that the buoyancy of water negates to some extent the effects of gravity. Therefore, sea-dwelling creatures can attain very large sizes without the same muscular, respiratory, or skeletal structures that are required by similarly sized land-based animals. And this is the primary reason that the largest animals to ever exist on Earth are all aquatic species."

"A Patagotitan might disagree," Ollie shot back. "It was a genus of titanosaur dinosaur from Patagonia, Argentina, around a hundred million years ago. It was one of the, if not the, largest known land animals to ever exist and had an estimated length of a hundred and twenty-one feet, weighed in at sixty-nine tons, and..."

"And lived in swampy areas and probably spent most of its life in or on the edges of lakes." Hiro raised an eyebrow. "Yes?"

"Yeah, possibly." Ollie sat back.

"So, bottom line, there could be giants down there," Morgan said. "But they may never come up for us to see them, as we'll just be skimming the surface."

"Maybe they'll be intrigued enough to come and find us," Angie suggested. "If they're as curious as we are. Remember Nemo."

"We'll still need luck." Morgan half smiled. "And here's a fun fact: our oceans, Earth's oceans, cover seventy percent of the globe's surface. But did you know of that, eighty percent of that total is what's called the abyssal zone, the dark and deepest part of our oceans. Places we still can't get to. Or get to easily." He smiled at each of them. "That means, over eighty-three percent of our own world's oceans have never been explored. Who knows what's down there. Or how big anything really gets down there."

"We get it. Europa is a lot bigger and deeper than Earth's oceans, so there are more places for them to inhabit, and grow ... and hide." Nina shrugged.

"*Them.*" Angie smiled dreamily. "I can't wait."

The crew sat in silence for a moment, mulling over what they had just been told.

"And now..." Morgan opened the bag he had brought and lifted out a bottle of champagne. "This was hard as hell to bring and luckily I know people in high places."

The group clapped, drained their coffee and wiped out their coffee mugs.

"Thank you, Brad. Or should we thank your brother?" Nina grinned.

Morgan laughed softly. "Okay, yeah, thank you, Greg." He poured them all an equal measure and raised his cup. "Here's to making new friends."

The group sipped, and then Nina held up her cup. "We're just here to skim the surface. So here's to luck."

CHAPTER 06

The Traveler spacecraft was in its terminal, slow orbit around Europa, and final prep was being undertaken before Morgan would need to strap everyone in for descent. He had a little over an hour to go as Europa having an equatorial diameter of only one thousand nine hundred and forty miles, even smaller than our own moon, meant circling the small blue ball was fast.

He still remembered the footage from the last probe's voyage below the ice – there were the lights, or maybe clusters of eyes, they had counted eight of them. But even with a computer clean up, the shape was too amorphous to provide any tangible description.

Even the size was hard to judge as one second it seemed to be a dozen feet across, and then next to be closer to a hundred – and then it either expanded or broke apart.

It had seized Nemo. And then travelled down into the mysterious Europan depths. Taking Nemo with it.

Morgan drew in a deep breath and let it out slowly.

Would it try and do that to them? They would be in a much bigger and more powerful craft, so would it be able to?

They had a few defensive mechanisms this time, but he'd be loath to use them in the event the creatures were more fragile than their earthly cousins. He'd hate to be known as the only man in history to have met a being from another world… and killed it.

His wrist comm beeped, letting him know it was time to take to the cockpit as they were coming up on their landing site. They only had five days on Europa, and the first day was literally just checking they had landed in one piece, preparing the two vehicles, sending and receiving any final instructions from home, and then most importantly getting some rest for what lay ahead.

Come the morning, at least Earth time morning, as it takes eighty-five hours – three and a half Earth days – for Europa to rotate on its axis for one of its days, so time would be judged on the Earth-Sol orbital rhythm – then they would load up their respective vehicles, leave the Traveler, and head to their mission zones and commence their real work.

Morgan felt proud, exhilarated, and a little nervous. Though he was curious as all hell to know what was down there, his priority would always be to get everyone home safely. Only then would the mission be a success.

Morgan headed up to the top level of the craft that was shaped like a large, stretched disc bristling with sensors and cameras. Above him was the small layer set aside for the escape pods, below that was the pilot deck, crew quarters, hibernation bays, and mess area. And then in the final section was the machine room and the two cradles holding Bruce and the Rover.

Morgan took to his chair and rotated it to the front. He strapped in and the first thing he did was reopen the meteorite impact doors over the huge viewing screen, and as it slid back, it showed the glowing ball filling their view.

"Hello, beautiful," he breathed.

He couldn't deny it was a magnificent sight – it was a soft, luminous blue tint and there were spidery veins running all over it with the odd splotch of red and brown thrown in. His macabre imagination kicked in and he couldn't help being reminded of a huge eyeball staring up at him.

He opened the ship-wide comms.

"Good morning, ladies and gentlemen, this is your captain speaking." He smiled. "If you'd like to take your seats and then check your viewing screens, you'll see our home away from home for the next few days. It is a fine morning on Europa, and temperatures are expected to be a balmy minus-two-hundred and thirty-two degrees."

There was a glint from the surface, and he frowned as he watched it coming up on his starboard side – there was something there that didn't look natural. At least as far as natural from a Europa perspective.

He opened the comms. "Nina, starboard side. You seeing this?"

"I got it. Amplifying," she replied. "Looks like a landed, or downed craft."

"The Russians? That two year ago mission that vanished," he guessed.

"The Gorbachev II. Maybe," she replied. "Had to be a reason for the Russians stopping all ROSCOSMOS press announcements about it just when it was due to land."

Morgan knew that the Russians had launched for Europa before them and made a big deal about what they were going to do. They liked nothing better than beating the US to the punch. But then when their ship was close to Europa and ready for landing, all communications ceased. He knew that you only did that when things went wrong. Very wrong.

The ship passed by, and he judged it to be about fifty miles from their own landing site. Close enough to get to in their rover. But only if they had spare time. They had a full dance card as it was.

Morgan looked again at the image of Europa, and he opened the mic again. "Our baby-blue world awaits us. As well as history."

He checked the instruments one more time, and everything was green across the board. Morgan drew in a deep breath. "And. Here. We. *Go*."

He initiated the thrusters to allow them to break orbit and the Traveler began its descent.

***

The two hundred foot long silver disc-shaped craft started its descent to the icy surface, coming in at a downward angle of one-twenty degrees and traveling at three hundred miles per hour.

On the tiny moon's frozen surface there was no sound, no movement, and no change. But below the ice something watched the craft, and then kept pace with it, moving swiftly beneath the ice crust to meet the new arrival at its landing site.

CHAPTER 07

The drop was a gentle drift down to the icy surface of the moon. Their designated landing site was not far from where Nemo was launched and was on the edge of a large sea – an area of smooth ice called a 'sea' even though it was actually a massive, flat area of surface ice probably from an ancient meteorite impact and upwelling of warm, subsurface water that had spread out smoothly and then refroze.

It was also close to some colorful streaking which would be the first stop for the ice rover to explore and analyze. Another advantage was that the ice on the meteorite impact site was particularly shallow at only eleven hundred feet thick – given that some areas had a supreme density of up to fifteen miles, this would be an easy and quick-drill melt place for them to be able to enter the ocean.

The Traveler was one-twenty-feet long, and eighty wide, making it a stretched circle shape – he bet if he arrived over Earth, many people would have claimed to have seen a flying saucer – and they'd be right.

There was little turbulence in the thin atmosphere, and Europa, like Earth's moon, had no weather, no storms, no wind, or sky colors – looking up at any time of their day or night would just show a black, starlit sky.

Coming in he slowed the craft. There was one other thing he needed to be conscious of – Europa having an ice surface meant that they couldn't use rocket thrusters on landing as it would have melted and sunk them into the ice. When it refroze, then they would have had their skids locked in by the new ice.

However, the Traveler's air-jet landers could lower them gently in the thin air which is what Morgan used now.

"Eighty feet," he intoned.

The craft gently lowered with barely any feeling of movement.

"Fifty," he said.

"All clear, all scanners," Nina added.

"All good." Morgan's eyes stayed fixed on the readout screens.

"Twenty."

And then with a gentle bump, they were down.

"Cutting engines." He shut off the thrusters.

There came the usual squeaks and groans as the craft's superstructure adjusted to gravity after the years in space. It was only thirteen percent of Earth's gravity on the surface, but the craft complained regardless.

"We have a secure touchdown, everyone." He breathed a sigh of relief.

The crew cheered, but he quietened them. All they'd done is pass the first test.

"No one moves a muscle until we do a full integrity check. Nina, you're in charge." Morgan shut down a few other landing systems, and the huge machine quietened around them.

"Aye aye, Captain," she said and began issuing orders.

Morgan sat in the chair for a few more moments feeling something like an electric charge run from his toes to his scalp. This was the biggest moment in space history since Yuri Gagarin orbited the Earth, or Apollo 11 landed on the moon.

"Ladies and gentlemen, boys and girls, we just made history," he whispered to himself, slapped the arm rests, and then got to his feet.

This is where it all gets real, he thought.

CHAPTER 08

After an hour's workout and the first solid meal he'd had in over two years, Morgan and Nina were down in the belly of the ship to check on their two research craft.

Morgan folded his arms and smiled as he looked at the pair of formidable machines – they were heavily armored for what they were built to do, but with radical different designs. His, Bruce, was on a sled that would transport it out of the machine bay of the Traveler and was like a giant torpedo-shaped fish complete with fins. Just like with Nemo, there was a drill nose cone that could be heated to four hundred degrees to melt their way through the ice down to the subsurface ocean.

Once there the nose cone would be ejected, and he would power it free. Joining him as his aquatic team would be Angie Sommers, Hiro Nakagawa, and Eddy Bourke.

Nina would have as her crew in the rover, Heather Winterson, Jake Wesley, and Ollie Masters. Staying at the controls in home base would be Benny Giordano.

Nina ran her hand along the tank-like land-based vehicle. It was shaped like an armored troop carrier but was bristling with sensors.

It had six huge silica-enriched rubber tires run through with Kevlar thread. The compound tires were near indestructible and remained flexible in frozen temperatures, thus enhancing their traction. Unlike Morgan's craft, her vehicle had opening doors for them to leave the rover when out on the surface so they could investigate their environment, collect samples, and undertake experiments.

Though Morgan and his team were able to exit the craft it could not be done in water so he would have to be satisfied with using robotic arms to grab things and place them in different enclosures which could then be drawn inside the craft for analysis.

"Radiation insulated, and its armor plating can withstand micrometeorite impact." Nina banged the toughened steel exterior of the rover with her fist. "High risk, high return. And a very big price tag," she said. "And we'll be leaving them behind."

"Damn shame," he replied.

She nodded. "What I would give to have this big bad boy sitting in my driveway." She raised her eyebrows. "Hey, I've got five bucks that says I find proof of life before you do?" She grinned and held out her hand.

He scoffed, and grabbed and shook her hand.

She grinned. "Easiest five bucks I'll ever make."

"You've seen the Nemo footage, right?" He let her hand go and tilted his head.

"Could have been something." She turned to him. "I'm betting the surface discoloration is a form of biological matting – life. And yours? Could have been nothing more than ice crystal reflection."

"Yeah sure." He lifted his chin to her. "You do know that no one gives the go ahead to spend billions of dollars on the basis of ice crystal reflection. Drinks will be on you, beautiful."

"Well…" She turned to him, leaning in closer. "Then if either of us are first, we both win."

He nodded. "Agreed. Let's ready the teams. We've got work to do, and the clock is ticking."

***

The crew donned their suits. The surface gear for Nina's team would be the bulkiest and had thermal inner linings that had heat ribbing from the toes to the fingertips. They could be temperature controlled to increase and decrease the temperature. If one of the passengers was to exit the craft, the heat could be jacked up – after all it was between two-twenty and two-sixty degrees below outside so anything exposed would be snap frozen in the blink of an eye.

For the underwater crew, their suits were far less bulky. The upside of the smaller scale suits was they had a lot more mobility and therefore comfort than the overland suits. They still had heat pads, but the water was basically three times as warm as the surface otherwise it would have frozen. If, for whatever reason, they needed to leave the craft at depth, they all knew they needed to be in shallow water, and even then if they had to travel more than a few hundred yards, their standard suits would not be enough insulation. However, there was a single deep water heavily insulated suit that looked more like a muscular robot than an outfit. It would be for emergencies only with a maximum airtime of just two hours.

On completion of their mission they would need to rise to the ice ceiling and then burn their way back to the surface. This would be archived by using their remaining power to heat the skin of the entire craft. The rover crew would be assisting. Then they planned to simply walk back to the rover and then drive back to the Traveler lander. Bruce, like the rover, would not be coming home.

Morgan was already in his suit and spoke softly to Nina as he performed a suit-check on her.

Everything needed to be buckled down, zipped closed, and tape sealed. Even a fraction of an inch exposure would be enough to create a needle of pain that could soon turn deadly.

In the rover, she would be embarking on multiple mission trips, returning each day to the Traveler mother ship. But once he was down, he'd be staying down with his crew until the day of departure. They'd rendezvous at another ice sea twenty-five miles from where they launched and melt their way back up, with Nina waiting for them. And as a plan B, if needed, the topside crew would blow a hole in the ice so they could emerge. They needed to work together. Or Morgan and his team would be staying.

Satisfied with her suit prep, he stood in front of her. "Three days," he said.

"Nervous?"

She stepped in close to him, looking up with eyes near luminous with anticipation and excitement. Morgan thought she looked like a school kid waiting for the bell to ring for summer vacation. He couldn't help it, he adored her.

"Nope." She smiled up at him as she grabbed the front of his suit over his stomach. And then: "Yep."

"Me too." He placed his hand over hers and looked down at her. "This is going to be something to tell our kids."

She kept holding onto his hand. "Our kids?"

"You know what I mean," he replied.

"I do." She nudged him. "And I like the idea…" she half turned but paused to glance back. "…whichever way it turns out." She lifted an eyebrow.

They finally released hands, and their eyes lingered for a moment more, before Morgan straightened.

"Okay, let's round the gang up; we got work to do."

***

The individual teams stood by their respective craft. The powerful machines were lined up with the land based rover in front, and Bruce behind.

The rover would head out to the first of the discoloration marks for its initial mission of sample gathering. It would spend six hours out on the icy surface, gathering information. It would also plant relay spikes that would allow them to remain in contact with the underwater team, even as they went farther and deeper away from the lander home base.

It only took them another hour for the teams to be ready even though the excitement made their fingers shake.

Benny Giordano had joined them, but he would soon take to the command deck and seal himself off so he could lower the ramp and expose them to the harsh Europan atmosphere for the first time.

Benny stood with Morgan and had a computer pad in his hand and looked down at the ice moon's stats.

"A nice mild morning at two-four-two below zero." He looked up. "Wish I was coming with you guys." He held out a fist. "Good luck, boss."

Morgan bumped fist with his comms man, Morgan's in the oversized gloves and Benny's bare fist. He had his helmet visor up inside his helmet, same as the other team members. For his aquatic team, if they needed to deploy their face shields it meant they were in the shit. The land team would need to deploy theirs often as the individual team members would be disembarking and opening the rover's inner and outer hatch door to the surface. Though it was all double sealed, there was still the chance over minus two hundred degree atmosphere might sneak in, making it uncomfortable. Or if any longer than a few seconds, deadly.

"Thanks, Benny. We'll see you in four days." He thumbed at Nina. "They'll be back for coffee this evening."

Nina grinned and saluted.

Benny chuckled, and then began to walk amongst the teams, giving a word here and there to individual team members, and then headed up the steel steps to the upper deck.

Morgan turned to his team. "Listen up, everyone."

The group immediately silenced and faced him.

"When that door opens we travel out into history." He half smiled. "In fact, getting here is history, everything we do from now on is groundbreaking, history making, and will be studied for generations. We will write the first rule book on Europa."

He looked along their faces. "What we discover will affect and determine what direction humans will take for generations. The question of, 'is there life' other than on Earth, that humans have held for generations now could be answered in the next few days. And if there is life, is it intelligent? And what could we learn? What could *they* learn?" He glanced at Angie Sommers, their linguist, and nodded, then half smiled. "It's time for us to provide some answers."

He sought out Nina. "Sub commander."

Nina nodded and everyone's eyes shifted to her. "You might be nervous. I certainly am," she said. "But it is a nervous energy that is filled with excitement, hope, and anticipation." She smiled. "One more thing. Our people back home paid over one-fifty billion dollars for this little adventure. So let's give them their money's worth."

Morgan clapped his hands together once, loudly. "Let's load em up."

The crews entered their respective craft, and the doors closed with a slight electronic whine. Both commanders checked all the seals, checked the crew, and then took up their pilot positions.

Finally, they sat with hands on joysticks or U-shaped wheels and waited for Benny to release them.

There was an audible pop as the ramp door opened and the Traveler's warm air met the freezing Europan atmosphere, plus differing density. The water suspended in the air snap-froze and turned to a glittering powder that fell like snow. There came a slight vibration as the rear ramp began to lower.

Morgan stared, his hands tight on the U-shaped wheel. It was a strange sight – the ground was a near luminous white as it was bathed in a weak sunlight, but already they could see the sky behind was pitch dark with a few pinpricks of stars.

This one's for you, big brother. I'm going to find you your angel, Morgan thought. He smiled.

"And. Here. We. Go." He pressed the accelerator.

CHAPTER 09

Brad Morgan piloted the submersible's sled across the terrain at around three miles per hour. His target was a preprogrammed site, and on his screen in front of him there was an image of his progress and a red bombsite which was his drill point.

As he travelled, the front window, though heavily fortified, was covered in a form of blast shield for when it burrowed and melted its way down to the ocean. So Morgan turned to one of the still exposed side windows and saw the over-the-surface rover making its way toward a line of what looked like razor-sharp valley walls that were probably massive ice crystals thrusting up from below the ice sheets.

The rover's six tires were heavily treaded and the Kevlar-impregnated rubber would resist freezing while giving maximum grip. It had more power over the land and a better speed. His own craft ambling along slowly on the sled would be more at home below the water.

Morgan's screen showed him he was coming up on his target site, and he slowed the sled. The scanners had told him that the ice depth was as expected – four thousand, eight hundred feet, and there were no obstructions.

Like our planet, Europa was expected to have an iron core surrounded by a rocky mantle, and that was covered by an enormous subsurface ocean of salty water. And then a thick layer of ice.

He piloted the sled another few dozen feet and then stopped.

"Ready the drill," he said.

Eddy Bourke's hands moved in a blur over the small console and out front the sharp tip began to rotate. Morgan knew it would also be heating.

He pressed the sled's control buttons and the carriage began to gently tilt. When they were at a forty-five degree angle, Morgan drew in a huge breath, and then disengaged the cradle and they began their slide toward the ice.

The rotating tip was at speed and was giving off a slight pink glow as the thermal drives engaged. Before they even touched he saw some of the ice melt and begin to form a small pond under the tip. And then they began their slide into the ice.

The entire craft would be warmed so the ice wouldn't refreeze around them. But it was the heated tip that would blaze the trail.

"And… here we go." Morgan increased the rotations, and the screw head began to drill and drag them down.

The viewing screens went white, and he knew at the slow walking pace of around four miles per hour it would still take them only around thirty minutes to glide through the single mile of ice.

It was smooth traveling, and Morgan knew that they were in a combination of drilling and swimming downwards in a tunnel of heated water. Behind them was not more than ten feet of water, that would cool, and first become slushy, and then freeze solid again. As there was no heaters in their rear end, there would be no reverse.

Morgan checked and rechecked his instruments, and as the minutes rolled on his mind drifted a little, drifted all the way back home to his father, Clay, on the farm. And then back to his brother, Greg, and also to all his friends. He wanted to say to them, 'we did it, we're here', but it would have to wait. At this point in time, he had no fears for his safety or thoughts of his mortality. He just didn't think there was a scenario where he didn't make it home.

"Nine minutes to emergence," Eddy Bourke intoned.

"Roger that, he replied automatically, suddenly realizing he had been daydreaming for ages, and they were now already most of the way through.

There had been no change in the ice, either its density, hue, or mineral content. This was partially due to the area being a refreeze zone from a previous melt, probably from an asteroid strike that caused enough frictional thermality to melt a large open crater a quarter mile across for a while. Or perhaps it was a powerful geyser upwelling that came from the warmer depths and with enough force to melt and blast a hole and then smooth it over when the water settled back to the moon's surface. Either way, the surface ice here was young, less dense, and a fraction of what it could be elsewhere.

"Three minutes," Bourke said.

"All hands, everyone. Prepare to go aquatic," Morgan said.

Everyone's alert level rose and he counted down the seconds, from ten, nine, eight, seven, and then…

With a surge and a clearing of the visual scanners they dropped into the midnight black water.

It felt like constraints had been lifted from them, and Morgan felt the freeness of operation as Bruce was finally allowed to do what he really was designed to do – swim.

"Lights up," he said, and switched on all the front, rear, and perimeter lighting.

But other than the ceiling of illuminated ice above them, there was nothing to see in the ink-like blackness.

Morgan half smiled as he read the stats on his screen. "Temperature is twenty-four degrees, and we are at a depth of six thousand four hundred feet. Below us is dark water down to forty-two miles." He turned. "And this is regarded as one of the shallow areas."

Morgan rotated the craft. The lights were powerful beams that stretched out into the darkness, but there was nothing to see. His scanners told him that except above them there was zero obstacles for miles in any direction.

He knew there was a lot to do, and a long way to go. He should have been exhilarated just to be here, but he prayed for something, anything, other than four days of black nothingness.

"Angie, give me a hull integrity check."

"On it," the woman said and had the system scan both the inner and exterior seals. If there was even the slightest leak or pressure compromission, then their choices were to abandon their trip, or to stay skimming the surface.

He waited and breathed a sigh of relief when Angie gave them the all-clear.

Morgan looked down at his screen that showed him his first day's mission route. It was to mirror Nemo's, and perhaps encounter their own angel in the darkness.

Here's hoping, he thought.

"Proceeding at ten knots." He tilted the U-shaped wheel forward, and then smiled broadly. "To infinity and beyond."

***

Jake Wesley drove the hulking rover, and Nina read off the data from the myriad of sensors covering the craft that was streaming in after every foot they travelled.

They powered along at about fifteen miles per hour even though they seemed to have clear running ahead. It wasn't their top speed, but everything was unknown right now, so caution overrode the need for speed.

Though everyone onboard had tasks to perform collecting and analyzing all the new information coming in, they all stopped from time to time to simply stare out the windows at the bizarre and magnificent landscape as the heavily armored machine lumbered along.

Nina also stopped what she was doing and looked out of the front window – there were towering ice crystals ahead that reminded her of the five hundred foot tall Washington obelisk monument. There were also shimmering surfaces that glistened like rainbows, and areas of ice that were deep blue, sea green, and even as purple as an angry bruise.

She stared in wonder at the walls of sheer ice that looked like it had cracked and broken open, and in some areas created tunnels that were dark and mysterious holes. Everything was being filmed and recorded in their personal diaries for study back home and she allowed the crew to gather round to stare out over her shoulder for a while – she understood what they felt – it was all just so mind blowing.

From time to time they saw things stuck to the ice that looked like fist-sized pompoms.

Heather Winterson snorted. "You know what they look like?" she asked. "When you throw a snowball and miss."

Nina chuckled. "They do, don't they?"

"Everything is so… different," Jake said. "I mean, I want it to be, and expect it to be, but seeing it makes me so thankful to be here."

"It's beyond what I could imagine," Heather whispered.

Nina half turned to her. "There is no life I know to compare with pure imagination."

Heather nodded. "That's beautiful. Who said that?"

"Willy Wonka, who else?" Nina grinned. "It's beautiful out there. And we only just arrived."

"How much more to go until we reach the first analysis site?" Jake asked.

Nina looked down at one of her screens. "Still about fifteen minutes."

The rover bucked as it ran over something like an ice bolder and the standing crew were jolted.

"Yeah, better take your seats," Nina said. "It would really rain on your parade if someone got a broken wrist or ankle in our first hour out."

The crew sat down and reviewed their equipment again. Nina knew that they would be soon stopping the rover and then she would be sending Jake out on the surface to collect interesting samples. He'd bring them back for some preliminary observation, and the rest to take back to the Traveler for detailed study.

They also had another task to perform on behalf of the aquatic crew – they needed to deploy relay spikes that would boost their communications signals – that would give them a loud and clear channel to the lander, but also allow the rover to stay in contact with Bruce under the ice.

They continued along, a valley of ice crystals towering over them like massive gem stones and then exited onto a huge plain of ice that from space had looked as smooth as an ice rink. But now up close they could see it was crisscrossed with lumps and bumps and spider veins like the roots of a large tree.

The veins were brown, gold, and the burnished red of a deep rust color. Though there was only a thin atmosphere, the weaker sunlight shone down making them almost fluoresce. At this point they had no idea whether they were a mineral composition, algae, or some form of clumped microbial growth.

Nina stopped the rover, and the crew joined her to stare out front.

"Beautiful," Heather said softly.

"She sure is," Nina replied.

"I was also going to say, *wow, and we're the first people to see this up close*." Jake raised his eyebrows. "But everything we do is a first for the human race."

"Except for the Russians." Ollie raised his eyebrows.

"True, but at this point we don't know if they even survived their landing," Nina replied.

"Maybe we'll get a chance to check them out," Ollie said. "I'm sure Russia would like to know what happened to them."

Nina looked over her shoulder at the man. "They probably already know." She turned back to the front. "Focus, people."

The group all studied the huge plain, many miles across and edged with a forty to fifty feet rim like a crater. But this area was not created by an impact, but instead by an upwelling where heated water had blasted up into the thin atmosphere before falling back to the surface, spreading, and then refreezing. And as it did it settled smoothly.

Perhaps in another million years or so, with meteor impacts and more upwellings, it too would look all chopped up and craggy again.

There was silence as they looked out over the plain. Until.

"Movement," Ollie said sharply.

Everyone froze for several seconds as the concept sunk in. The group stared fiercely out at the ice, and then Nina slowly turned to him.

"Ollie, what and where?"

Ollie's hands were a blur as he checked and double checked. "Sixty degrees, east-north-east." He began to shake his head. "Small signature... nothing now." He scoffed. "Was there and now gone."

Everyone turned to the direction Ollie had indicated, but now there was nothing but white on white.

"This is Europa, no rain, no breeze, no weather," Jake said.

"But there is gravity," Nina replied. "Even though it's lighter than home, it's still there."

"Falling snow drift?" Heather raised her eyebrows.

"Probably. Maybe the vibrations from the rover shook something loose." Nina turned in her seat. "But our boy Jake here can have a look on his surface walk. Right, Jakey?"

Jake saluted. "I'll take my net just in case I spot a Europa penguin."

Nina chuckled. "I'll be happy if you bring us back some algae. Or anything living would be a good day's work in my book. I have a bet with the commander. And I want to win. So suit up, Mr. Wesley." She turned back to the front window.

"Yes ma'am." Jake turned to smile widely at Heather and then headed to the rear of the craft.

Heather also rose and headed back.

***

Jake had double checked his suit seals, gathered his equipment and donned a belt. He would also take a box-case that contained various sized sample jars and test tubes, plus he also had the six foot tall communication spike.

He felt Heather behind him checking his suit's seals and generally fussing over him. He turned around to her and she pulled one of her most concerned expressions.

"If there's even the slightest sensation of cold, you come back. Got it?"

He smiled. "Yes, Mommy."

She punched his chest softly. "I mean it. If you feel cold, means you've got a leak. If the leak turns into a hole, losing some flesh to necrotizing freezing will be getting off lightly." She reached down to punch his groin lightly. "And some things I'm betting you do *not* want to lose."

"You're right, I need that. At least when I get home," he chuckled. "And yeah, I know, I did the same training as you did." He placed a huge, gloved hand over hers. "This is just the initial walk. I'm only out there for about thirty minutes to survey the surface ice, take a few samples, and jam the spike in. I'll be back before you know it."

She snorted softly, still not looking mollified.

He turned back to her. "But the biggest issue I have is..."

She waited, and his face broke into a grin.

"Thinking of something to do or say that'll make me look cool in the history books," he chuckled.

"You conceited ass." She pushed him in the chest.

In another few minutes he was ready. And weirdly, it was only now the nerves began to kick in.

Jake walked to the single airlock, which was little more than a tub that rotated open to allow a single occupant at a time.

He paused and looked over his shoulder. "Hey, Nina, what happens if I meet an alien?"

"Here, you're the alien, Jake," Nina smiled. "And remember, we come in peace."

"I hope you do meet one," Ollie said. "Means we're not alone in the universe."

"First contact," Heather beamed. "It would be so cool."

"Yeah," Jake grinned. "It would." He turned back to the decon chamber.

There should be no breach of atmosphere but as a precaution everyone onboard would shut their visors sealing themselves into their own cocoon habitat. It was just the cylinder which would pressurize, flush air, and then rotate open to the external site. On the way back in, it would also decontaminate him.

Jake stepped in. It was a tight fit in the bulky suit, but the airlock had a bank of instrumentation and was well lit.

He heard Nina come online.

"Okay in there, Jake?" she asked.

"AOK, and ready to roll," he replied.

"And here we go, on a, three, two, one…"

There was a hissing of gas, and he felt his body become lighter as the gravity changed. And then the cylinder rotated open. Jake felt the breath catch in his chest as he instinctively held his breath for a second or two.

"Good luck, stay safe, and bring us back something interesting. We'll be watching," Nina said.

He blinked a few times; the vista was weird, different, and even though he had seen it out the rover's front viewport, having it right in his face now was truly breathtaking.

His face plate immediately darkened a little as even though there was no bright sky, the white snow and ice seemed so bright it was almost glowing. The unfiltered sun, sol, further away here than from Earth but still reflected on the frozen surface. And that sunlight caught a million different refractions making diamond-like glints and rainbows everywhere he looked.

Stairs telescoped out from the side of the craft and Jake carefully walked down them.

He knew there were cameras on him, recording his every word and step. He was working his single line over and over in his head as he reached the bottom.

He put his foot on the surface and moved his weight forward. It was a lot more slippery than he expected and his foot immediately skidded forward.

He didn't fall, but he did the splits, painfully.

"*You bastard!*" he yelled.

"Mr. Wesley, are you okay?" Nina immediately asked.

"Yeah, yeah." He got to his feet. "It's like stepping on wet glass out here."

"Or ice," Heather giggled. "Beautiful, Jake. That's going to be right up there with Armstrong's *'One Small Step'*."

Jake cleared his throat. "We people of Earth seek knowledge, and we will cross a million miles to find it."

"Nope, sorry buddy, but we're going with *You Bastard,*" Ollie said.

Jake turned, giving the finger to one of the rover's cameras. Then he turned back to look over the Europa icy surface. He spotted a particularly rich vein of rust coloring about a hundred feet further out on the ice plain. It would also be a good place to plant the first comm spike.

"Going to head out for first sample site." Jake turned to salute.

He moved out from the rover, walking carefully across the ice. He used the five foot comm spike like a walking staff at first, as he was now aware of how slippery it was. But he adjusted his gait and soon was walking fine.

If he had turned around, and by chance then looked real hard at his footprints, he would have seen they were now filled with tiny thread-like things that waved and swayed as if looking for whatever had made the warm indentations in the million year old ice.

Jake saw the first patch of discoloration and stopped at its edge. It looked like the roots of a plant if you viewed it from the underearth side and were looking up. There were spidery-looking veins branching out, that were primarily a burnt red color at the filament end and moving to a deeper brown at its center.

He knelt. "First sample." He looked at his wrist computer and took an imprint of the time and exact location. He then pulled a small flag from his thigh pouch and pressed it into the ice.

Jake opened the case and took out a sample jar, removed the lid, and used a steel scoop to rake up some of the rust-colored material, trying to get underneath it to retain its structure.

He lowered it into the jar, sealed the lid and held it up – he couldn't quite discern if it was a line of mineral stain, or actual threads of something, perhaps living and growing.

"I hope you are," he whispered as he stood.

He looked around – *good a place as any*, he thought.

"Going to plant the comm spike."

"Roger that, Jake," Nina replied.

He held the sharpened spike over the ice and pulled a small steel mallet from his kit. He looked at the shiny piece of steel – nine thousand dollar NASA hammer, he bet.

He began to hammer the long spike into the ice.

It took four good strikes before it sunk in about eight inches and was enough to keep it firmly upright. He didn't need to worry about it blowing over, or earthquakes. And as for upwellings, well, they occurred once every few thousand years. Time enough for them to do what they needed to do.

"Comm spike planted." He switched it on, and a small light flickered for a moment, and then went green. "Transmitting now."

"We see it. Continue," Nina replied.

Jake let it go and just as he was about to turn away he paused, frowning –

did he just see that?

Below the ice at the base of the spike he thought he saw something, a flash of lights, or a glow momentarily, before they vanished. Or closed. Like eyelids closing.

"Let's not go spooking ourselves now, buddy," he said softly.

"Repeat that, Mr. Wesley?" Nina asked.

"It's okay, moving on to the next collection site," he said.

Jake continued on toward his next target – it was a patch of ice that lumped up a little higher than the rest. It had the appearance of a large pimple, with a yellowish base, deepening to rust-red at the edges, and then with a lighter colored tip.

"Coming up on the boil," he said. "Are you seeing this?"

"Weird," Heather said and then added with a grin in her voice, "Don't pop it."

Jake walked around it, studying it. Below the lump at the center there was something dark and more solid, and he crouched just as the lights came on below it again.

He shot to his feet. "What the fuck?" He turned to the rover which was a good two hundred feet from him now. "You guys see that?" he asked.

"We saw nothing, Jake. What did you see?" Nina asked carefully.

"Those damn lights under the ice. They were here again. Watching me." He groaned, immediately regretting saying that.

"Did you say, watching you?" Nina asked carefully.

"Come back," Heather said.

Jake looked around, not seeing lights now, or anything moving. "Ah… no, nothing. Forget I said that. Must have been the reflection," he said.

"Mr. Wesley, are you okay?" Nina asked.

"Yeah, yeah, proceeding with collection," he sighed.

I'm just sounding stupid or panicked now, he thought. *Pull up your big boy britches and dial it back a few notches.*

Jake knelt and opened the sample case again. He selected a couple of jars, and took scrapings from the varying colored areas, once again trying to retain its structure for analysis.

He then probed the central section and found the scoop wouldn't penetrate it. Whatever the material's composition, it was rock solid.

"Central core is hard," he said. "Don't think it's ice."

"Compression and pressure can make some ice harder than others," Nina said.

"Maybe it's a meteorite fragment. Just like in Antarctica," Ollie suggested. "On clear days after a katabatic wind has blown away the top layer of snow, the snow is littered with small meteorites that had fallen over thousands of years ago. Many iron based," he remarked.

"Or it could be something from the sea bottom that was ejected in the upwelling," Heather suggested.

"Ooh, even better," Oliver replied. "Can you get a sample, Jake? Try and break off a small piece. Could be important."

"I'll try." Jake took out the metal mallet he used to pound in the comm spike.

He gripped the metal scoop in his other hand and then used the pair of instruments as hammer and chisel. It took him a moment, but he broke away a two inch by two inch piece of purple-looking matter that looked like crystal.

He held it up. "Beautiful," he said.

"Looks a little like garnet," Oliver remarked.

"A seabird?" Jake frowned.

"That's a gannet, you philistine," Oliver snorted. "*Garnet*, it's a translucent mineral. A crystal that's usually a deep red or purple color." He chuckled. "Like that."

"Oh yeah, I know." Jake dropped the piece into a jar.

He replaced the samples in the case and then looked at his fingers. They were covered in what looked like tiny, white threads. He looked back at the ground and squinted – around the peak of the lump there were more of them, though it was hard to see.

He crouched – they looked like hairs and on closer inspection they even had a dark spot on one end like a follicle. He craned closer at his hand again and saw that all the dark spots seemed to be turned toward him.

He'd heard of something called hoar frost, that made the ice form a shape like hairs.

"Weird," he said softly and stood.

"Come on in now, Jake," Nina said.

He took one last look around. "It's a nice place to visit…but I wouldn't want to live here."

Jake headed back to the lander. He never noticed the rust-colored stain on his knee. Or the few threads with a dark spot on the end stuck within it.

Coming back inside he was in the circular tube prior to entering the rover. It flushed him with a strong disinfectant, dried him, and then bathed him in ultraviolet light.

But by then the stain on his knee, and a few of the tiny white threads, had already opened a pinhole-sized hole in the tough suit fabric, and were in.

CHAPTER 10

Morgan stared out at the pipe of light leading them into a lightless void of nothingness. They had been traveling for an hour now, and everything was unchanged.

Above them was a ceiling that looked like clouds, but was really the floor of the ice shell that completely enclosed the planet. It was an upside down world, where the ground was above them, and the inky blackness of the near bottomless sea was the sky below them.

Their route would avoid the super thick areas where the ice canopy was fifteen miles thick, but below them the depths were mind blowing – right now it was just on sixty miles deep. But there were other sea basements that dropped to over a hundred miles. That was basically the equivalent distance of New York from Philadelphia.

They glided on until they came up on the position where little Nemo encountered its 'angel'. Morgan was energized just at the thought of it.

Angie came and placed a hand on his shoulder. "How much further?"

"Four point two miles. Maybe twenty minutes." He turned to her. "Feeling lucky?"

"I'm a realist." She shrugged. "I'll reserve my enthusiasm. It's like spotting a blue whale out in the center of the Pacific Ocean. And then twenty years later you go back to that same spot hoping to see that same blue whale again. It's a long shot."

He nodded and faced the formidable composite glass window in front of them. "Unless it was on a whale migration route."

She laughed softly and squeezed his shoulder. "That's my glass-half-full kinda leader."

Morgan looked down at the screens in front of him. "Better strap in. Just in case."

They were now just a mile out. The short range scanner showed nothing, but further out there was a few impressions, but they weren't solid masses, and the expectations were they might be mid-water floating bergs, with some of them being the size of entire office blocks.

"And, here, we, are…" Morgan eased back on the thrusters and just allowed the small stabilizer jets to operate.

Bruce hung in the water, a tiny metal dot in a moon-sized ocean.

"Rotating," he said and slowly turned the craft three hundred and sixty degrees.

"All clear on scanners, all quadrants," Hiro intoned.

After ten minutes, Morgan sighed.

There was nothing.

But there was one more thing he could try. "Switching off all thrusters. Silence in the craft. Putting hydrophone over internal speakers."

He switched on Bruce's external ears, and everyone sat in silence and just listened.

There was popping and slight cracks, which was probably ice shifting. There came some deep grating which could also have been bergs crashing up against each other.

Morgan breathed slowly, his eyes closed, listening to the sounds of the colossal oceans of Europa.

And then he heard it.

The song.

His eyes flicked open. He tilted his head, his brows drawing ever so slightly together as he concentrated.

It could almost have been a human voice, intertwined with a musical instrument. Morgan had heard whale song before, the booming groans, squeals, and clicks of the great cetaceans. But this was nothing like that. This seemed more, refined.

He slowly half turned in his seat to raise his eyebrows at Angie Sommers, their bio-linguist.

She nodded, her eyes shining. "It could be," she said softly.

He pressed a series of buttons on the console. "Recording."

They listened for several more minutes and the cadence ebbed and flowed. It was the same but different. Not so much a repeating sound, but a stream of lyrical notes that rose and fell, in no particular pattern.

"It's beautiful," Eddy said. "I could listen to this all day. It's just so… relaxing."

"Speak to me, Angie," he said.

"It could be biological. I can't think of any natural sound that might be like that." She leaned forward. "But this place is rewriting all the rule books from Earth."

She typed on her console for a second or two. "I'm looking for pattern recognition to determine if it could be a natural episode."

She fiddled with the external speaker controls, modulating and tweaking, but after a moment, she sat back.

"I'm not seeing anything. And neither is the program." She looked up, grinning. "It sounds like it might really be organic."

"*Hmm.*" Morgan sat staring into the darkness for a moment and then spoke over his shoulder. "Mr. Bourke, give me a direction of that aural emanation."

"A voice," Angie inserted.

"We'll see," Morgan leaned back.

"West-north-west," he replied. "Hard to get a precise reading of where its exact emanation point is. But it's at a depth of around eight thousand feet."

"Deep. Almost to our limit." Morgan whistled. "Okay, well, let's go see who's calling."

He restarted the engines and pushed the U-shaped wheel forward and Bruce scooted ahead through the near impenetrable blackness. He increased speed to around twelve knots, and then angled it down.

Chasing angels, he thought. *That's why we're here.*

Morgan continued to stare straight ahead. If it wasn't for the feeling of motion from the engines giving a soft vibration throughout the craft, it would be impossible to tell they were moving at all.

They travelled in silence for the next thirty minutes, either working on their individual consoles or lost in a myriad of thoughts.

Morgan had lowered the internal temperature slightly as the warmth was making him a little drowsy without any other stimuli. But even then he felt his eyes growing gritty and had to blink them several times.

"Contact coming up," Hiro read from the scanner and then checked some other instruments. "Not the source of our noise and I don't think it's biological."

"Clarify," Morgan requested.

Eddy Bourke had opened the long range scanners. "Free floating. And there's more than one. Big. Real big." He frowned. "Hope it's not a blockage."

"Can't be," Angie replied. "Depth here is sixty-seven miles."

"Doesn't need to go all the way to the bottom. Just drop down below our basement level and we couldn't get under it," Morgan replied. "We'd need to go back. Or try and go around."

"First coming up on port side... *now*," Eddy said and turned to look out the port side view window.

Morgan slowed the craft and switched on the port side spotlights. They saw, looming out of the darkness, a huge white rock that sparkled in Bruce's light beam. It was like an iceberg, but one that had some sort of neutral buoyancy as it remained stationary, as it was suspended mid water.

"*Ho-ley-shit,*" Eddy breathed. "That is one big ass chunk of ice."

"Diameter around two thousand feet. Like an office block," Hiro said.

"Can we get closer?" Angie asked.

Morgan half turned. "Could it roll?"

"Unlikely. Our icebergs roll because the bottom half melts creating a weight disparity. It then rolls to rebalance itself. Down here that can't happen – if it was going to melt it'll melt uniformly." He shrugged. "On paper, should be stable."

Morgan nodded. "Okay, then let's go in for a closer look."

He veered the craft nearer and angled the side spotlight on the floating ice mountain. Up close they could see it wasn't pure white but had speckles embedded in its matrix.

"Animal, mineral, or vegetable?" Morgan asked.

"Can we get a sample?" Hiro asked.

"Let's see." Morgan slowed and used the small thrusters to edge them in closer. "Eddy, get on the claw and grab us a handful. Try and get some of the dark matter."

"On it." Eddy changed seats and pulled out a keyboard and joystick controller. Then he leaned forward to place his eyes over a view screen. From the side of Bruce a small door opened, and a claw arm extended from within the dark portal. "Say the word," he said.

Morgan piloted them in so close the floating ice chunk filled their screens.

"Coming up on a collection of that debris that looks closer to the surface now. I'll hover." He eased in another few feet and then held the craft's position.

Eddy extended the arm, and the claw's steel fingers opened. It reached out slowly and dug into the ice around a speckled area. The claw tightened, but the ice didn't break away.

"This sucker is tough," Eddy said.

He changed angle and gripped again. But once again the chunk he gripped refused to come away.

"Hang on. And I mean *hang on*." Morgan used the thruster to move Bruce away from the massive iceberg. The claw extended another inch momentarily and then a small fist-sized chunk came away in Eddy's mechanical grip.

"Got it," Eddy said, grinning. "Reeling it in."

The claw retracted back into the craft and then he spent the next few minutes depositing the sample in a small container which would be sealed and then brought into the submersible's interior for basic analysis.

In minutes more a green light came on one of the panels and a small door opened revealing a sample jar still freezing cold and wet.

Eddy went to it and lifted it. Beside him Hiro, their biologist, was already trying to take it from him.

"Show me, show me," Hiro said

Eddy handed it over and the Japanese biologist held it up. "*Ahhh*, yes. Could be."

Inside the warm craft the surrounding ice rapidly melted to mush, and then to clear liquid leaving the speckled debris free floating. He swirled it.

"I don't think it's algae or bacterial. But it could be. It could also be mineral." He turned. "But the Earthly rules don't apply here."

"Unfortunately, you only get to do an external investigation. We can't open it until we get back to the Traveler and have had it isolated," Morgan said.

"I know, I know," Hiro said and hunched over a scope with the jar having a strong light beam focused down onto it, making the tiny specks in the jar sparkle.

Morgan powered on, and Eddy warned him of more floating ice ahead. It was in the next hour that whatever was coming up was no office block-sized chunk this time but a gargantuan wall that was around five miles in circumference.

Morgan was prepared to plot a path around it, but Eddy pinged it.

"Hey, this is going to sound weird, but I think there's more depth at its center. And warmth." He frowned. "What does that mean?"

Morgan snorted softly. "Means there might be a cave in there. A big one."

"And warmth?" Hiro asked. "Salt water and warmth are two of the basic ingredients for life."

Morgan turned and smiled. "A micro-climate niche."

"Now I'm really interested," Angie said.

***

The aquatic craft's sensors screamed their collision warning at him as he approached. Morgan slowed, but didn't need the electronic eyes to tell him what was coming.

From out of the gloom the wall of greenish ice appeared. But just off center was a dark void that wasn't its edge, but its core.

The hole in the five mile-sized iceberg was about a hundred feet in diameter.

"And there it is," Morgan said.

Eddy Bourke straightened in his chair. "Hey, hey, hey." He turned. "You're not going to believe this, but the motion scanners are picking something up." He pointed. "Coming from deep inside."

Morgan turned to Hiro. "That sound we heard before. Could it have…?"

"Yes." Hiro turned to him. "It could have come from inside that ice cavern."

Morgan turned back assessing and thinking it through. This was not on their prescribed route. But the inferences of warmth, movement, and the audio was exactly the reason for them being here.

He decided, and half turned. "Hiro, let Benny know what we're doing and tell him we may go radio dark for a while."

Morgan faced the front. "Well, this is why we came, ladies and gentlemen," he said. "Everyone on high alert. This is right off the risk charts." He placed both hands on the U-shaped wheel. "We're going in."

CHAPTER 11

Back in the Traveler, Benny saw the communication spike come online, and immediately the sonar image of Bruce sharpened. He bet if he needed to contact them, the channel would be crystal clear.

He hummed as he then switched screens to check on the rover and saw it had stopped on the edge of an ice plain, and he guessed they were taking their first samples there and where they sunk the first spike.

"A-*aaall* good."

He eased back in the captain's chair. Everything was where it should be and proceeding to plan. He looked out the huge window at the Europan surface – the scene looked a little like he would expect it to look in the Antarctic except everything was oversized – the ice mountains, the expanse of the ice seas, and the gentle blue that from space seemed near luminescent, but now was more crystalline white.

A light blinked on his console, and he turned to it and frowned. It was a warning light, but for a few seconds he could not even remember which warning it was trying to give him.

Benny leaned forward to read the code and saw the lettering: *TOT.* And then he remembered – TOT – Topological Proximity Tilt, and it was blinking.

Impossible, he thought. That would mean the Traveler had started to change angles.

"How the fuck?" he whispered, and started checking other sensors.

They had set down on firm, thousands of feet thick ice, so how was the craft settling or tilting? But sure enough, he saw that the gimbal had indicated a rotational accent of now twelve degrees.

He switched on the banks of cameras underneath the huge craft and scanned for fissures, cracks, or anything to give him a clue. But the ice surface was uniform.

And then he looked closer to the ship – and saw it – the four landing struts had sunk, no, were *sinking* into the ice.

He knew they weren't hot, so they couldn't be creating a melt to bring that about. But something was making the ice around the strut pads melt.

He squinted. *Were those lights under there?*

The pools of water continued to grow around each of the four struts. And that foreshadowed a huge problem.

"No, no, no…" Benny shook his head. "Don't you dare fucking refreeze on me."

But they didn't. And the Traveler continued to sink lower into the ice.

CHAPTER 12

Morgan eased the craft along the ice passageway. There was plenty of clearance and no current, so he thought the risk level was acceptable.

The ice walls were smooth, and devoid of anything interesting and he piloted Bruce slowly and smoothly.

"Speak to me, Eddy," he said over his shoulder.

The young engineer read off data. "Big cavity. Five hundred feet until we come to, *ah*, a change."

"A change? Like what, a wall, or the other side of the berg?" Morgan asked.

"No, not sure what I'm reading here," he sighed. "It's telling me there's a change in approximate density coming up."

"Give me your best guess," Morgan asked.

"My best guess is…" Eddy looked up, "…an air pocket. Big one."

"How big?" Morgan asked.

"Could be thousands of square feet." Eddy shook his head. "Unbelievable."

As Morgan was processing what that might mean, in the light of the front beam, something that looked like a snowball drifted into view.

It floated down and then was right in their path. In seconds the nose of Bruce touched it, and the thing stuck.

Morgan watched it, but it did nothing but sit there. He was surprised that the snowball didn't get buffeted away by their movement. He was prepared to ignore it, when another appeared. Then another.

"Are those things natural?" Angie asked.

"Natural for Earth? Or natural for Europa?" Morgan asked.

As he watched every single one of the snowballs now stuck to their craft.

"And no, I don't think they are," he said.

By now there were about fifty of the things adhering to the skin of the submersible. One of them moved position, and he was about to ask Eddy to grab one but he saw that where it had been there was now a polished area of steel, as the paint had been somehow worn away.

"Lifeform," Hiro said.

"Yes, and I don't like what it's doing to Bruce's skin," Morgan said.

He hated to do it, but… "Going to give them a little encouragement to leave us alone. Give them a little jolt."

He flipped up a clear cover over a button and placed his finger on it, ready.

He hoped they wouldn't be damaged, but he felt he had no choice. If these things could degrade the paint in seconds, if they stayed for ten minutes then they might start to sink into the steel. And then…

"*Jolt* on three, two, one…*jolt*." He pressed the button.

An invisible electrical current passed over the skin of the ship. Nowhere near as powerful a charge as he could have discharged, but enough he hoped to make it uncomfortable for them.

All the fist-sized pompoms exploded.

"What the hell?" Morgan scoffed.

"We come in peace," Eddy chuckled.

"I think your plan to dislodge them was a success," Hiro said deadpan.

Morgan sighed as he stopped the craft and hovered in the water. Around them more of the snowballs drifted closer, but now they kept their distance.

"Looks like they got the message," Eddy said. "Don't fuck with Earth."

"They were fragile. Maybe all life here is the same," Morgan said.

He looked down at the nose of the craft and saw all the silver spots where the pompoms had been corroding it. Maybe they weren't so fragile, after all. He pushed the wheel forward and Bruce began to move ahead in the still water.

After traveling for another few hundred feet Morgan slowed as more debris began to appear. Then something began to stroke past Bruce's glass shield that looked like a four inch long bug and used its ten legs like oars.

"Hey quick; Eddy, think you can catch that?" he said over his shoulder and rotated the craft to keep the bug in sight.

"I can try. I'll use the pump," Eddy said.

He worked a control panel, and a long tube extended from the side of the ship. Its nozzle had limited movement, so Morgan had to try and tilt and lift the craft to line it up.

"Here's hoping it's not as fragile as the powder puffs," Angie said.

"We're going to suck it into the tube, not electrify it." Eddy grinned, keeping his eye on the thing. "Little higher," he said.

Morgan complied.

Eddy's lips pressed together as he worked the vacuum's controls. "And...*got it.*"

The insectoid-looking creature was sucked into the tube. Even stroking furiously against the current it was no match for the inward surge and soon found itself in a sample jar that was automatically sealed. The machinery then drew it in and handed it over to Hiro's workspace.

In seconds more, Hiro retrieved the jar and using gloves held it up. "*Ooh, you magnificent thing,*" he breathed.

The bug had no eyes anywhere on its body, but it seemed to swivel in the jar to face Hiro.

"Arthropodic appearance," Hiro remarked. "Ten legs, feathery limbs for aquatic movement. Has an external carapace, and I'm betting it's used as an exoskeleton." He scoffed. "Could be proof of Europan convergent evolution."

"Say again?" Eddy asked.

"Convergent evolution," Hiro said. "It's evolution of similar biological features and structures occurring in different periods or places. Creatures evolve with the same form and features, even if separated by time and geography. This is big news."

"No eyes," Morgan noted. "Means it's used to darkness."

"That's right." Hiro nodded. "Why would you need eyes in permanent darkness? Just like cave dwelling bugs on Earth." Hiro brought a small probe light close to the jar and the thing shied away from it.

"Must have other sensors," he said.

"For something that has only ever known darkness, light is an abomination," Angie said softly.

Everyone turned to her.

"Well, that's dark." Eddy grinned.

She waved it away. "Just a quote from a favorite author of mine."

As Hiro stared in at the thing it came closer and attached itself to the side of the jar under where his thumb was.

He squinted. From its head end a small spike shot out to try and pierce either the glass or his thumb.

"Hmm, it can't see me, but it knows I'm here. It seems to want to get a taste of my thumb." Hiro tilted his head. "I wonder if it is my body heat that is attracting it."

"Things without eyes usually have a myriad of sensors for detecting movement and warmth. Maybe even infrared. That's how it finds its food," Morgan said.

"Things are getting interesting," Angie said.

"That they are. And we've only just arrived." Morgan turned back around. "Moving ahead."

It was in another fifteen minutes that Eddy told them that the density change was just up ahead. Morgan increased the illumination and saw the wall of green ice approaching. But the sensor told him there was more space there.

When he was just twenty feet from the ice he had slowed and then stopped. He craned forward.

Hiro had joined him. "Are you thinking what I'm thinking?"

"Yep," Morgan said and craned forward, and then up. "There's an air pocket up there."

"Not just an air pocket," Eddy added. "But a void. A big one. And I'm talking big – several miles."

"The berg is hollow," Angie said. "This could be what we've been waiting for. Go up, go up."

Morgan smiled. "Rising, all slow." The craft used its hull jets to slowly lift them.

It was still dark as Hades above them, but there was a reflection from their own lights making a mirror-like effect as they rose toward an image of an upside down Bruce above them.

And then in seconds more they breached. From the glow of their own lights they could make out an ice shoreline, but that was all in the sunless void they had risen into.

"Initiating all external lights," Morgan said, and switched on every external light they had. The multiple powerful lights cast a glow for hundreds of feet in every direction, and it was enough to see what was hidden in the mountain-sized iceberg.

"I don't believe it," Hiro said, his mouth gaping. "It's another world in here."

CHAPTER 13

Heather sat next to Jake in the back of the rover as Nina piloted them to their next analysis site. He still wore his bulky suit but had removed his helmet. He gently scratched at his knee.

"I wish I could have come with you. Out on the surface." She smiled. "Maybe we can go out together next time." She lowered her voice, "If Nina lets us."

"I can hear you." Nina turned to smile. "And everyone will be doing work out on the ice at some time or other over the next few days." She turned back. "Got a few hours now before we reach the next site. Why don't you all catch some shut eye, and I'll shout when we're closer."

"Now you're talking," Jake said and settled back in his chair.

"Sleep?" Heather scoffed. "We're hundreds of millions of miles from Earth and the first humans on Europa, and you want to just go off to sleep? How do you even do that?" She grinned.

"It's an art," he chuckled, meshed his fingers over his stomach and leaned his head back. He turned to her and opened one eye. "See you in my dreams."

Heather beamed and reached across to squeeze his arm. She obviously decided to try and do the same as she also leaned back and closed her eyes, still clinging to his arm.

Ollie also sighed and began to slump in his chair.

"Not you, Mr. Masters," Nina chuckled. "I need you up here."

"No rest for the wicked," he groaned and went to join his team leader.

PART 04
FIRST CONTACT

CHAPTER 14

The single, thread-like creature lifted one end of its tiny body. On that end there was a dark spot. That spot was more than an eye. It was a brain and sensory apparatus.

Alone it was small, weak, and vulnerable. But it knew it could split, and multiply, provided it had enough sustenance. It acted independently, but it was little more than a fragment, a cell, part of a larger horde. Right now, it was hungry and needed to feed to fuel its expansion.

Though the heat of the cabin was not to its liking, the liquid pulse of the large biped being attracted it and it needed to be inside the thing's shell, and feeding.

It slowly worked its way up the body from the leg in a peristaltic motion, almost imperceptible to the human eye.

It took nearly an hour, but it finally reached an opening on the side of the head of the massive creature. In seconds more it had entered.

***

Heather opened her eyes and smacked her lips together. Her mouth was dry, and that was the expected side-effect of being inside an area that had bone dry, recirculated air. She reached for her water canteen and took a sip, re-screwing the lid, and turned to Jake, seeing his eyes were also open.

She nudged him with her leg and held out her canteen. "Good samples you collected. I can't wait to get them back to the Traveler and start work on them."

He ignored her canteen. But after a moment, he nodded, his expression still blank.

"I can't tell if the samples contain something that is animal, vegetable, or mineral. Just looks like black headed rice. But even that is exciting."

She continued to look up at him and her brows slowly came together. "Are you okay, Jake? *Jake*?"

After a moment he blinked. "Hot," he said so softly it was little more than a breath.

"Hot? You're hot?" She leaned a little further around in front of him.

Then she reached up and put the back of her hand on his forehead. "You feel cold. Very cold."

"Everything alright back there?" Nina asked.

"Jake says he feels hot but he feels really cold to touch. Too cold," Heather replied.

"Jake, how do you feel?" Nina asked.

"Hot," he repeated.

The crew still wore their environmental suits, but no helmets in the rover. However, Jake began to work at one of the fasteners at the top.

"Hot," he said again.

"Don't do that, Jake. You know the protocols," Nina warned.

The young man continued to work at his suit, his movements getting faster. In seconds he managed to get the top open, and he worked at sliding his torso out of it.

"Mr. Jake Wesley, you will stop that right now." Nina's voice was forceful, but he ignored her and continued to pull the suit off his top half. She turned to Oliver Masters. "Ollie."

The physicist nodded and got to his feet. Jake was younger and probably outweighed Ollie by fifty pounds, so the older man approached cautiously.

"Hey Jake, why don't we just settle down, buddy. Let me take a look at you." He held his hands up as he approached.

Jake got to his feet, his suit now down around his waist, revealing himself to the crew.

"Oh god." Heather put her hand to her mouth. "Jake?"

His body was covered in patches of what looked like hair, or short white fur. But on each hair-like tendril was a black tip, and they all undulated and waved like seaweed in a slight current.

"There's something on him," Heather squeaked.

Ollie tried to grab him, but Jake batted him aside as if he weighed nothing.

"Hot," he said again and turned about.

His eyes alighted on the exit decon tube. In a blink he moved towards it and placed his hand on the panel to open it.

Nina spun and yelled. "Restrain that man."

But in a blink he had opened the cylindrical airlock door and locked himself in.

"Don't you dare." Nina jerked the rover to a stop and leapt from her seat. "Don't you fucking even think about it, Mr. Wesley. You come out right now!" she yelled.

Jake ignored her as Heather wailed and Ollie banged on the airlock tube. But Jake seemed oblivious to everything and simply turned to the system controls.

"*Shit!*" Nina yelled. "Helmets on, *now*."

Everyone scrambled for their suit helmets and quickly put them on as Jake flushed the air and gravity. And then opened the outer door.

Heather's voice was one long howl, and Nina turned. "Ollie, I'm going out to get him. You follow me."

She turned. "Heather." The young woman babbled. "*Heather*." She roared at the young woman.

Heather looked up with trembling chin and red-rimmed eyes.

Nina pointed. "Get on the mic and contact Benny back at the Traveler. Tell him we're coming in hot with a casualty. Now!"

She resealed the door and turned the exit tube around. When it had re-flushed the air she opened it and stepped in. "We got seconds," she said, and then thought, *No we don't. He's probably already dead.*

Ollie nodded. "Right behind you."

The cylindrical door rotated and then Nina opened the external door.

***

Nina felt her heart beating like a bass drum in her chest as the door opened. The white ice and snow was glaring and her helmet immediately darkened to compensate.

She expected to see the body of Jake at the foot of the stairs, but unbelievably, *impossibly*, he was staggering toward an ice flow some fifty feet from her.

Other than the air being unbreathable, the temperature was around minus two-forty degrees – he should have been snap frozen before he took two steps.

She didn't wait for Ollie, who she hoped would follow her out in under a minute, and went after her young engineer.

"Jake," she called over her mic, and then switched to external audio as the man didn't have his helmet on. "*Jake!*" she yelled.

Behind her she still hadn't heard the external door of the rover open and needed Ollie's help. But she couldn't wait and strode forward just as Jake slowed.

Up closer now she saw that his body that had just been covered in only patches of the strange growths now seemed to be completely coated in moving white hair. And as she watched they spread, multiplying, growing, his body getting a hairy pelt look. But at the end of each was a black dot, and even though they waved and rippled in no breeze at all, they all seemed to point toward her.

Her mind screamed: *they're eyes. And they're all looking at me.*

Jake finally stopped walking. He threw his head back, arms out. "It hurts," he screamed.

Nina stared with a stomach roiling from fear as she watched the tiny rippling hairs cover his face, nose, eyes, and some even crawled into his mouth.

No, not into his mouth, but *out* of his mouth – it seemed the thread-like growths were growing from inside the young engineer as well as from the outside.

Then a long moan exited the vanishing hole where his mouth used to be.

"Jake…" Nina said softly and took a step forward. She held her hand out.

And then Jake just burst apart.

It was like a blizzard of white threads with black tips. One minute the young man was there, and the next, all that remained was the bottom half of the suit, which toppled forward, disgorging thousands or millions of the tiny revolting things.

Suddenly there was puffing breaths from behind her, and Ollie appeared.

"Where is he?" the physicist asked.

"I… I don't know," Nina replied.

She pointed at an area of ice that contained an empty space suit and lumps of white fur-like mounds. It was just another stain like so many others on the Europan ice sea.

Ollie walked closer and got to the edge of the lumped stains and looked down. He walked toward the empty suit, nudged it with the toe of his large boot, and then looked around for a moment.

He turned to Nina and held up his hands. "Where? Where is he?" he shrugged. "Did the cold do this?"

She shook her head, not knowing how to describe what she had seen. In fact, she was starting to doubt what she had just seen with her own eyes.

"Is he okay?" Heather sobbed. "I can't see him anymore."

Nina sighed at hearing the young woman's small voice in her ear.

"Did you get him?" Heather asked.

She turned and in the fortified front window of the rover she saw Heather's outline. She didn't know yet what to tell her.

"What do you want to do?" Ollie asked.

"What can we do?" Nina felt defeated.

She looked at the empty suit debating whether to bring it back. Or to take some samples of the debris stain that was once their youthful engineer.

As she stared, she thought she saw one of the small mounds of white move. She blinked and focused.

The white mound began to flatten, and tiny threads seemed to be stirring over its surface. As she watched, they began to organize themselves, and in lines they started to migrate toward Ollie's boots.

"Hey!" she said.

"Huh?" Ollie turned to her.

"*Hey*!" She pointed. "There… on the ground."

She started to move forward as Ollie looked down.

The white threads were coalescing around his boots. As Nina watched, they started to surge up over them and onto his pants legs.

"Hey!" Ollie started to stamp his feet and back away. "What the hell."

He glanced up at Nina, perhaps for answers. But she had none. He then reached down to try and brush the hair things off, but all he did was manage to get them on one of his gloves. Where they stuck. And then began their march up his arm.

"Help me." He began to smack at them.

Nina was now not more than six feet from her crewmate but stopped, not wanting to get closer as a primitive self-preservation reflex took over.

At a base level, she already realized these things were no natural geological phenomena but some sort of thread-like worm. And after she saw what they did to Jake, she knew they were a dangerous and aggressive one. She also knew what was in store for Ollie.

Ollie now danced and brushed at himself.

"They're inside, they're inside my suit." He put his hands to his head.

"That's impossible. Stay calm." Nina held up her hands, waving him down. "The suit will protect you. We need to…"

But she had no plan for him, as there was no way she could allow him back in the rover with those things on him.

"*Ah*, roll on the ground, dislodge them," she urged, hoping that might have the same effect as putting out flames on a burning body.

Ollie just danced and flapped his arms down at his sides. Then, right before her eyes she saw his tough suit begin to deflate.

Nina stopped dead. "Oh no," she whispered.

The man's suit began to show small pin holes that released jets of warm air out into the freezing atmosphere of Europa where it firstly steamed and then floated to the ground as the gas and water particles solidified.

"Ollie!" she shouted uselessly.

"*It hurts.*" Ollie began to scream and wail as his suit continued to disintegrate. It was a pitiful sound of pain, anguish and fear and tore at Nina's soul. And it was exactly how Jake had screamed just before…

The short man punched at his helmeted head. And then he gripped the helmet at the neck and began to twist.

"No, no, Ollie, please." Nina stepped forward, but the man ripped the helmet off and flung it to the side.

Nina's eyes widened as she gasped in horror.

Ollie swatted and vigorously wiped at his face and head. But he was quickly covered in white hair, and further, some were swarming higher, searching out his nostrils, mouth, ears, and eyes.

She gagged a little as they vanished in the orifices and bet they'd be finding any other egress holes on his body further down.

His eyes were still wide open and they froze solid, turning a milky white, and just like Jake, he threw his head back and opened his mouth, perhaps to scream, but his tongue and throat would have turned to brittle ice by then, and nothing escaped but a small ghost of warm air, as if it was his soul exiting his body.

"What's happening?" Heather asked in a voice that sounded like it came from a little girl.

Nina couldn't respond or even speak and began to shake as she watched Ollie's entire head just shrivel back into the neck of his suit. For a few seconds there was a ghastly image of a headless man standing, hands opening and closing, before he fell back, and just as with Jake, there was a sudden disgorging of frozen flesh and white thread-like worms that burst from the neck of his suit and sprayed in a plume to stain the ice.

Nina felt rooted to the spot. Then her stomach rebelled, and she vomited in her suit.

Nina at least managed to tilt her head a little and thankfully the warm thick liquid didn't coat her visor, but it still filled her suit with eye stinging bile.

Small pops of light were going off behind her eyes and she knew she was going into shock.

You will not fucking pass out, she demanded of herself. *Not here.*

As she stared, she saw that her colleague's suit rippled and pulsed as the remaining creatures poured forth from the suit neck to spread out. Then they seemed to gather themselves and to organize, and then they turned in their long lines like pale army ants.

In a small wave, they began to move in a peristaltic motion over the ice. Toward her.

"Fuck no."

Nina's muscles unlocked and she began to back up. She had no weapon, nothing to defend herself with. She had seen how they penetrated Ollie's tough suit, and they probably did the same to Jake's. She knew she was basically defenseless before them.

Nina desperately wanted to wipe the vomit from her chin but couldn't. She backed up a step, then two, walking backwards.

"Nina, what's happening?" Heather asked again in her tiny voice.

"Heather, listen to me. Start the engine." Her own voice cracked with fear.

"I don't know what's happening," Heather sniffed wetly. "Where's Jake and Ollie? I can't see them anymore."

"Just start the fucking engines!" Nina yelled so loudly it hurt her already raw throat from vomiting.

She looked down and saw that the white thread-like worms had begun to pick up speed, moving with purpose and flowing like liquid over the ice.

Nina turned and ran.

In seconds she hit the outer airlock, entered, and waited impatiently while she was deconned. As soon as the process completed she ripped her helmet free to drag in clean air and wipe her greasy chin.

The circular tube door slid back, and she burst out to find Heather waiting for her and not at the controls.

"Where are they?" Heather begged.

Nina pushed past her, heading fast for the rover pilot controls.

"I saw them fall down." Heather wrung her hands. "Is Jake okay?"

"They're gone," Nina said as she started the huge machine and began to back it up.

"Gone?" Heather came and grabbed her shoulder. "Gone, *where*?"

Nina shrugged her off, fury beginning to animate her now. "*Look*." She pointed out the main screen.

There was a white wave, like a snow drift, moving over the ice toward the rover. Nina had no doubt it would get inside if it wanted to – armor plating, seals or no seals – and she bet it wanted to.

"You see that shit?" she yelled.

Heather's lips pressed together as she glanced out and finally nodded.

"That shit is alive. And that's all that's left of Jake and Ollie, because it fucking just ate them." Nina gritted her teeth as she wrestled with the controls to turn the rover around. "And if we don't get the fuck out of here, that'll be us as well."

"Where are we going? We're supposed to rendezvous with Bruce." Heather sat down slowly in her chair.

"We're going back to the Traveler. We need to warn the teams. There's danger here." Nina gritted her teeth as the massive machine began to come out of its turn.

"Stop!" Heather yelled.

Nina was shocked at the force from the young woman and saw her looking out of the corner of the front screen as the rover completed its arc.

"*They're alive!*" she screamed.

Nina looked back to where her crew mates had fallen and froze in her seat, a shock running from her toes to her scalp – there were two people standing there. Her heart pounded as her brows came together. She saw that they both looked stiff and unnatural.

"No. That's not them," Nina said, feeling short of breath.

She suddenly felt a little dizzy as if she was about to black out from fear. If she did, she knew they were both as good as dead.

Heather grabbed Nina's arm and jerked on it. "It is them. We have to go back."

"Look." Nina yanked her arm away. "Neither of them are wearing helmets and it's nearly two-fifty-degrees below zero out there. *That. Is. Not. Fucking them.*"

"But, Jake…" Heather stared, her eyes glistening. Her mouth moved but no words came.

Nina saw the two figures begin to shamble towards them. She concentrated and saw one of them carried something that looked like a pustulous yellow sack in its hands. It was about the size of a basketball and was softly pulsating.

"Fuck that. We're outta here." She accelerated away from the horrifying scene.

CHAPTER 15

Benny ran from one scanner to the next. The Traveler was sinking lower into the ice, and he knew that it wasn't melting its way down, instead something was liquifying the ice just around and under the landing pads and was somehow drawing it down.

He checked the belly cameras and saw the hint of lights still deep down below them. It was as if there were eyes looking up at him, watching, and waiting.

"Nope. No way," he said and stood.

He had been tasked with acting as the relay center for messages. But in absolute shit timing, the boss had gone radio silent as they entered some sort of communication blackout zone.

"That's it, no more fucking around."

He went back to the pilot's chair and sat. He engaged the engines. The drives were a powerful form of air jets just so they would avoid a fire burn to melt the ice, exactly what was happening now. But he could still bring a huge amount of lift to bear, which should do it as the ice around the struts was still liquid.

"Let's just pick her up and drop her a few hundred feet from where we are now," he said to the control panel.

He glanced at the cameras and his eyes widened.

The pools of water around the struts had changed color – it wasn't the shimmering pools anymore, but a mushy white. It was beginning to freeze. It was as if whatever was below the ice knew exactly what he was planning.

"No way. No way." He increased the engine power and pushed the lever gently forward on the panel.

The Traveler should have gradually lifted. But she didn't move.

On the console beside him he saw the light come on letting him know that there was an incoming message from the rover. He shook his head and spoke through clamped teeth.

"Not now, Nina, not now. Got a big fucking problem here."

He pushed the power lever forward a little more and the entire craft shook and vibrated as a battle between the strength of their engines fought with the grip of the ice.

"Come on, baby, you can do it," he said and gave the lever another push.

The whine of the Traveler's engines lifted in volume along with the vibration throughout the hull of the craft.

Benny's teeth showed as he willed the Traveler to lift. And then with a groan she began to rise.

But only a few inches as, like a bird being held by its legs, it couldn't break free of Europa's icy grip. And then the noise every ship's pilot dreads – the sound of tearing steel.

With a crunch and crack, the ship's front landing pad snapped free from the leg, and the back ones were beginning to stretch as metallic tendons and bones were starting to tear and break.

For Benny it was a lose-lose situation – if he continued to lift he'd lose all of his landing pads and most of their struts, meaning he couldn't touchdown again. And if he settled now, he wasn't free of the ice that was trapping him.

He guessed that if he resettled, at least they'd have legs under the ship, and when both teams got back it might take a manual effort to dig them out when they had all hands at the ready.

Unless the melting started again, and this time swallowed the entire spaceship.

"*I don't fucking know!*" he yelled.

The grinding and cracking got louder.

"Fuck it." He pulled the lever back slowly, reducing the engine's power and the huge craft began to resettle.

The front strut's pad was missing, and the Traveler had a forward tilt, and Benny could tell by the sound of the rear ones taking the weight that they had suffered damage as well.

"Oh, what did you do on the mission, Benny?" he said with turned down mouth. "Well, while everyone was away doing important jobs I just destroyed part of the ship." He cut the power, and the craft groaned, tilted, and settled with a forward slope so he was angled down toward the icy ground.

"You had one fucking job, Benny." He blinked watering eyes. "And you fucked it up."

But as a final insult the tilting didn't stop. The Traveler began to sink even lower as the ice liquefied once again, this time all around the frontal command area of the ship.

"*Stop fucking doing that!*" he screamed.

He rubbed his face, hard, and looked out the front screen, and now that it was pointing down at the ice he was sure he could see the lights again, several of them.

And they looked like eyes, staring up at him.

He only then noticed the comm system still trying to get his attention – it was still the rover.

"Not a good time for a chat, Nina," he sighed and then decided to answer it.

Benny listened with growing alarm and his own problems seemed nothing compared to what she was saying.

But what she was telling him didn't make sense, and he had a million questions. But by the sound of her voice she was in no mood for conversation.

"I'll be ready for you," he said and jumped from his seat.

He stopped. There was no way he could lower the ramp with the ship sitting lower and at an angle. They were going to have to walk it in.

Benny grabbed his helmet and headed for the hatch. They'd only been on Europa for a day and already things were going to shit. He just hoped Commander Morgan was having better luck than they were.

CHAPTER 16

The crew of Bruce crowded the front window and looked out at the wonderous scene – the ice cavern they were in was beyond both their imagination and the extent of the craft's lights as it didn't have the illumination strength to extend to its full height or sides.

There were walls of meshed ice crystals, and also things that might have been a type of unique ice formation or perhaps even a growing plant life form. It was all mostly white, and draping strings of glittering icy beads to a carpet of what they at first thought was snow but could have been a form of living ground cover.

"A world within a world," Angie said. "How?"

"I got movement. Lots of it," Eddy said and looked from his scanner to the window again. "Forty degrees, north-west quadrant."

The group looked to where he indicated, but there was nothing but stillness. Even a low lying mist stayed as a blanket a few feet over the ground.

"External sound on," Morgan said.

Hiro switched on the audio sensors. And they listened to the sounds of inner Europa.

"Oh my god," Angie whispered.

There was a hissing, and a low moaning, perhaps like the sound of a breeze through the brittle limbs of twisted trees in a midnight graveyard.

Morgan shook away the morbid thoughts.

"Well, that is creepy as hell," Eddy scoffed.

Morgan folded his arms. "Nothing in life is to be feared, it is only to be understood." He half smiled. "So said Marie Curie over a hundred years ago."

"Had she ever been to Europa?" Eddy grinned.

"It's because of scientists like her, that we're all here now." Angie scowled at the young man.

"I don't believe it." Hiro swung away from his analysis panel. "The air out there is breathable. Oxygen component is a little high, but very breathable."

"We need to take a look," Angie said. "I mean, that's what we came for."

Morgan crossed his arms, thinking about it. It *was* what they came for. But that was supposed to be the rover crew's job, not the aquatic crew. Though they could exit the craft, their suits weren't the heavily armored enviro suits like the ones the rover crew wore.

"It gets my vote. What do you think, boss?" Eddy asked.

He drew in a breath and let it out slowly. Then turned in his chair. "Eddy, I think I have good and bad news for you." He half smiled. "We are going to do a short external exploration. But someone has to stay in the craft.

"*Aww*, no way." Eddy sat heavily.

"Sorry, Eddy, but I need my biologist, and linguist, just in case." Morgan sat forward. "And I need a competent pilot who I can trust to look after our ship. If anything happens to it, we're stuck here, and nobody is going to come for us. Let alone even find us."

Eddy closed his eyes and let his head tilt back on his neck. After a moment he nodded.

Morgan got to his feet. "Suit up, people."

***

Morgan brought the craft's side in close to the ice shelf. He then instigated a small pulse of warmth over the skin of the vessel that melted through the wafer-thin ice surrounding the thicker ice of the shelf so he could nestle in against it. This meant they didn't have to enter the water or have to leap across thin ice to get to the solid ground, while they still had plenty of water underneath them.

Morgan handed control of Bruce over to Eddy. "We'll stay on comms. You too. Keep watching the hull sensors. I don't want anything creeping up on you." He half smiled. "If anything happens to you, we can't even walk home."

Eddy returned a quick salute. "Don't worry, I'll stay alert." He lifted his hands. "Just wish I was coming with you."

"Next time," Morgan replied.

The trio headed to the airlock. Their suits weren't as bulky as Nina's ground based crew in the rover, but the temperature inside the berg-world was a lot warmer. Plus there was oxygen levels that should be breathable.

Hiro had already performed a scan for free-floating microorganisms and found it to be clean, so if they wanted to take their helmets off, it was possible. But whether they did or not would be Morgan's call.

"Ready?" he asked the small team.

Nods from both and they affixed their helmets.

This time they didn't exit from the ramp, but climbed a ladder to the upper airlock door, and one at a time went out with Morgan leading them.

One after the other they stood on the ship's surface and walked forward a pace or two to stare out at the strange, alien scene – there was an ice forest, or what Morgan's Earthly imagination made him think of as one. Their halo of light only illuminated a hundred feet in all directions, but the place must have been huge, because as the shadows intruded further out, the place seemed to get bigger. In addition, the clang of their footfalls on Bruce's skin created a distant echo that seemed to bounce away for miles.

Morgan turned slowly looking out over the eerie frozen landscape that was illuminated by Bruce's powerful lights but still left too many shadows.

Movement, Morgan remembered Eddy had said. And in his gut he felt something was out there – it might have only been falling crystals out in the darkness. Or it might have been a life form.

Gotta win my bet with Nina, he thought. The smart money was on him to find traces of life first, so he was still feeling confident.

Morgan turned on his helmet camera so everything would be recorded along with their personal diaries. Hiro and Angie would do the same. This was history making, unexpected, and damn wonderful.

Angie and Hiro had brought sample jars and analysis kits. And he had brought a long flashlight, that would double as a club – a meagre weapon if he really needed one.

"Wonderful," Angie laughed softly. "I never ever expected to see something like this. And I'm so happy that I got to."

"How could we know it even existed?" Hiro said. "It was hidden from us."

"Well…" Morgan said and leapt down to the ice. "One small step."

Once Angie and Hiro joined him, they already had their helmet lights on, and each used strong lanterns and flashlights.

Shining them around Morgan assessed his best path. There seemed to be a break in the ice flora, and he pointed. "That way."

They headed in.

They soon moved out of the radius of the submersible's light and had to rely on their own lantern, flashlights, and helmet lights.

Hiro read off the information and the oxygen levels remained consistently benign, and the warmth was staying the same at a cold, but not freezing, forty-two degrees.

It was after another few minutes they came to the pool of water – open and unfrozen. Hiro crouched beside it.

He focused his beam on it, and then pulled out a probe and got down on his hands and knees to bend forward.

"You see this?" He dragged the probe along the edge and held it up. There was something draped over it that looked like whitish, glutinous snot.

"I think this is either a microbial mat, or some form of primitive algae that doesn't require light."

"Bring some back," Morgan said. "If that's life, I might have just won my bet."

Hiro collected a sample, and also some water into another jar, setting them aside. He looked up at his crewmates.

"If this is biological matter similar to that on Earth, then it is the basis of a food chain." He looked back down into the pond. "I'm betting just like on Earth, there are minute unicelled organisms in there, simple creatures like amoeba, sporozoans and flagellates. On Earth, they're known for living deep in caves."

"How do they survive in the darkness?" Angie asked.

Hiro held up the jar with the slimy-looking strands inside. "Green plants use the sun's energy to convert carbon dioxide into organic compounds such as sugar in a process called photosynthesis. It's the same process that algae and many bacteria learned how to do. But some free living algae in deep caves use different metabolic pathways to survive without light. They find or capture organic matter in the water that can be used as a substitute for photosynthesis."

"Carnivores," Angie replied.

Hiro nodded and smiled. "This is important. This form of biological matter is the basis for all food chains. There will be things feeding on this matter, and of course, other things will have evolved to feed on them."

From behind them there was a soft snap that sounded like a twig breaking off somewhere in the darkness. The three people turned to it, shining their lights over the white, crystalline landscape, but there was nothing.

After another moment, Morgan turned away. "I guess we might find out just how big that food chain is, and just what sits at its top."

Angie turned from their icy surroundings. "What do you want to do?"

"We give it another few minutes. I don't want us to get too far from the ship," Morgan said.

Hiro stood, keeping his eyes on the pond. "I'd love to know what is in the deeper parts of that pool of water." He turned. "These suits are watertight aren't they?" He grinned.

"Don't even think about it," Morgan laughed softly, and then pointed with his light. "We take that pathway, towards the tall things that might be trees or might be crystalline growths."

"I hope they are trees." Hiro packed away his samples.

Morgan then led them on, and they first rounded an odd-shaped boulder and headed further in.

***

As they passed, dark adapted eyes observed them. To the watchers the bipeds were flaring red as their body heat was like a beacon to everything inside a world that was perpetually frozen.

The thing they had thought was a boulder lifted, and from underneath, a knot of eyes extended on stalks like some sort of mollusk, they all bent in the direction of the moving animals. Then the thing lifted on dozens of sharp pointed legs and began to follow them.

***

Morgan led them on until Hiro stopped cold. "There," he said.

Underneath an overhang of rock there was a cluster of rounded objects all glued together. Each was about the size of a basketball, and they were totally white.

"What do they look like?" Hiro grinned.

"Eggs." Angie grinned back.

"Big eggs," Morgan added and looked about. "I'm not sure we're equipped to run into whatever laid them."

"Can we take one back?" Hiro asked.

"And what if it hatches in the ship?" Morgan replied. "Do we want some sort of pet running around on the Traveler? We can't even freeze it to slow down its metabolism, as it's already bone cold in here."

"Yes, this is true." Hiro made a guttural sound in his throat. "Next time we will be ready."

As they headed in further they stopped as a stream of weird bug-like creatures crossed their path. They were around two feet long, seemed to have no head, and had armor plated white shells. As they went by, they scoured the ground clean, leaving behind a totally smooth and polished surface.

Morgan smiled. This place was alive. He couldn't wait to tell Nina.

"They look like slater bugs," Hiro said. "Or maybe isopods. They live in the bottom of the ocean in complete darkness and the deeper you go the bigger they get."

"Their mouths must be underneath them," Angie said. "Maybe they exude their stomachs and eat as they forage."

As they waited for the line of bug things to pass, one of them looked damaged.

"Is that a bite mark?" Angie asked.

"Looks like it." Morgan's eyes narrowed. "Something definitely has a mouth with teeth in here. Guess these guys aren't top of the food chain."

The small group spread out a little and Hiro walked toward a wall of ice which might have been one of the perimeters of the berg-world.

"So smooth," he said as he lifted his light.

Morgan came and joined him and the trio looked up at the monolithic wall of ice that lifted hundreds of feet into a layer of darkness their lights couldn't challenge.

"I guess this is the end of one side of our floating world. The ocean might be beyond that barrier." Morgan walked closer, feeling the cold emanating from the wall. He lifted a hand to place it against the ice and looked up.

He stood there feeling, *something*. He had a prickling feeling on the back of his neck as if there was someone close behind you in a dark room, but you couldn't see them.

After a moment he dropped his hand, turned, and walked back to Hiro.

"Let's go."

***

Behind Morgan and Hiro the massive ice wall flickered and moved.

In another moment, several orbs of light started from dots to grow to many feet across as something with luminous eyes gazed into the berg world from the ocean outside. It stayed there for many minutes, watching, assessing, and learning.

After a while it receded back into the black water beyond the wall of ice.

***

Hiro and Morgan examined something that looked like tracks in the crushed ice when there was a sound from overhead and Morgan pointed his flashlight upwards. As the trio were focused there, something darted through one of their light beams.

"*Hey*, did you see that?" he asked.

Then from behind them as the last of the two foot long bugs were passing there was a cracking sound and they spun to see the line had been interrupted and there were deep scratches in the ground, now leaving an open space in the line of critters.

"Did..." Angie frowned. "Did, some of those bug things just vanish?"

She stepped out from under the ice rock overhang – immediately something came out of the darkness and landed on her back. She screamed, Morgan swore, and Hiro stumbled back onto his ass.

The creature that landed on Angie was big, easily a four foot wingspan and humped muscular back. The body of the thing looked like someone had thrown together bat wings over a shelled octopus with sharply pointed crab legs.

"Visor!" Morgan yelled. Thankfully, Angie heard him, and she engaged the hardened clear material that closed over her face.

The thing then tried to lift off with Angie, and her feet left the ground for a few seconds such was its strength. Morgan reacted quickly, with Hiro running in to also help and the pair leapt at the furious creature.

The back was armored, but the front was soft, wriggling tentacles and at their center was a hooked beak apparatus that it was frantically using to try and crack Angie's helmet open. While that happened dozens of small writhing limbs worked at every joint, angle, and armor plate, looking for an opening.

Morgan used his flashlight like a club, smashing it down on the thing. But it bounced off as the shell was like iron.

He gave up and grabbed it, tugging, but all that did was have the strange beast wrap muscular tentacles around his own forearms.

Morgan then felt the temperature of the thing through his suit – it was near freezing – and he also felt the power as it gripped him. They hurt, so he knew Angie must have been both scared out of her wits, in pain, and seriously had a chance her suit would be compromised.

Hiro threw his pack off and quickly tugged it open – he had no weapons, but he did have the next best thing – a small welding-type device that he initiated and then leapt back in to the fight over Angie.

Hiro touched the creature on its head. There was an audible sizzling sound and a shriek that Morgan would remember for the rest of his life.

The revolting beast unwrapped its tendril grip on both people and flapped heavily up into what passed for some tree-like growth in the ice world, and sat facing them, and Morgan bet if it had eyes it would have been glaring back at them balefully as its front tentacles coiled and agitatedly stroked the burned area on its head.

"Good thinking, Hiro," Morgan said and then tended to Angie who was down on her hands and knees. He got down next to her. "You okay?" he asked.

The woman got haltingly to her feet. "I hurt all over. Feels like I just did a few rounds against a grizzly bear." She reached up to touch her visor where there were several deep gouges in the super toughened material.

"Glad you didn't let us take our helmets off and you gave me the heads up about my visor. That thing would have ripped my face off." Angie felt all around the seals of her suit.

They turned to where the thing sat facing them and they all knew that even though it didn't have eyes it was somehow staring back. The greyish-white sack-like head pulsated and the shell shone like it had a coating of oil.

Hiro stepped closer. "No eyes. Again." He observed, then said, "I wonder if these things find us through heat sensitivity. Maybe what they can see or sense is a thermal image."

It then emitted a sound, this time not just shrieking, but more like babbling and with high-pitched, sibilant hisses.

Morgan turned to Angie. "Language?"

Angie stared for a moment, listening. "I can't tell. It sounds pissed off. But it definitely sounds like it's communicating."

The thing raised its voice, shrieking louder, and the sound echoed throughout the enclosed ice world. Then from somewhere in the darkness above them came a noise like heavy canvas sheets being whipped by the wind.

"It is communicating," Angie said. "Just not with us."

"Oh great," Morgan scoffed. "Reinforcements."

With heavy flapping another of the creatures landed beside the first. It ambled closer, and its tentacle touched and gently tapped over the original beast's body, and then felt along the burn on the back of its head.

"This might be proof of pair bonding," Hiro said. "I think we…"

His mouth snapped shut as another of the things landed close to the first two. The babbling and hissing became a chorus.

Hiro half turned. "I only have one small welder."

"Well, we had trouble with one of them. Three is going to be a fight we might not win." Morgan looked over his shoulder. "Okay, guys, I think we'll wrap it up for today. Nice and slow now."

Morgan knew that the powerful beak it used to scratch Angie's tough face screen might be able to bite right through the suit material. Or if they managed to get hold of a finger or hand it could break all the bones right through the glove.

"Back up. Slowly," Morgan said as the trio began to edge back in the direction of their ship.

Morgan kept looking back over his shoulder to keep on the pathway back, while Angie and Hiro watched the beasts. For every dozen steps they took, the three weird-looking creatures took off to fly closer, staying within reach.

"They're going to follow us all the way back, aren't they?" Angie said.

"Probably," Morgan said and glanced over his shoulder again. He moved around a huge boulder that was in their path. One he didn't recognize when they came in, and it made him think they might not be following the same way back.

"Hiro, keep the burner handy, we might need it for a little discouragement." Morgan's grip on his club-like flashlight tightened.

"Got it." He held it up, and that elicited some louder shrieks from the original creature. "Ah, you remember that, do you?" Hiro spoke to Angie out of the side of his mouth. "Sign of intelligence."

Morgan turned to her. "That might be a language after all."

"Yep, I'm recording," she replied.

There was a sudden flapping sound and a swirl of frigid air as the three creatures launched themselves at the trio again. In the seconds that Morgan was facing Angie, they struck. But not at the people. Instead this time they went for Hiro's small burner, and in a flurry of leathery wings and hard shelled bodies they attacked, wrestled, and then snatched it from his hand.

"Now we know what they were talking about – they were planning their attack. Clear intelligence," Morgan sighed. "They remembered that burner, and knew it was a threat to them. Probably the only threat. So they disarmed us."

"Now what?" Angie asked.

"I'd say *now we run*, but they'll overtake us." Morgan hefted the flashlight. "Be prepared to fight. If they come at us, we need to stay close together, and not let them separate us. If one of them nearly got you into the air, two, and you might end up back at their nest."

"I'm not staying here," Angie replied.

Hiro slowly rummaged in his kit and pulled out a metal probe which was little more than a twelve inch spike, and held it like a dagger.

Then, just as the three people rounded another huge boulder, as one, the creatures came at them, and fast.

As the people readied for the attack, the boulder next to them lifted, and from underneath the fake rock was a mass of dark eyes on stalks beside crowded, sharp-pointed legs. A spike shot out that was as thick as an arm, with a spear tip.

It impaled one of the creatures that fell to the icy ground flapping and screeching in pain. The other two must have immediately recognized the threat and flew away into the darkness.

As the three people staggered back from the new horror, they watched it reel in the caught prey, and once close enough the fake rock shell slammed down over it.

The trio continued to stare for a moment, until Hiro cleared his throat. "Camouflage ambush."

"We walked right past that thing," Angie said. "That could have been one of us speared."

"Maybe it didn't recognize us as prey animals," Morgan said. "And something else; I think we went past more of them."

"Yes, you might be right," Hiro said. "Did you notice something different about this new creature?" He turned to his colleagues. "It had eyes."

"That's a good observation," Morgan replied. "Why?"

The trio put distance between themselves and the ambush boulder. Hiro turned about briefly.

"Are you brave enough to conduct a quick experiment?" he asked.

Morgan scoffed. "I'll let you know when you tell me what it is."

Hiro grinned. "Everyone turn off their lights for several seconds. See what happens."

Morgan took a quick look around and saw nothing. But after the fake boulder, that just meant they didn't see or recognize the danger.

"Okay, everyone get in closer. Lights off for thirty seconds." Morgan turned to Hiro.

"That should be enough time," Hiro replied. "On, three, two, one…off."

The trio turned off their lights and were plunged into a complete darkness. After just fifteen seconds Morgan began to get nervous.

"Wait," Hiro said.

And then it happened.

A soft green glow began to suffuse the icy environment. It created a deep twilight, and left a lot of shadows and dark places, but it was enough to see by.

"What is that?" Angie looked up at a ceiling, many hundreds of feet above her head, that seemed to be undulating with waves of light. "Is it biological, or chemical?"

"Could be some form of bioluminescence. And there are also some rocks that are iridescent. But then again it might be something we've never seen before," Hiro said. "I'll take a sample back for analysis."

"Explains why some of the things in here have eyes – vision is still useful," Morgan said. And then, "Lights on."

The pipes of light returned to cut the returned darkness. Though Morgan knew he could have navigated within the weak light, it left far too many shadows and they had already had a few lucky escapes from some of the locals inside the berg-world.

The group moved quickly back to Bruce, and in a few more minutes they saw the ship. Angie waved at the form of Eddy sitting in the window. He spotted them and waved back.

Morgan turned. "This place is habitable. It has predators, but no more than any primitive forest or jungle. If we had weapons, we'd be more secure." He turned to his crew. "This will be a place for future study."

Hiro nodded. "Everything seemed to be arthropod based. At least in form and structure. It might be a totally different species base altogether, but it makes sense, as arthropods are some of the most durable and adaptable creatures on Earth. Why not here too?"

"I wonder how many more species there are in here?" Angie asked.

"And another question – are there other floating iceberg worlds drifting within the massive ocean of Europa? And will the creatures inside be the same as these or have they evolved differently?" Hiro tilted his head. "I could spend my life here studying these worlds." He smiled. "And be content."

"Sorry, Robinson Crusoe, you're coming home with us." Morgan smiled as he checked his timer. "Okay team, let's go, we've done enough for this day." He turned and waved Eddy to bring Bruce closer as it had drifted a few feet out from the ice shelf.

They each leapt across and scaled back down into Bruce's belly, Morgan being last and lingering for a moment more as he looked over the once again dark landscape. The lights of the ship robbed them of the strange green illumination, but he still felt like they were being watched.

The samples and the film they had would keep the scientists back home busy for years to come.

Morgan dropped back down, and Eddy was waiting for him.

"Well? What happened out there?" he pointed to the deep gouges in Angie's face plate.

Morgan shrugged. "We saw a pond with some sort of primordial goop in it. Then had to wait as a line of ice bugs crossed our path. Then Angie got attacked by a flying mollusky thing." He rubbed his chin. "Oh, and did I mention a giant fake rock creature ate one of the flying mollusks?"

Eddy's mouth dropped open in a wide grin. "You gotta be shitting me?" He straightened. "Right, that's it, next time I'm definitely coming."

Angie handed him a small disc. "Here's my helmet cam data with images. Check it out."

"Thank you." He took it from her and immediately headed to a view screen to plug it in.

She joined him to watch from over his shoulder and add any comments. "You can take my slot next time." She rested a hand on his shoulder. "I nearly got carried away by the little monsters."

Eddy turned. "You should have told them that you just came in peace. Seems to work in the movies," he scoffed.

She cuffed the back of his head. "Oh, we came in peace. The problem was they wanted me in pieces." She shrugged. "And we had no weapons."

"Let's get going." Morgan took his seat in the command chair. "We've got more ocean to explore, and we need to make it to a rendezvous point with the rover this time tomorrow."

Hiro turned with a satisfied look on his face. "I knew our aquatic mission would be more eventful than theirs." He turned back to his console. "I wonder if they've found any boring microscopic bacteria yet." He laughed and turned back around.

Morgan grinned. "For all we know they're having tea right now with some Europa moon men." He nodded. "Be good to catch up tomorrow and compare notes."

He dropped the ship down around fifty feet in their landing pool and then pivoted around to face the long tunnel to the exit. He engaged the engines. They had work to do, and as yet they still hadn't seen any sign of their angels.

Once they were out of the radio black spot, he'd check in with Benny and see if any news had come in from the rover, or from Earth.

He smiled; things were getting interesting.

He checked the pulse sonar telling him the shape of the tunnel of ice they were in – *not long to go now*, he thought. Then they could head off once again into the ink-black icy water of the massive Europa ocean to their rendezvous point. And Nina.

He smiled at the thought of her. He couldn't wait to see her, and did he ever have some cool things to tell her.

***

From out in the darkness small lights came on – eyes – two at first, then a cluster, and then more.

They hung in the water watching the submersible for a while, before most blinked out. Then they began to follow.

CHAPTER 17

Nina drove at maximum speed and the rover bounced and bucked as it struck sharp edges of jagged ice. She prayed they didn't rupture anything, and she forced herself to breathe in and out slowly even though she felt her heart hammering in her chest and her mind fraying to the edges of just blowing apart.

What had happened to Jake and Ollie? They were dead, gone, she knew it. But their bodies were standing there watching them as she sped away.

No, not their bodies, her mind rebuked. Just their suits. Their suits filled with something that wasn't flesh and blood. That wasn't human at all.

Those tiny white threads with black heads. *Or eyes*, her mind screamed. They had somehow consumed them, and then replaced them.

Were they separate creatures all working together? she wondered. Or was it a single organism and those threads were its individual cells all working in unison?

They were just a few klicks out and Nina opened the comm system. "Benny, Nina Barker here. We are coming in hot. We have casualties, and need urgent attention. Over."

She waited, but there was no response.

She tried again. "Benny, do you read? Over"

There was still no response.

"*Benny, where the fuck are you?*" she yelled.

"Is everything okay?" Heather mumbled from behind her.

Nina let out a harsh breath. "Yeah, sure it is. Just must be a tech problem."

"Or maybe those little white things got him too," Heather's voice was barely a whisper.

"Don't even think that," Nina shot back, and accelerated, because that was exactly what she was thinking.

In minutes more they came out of a forest of crystalline growths, and she saw then why Benny hadn't responded. The Traveler was down on the ice on its belly. And there was Benny surveying the damage or trying to do something with one of the heat torches.

The man stood and turned when he heard them approaching. He raised a hand but waved them down to slow. Nina pulled back on the throttle and the bulldozer-like machine slowed to a crawl.

"Visors down," she said.

They were already in their suits but engaged their clear visors and went to circulated air. Nina was first into the decon airlock and one after the other she and Heather stepped out as Benny approached.

"What happened?" Nina pointed to the Traveler.

He looked past them. "Where's Jake and Ollie?"

"Gone," she said and lowered her head for a moment. "We were attacked, and they got…" she shook her head. "They're just gone."

"Attacked? Gone? Gone where?" Benny's voice rose. "What does that even…"

"*Shut up!*" Nina barked. "We don't have time for this. We need to get Morgan on the line. I can't reach him." Her head jutted forward. "We've got serious problems, and we need the Traveler. What the hell happened here? Why is she laying on the ice, Benny?"

Benny shook his head. "She isn't. The landing struts are down. But they melted, or rather the ice melted around them, and the Traveler sunk."

"What? How?" Nina walked forward.

"I have no idea," he exhaled. "But as it was melting, and she started to sink, I tried to lift off. But then it snap froze and held on. When I powered back down, and settled, it began to melt again, and we sunk. It was like it was done by design."

"Oh no, oh no. This can't be happening. *Are we stuck here?*" Heather wailed.

Nina spun. "Jesus Christ, Heather, will you keep it together?" she growled. "We've got other priorities." She turned back to Benny. "Are we still operational?"

Benny nodded. "We're stuck, for now. But everything is online."

"Good," she replied. "Let's try and contact Morgan. And send a message to Earth base." She turned to look back at the rover. "We still need to rendezvous with the aquatic team. When we have them, we'll make a plan."

Nina turned away. *Once Morgan is with us, everything will be alright,* she told herself.

But she had a dilemma – she'd just lost two of the most physically strongest team members, and there was some heavy lifting work that needed to be done at the rendezvous point. She needed Benny. But if she took him, what happened if the ship started to sink more? And she certainly couldn't leave Heather behind by herself. With her frame of mind, she was liable to get spooked by something and decide to try and lift off.

She decided – she and Heather would just have to manage.

Nina turned. "Benny, we're going to head out to the rendezvous point. You need to monitor the ship and not let its belly become trapped in the ice. We can lift off and get home without the landing struts. But if we tear the belly out of the Traveler, we're fucked."

Hearing that, Heather made a small squeak in her throat.

Nina glanced at her and then back to Benny. "Send a message to Earth base. Tell them we have encountered a hostile indigenous species. And two of our team have not survived the experience."

"Jesus." Benny went a ghastly color behind his visor.

Nina stepped in close to him, jabbing him softly in the chest with one knuckle. "Keep trying to raise Morgan. Tell him we'll be there to meet him. But once he surfaces, we are heading straight back, and I recommend an immediate dust-off. Got it?"

Benny nodded up and down mechanically for a moment. "Yep, yep."

Nina glanced around. She wished they had weapons, but they never expected they would ever need them. Why would they? If they did find life, they were thinking it might be little more than microbes or algae.

"Okay." She turned then to Heather. "Ms. Winterson, are you okay?"

Heather's mouth turned down as she shook her head.

No, she mouthed.

Nina walked over to the young woman and grabbed her by both shoulders. "Heather…" She shook her softly until Heather met her eyes. "Heather, you need to be strong now. We all do. As they say, the shit just got real. We finish our job and we get home. Safely. That's it. Are you with me?"

She nodded.

"Ah, Nina…" Benny swallowed noisily. "What should I look out for? I mean, for these deadly indigenous creatures."

Nina thought for a moment. "Threads, hairs. White. And thousands of them. There's no breeze out there. So if you see a snow drift moving toward you, then that's them." She was about to turn away but paused. "And they can clump together, make shapes, like…" She didn't really want to say it, "…like living things."

Benny swallowed again. "If the ship is under attack, should I…?"

She knew what he was asking.

"Yes," she said. "Get the Traveler into orbit. If need be we'll give you a new landing site. But whatever you do, do *not* let these things into the craft."

"Okay, okay, I got it. But, uh, you want me to lift off without landing struts?" he asked.

"No choice. The Traveler will be a lot lighter now that Bruce and the rover is out of its hold. If the struts are gone, she can survive a belly landing." She looked at him from under her brows. "You can do this, Benny. I know you can." She saw the man was still pale as a sheet and decided to dial it back a notch. She smiled. "But I doubt it's going to come to that."

Nina drew in a deep breath. "We've all got work to do." She checked her wrist panel and saw the countdown until Morgan and his team reached the resurface burn point. They would melt their way back to the ice floor, and in doing so would use up their remaining fuel. To assist, the plan was that the surface team would blow a hole in the rest of the ice and make a crater. In effect, burrowing down to meet them.

They could still do it, she thought, bolstering her own confidence. It was time to get going.

"Heather, let's go." She saw the absolute fear in the young woman's eyes.

"I can't." The words were little more than a squeak and Heather just looked down at her boots.

"Of course you can," Nina smiled reassuringly. "Listen, we go out and get them, bring them back to the Traveler, and then we all go home. How does that sound?"

Heather just shook her head, and then sat down on the ice. "Sorry, I can't. I'm so scared I feel sick and can't think straight. I won't be any good to you."

Oh shit, not now, Nina thought and felt a surge of anger.

"*Listen…*" Nina was about to order the young woman to follow her but knew that would just cause a mini mutiny.

"I'm sorry," Heather said.

Nina crouched, looked into her face, and reached out to rub her arm. "It's okay. You stay here and keep Benny company." She turned to Benny. "Look after her. And look after the Traveler."

Benny nodded.

Nina saluted, turned and walked stiff legged back to the rover. She reentered the vehicle, took off her helmet, sat, and then faced front. She just hoped that Morgan and his team were safe and were at the rendezvous point as expected.

And if they weren't?

Her mind raced off into risk management planning.

If there was a worst case scenario, and something had happened to Morgan and Bruce, then she would turn back, board the Traveler and head home.

And if the Traveler was incapacitated? Her mind whispered the doleful question and it gave her a heavy feeling in the gut.

Then…?

Then she and everyone else remaining here were dead.

Nina's vision blurred as the tears welled up. She hated the feeling of losing control, and her entire life had been one of success, and mastering all manner of situations. But right now, she was lost.

She leaned forward and rubbed her eyes with the heels of her hand.

After a moment she sat back. "I'm not fucking dead yet."

She wiped her eyes with her sleeve. Right now her priority was the resurfacing submersible and seeing Morgan again.

Come on, Brad, she thought.

She liked him, a lot. And they'd whispered many shared promises for when they got home. But right now she didn't just miss him, she needed him.

Please be there, she prayed.

She looked over her shoulder at the empty rear of the rover. She also wished she had Heather with her, but the young woman was closing down, and she just hoped that some quiet time with Benny allowed her to get herself together.

Nina was just glad Heather didn't see first-hand what happened to Jake and Ollie. That might have pushed her right over the edge.

Nina checked her position on the grid console – the rendezvous point should have taken them half a day to reach. But there would be no stops for sightseeing or gathering specimens now, or at any time. Also, they had arrived on Europa at sunrise, and the days were eighty-five hours long.

The daytime temperature was a balmy two hundred and twenty to two sixty degrees below zero. But the night time temperature was down to three hundred and fifty below zero. Even their thickest enviro-suits weren't really designed to be able to deal with that drop in temperature.

They expected they would be gone by sundown, or at least safely all inside the Traveler. But if for whatever reason they ended up staying longer and being caught outside in a Europa night, they'd all be frozen solid.

"We can do it," she muttered.

She checked her destination settings – still twenty miles to go and she prayed she didn't run into any obstacles. Once they arrived at a large flat and shallow area of ice, the plan was for Bruce to initiate a full burn by using all its remaining energy stores on heating the skin of the ship and literally rising up through the ice sheet.

It should take several hours and if all went to plan, they should make it all the way to the surface.

But if it was thicker than their estimates or they ran into something unexpected, then the rover team were supposed to plant charges, and blow a hole in the ice to break it up and reduce the amount of thickness above them so they can breach quicker.

Forget it, she was going to blow a hole in the ice anyway to speed up Bruce's ascent. Speed was critical now.

She cursed; Jake was supposed to plant the charges and all four of them were to work on the retrieval if they created an ice crater to help Morgan and his team climb out of the pit before it refroze and trapped them forever.

Now it would be just her, doing everything.

Just her. She sniffed wetly, feeling a little overwhelmed by the morbid thought.

Nina looked over her shoulder at the empty cabin again – she couldn't help her mind going back to the loss of her crew members. And what happened afterwards. She had seen them, or their bodies, or at least their suits, standing there. Had the thread-like things somehow created an approximation of the flesh and bone and were animating it? Were they trying to *be* people? she wondered. And to what end? What did they want?

They had somehow consumed everything that was her friends and then inhabited the spacesuits. They even had their height, weight, and build right.

Did they think that was going to fool the rest of us into letting them inside? And if that's what they wanted, then what would happen if they made it inside?

Nina swallowed and shook her head. Bile threatened to rise into her throat as her stomach roiled. She wished they had weapons as she felt they were all vulnerable, and if their only defense was to run away, that only worked as long as they could stay ahead of the threat.

Her console lit up with an incoming message from Benny. She glanced at the landscape; seeing everything all clear, she leaned forward to read from a small screen.

Benny said he wasn't able to send a message but he did get an incoming information squirt from Bruce. They were closing in on the rendezvous point – she scoffed as she read the next part – they had found life.

"*Life*," Nina sighed. "Yeah, so did we."

She checked the destination map again. She was making good time, and there was only eleven miles to go.

The rover approached a towering ice formation that created an arching bridge which she passed underneath. For a brief second she thought she saw something move up there, but blinked and refocused and wasn't sure if it did or was just the strange light beaming down from a cold black sky onto the ice surface.

Come on, Nina urged and stared straight ahead as she gripped the U-shaped wheel so hard her hands ached.

Just a few more miles to go, she begged.

***

Several hundred feet out from the rover one of the snow drifts moved. It rose up into a lump as she passed as if straightening itself to get a better look at what just passed it by.

Once the hulking machine passed, the lump settled back to the surface to become invisible. But then like a small wave, it began to flow over the ice, following their path.

CHAPTER 18

Morgan's brows came together as they travelled along the passage of ice to the exit. He slowed Bruce as he stared out from the front viewing window.

"Hey, was that there before?"

Angie, Hiro, and Eddy turned to look out from the front window.

One of the walls were etched with deep carved sworls, strokes, and dashes. They were all assembled in a single box-like frame and stood fifty feet high and that much again wide.

"How did we miss them?" Angie scrambled forward.

"We didn't. Not a chance," Eddy said.

"Were they just done? While we were in the cave?" Morgan turned to him. "If that's true, then it's a message. And it's a message just for us."

"Definitely looks like writing to me. But none I can even guess at." Angie had the external camera capture the huge images. "Going to run them through the universal translator."

"What are your chances?" Hiro asked.

Angie bobbed her head. "The language translation algorithms are based on the famous linguist, Matt Kearns' translation engine. But it's bolstered by AI, so can make some best guesses at what the artificial intelligence thinks it is or might be."

Morgan hovered. "How long?"

Angie shook her head. "An hour, a day…never."

"Okay, we'll continue on. But everyone keep an eye on your sensors as something out there is intelligent, close by, and might be trying to talk to us."

***

They exited the huge ice cavern in the floating berg-world a while ago now and were back in the stygian black open water. They still had miles to go, but they had run down the clock on their exploration route inside the ice world. Timing was everything.

Morgan was extremely satisfied and knew it had been worth it as they had discovered proof of life, and diverse life, and further, had identified a magnificent area for future scientific research.

Right now, they would head directly to the rendezvous point and if they saw their angel in the darkness, that would be the icing on the cake. But it didn't matter so much anymore.

"Any more berg worlds?" Morgan half turned to Hiro.

The man shook his head. "All clear all quadrants," he replied. "I wish we had more time. It would be interesting to see if there were more of those floating worlds, and if the lifeforms were the same in all of them or different, showing evolutionary differential development."

"Not this trip," Mogan replied. "But what we have discovered ensures there will be more visits in the future. It's a scientific goldmine."

Morgan's control panel pinged, and he glanced down at it. "*Hmm.* You seeing this, Hiro? I thought you said *all clear.*"

"It was." Hiro began to work quickly on his panel. "Whatever that is, it wasn't there before."

Morgan lifted his gaze form the panel scanners and looked out into the dark water. From way out in the blackness, Morgan saw the tiny dots of light.

"Here we go, people. *Contact.*" Morgan headed towards the dots. "Speak to me, Hiro, Eddy."

"Big signature, range is two thousand feet at twenty-degrees starboard. Speed is five knots." Eddy said. "Three hundred feet, end to end. And coming right at us."

"Got it," Morgan said. "Let's go dark. Everyone keep internal noise to a minimum."

He switched off all external lights, and internal conversations ceased.

Morgan thought it might be best to vanish. He had no idea if the thing hunted by sight if it lived in perpetual darkness, or whether it had other senses to detect motion, thermal, or sound, but at least he could make them less of a target if it was a predator.

"Bogey is closing," Eddy said softly. "Holy shit. Speed has increased to ten knots."

Morgan thought for a moment. If ten knots was its top speed, then they could stay in front of it as theirs was twelve. But if it had more in the tank, then it could run them down. And did he really want a three hundred foot Europan whale meeting them in the dark – especially if it turned out to be the carnivorous variety.

"Turning to port side. Let's put some distance between us and whatever that is." He half turned. "Hiro, launch a light probe."

"On it." Hiro readied the small probe.

Small doors opened underneath Bruce and the device was launched to drop down a dozen feet. It was a mere three feet long and little more than a guided torpedo-shaped camera with a strong light at the front end.

Morgan could have just used its thermal or infrared vision but decided to immediately use the bright light to maybe draw in and away whatever the thing was that was tracking them. The bonus being that they might get an up close look at the damn thing at the same time.

"On three, two, one… *launch.*" Hiro used a small joystick with finger controls for operating the probe that shot away from them already doing ten knots – its destination was the cluster of lights out in the darkness.

"Intersection in three minutes and twenty seconds, and counting," he said as he watched a screen that was just dark and blank. For now.

"Put it up on the main board," Morgan said.

"Switching. Now," Hiro replied, and the images went to the major screen at the front of their craft.

As Morgan steered Bruce away from the huge thing, they saw the multiple dots of light in the distance of the probe's target, growing steadily bigger.

Though the probe had an extremely high light scale of around ten thousand lumens, still, its light was only reaching a few hundred feet out in front of it. And given what it was approaching was three hundred feet across, it could never be able to take it all in.

"Five hundred feet and closing," Hiro said.

There was silence in the craft as the probe approached the invisible leviathan.

"Bogey is slowing. It must sense the probe," Eddy said.

The probe's camera focused on the lights out in the darkness – they went from two, to three, then eight, and then a cluster. They formed into different patterns, and then spread in a recognizable form.

Brad Morgan smiled, immediately thinking of his big brother Greg, who witnessed this twenty years ago and from millions of miles away in the NASA tech rooms as they piloted the small probe, Nemo, through the Europa depths.

Morgan's gaze was unwavering. "And there it is, ladies and gentlemen; our angel in the darkness."

"Beautiful," Angie said reverently.

"Three hundred feet. Bogey has stopped," Eddy said. "Slow it down, Hiro, or we'll crash into it. And that might piss it off."

"Or frighten it," Angie added.

"Slowing to three knots," Hiro replied. "Two fifty feet to signature. We should be picking up visuals soon."

The dots reassembled again, all in a cluster now about fifty feet across.

"Here we go," Hiro said softly.

Images began to be revealed in the darkness. The lights weren't eyes. They were glowing globes on the end of long stalks that all grew from the head of an animal that had multiple black orb-like eyes each dozens of feet across.

The stalks were all plotted around a mouth fifty feet wide and lined with dagger shaped, glassine teeth.

"Just like a deep sea fish," Morgan said. "But on a scale fitting an ocean world with seas a hundred miles deep."

"It must come up from the depths to hunt," Hiro said. "Those lights probably evolved to draw its prey closer. Just like our own angler fish."

All the lights went out except for one in the center that began to move back towards itself. To its mouth.

"Come on, little fishy." Eddy grinned. "He wants to play."

"We should back up," Morgan said.

But then almost faster than they could react, the monstrous fish lunged forward, its mouth swinging open as it gulped. The sudden inflow of water created a massive suction effect and in the blink of an eye, the probe was sucked in.

"And that's what happened to Nemo over twenty years ago," Morgan sighed. "Okay, we've seen enough. I do not want to be next on the menu."

He powered up Bruce's engines and then continued to move away from the massive aquatic creature.

"It's following," Hiro said.

"How can it see us?" Angie asked.

"Do you know the thing about angler fish is they have very weak eyesight, but they also use other senses to locate and catch their prey." Hiro watched the screen intently. "They have a lateral line system that helps them sense their environment through water pressure and vibrations. They can *feel* their prey moving in the water without seeing it."

"That ain't good," Morgan said. "Okay, let's get the hell out of here."

He accelerated the craft to its maximum speed and it surged ahead at twelve knots in the lightless water.

After a moment, he half turned. "Hiro, how we doing?"

"Not good. It's still coming after us. Now doing fourteen knots." Hiro shook his head. "It's running us down."

"*Shit,*" Morgan said under his breath.

Bruce had a few defensive mechanisms. He could electrify the skin of the ship. Or he could heat it. But he doubted either of those would be effective against a creature that was three hundred feet long and probably weighed over five hundred tons.

What he really needed was torpedoes. And that was not something the builders thought needed to be fitted at the design stage.

"Talk to me, Hiro," Morgan said.

Hiro and Eddy were glued to their sensor screens, and Angie came and sat in the copilot chair beside him.

Hiro spoke without taking his eyes away from the screen. "Three hundred feet from our stern, speed unchanged at fourteen knots to our twelve."

"Confirmed," Eddy said. "Based on current heading, time to intersection is forty-two seconds, and counting down."

"Launching another light probe," Morgan said and prepped and then ejected another of the small aquatic swimming eyes. It sped away and then followed its preprogrammed course, looping around and heading back at the mountainous creature looming up behind them.

Morgan started to move the submersible in a zig-zag pattern, but there was no more speed to squeeze from the engines. He knew if they went inside that massive mouth, they were all dead and gone.

He glanced at the screen as the tiny dot of light from the probe sped toward the monster. As it did the lights on the end of the creature's feelers or tentacles came to life and drew together as though trying to attract the tiny probe in closer.

Morgan sent an instruction to light up the probe's globes in a single massive flash and when they all came on for a brief second or two they illuminated the massive gargoyle-like face of the monster fish. A shiver ran down Morgan's spine just at the sight of it.

"Oh god," Angie whispered.

Morgan had one more trick up his sleeve and his finger rested on the self-destruct button.

He waited until the maw opened and the probe's dot of light entered.

Now.

He pressed the button, and a tiny flash, followed by a small bloom of bubbles came from the closing mouth. If the monster even noticed it didn't react, and instead now just focused on the fleeing, much bigger, morsel of Bruce.

Shit, we're about to become Jonah, Morgan thought as the beast came after them.

They were seconds away from being eaten and he spoke quickly over his shoulder. "Hiro, any more of those floating berg worlds close by?"

Hiro widened his scanner search, but then shook his head. "No, nothing. Just miles of clear water. Just us and that giant thing behind us, and…"

He stopped.

"And what?" Morgan asked.

"Now, there's something else on the sonar," Hiro said and his eyes widened.

"What, where?" Morgan asked as the massive mouth was just a couple of hundred feet behind them and he was starting to feel the pressure wave from the thing catch the back of Bruce.

"Coming up from below. Big, very big. Bigger than the thing chasing us." Hiro pulled back. "Impossible."

Morgan put the submersible into a hard turn to starboard, and from the side of the front screen he saw the colossal beast following them.

"Does something else wanna eat us?" Morgan yelled, still turning the ship.

"Not us…" Hiro said.

There came a massive underwater impact as something struck the monstrous gargoyle fish chasing them.

Right through the structure of the ship they felt the vibrations of its squeal of fright or pain, and as Morgan completed his turn to face it, they all saw the amazing sight of the biggest creature they had ever seen, being held tight by something even larger.

Reaching up from the Hadean depths, it looked like a giant worm, two hundred feet around, that ended in a four pronged fang-head, that now gripped the monstrosity tightly.

There didn't seem to be any eyes on the giant sand worm-type beast, and it seemed just an endless pipe of muscle that had a mouth and gripping apparatus on one end.

"Big prey, bigger predators," Hiro said in awe.

The four taloned claws, or tentacles, or prongs dug in. The thrashing angler fish-type thing that had been following them thrashed and jerked, and it disturbed the water so violently it created pressure waves that buffeted Bruce, and Morgan had to use all the thrusters and his skill to keep the craft from tumbling bow over stern in the water.

There was an audible crunching sound as the prongs dug into the flesh of the beast, and the dark water began to become discolored with blood. And then the great worm-like colossus began to drag its prey back down into the seemingly bottomless depths.

There was a fight for a while, but bit by bit, the pair of monsters sunk below them.

"Did that just really happen?" Angie asked softly

Eddy laughed nervously. "Anyone else need a change of underwear?"

"Everything here is on a monstrous scale," Morgan said. "We're floating dots, dust, maybe like krill or just a sardine."

Morgan realized he was perspiring and lifted a forearm to wipe his brow. He turned to Angie who looked pale as a sheet.

She smiled. "I feel a bit lightheaded."

"You and me both." He turned in his seat. "Hiro, anything on sonar?"

The man checked his sensors and slowly shook his head. "No, nothing. Just us and a lot of open water."

Eddy slumped in his chair. "I'll tell you one thing. I can confirm that the angel in the darkness did *not* meet my expectations."

The crew laughed, and Morgan checked his recording equipment. "We got it all on tape, there's a few people back at NASA who will be very interested in what we've found." He checked his equipment one last time.

"Our energy reserves are at the minimum baseline for a burn to the surface. I suggest we plot an event free trip to our rendezvous site, and head back to the surface." Morgan looked up. "Everyone okay with that?"

"Let's go home," Angie said. "Our work here is done."

Morgan nodded. "Plotting a course to exit site. And Mr. Nakagawa and Mr. Bourke, please keep your eyes open for any more big bad monster fish. Next time we might not have a giant carnivorous worm as our cavalry."

Morgan checked the scanners and saw a course plotting to where they needed to get to – it would still take them six hours without interruptions. He was looking forward to seeing Nina but doubted her topside mission would have been as exciting as his was.

Morgan tried the direct comm link to the rover but got nothing. He should have been able to pick them up if they had deployed all the relay spikes they were meant to. If they hadn't deployed all the spikes and still being under thousands of feet of solid pack ice it also meant he was out of reach of the Traveler's communications.

A tinge of concern bloomed in his belly. There was nothing he could do now and was headed directly to the rendezvous point. He just prayed Nina and her team would be waiting when he got there.

CHAPTER 19

Benny made Heather a coffee – not too strong as he thought she looked jittery enough already. They were in the Traveler's command section before the large front window, and he handed her the steaming mug and sat down in front of her.

"Rough mission?" he simply asked, waiting on her to talk it out and perhaps purge herself of the memories.

Heather nodded. "Jake got sick." She stared down at the swirling dark liquid. "He said he was hot, and then he just…went outside." She looked up. "Without his helmet."

Benny nodded. "Maybe the pressure, the cold, or some other factor affected his mind. It happens." He meshed his fingers together. "Then what happened?"

"But it was around two hundred and fifty degrees below zero outside. He should have died instantly. But somehow he didn't." She slowly shook her head. "At least that's what Nina said."

"You didn't see?" Benny asked.

"Not really. The rover was faced away from them. But then Nina went out after him. And Ollie followed." Her mouth turned down. "But I could hear Nina on comms. She was shouting at Jake."

Benny frowned. "He was still alive?"

Heather hiked her shoulders. "Yes, maybe… I don't know, I didn't hear him. But I heard Nina; she screamed at Jake. And then a minute later Ollie was out there with her, and that's when things got really weird. It sounded like they couldn't find him. Then she was yelling at Ollie. And I heard him yell for help, then scream." She grimaced as she screwed her eyes shut. "Then he made this weird, strangled noise." She sobbed. "He sounded so scared."

Heather sniffed back tears, and Benny saw her hands begin to tremble. "Take it easy, Heather, you're safe now," he said in his most soothing voice. "What happened then?"

She looked up, her eyes red-rimmed. "Then Nina came back. Alone. And her eyes were wild. She yelled at me to start the rover. And when I asked where the others were she said that they were dead." She sobbed again. "Just like that. They were dead, gone." She straightened. "And I was supposed to just believe that and say, oh, okay, that's fine then."

"Because you didn't think they were?" Benny leaned forward.

Her eyes were on him, as she shook her head. "As we pulled away in the rover, I saw them. They were standing there."

"Alive, without helmets?" Benny asked gently. "In an unbreathable atmosphere that was hundreds of degrees below zero. You know that's impossible, right?"

"I don't know what's possible in this place anymore." She closed her eyes.

Benny sighed and sat back. "Me either."

He'd let her decompress for a while longer and then get her to do some basic maintenance tasks around the ship to keep her mind occupied.

Right now, he just hoped Morgan and his team could surface safely, and Nina made it on time to somehow assist him. Then they came back quickly. Because frankly, he was done with this place.

He checked his wrist computer noting the time, and saw they were coming up on an Earth-Europa complementary communication orbit, and he should be able to get a long range message off to Earth.

"Take it easy." He put a hand on Heather's shoulder and rubbed softly. "I'll be back in a few minutes."

She nodded, but her eyes remained on her coffee.

He went to the pilot's chair and began to prepare the communication delivery. He would make sure it was concise and provide a thorough update for the NASA teams back home. Things were so complex, that he'd need to gather his thoughts before speaking to ensure he didn't sound insane.

He didn't doubt what Nina had told him. But it was all so bizarre that he didn't quite know how to explain it either. Perhaps he would leave those details for Morgan to deliver to home base once they were all back in the Traveler together.

Ping-ping-ping.

The alarm made Benny jump.

As well as the alarm, the proximity warning light was blinking on the control panel. Benny checked it and saw that his sensor net was telling him that objects were approaching the Traveler from the direction Nina had come in on.

He checked other sensors and couldn't get a read as the thermal scanner wasn't picking anything up. Also, there was a communication void so whatever was coming at him had no comm equipment.

Benny saw that the movement was coming out of the ice crystal forest and he moved the external cameras to focus on the area. He craned forward, staring so hard and for so long, his eyeballs began to dry out. After another minute or two, he used one of the cameras to amplify the image. Then amplify it again.

Then he saw – just appearing from the edge of the crystal forest were two figures, human, or human shaped, and walking in a shuffling gait.

"Holy shit," he whispered.

"What is it?" Heather asked.

Benny regretted talking out loud as Heather came and looked over his shoulder. The people were close enough now to be seen with the naked eye from the corner of the front view screen.

"Who is it?" Benny asked.

Heather's eyes widened. "It's Jake. And Ollie."

Benny stared for a moment more, and then his hands went to the onboard cameras again and he focused in on the pair. They were still a way out, but he enlarged and sharpened their image.

"If it is Jake and Ollie, did they just walk ten miles without helmets?" He shook his head. "That isn't possible."

Heather backed up a step. "We have to help them."

"They don't look right," Benny said. "It doesn't look like them. Their faces…"

He turned, but she had gone. "Heather?" He swung all the way around but she had left the command deck. "Oh shit…" He leapt to his feet. "She's going for the freaking air lock."

He sprinted down along the corridor heading for the lower deck where the smaller airlock was. The Traveler was now sitting on the ice, so they couldn't use the large airlock anymore. But the smaller one could still accommodate several people at once.

Benny wasn't sure what was going on, but he had doubts that the two people coming in were actually his crew mates. And given what Nina had told him, she had warned him to be alert.

As he arrived on the lower deck, he saw Heather with her hand on the opening-release button.

He stopped and pointed. "Heather. *Don't!*" he said.

She turned to him. "It's okay. They're here now." She turned back.

"Please, please, don't." Benny held his hands out as he approached. "We don't know…"

"It'll be okay. We can take them to the med bay." Heather smiled as she pressed the opening button and the external door to the airlock opened.

"No!" he yelled and ran at her as she had already shut the external door. And he saw someone was inside.

But before he could get to her, she initiated the internal one.

The circular airlock and decon system rotated and the two beings were standing in the tube.

Heather's smile fell away and she put her hand to her mouth, a frozen scream trapped there.

Benny tried to make sense of what he was seeing – there were two human-shaped things standing before them, but that was mostly because they inhabited the space suits.

Ollie's was complete, but Jake's was just the bottom half and where the suit ended on both of them, there was something like thick, white fur, that bristled and waved, like it was some sort of pond weed in an underwater current.

With the inner door now open, the beings came inside.

"Get back!" Benny yelled and a wailing Heather started to walk backwards with her hands pressed together in front of her as if praying.

"Jake. Jake, are you in there?" she asked forlornly.

"That's *not* them!" Benny yelled.

He quickly looked around for some sort of weapon, or anything he could use to keep the pair of abominations at bay. But all there was in the entrance dock was a fire extinguisher, and he doubted a being would be deterred by a coolant considering it just came from an environment of super cold.

But heat might do it. And there was heat in the kitchen area. But even better, in the maintenance area there was a miniature welder.

The two beings seemed confused about their surroundings. Maybe it was the sudden change in atmosphere and temperature they were adjusting to, but so far they hadn't moved out of the airlock.

We still have a chance, Benny thought.

He began to carefully back up, determined not to make any sudden moves that might rouse the pair into action.

He half turned. "Heather, get to the command deck and seal yourself in," he said as he took another two small steps backward. "I'm going to get something to ward them off and will meet you there."

"I can't." She had her arms down beside her body and fists balled. She only took a baby step backwards.

She's freezing up. Not now, please not now, he silently begged.

"Heather, listen to me. We must keep these things away from us. Nina said Jake infected Ollie by touch. You'll be safe in the command deck once you seal yourself in. We can contact the others and NASA from there."

She took another baby step backwards.

As if sensing her, the tallest creature, the one that must have been Jake, stepped from the tube and turned toward her.

"Oh, Jake," she whispered.

"*It's not fucking Jake,*" Benny seethed.

The smallest one also stepped out and began to lumber toward Heather as well.

Benny turned and saw a coffee mug on a benchtop, picked it up and threw it at the smaller one – it was a good throw, and he hit the thing's face, or where the face should have been, as the visage was blank as a store dummy.

But instead of making an impact, the mug went inside the white mass and vanished. And never came out.

There was a hole there for a few seconds and then it closed as things like threads wove themselves back together. It began to approach again; this time the small one was coming at him.

"Fuck this," Benny said. "*Run!*"

Heather's muscles finally unlocked, and she turned to sprint toward the command deck. Benny went the other way, heading to the maintenance room.

He went through a hatch door and into the maintenance room and tool section. He knew where and what he was looking for, and in a drawer there was a two foot probe-like device with a bulb of gas attached to it.

He grabbed it out, and flicked it, sparking the initiator and creating a three inch flame with blue center. Benny quickly altered the settings and then saw he could bring the flame in tight or lengthen it to about two feet. Right now, he wanted these revolting things as far from him as he could manage.

"Fuck you, burn." He turned, heading to the command deck.

He just hoped Heather had made it, and also when he re-entered the room with the exit portal, he hoped to see the two things still standing there. His plan was to use the flame to force them back into the airlock and then jettison the pair back out onto the Europa surface.

But as he came back into the room he saw they had both vanished.

"*Dammit,*" he whispered.

He looked about. *Did they go after Heather?* he wondered. Okay, then, Plan-B – get to the command center and seal themselves both in to buy some time.

He ran hard, going through doors and along corridors in the ship until he reached the command center. But there they were, both of them, standing motionless against the wall as though hiding in wait for him.

Benny sidled past them to the door. He kept his eyes on them, and for the first time noticed that facial features were forming on the once blank heads – the hint of eyes and the lump of a nose, and the beginning of a hole where the mouth should be. *Were they trying to get better at copying them*? he wondered.

"Okay," he breathed.

Then he quickly spun to hit the button. But the door refused to open.

Okay, good, smart girl, he thought, she'd sealed it to make the command deck secure.

Benny banged on the door and then looked through the clear portal but didn't see her. "Heather," he shout whispered. "It's me. Open up, quick."

He turned and saw that the creatures had moved. Toward him. They came in an odd fluid movement as though their bodies were boneless. It made his stomach flip.

He turned back and banged on the door again. This time he looked in through the portal and saw her there, staring at him. Her face was wet with tears and perhaps perspiration, and the expression she wore was ripped with fear.

Heather Winterson wrung her hands and moved from foot to foot, her wet lips moving as if mumbling and her face crumpled in abject terror.

"Please." Benny was becoming frantic, and he looked over his shoulder and saw the things were so close now he could finally see that what covered them wasn't fur but something alive that wriggled and squirmed and had a black head or a single eye on its tip.

Benny pressed himself up against the door so hard it hurt his chest, and he banged hard with his fist. He thumped the door, begged, pleaded, but saw Heather just begin to cry and shake her head.

I can't, she mouthed.

He dropped his hands, knowing it was all too late. He wouldn't dare turn around, couldn't even if he wanted to. But suddenly he felt something bone chillingly cold behind him.

***

Heather felt ripped with fear and indecision. She couldn't open the door and perhaps allow the command deck to be contaminated. That was protocol, wasn't it?

Benny was her crew mate, and a friend. And she needed him. If she was out there, he'd probably risk it and let her in. But he was out of sight for so long, how did she know it was really him? He could be one of those things by now.

She agonized over what to do, tormenting herself.

Heather backed away from the pounding on the door. Before Benny had come back, she had seen those alien things looking in at her, with those horrifying unformed faces. And Benny's face had features, and he was so scared. So, so scared. That couldn't be faked, could it?

She tried to judge how much time she had to open the door, allow Benny to slip in, and then reclose it, without the horrors following. She tried to think, but Benny pounding so hard, coupled with his shouting and wild eyed face pressed to the portal window, was scrambling her mind.

"I can't," she said wetly.

And then as she stared, Benny's face was gone as he seemed to be enveloped by a white wave that totally covered him for a few seconds. But she could still just make out his face, screaming, and looking like he was in agony.

As she watched she saw the flesh on his face become mottled red, as the things poured into his mouth, nose, and around his bulging eyes. And then it was like he just came apart, and bits of his face were pulled in different directions to leave nothing but a squirming white horde and when the mass pulled back Benny wasn't there anymore.

"No, no, no." She backed up, shaking her head, not able to think, barely even able to breathe.

Tell someone, her mind shrieked.

Benny had said they were nearing a complementary orbit with Earth. Heather raced to the console and sat down. She began the long range communication protocol for an Earth message even though they weren't in the perfect orbital alignment. It meant the message would take longer to get there, but that didn't matter anymore.

As she did she heard a liquid sliding coming from behind the door, and then the groan of steel under pressure as if some huge weight was pushing against it.

It's trying to get in, her mind shrieked.

She turned and froze. Benny was back, staring in at her. His face was calm, but there was something wrong with him.

She didn't want to, but it was as if her legs had a will of their own and drew her closer – she had to know.

"Benny? Benny, are you okay?"

As she drew near the small portal window she could see that his skin looked different, more granular, and then she saw what it was – it wasn't skin at all, but thousands or millions of tiny worms all working together to create an *image* of his face.

And they were all alive.

Benny's mouth opened, looking like he, or them, were trying to say something. As she stared, he pressed against the door, and whatever he was now far outweighed the smaller, slightly overweight man she knew as the steel groaned under the titanic pressure.

"Please don't, Benny," she begged.

As she watched, the man's left eye vanished to leave an empty socket. Then it refilled to form another eye, but this one higher up on the forehead, as though it forgot where the other eye was supposed to be.

Then crowding in at the window, Jake's face appeared. Then Ollie's.

They were near perfect now as if the monstrosity had learned how to make them. But that was where the sanity ended because the other faces, the other heads, were growing from Benny's thickened neck – all three of the men were now inhabiting the single body that was a mess of limbs, misshapen bulges, and patches of tangled hair.

The door groaned again, then there came a thump that was so powerful it went right through the ship's substructure, and she even felt it beneath her feet.

Get help, her mind screamed again. *Warn them. Call Nina. Get help*, her mind babbled with all messages falling over each other in her chaotic mind.

She opened the long range channel and began to scream and yell about what was happening. She glanced over her shoulder and to her horror saw that around the door frame there was movement, and something like white hair was beginning to sprout.

She turned back, screaming. "It's getting in, it's getting in."

She left the channel open and also opened another channel to Nina in the rover. And another to Morgan in Bruce.

"Help me!" she screamed. "He-*eeelp!*"

There was no response, and she jumped to her feet, and ran to the pilot's chair.

"Nina, what should I do?" she screamed.

But the return comms was silent.

And then: *what would Nina do*? she asked herself.

She'd kill it, any way she could, she answered.

Heather began to initiate a launch sequence. While she did she opened all the external doors, allowing the Europa atmosphere to seep in.

"Vent it into space," she babbled. "I'll fucking show you."

She glanced back and saw the white threads begin to drop to the floor.

She'd take off, just high enough to make it out past the weak moon's atmosphere. Then she could let the vacuum of space take care of them. *Nothing could survive that, nothing*, she thought.

She put the Traveler into takeoff mode. There'd be no gradual rise, instead a hard liftoff. The engines roared to life.

But the Traveler stuck hard for a moment as the struts were all glued in place by the ice that still held them tight.

"Fuck it." She pushed the engines to maximum, screaming her frustration as though she was taking on the physical exertion herself.

The Traveler lifted, and with a sound of crunching steel broke two of its rear landing struts, with another already damaged from Benny's previous attempt, and the final one clinging, still held firm by Europa's surface.

With engines at maximum and with the final one still holding tight, the craft lifted at an angle and with the full power deployed to the thrust, it began to lift anyway, higher. And then the remaining caught strut acted as an anchor and caused the large ship to turn on its side.

Heather felt the craft tilting, and then start to turn right over. She grabbed the arm rests of the chair she was now seated on, and just as she did she turned to the door and saw it was beginning to crumple inwards.

"Fuck off." She held tight as the craft gave one final lurch, picking up speed while still tethered by one landing strut, and then completely flipped over. But

the jets kept pushing, and with the Traveler's world turned upside down there was only one place left to go.

The massive craft was thrown down onto the Europa hard icy surface, where it crumpled. And then detonated.

In seconds, the mega-ton Traveler craft became a massive fireball of molten steel and gas as debris flew into the thin atmosphere and rained down over a half mile radius. At the ground zero point of the explosion the ice liquified, turning into a lake for several minutes, which quickly claimed the torn shell of the space craft.

In minutes more, silence and the deadly cold returned.

CHAPTER 20

Nina reached the outer limits of the Bruce-Rover intersection site, which was a mile wide sea of ice that was probably an ancient spot where the warm water vented from below at some time in Europa's history. Now, the ice was glass smooth, and relatively thin for Europa with it being only an eight hundred foot thick skin.

Nina knew that Bruce should be able to melt its way to the surface, but she had to help to speed the process. She needed to deploy explosives and take some of the surface ice away, then plant a location spike so they came up into the pit she would have dug.

Unfortunately, she was by herself, so it was going to take extra time and a mountain of effort. However, she was ahead of schedule, so she could still make it.

Nina sat looking out at the ice for several minutes, praying nothing was out there, and also bolstering her courage. After a moment she drew in a deep lung-filling breath and let it out with a whoosh.

"Let's do this." She rose from her chair.

The mission second-in-command went back to the rear of the large tank-like vehicle and grabbed the digging equipment, explosive charge packs, and the comm spike, and dragged them forward to glance out once more at the ice – there still didn't seem to be anything moving, and no snow drifts.

"Please be empty," she whispered.

She straightened, breathed in and out three times as if she was about to submerge herself in water, and then put her helmet on, locking it in place.

The sooner I start, the sooner we all get home, she thought.

She exited the rover and, dragging all the equipment, headed to the designated point of Bruce's potential breach.

By then it was too late to see the incoming message button begin to blink in her control panel.

***

Nina strode out a hundred feet onto the ice and stopped to check her positioning. This was the approximate area they had agreed on for the submersible rendezvous.

She turned slowly, looking out over the flat ice with the yellowish mineral striations like veins. The strange black sky even with the sun shining down, the lack of anything moving, and also the dead silence was all so ominous and alien now.

When she had first arrived it had seemed fantastic and magnificent – a wonderland – but now it made her scared right down to her bones. There was something out there, that consumed them. And then replaced them.

She sighed and then blinked several times as her eyes watered.

She had work to do; Morgan would be piloting Bruce to this point, and she needed to excavate a hole and then place a beacon spike so he came up right under it.

He would do the bulk of the heavy lifting by melting ninety-nine percent of the way up to meet her. But the expectation was he would be cutting it fine on fuel burn. He might be able to make it on his own, but best for him to surface with some reserves into a cavity made by the rover team, rather than run out of energy before they reached the surface, and then become entombed below the ice. Or worse, *within* the ice.

Because no one was coming to save them. Or even could.

Nina had to drag the heavy cases by herself with each one weighing in at about eighty pounds. And there were four of them. It meant four trips, and each one got slower as the cases seemed to get heavier the more worn out she got.

On completion, she had to arrange the explosive packages in a circle about fifty feet apart, rig a simultaneous detonation, and all via a timed switch. And before that even happened, she needed to have gotten the rover to a safe distance.

It took her an hour, and her suit was working overtime to keep her cool as she strained and perspired. By the end of it she was feeling sore and dizzy, and felt like sitting down, but the ice creeped her out, and instead she stood, turning slightly, looking for the slightest movement on the ice.

And if she saw something, what could she do?

Run to the rover and hide inside. And what about Morgan in Bruce?

Fuck it.

She blanked everything out and set the detonation to ten minutes to give her time to get good clearance, and then straightened, putting her hands in the center of her back, feeling it creak.

Nina then felt something rather than heard it on her audio pickup – in the distance she thought she saw a glowing ball just over the horizon. It had come from the direction of the Traveler.

"Oh no. Please no," she whispered.

She took a few paces toward it as though to improve her view.

She opened a channel with her helmet mic but knew it had limited range. She tried anyway. "Benny, Heather, come back?"

She took a few more paces toward the glow but then remembered there was about to be a real detonation. Right underneath her.

Nina looked to the detonator, judging whether she should stop the explosion as she desperately wanted to go and check out the glow on the horizon. But knew she couldn't. Timing was everything now – they had one chance to evac Morgan and his team onto the surface before everything filled in and iced over.

She glanced again at the glowing horizon – she was torn – she banged a gloved fist down onto her thigh several times.

"*Fu-uuuck!*" she screamed.

Nina turned and ran back to the rover. She climbed inside, and started to draw the hulking machine back to a line of massive ice crystals that would form a barrier between her and the excavation explosion.

She skidded to a stop and opened a channel to the Traveler. "Benny, come in?"

There was nothing but static.

"Benny, Heather, are you reading me?" Her teeth chattered a little, but not from cold.

She tried again and again but got nothing.

She glanced at the timer – seconds – she braced herself.

The explosion shook the ground, and the rover rocked as ice crystals rained down from above. They shattered like glass on the machine's tough skin and though the sound was near deafening, there was no damage.

The crystal barrier also sheltered her from the massive chunks of ice blown free from the detonation and they thumped to the ground like a titan's footsteps. She gave it a full minute before starting the rover and heading out to check on the result.

Smoke or mist still rose into the dark air, and there was a vapor cloud hanging over the flat ice plain. She stopped the rover about two hundred feet from where she had planted the explosives and exited the vehicle, walking cautiously across the ice.

She had brought with her a large case that she struggled to carry, and in minutes she came to a lumped wall of ice and snow around six feet in height – she knew what it was – a crater wall from the explosion. She had brought a flashlight, switched it on, and she climbed up over the rim to stare down.

The mist finally began to settle, and she saw the massive pit in the ice some two hundred feet deep, and at the bottom it was smooth as the detonation had blown hundreds of tons of ice out, but the heat from the explosion had melted the core, liquifying it and now the basin bottom was smooth as the residual water refroze.

She opened the case and took out the roll of ladder and hammered in two large spikes to secure one end of it. She then rolled the other end into the crater pit where it unfurled all the way toward the bottom.

She watched it drop – *yes* – just enough. She silently congratulated the back room technicians at home who worked at the precise measurements on a computer to the fraction of an inch.

Nina stood up on the rim and looked once again to where the Traveler was – there was no more glow on the horizon.

Please be okay, she prayed.

She looked back down into the crater. Ice dust was already beginning to settle into it. She climbed down with the communication spike strapped to her back. It was tough going down, but she knew it would be tougher going back up.

This was why she was supposed to have a team with her. Now she was wishing she had made Benny and Heather come with her – she left them behind to be safe and guard the ship, and now she doubted they had done either.

At the bottom she hammered in the spike and switched it on. The small red light flicked on at the top to create a destination target for Morgan in the submersible. She put her hands on her hips and stared at the small light for a moment.

"Okay, baby. It's up to you now."

She turned then to climb back up, hand over hand, one agonizing foot after the other. It took a lot longer than she expected. Once at the top she climbed over the crater rim on her hands and knees and turned to sit with her head down and elbows on her knees for a moment. Her heart beat like crazy, and she sucked in deep breaths.

Everything will be okay when Morgan gets here, she promised herself.

Nina turned to look out over the landscape; it was silent as a tomb, and still as death. She then tilted her head to face the black sky and tried to guess which tiny dot of light was Earth.

She sighed. "I want to go home," she said softly.

CHAPTER 21

Morgan smiled. "Got it."

The intersection point beacon showed up on his scanner and was only five miles out from where they were now.

He had previously scaled back the speed to eight knots but was tempted to increase it again as he was impatient to see Nina and the rest of his team. He had a lot to tell them, and was also keen to hear what they had seen, done, and experienced.

But logic overrode his desires as he knew that their fuel reserves were a lot lower than where he wanted them to be. Being chased by that monster fish had drained them of valuable resources, and he prayed they had enough burn left to raise them to the crater bottom.

The worst case scenario was they ran into an obstacle or thicker than expected ice and their bubble of warm water they were traveling in as they melted their way to the surface, cooled, refroze, and marooned them hundreds of feet below the surface. If that happened, they were doomed.

As they travelled they passed many smaller floating bergs, some of them with colossal sea fan-type things straining the water for anything they could siphon. In addition, more creatures had come to investigate them, some small at around a dozen feet, and others of huge proportions that just stayed on the periphery of their scanners.

Morgan wondered at the sterile surface of the moon – life was enormously resilient and adaptable, and he couldn't understand how there was no significant lifeforms topside compared to the abundance down below.

He guessed it would be up to smarter people than him to work out why that was the case.

They ate up the miles to their destination. As yet, he had not been able to raise Benny back in the Traveler, but knew Nina would be waiting for him as the signal spike had been planted and initiated.

"I'm coming home, baby." He smiled.

"You talking to me?" Eddy chuckled from behind him.

"Maybe a baby pumpkin." Morgan grinned. "Give me some stats, Ed."

"One mile and counting down. Signal is loud and strong," Eddy replied.

Morgan nodded. They had come to make history, and the wonderful things they had seen and recorded would do that a hundred times over. They had found life, and unlocked mysteries from our solar system that generations before them had only dreamed of.

The mission was a success. Now they had one part to get right to tie it all off – get home.

"On target," Eddy announced.

"Roger that." Morgan felt a bloom of happiness in his stomach. "Prepare to surface."

Morgan piloted the craft towards the ice ceiling that was illuminated by his top spotlights. On his control panel was a screen that showed where he was in proximity to the ice, and also a red dot with targeting rings showing where he needed to be to line up with the signal spike.

He knew that saying he needed to line things up was an understatement given the crater he would be surfacing into was only about a hundred feet wide, and he was rising through nearly a thousand feet of ice, fractions of an inch mattered.

Morgan slowed, looking from a small camera to the bombsite crossed-circle of where he needed to touch.

"Ready for burn," he said.

Then the ship stopped in the water, and alarms sounded.

"What the hell is going on?" Morgan turned about. "Why have we stopped?"

"I've got a proximity warning," Hiro said as he stared at a small screen. "Front, sides, and below. Like we are caught in something."

Morgan switched on all the external lights and cameras and saw that there were almost transparent ropes or tentacles wrapped around Bruce in multiple places.

Over the hydrophone there was a deep booming noise, that made him wince at the volume.

"Holy shit," Eddy grimaced. "Sounds like a whale on steroids."

Out of the front viewscreen something started to take form.

"Contact," Hiro said in awe.

"Not now, dammit," Morgan said through gritted teeth.

Angie left her translation work on the strange glyphic symbols from the wall of the ice cave and came up to join him. In front of them something started to swirl like fireflies swarming around a porch light.

"It's not another monster angler fish, is it?" she asked.

"Can't tell yet." He shook his head. "It's just holding us in place. Not trying to drag us down."

"Maybe it's not trying to drag us down, because it's coming up," Eddy said.

"I don't know if that's any better," Morgan scoffed.

Then the swirling fireflies seemed to coalesce and form into something like lines, sworls, dashes and dots.

They hung in the dark water like a laser light show made by a million tiny drones.

"Oh my god," Angie said and rushed back to her small screen. She looked from it to the front window.

"It's the same." Her eyes were blazing. "It's the same type of writing that was on the cave wall."

"Any chance…" Morgan turned to her.

She shook her head. "No translation from the application yet. But something is desperate we read it and understand them."

Then Bruce started to be dragged down.

"No, no, no." Morgan applied a little more thrust, but they continued down, unable to fight the strength of the thing.

"Whatever they are trying to do, they're going to end up drowning us." He tried to think of options, but there was only one.

"Going to have to apply a little discouragement."

"No, don't," Angie begged. "Some type of sentience is reaching out to us."

"Can we afford the power?" Eddy asked.

"Yes and no." Morgan half turned. "We can't afford to be dragged down, and if I don't give them a little disincentive, we'll be dead anyway." He faced Angie and saw her face was ripped by his decision. "They might not know we're airbreathers. Sorry, but they'll kill us."

"Do it," Eddy said.

Morgan turned to Hiro who just nodded once.

"Okay, surface discharge in three, two, one...*now*." Morgan hit the button, and several hundred volts ran over the skin of the ship.

The lights out front went dark, and whatever held on released them.

"Free," he said. "Sensors?" he asked.

Hiro and Eddy checked the external eyes and ears.

"Nothing," they agreed. "All clear."

"Then we're out of here," Morgan said and quickly rose again to the ice ceiling. "Hiro, prepare for ice burn.".

"Roger that." Hiro prepared the fuel cells to run a thermal charge over the skin of Bruce. It would heat the craft to one hundred and twenty degrees, not a lot, but given the water outside was only just above freezing, and the ice lower than that, it would be more than enough to melt a hole in the ice cap.

Then they would generate a bubble of warm water that would be an envelope of liquid all around them and refreeze below them – it worked on the way down, it should work on the way back up.

Morgan slowed Bruce as they were almost right under the lift zone.

"Okay people, shutting down all unnecessary equipment and components." He then took everything offline except life support and switched all resources to the thermal layer surrounding the submersible.

Morgan took a quick look at his personnel. Angie smiled and nodded to him. Hiro was still busy looking at one of the samples through a microscope. And Eddy sipped a coffee, the last he'd have before they got topside.

Eddy raised his cup in a toast. "Up, up and away."

Morgan nodded. "Initiating thermals. Lifting, now."

There was no change inside Bruce, but externally the ribbing started to glow and they began to rise. As they did, the ice above them quickly melted away, and after a few seconds began to form a large cavity that Bruce lifted into.

Soon the cavity became a tunnel, and they rose into it, creating more tunnel as they went. After just five minutes, behind them the hole grew opaque, thickened, and then turned back into solid ice. But a bubble of warm water, containing the eighty-five-foot submersible, was rising steadily toward the surface.

Morgan sat back; he kept one eye on the depth gauge as they slowly headed to the surface that also showed the feet of thickness between Bruce and the target beacon. And his other eye was on their energy levels.

If they hadn't needed to burn so much fuel escaping a monster fish, or dissuading the thing trying to communicate, they would have easily had enough to make it to the surface, and maybe some in reserve for any unexpected anomalous events. But now it was a race to see if they made it to the crater pit before they ran out of energy. And everything was out of his hands.

"Four hours, twenty seven minutes, people," Morgan said. "Keep movement to a minimum, and no unnecessary use of equipment that draws power. We have one shot at breaching."

Hiro went and lay down on one of the rear bunks, meshed his fingers on his belly and either slept or lay there meditating. Eddy still sipped the remains of his cold coffee – there'd be no more until they hit the surface. Even then if their fuel was exhausted, he'd need to wait until he was in the rover. And Angie still worked on her translation, but by the look on her face it just wasn't becoming clearer just yet.

Morgan stared straight ahead at nothing but blackness outside. If he switched on the external lights, he would see the opposite – nothing but the glaring whiteness of the ice.

The computer's risk algorithms estimated it would be close, but they should make it. Unless they hit an obstacle. Unless they missed the pit the rover team had dug. Unless, unless, unless…

He shut his eyes and rubbed them with his fingertips. Everything was in the hands of the technology and fate. So he should just relax and enjoy the quiet.

Morgan let his mind drift back to his father, his brother, and the farm. He looked forward to another cookout, and beers together on the old wooden porch steps after a long day rounding up cattle, hay bailing, or just attending to general duties on the huge property.

He pictured Greg, his brother, listening to him with rapt attention, asking questions, and Morgan having all the answers he had sought for so many decades. Greg would have given anything to be in his shoes.

His father, Clay, had been so proud and supportive, but just in the days before he was due to leave, he remembered one of the last things his father had said to him: *Don't go, Brad.*

Morgan smiled. He had explained that he was probably going to be safer on Europa than if he drove on a city street at peak hour. But his dad didn't look convinced. He was even more upset when he told his dad that he'd be away around four years.

Morgan sighed. He just hoped they were both there, happy and healthy, when he got home. This time he might invite Nina out to the farm. Show her off, and give his dad someone else to fuss over.

Just thinking of Nina made his soul happy. He had kept the relationship mostly low-key and professional when they were leading up to their trip. He knew she felt strongly about him, the same as he felt about her. But once they were safely on their way home, well then, things would be allowed to be different.

Morgan leaned back and rested his head on the chair rest. He looked forward to seeing what adventures and interesting things his surface team had discovered. Whatever happened, this voyage would go down in history.

***

Ping – ping – ping.

Morgan opened his eyes, disoriented for the moment. Hours had gone by. He immediately looked from the surface gauge to the energy levels.

"*Shit,*" he muttered.

"What is it?" Angie asked.

"Nothing good," Morgan replied.

They were still two hundred feet from the surface, and the fuel reserves were depleted. Or near enough.

He sat forward and quickly checked all the ship's energy consumption and saw there was little being used other than a few internal lights, and the big one, the heating.

Then we have no choice, he thought.

"Rug up, people, about to get dark and cold." Morgan switched off the remaining lights and the ship plunged into darkness save for the glow from their control panels, making his crew's faces glow a ghostly green.

He then dialed back the internal heating to just above freezing. They only needed to deal with it for another half hour, if the energy burn lasted that long.

Then they needn't worry about it being just above zero, because if the fuel ran out, it'd be well below that in a few minutes.

"Everyone cross their fingers," he said and stared hard at his monitors.

Morgan's jaws ached from clenching his teeth – he hated not being able to do anything as, if he could, he'd get outside and row or drag the ship to the surface using brute force. He was damned if he was going to lose his team and the craft in the last hundred feet of ice after coming this far.

"Forty feet," Hiro said softly. "Still on target for the beacon."

"Come on, come on, Bruce, you can do it," Eddy whispered.

Morgan looked upwards, imagining Nina, Heather, Jake and Ollie standing up there at the edge of some sort of crater rim, watching the bottom of the crater they had made with their explosives. Looking for some sort of shadow or lights to appear.

He checked the fuel reserves – point-one percent remaining.

"Twenty-five feet," Hiro counted off. "Slowing."

"Damnit," Morgan cursed, and then flexed his cold and numbing fingers. The thermal was cooling down, but it was still bearable. But they needed a bit of kindling on the fire now.

"Sorry guys, shutting off all heating... and oxygen recirculation." He switched off the heating and other life support.

He guessed that the cabin would retain enough breathable air for about five minutes, and it would take a little longer than that for them to drop to a temperature that would be fatal. Either way, if they got too cold or ran out of air, they'd just black out.

He looked at the fuel reserves – it was now showing below the red line.

"Twenty feet," Hiro said and then coughed.

Morgan stared at the reserves. He saw his breath misting before him.

"Fifteen…" Hiro's teeth chattered.

Morgan put his hands under his arms.

"Oh no," Morgan whispered.

The energy level indicator began to blink on his console panel.

"Ten feet," Hiro said. "Slowing to zero rise."

Morgan wondered if they could break through manually.

"Eight feet. Come on," Eddy urged. "Seven."

Everyone sat motionless, waiting.

"Seven feet. Six feet, slowing, five feet, five feet, five feet..." Hiro groaned, "…and now we are stopped."

Morgan knew that the bubble of warm water surrounding them was already cooling as the skin of the ship lost its heat. It wouldn't be long until the bubble started to refreeze, locking them in.

"Suits on, people," Morgan said. "We're going to have to manually bust through."

Morgan used the last ergs of energy to lift the ship that punched into the ice at the top of the warm water bubble, with a crunching that shook the entire superstructure of the submersible.

They were lodged tight in the ceiling, but never broke through. Morgan looked up as though seeing through the ice to his surface team.

They were short by five feet, or less.

They could do it. They had to.

He turned. "Get the burners, axes, anything we can use. We're going to have to dig and dig fast."

The crew scrambled; they had minutes before the bone-chilling cold became deadly, and the ice settled to concrete hardness, and they were sealed in forever.

***

"*Yes.*"

Nina sprinted back to the crater and her heart leapt in her chest as she saw the dark shape begin to show at the bottom of the crater pit. She smiled, counting the seconds. But her smile soon fell away as it seemed to stop its rise.

There was the cracking sound of an impact as Bruce obviously struck the bottom of the ice, but then that's as far as it came, and before her eyes she saw the ice begin to whiten as it started to reset.

Oh no, no, no, she thought. *They've run out of fuel and are stuck.*

They were just right there, she knew.

Nina sprinted back to the rover to grab anything she could use – a large wrench, the only small burner remaining, and even a thermal blanket – it was all she had.

She tripped over her feet on the way back as she ran so fast. Then slid down the crater wall, not bothering to use the ladder, and thumped heavily at the bottom. She then raced to where there were lights showing, that were now dimming – another sign that the submersible's energy levels were depleted.

"Not yet you don't." She spread the thermal blanket over one area and turned it to maximum. Then initiated the small burner and began to use it on another area of the ice.

The heat turned the hardened ice mushy, and she scooped and brushed it away – inches by inches – every bit helped. Then she used the wrench to smash up more of the ice, and then brought the burner back again.

After a few minutes all she had done is excavate down another foot and she was already exhausted.

But when she next looked down through the ice, she saw lights – flashlights – waving back and forth and she heard digging.

"*Yes!*" she screamed. "Yes, yes, *dig*, I'm coming."

She picked up the wrench again and with two hands bashed it down on the ice over and over, furiously swinging with every ounce of strength she had remaining.

At about two feet down she felt her back and shoulders starting to ache and burn so bad she worried she would tear muscles and tendons. She thought she was going to have to slow up. And then she saw the hand, pressing up at the ice, waving, and she almost began to cry.

They were almost here. But time was against them, as she knew that without power, they would be locked within a freezing tomb within minutes more.

She stood, changing angles, and swung the big wrench down, once, twice, tears flowing now.

"Come on!" she screamed. "*Come on.*"

One more big hit.

And then her ice floor, and their ceiling, cracked – they'd broken through.

***

The submersible team were living inside their suits now, and each took turns working the ice above the small upper hatch at the top of the submersible – first Morgan, then Hiro, then Eddy, and even Angie took turns digging and smashing at the ice.

The submersible was now a dead hulk and had given them every ounce of its energy to get this far. The team used a long spike like a flat crowbar and worked furiously and fast as the ice was settling around them now, and inside Bruce it was becoming like a refrigerator.

While Morgan took his next turn, Angie stood with her arms wrapped around herself, jumping from foot to foot and breath steaming.

Chunks of ice smashed to the deck as it fell past the working people. At first it melted, but as the craft got colder, it stayed in solid form and the person at the top chipped and smashed, the guys at the bottom moving the fallen ice out of the way.

"I can see a light," Eddy yelled down at them as he took his turn. "Someone is digging down to us."

"That's the rover team; we're on the money," Morgan yelled up at the young engineer.

Morgan turned as there came a groan of steel as the pressure of the settling ice around the hull grew thicker. He doubted they'd have any compression problems, but worried as the ice hardened, and compacted, it might shrink and drag them down. Right now, even a few more feet of ice to dig through might defeat them.

Eddy's movements became slower, and Morgan knew he was done.

"Jump down, Eddy, I'm coming up," Morgan said.

Eddy came down, his face red and breathing hard. He handed over the spike. "Home stretch. I hope." He grinned.

Morgan took the spike and climbed the ladder. Once there he could see the light, but then it vanished. He began to dig, jamming the spike up, wedging it in, moving it back and forth and then levering out more ice chunks. Then repeating the process.

A large chunk of ice was dislodged and struck his shoulder as it travelled past him. It felt like a block of granite, and he groaned and reminded himself to pay attention; if he copped one of those on the head it might be lights out.

He went back at it, and it was hard work and agonizing on the shoulders and arms. His fingers were numb now and a small voice whispered for him to go and take a break, but this was turning into life or death now, and he was determined to not leave anything *on the field,* as the saying goes. If he did the field would be his grave.

The light appeared again, and he saw the watery figure there. Morgan jammed a hand up against the ice and waved. And then in the next second there was a *thump* and something punched downwards, narrowly missing his face.

"*Yes, we're through!*" he yelled over his shoulder.

Behind him the team cheered, and he worked at widening the hole.

The light appeared again and he heard his name called.

"Nina?" he asked.

"I'm here, I'm here, *thank god.*" She sounded breathless, and rather than being explosively happy at seeing them, she instead sounded nervous as hell and frightened.

He stuck his hand and arm up through the small hole and felt the embrace of Nina's gloved hand. She squeezed it and let him go.

He pulled his arm back and peered up through the hole. "Where's everyone else?" he asked, and then, "You okay?"

"Hurry," she just replied.

So he did, working like a madman. Then jumping down to catch his breath and handing over to Hiro so he could continue the fight against the ice.

In fifteen more minutes they had a hole wide enough for them to begin to squeeze through. Angie went first, then Hiro, then Eddy.

Morgan looked around at the now night-dark submersible.

"Thank you, Bruce. You did everything we asked of you and exceeded our expectations. Thank you for keeping us safe." He saluted his vessel, and then climbed the ladder.

A hand came down and he grabbed it and was hauled out to find himself at the bottom of a deep and wide crater.

"*Holy shit*." He looked around and then up at the steep walls. Morgan realized then that if they hadn't used dynamite, all his team would have been entombed far too deep to ever be rescued.

He looked for the rover team and just saw Nina. "Well done," he said.

She came and hugged him, and then stood back to look deep into his helmeted face.

"We must hurry, we need to get to the rover. A lot has happened." She turned to the ladder leading to the top of the crater.

"Nina, where's everyone else?" Morgan asked, feeling his trepidation rising.

"Not here. Once we're in the rover." She turned away and began to climb.

Morgan had Hiro go next up the ladder, then Angie, Eddy, and he placed one hand on the ladder rungs and looked back at the hole in the ice. There was no weather on Europa, no snowfall, or wind, but there were ice quakes, upwellings, and meteorite impacts. The crater might still be here in a thousand years, or it could fill in within the next day or so.

Bruce was always going to be left behind, but he was sad that they would not get to travel beneath the ice to those amazing oceans ever again.

He looked up to see Nina had already scaled to the top, and his team was nearly there as well. Morgan began to climb, feeling the strain of sore muscles from the digging they had done, but he guessed the hard part was over.

He was keen to see the other team members, and knew that whatever Nina was worried about, now that they were together they could work it out. The team would be united, and their job was done. Successfully.

Morgan began to climb quickly, and his spirits lifted. He felt every rung he travelled upwards was a step closer to home.

CHAPTER 22

At the top of the crater the group waited, and Morgan saw Nina looking around, not at the team, but at the landscape. He could see she seemed to be looking *for* something, but after another moment she seemed satisfied.

"Quickly," she said and waved them on.

She took them to where the rover was sheltered, and as they approached Morgan saw behind the large front screen that there didn't seem to be anyone inside.

Nina went in first and they all followed into the rover via the decon-airlock door, one at a time. Inside she adjusted the air and environmental conditions and took her helmet off.

Once Morgan entered he ripped his helmet free and stared hard at her ashen face. "Nina, what the hell happened?"

Nina straightened. "Jake and Ollie are dead," she said flatly. "They got infected by some sort of organism from the Europa surface."

"What?" Eddy's mouth hung open.

"It got inside them, and, just, took them over," she swallowed. "They sort of melted or were disassembled. And then, and then, they were rebuilt, but it wasn't them anymore."

"What are you saying?" Eddy's eyes blazed. "They got taken over by some sort of parasite? I don't understand."

"Where's Heather?" Angie asked.

"I don't understand either," Nina sighed and looked up with red rimmed eyes. "I took Heather back to the Traveler, but it was somehow trapped in the ice, sunk into it. Benny said the ice around the landing pads just liquified and the ship was drawn down into the pools. Then they refroze around the struts, locking them in."

She was talking fast now. "But while I was waiting for you, I heard an explosion from their direction. And then I couldn't raise them anymore." Nina grimaced. "But there was a glow on the horizon."

Morgan put a hand to his forehead and rubbed, as he paced for a moment. He stopped and turned to her. "We go to the Traveler, *now*."

Nina, given a clear objective, flew into action and jumped in the pilot seat, immediately bringing the rover to life. They skidded away, leaving a rooster tail of ice and snow in their wake as the huge machine ground and bounced its way over the Europa surface toward their ship.

Morgan sat in the copilot chair, his mind lost in thought. He knew they needed to see what they were dealing with. If the craft had suffered some sort of massive malfunction, and he didn't want to even think of a worst case right now, then they needed to see if there were casualties.

Eddy cleared his throat. "What happens if, *ah*, the Traveler is gone?"

"We make a plan," Morgan said and stared straight ahead, as Nina navigated the ice valleys, mountains, and crevices.

He turned to Nina. "Jake and Ollie. Tell me what happened to them."

Nina's normally glowing brown face was ghastly pale, but she nodded and spoke while keeping her eyes on the ice ahead. "Jake went out on the ice to collect samples. It all went to plan and he came back. But after about an hour he started to act strange. Said he was hot, and then ripped the top of his suit down."

She shook her head, wincing at the memories. "His body looked strange, covered in white spots and veins. He said he was hot."

"Hot?" Morgan asked.

"Yes, hot. And the next thing he jumped up and just locked himself in the decon tube." She turned. "And then opened the outer door. And goddamn stepped out."

"In two-forty degrees below zero? He should have been snap frozen," Hiro said from behind them.

"That's right," Nina said. "Ollie and I went after him. Me first. When I got out he was still alive and staggering toward the ice plain. He was covered in something that looked like tiny white hairs, that were alive and undulating." She sniffed back some tears. "Then he just threw his arms out wide, screamed, and, and, burst apart." She laughed a little madly. "Burst, into millions of little white maggot things."

Morgan just stared. Behind him, Angie made a small sound in her throat.

"Go on," Morgan said softly.

"By the time Ollie arrived Jake was gone." She stared ahead again.

"Gone where?" Eddy asked.

"Just gone. Sort of," she said. "Ollie went to check him out, and somehow the worm things infected him as well. Same thing happened. He took his helmet off because he was hot, screamed, and exploded into worms," she sobbed as she began to babble. "The worm threads got in them. Ate them. And then they fell apart because they were gone and there was nothing left but the worms. And then…"

Morgan didn't even know where to start with asking questions. It was all so bizarre and horrible he was dumbstruck.

"Did I miss something here? I thought it took over half an hour before Jake changed. But Ollie's, ah, transformation only took minutes."

"Yeah, and I don't know why," Nina replied. "Maybe they just got better at dealing with us."

"But that wasn't the end of it, was it?" Morgan asked.

"No." She blinked a few times, and then wiped one of her eyes with a forearm. "As we were getting the hell out of there, I looked back. I wish I hadn't." Her expression was dead. "They were standing there. I mean, I knew it wasn't them. It was their shape, but it wasn't them. They were made of the worm bodies all working together."

"Sentient parasite," Hiro said.

There was silence save for the sound of the rover's engines.

"That's fucking great. We're 390-million miles from home on a moon with a sentient parasite that eats you. And copies you," Eddy spat. "And we woke it up."

"Shut it, Bourke," Morgan scowled.

Hiro sat forward. "You said Jake took samples. Where are they?"

"In the containment chamber," she said and then turned. "Be careful. Do not open them in here."

Hiro nodded and went to the cabinet-like chamber and immediately found the samples. There were several glass jars, and he brought one out and placed it on the desk in a work area.

The rover was like Bruce in that it had small but limited work areas. But it only had a few pieces of equipment. Hiro quickly set them up.

Morgan looked across at Nina whose eyes were glassy and she gripped the wheel so hard her knuckles were showing white even through her brown skin.

"How long?" he asked.

She glanced at her control panel. "Forty-five minutes, give or take," she replied.

He reached across to lay a hand on her forearm, and it felt like corded wood such was the tension in her body.

"You be okay?" he asked softly.

After a moment she half turned to him, and her face was drooping with sadness. "No. Maybe," she scoffed softly. "If you'd seen what I saw, you wouldn't be okay either." She shrugged. "But I'm functioning."

"I know you are." Morgan lowered his voice, "We've got plenty of aces to play yet. Our priority is to get our team home. We focus on that."

Morgan turned to look back at Hiro, and then rose from his chair. "I need to see what we're dealing with."

Morgan headed down to Hiro's work area, sat in the spare chair, and leaned forward. "Mr. Nakagawa, what can you tell me?"

Hiro held up the sample jar. "Inside there are life forms. I can barely see them in amongst the ice, but that's melting now I have the jar out in the cabin."

Morgan could see thread-like things in the water at the bottom. They must have been around half an inch in length, were like thick, white hairs, and had a black tip at one end.

"Like a skinny black-headed maggot," he said.

Hiro nodded. "Except maggots are blind and carrion feeders. This thing hunts, and I think that dot is a combination of sensory organ, and brain. In fact, the brain to body ratio leaves us for dead. This thing is smart, and learns."

"How?" Morgan stared at the jar.

Hiro shrugged. "I can only hypothesize, but I think this thing, these *things*, are less like a maggot, and more like a flatworm. Those little horrors, flatworms, once they've been inside you for a while can cause anemia, and can damage the liver, intestine, lungs and bladder. They can even cause seizures, paralysis or spinal cord inflammation."

Hiro put the jar down. "But what I can draw parallels with is something called flatworm learning – they can learn from ingesting their host. Flatworms can solve puzzles and mazes. You train a flatworm to solve a maze, then grind it up and feed it to another flatworm, then guess what? The next flatworm already knows how to solve the maze."

"I know a bit about flatworms. My dad's farm had to deal with an infestation once. Killed a lot of his cattle. Ate them from the inside out. Turned their brains to mush."

"That's them," Hiro replied.

Morgan grimaced. "So these things ate Jake and Ollie, and then learned enough to sort of put them back together?"

"I don't know. It's clearly something we've never seen before." Hiro's mouth turned down and he hiked his shoulders. "Everything is theory and guesswork for now." He turned back. "But the thing is, they'll get better and better at their learning if they get to ingest more of us."

Morgan sat back. "I'm guessing they stay dormant on the surface until some poor sap like Jake walks by."

"Or some other lifeform." Hiro nodded. "From what Nina told us, it took them thirty minutes to break down Jake and then reform him. But only minutes to do the same to Ollie."

"Fast learning." Morgan nodded. "Well, then, we better not give them another chance to get at anyone else."

"There's one more thing that bothers me," Hiro said. "These things are tiny, but smart. But their brain, if that's what those dark spots are, is not nearly big enough to store all that complex information."

"That's good, right?" Morgan asked.

"Maybe." Hiro put the jar down. "Or it might mean they're not really individuals, but are more like the cells of a body, and somewhere else, some *thing* else, is the real central brain."

Morgan sighed. "Yeah, well, that's another whole level of nightmare I'll try not to think about for a while." Morgan stood and patted the man's shoulder. "Keep at it."

He headed back to Nina up in front. He needed to keep them all safe and away from these things, but had no idea exactly where they were, or how many there were.

Nina spoke without turning. "Fifteen minutes," she said robotically.

"Good." Morgan squeezed her shoulder, sat, and then switched on the comms once more. "Traveler, come back."

He waited a moment.

"Benny, this is Commander Brad Morgan, come back."

He waited again, but the feedback from the open channel was nothing but a grating white noise.

He switched it off and sat thinking through what Nina had told him and what might have happened – there could be some sort of interference. There could be a technical malfunction. There could even be human error, or human intervention. Nina had mentioned that Heather was a bit mentally fragmented when she was dropped off. What if she tried to…

Tried to what, exactly?

Worst case Heather had damaged something. Or even worse case, she'd hurt Benny. And then damaged something.

He groaned and sat back. In minutes they would know.

He half turned. "Helmets on."

In the rear of the rover, Hiro, Eddy, and Angie began to suit up. He did the same. And Nina would when she finished piloting the rover.

They came out between two jagged hills of ice and onto the plain where the Traveler had originally set down.

There was nothing there.

But then he saw it. "Oh god, no."

There was an absolute worst case, and one he had not even imagined possible.

He pointed with a shaking hand. "There."

About five hundred yards away was an impact site. And in and around it a lot of twisted metal debris. There was no smoke as it was obviously already cooling.

"What happened?" Angie said from right behind them.

Eddy was also out of his seat. "They crashed," he said morosely. "That's what happened."

When they were just a few hundred feet out Morgan called a halt, and Nina pulled the rover around to be side-on. The group sat looking at the debris pattern.

"I guess we're not going to be making that complementary orbit," Angie said softly.

"They took off, and then came back down. Hard," Hiro said.

"Did they? Come back down." Angie's brows were deeply knitted. "There's not nearly enough debris out there on the ice for it to be the Traveler out there. Maybe they grazed the surface, breaking away some external equipment and still managed to take off."

"Maybe," Morgan started. "Any movement on any quadrants?" he asked Hiro.

The man checked the sensors. "Nothing from the crash site." He looked a little more. "And all quiet for half a mile. Just us here."

"Okay Eddy, we're taking a look. Everyone else, sit tight." Morgan left his seat.

"What should I bring?" Eddy asked.

Morgan thought about it. "Just your wits."

"No, take a burner. Those things don't like heat," Nina said. "Just in case they're out there."

Morgan nodded. "Grab one."

He did as asked, and then both men exited the rover one at a time. On the surface, Morgan looked one way then the other.

"Nina, voice check." He turned and looked back at the people in the rover cabin window.

"Loud and clear," Nina replied.

Morgan gave her a thumbs up, and together he and Jake headed for the crash site.

It only took them a few minutes to come to the first pieces of the Traveler in the dispersal zone. For some insane reason, Morgan hoped it wasn't going to be their ship like Angie suggested. But after a moment he began to recognize more of the craft – and devastatingly, fragments from inside.

There were the charring and carbon discoloration remnants on the ice that was now polished like glass.

"Where's the rest of it?" Eddy asked. "Was Angie right? Did they get away?"

"No. We're standing on it," Morgan replied. "Nina said there was an explosion and if the fuel tanks had detonated then it probably melted the surface to water. It would have created a small lake for a while and the Traveler went down into it. Now its remains are sunken below the ice. Entombed." He walked a few paces forward. "Keep your eyes open. Though the fire might have killed everything in and on the Traveler, I don't know what the physiology of these things is. And if they're tough enough to survive on Europa, we don't yet know what they're capable of."

"I heard that," Eddy said.

The pair spread left and right, walking slowly.

Morgan spotted the scattered debris through the ice and saw that very little remained of the Traveler's superstructure, and knew there would be nothing salvageable. They had brought enough fuel for a trip to and from Europa with fuel consumption for landing, liftoff, traveling, and a small extra reserve for emergencies.

The tanks had been thirty percent of the entire craft's weight, with at least fifty-five percent remaining. That amount of fuel would have detonated like a massive thermal bomb and heated the temperature for hundreds of yards to well above freezing. The crash site would have become a boiling lake of fire dozens of feet deep before it refroze.

As if to prove his assumption, he stopped over a particular glassine area and could just make out a small human shape with long hair about six feet down. One of the legs was missing from just above the knee, and the suit looked blackened on that side.

"Oh Heather," he sighed. "What happened here?"

Morgan went down on one knee for a closer look and immediately saw something else; around the stump there was the discoloration marks of blood. it might have meant it was still pumping when she sank. She had been alive.

He looked over his shoulder. "Eddy, over here."

The young man jogged back over the freezing landscape and stopped, and also crouched. Morgan shone a light down into the ice and he was glad the figure was face down so he couldn't see her face.

"I think it's Heather," he said.

Eddy nodded. "That's her." He looked up. "Should we try and dig her out?"

Morgan looked down at the young woman's trapped corpse. "No, we don't have the equipment so would have to do it by hand. We'd expend too much energy," he sighed. "This will be her grave, for now."

"What about Benny?" Eddy asked.

"He might have been vaporized. Or is buried too deep for us to see." Morgan got to his feet. "Let's take a last look around."

The pair circled the crash site, and Morgan widened their search pattern. A few hundred feet from the crash debris he found the four strut legs encased in the ice, like the feet of a giant insect that had been pulled free.

He could imagine what happened – they had taken off, but the struts had held them in place. Until they finally snapped off. Then either Benny or Heather had lost control.

But why did they take off? he wondered.

The only reason they would was if they were worried about the safety of themselves or there was a risk to the ship.

But whatever the reason, the result was catastrophic, and his entire team was now marooned. No one would be coming to rescue them. Or at least not before their fuel, food, and air ran out.

Currently their entire fuel reserves and oxygen consisted of what was in the rover and their own personal suit tanks. That would probably only last another week. And that was only possible because half of them were now dead.

He remembered a saying from his dad from years ago: Things can go bad real quick.

"You're right again, Dad," he thought.

"Morgan, say again?" Nina asked.

Morgan forgot he had his comm link open. "There's nothing left. It's all gone." He turned to look back at the crash site. "We think we might have found Heather. Frozen in the ice. Too deep to dig out, so we'll leave her there."

Nina lowered her voice. "Was she…okay?"

He knew what she was asking. Was she still human? Or had she turned into something else?

"I think so. There looked like blood, and none of those white worm things. As far as we could make out." He turned back. "We'll give it a few more minutes and come back in. We need to work on a plan."

"Good," she said simply, and signed off.

Morgan thought about the white worm things that apparently got inside a body, and then made it do things. Hiro had suggested it/they learned from them, so each time it got smarter and better at copying them.

Thinking about his father reminded him of something else – the time his dad's herd had become infected by *Cysticercosis*, a parasitic tissue infection caused by larval cysts of the tapeworm.

He remembered that the larval cysts had moved from the gut to infect internal organs, muscles, and then even onto the brain. The flukes curled up in their heads in little pockets they made for themselves in the brain tissue and fed on the soft, warm brain. And in turn secreted a substance that kept the cattle's immune system from detecting them.

The cattle got confused, had erratic behavior and behavioral changes – some went from their usual docile selves to aggressive animals that attacked the other cattle, and in extreme cases, even taking bites out of them.

By that time up to a hundred of Dad's cattle had to be put down as their brains and flesh were overrun by the worms. They had a vaccine for it and a single dose of *Albendazole* had sorted them out. But that was something they didn't have here. Right now their only defense was to stay ahead of it.

"Eddy." He waved his arm at the young man. "We're heading back."

He turned and walked slowly to the rover.

He needed a plan to get them home. And he needed to keep his remaining crew safe from whatever indigenous life forms were out there.

Morgan looked about. White thread-like creatures that got inside you and remade you. White threads on white ice and snow – so, basically invisible.

He felt the start of a tension headache. He had a lot to do, and the clock was ticking on their life support systems.

Morgan tilted his helmet to look up at the black starlit sky in the direction where Earth should be. Maybe one of those dots was his home, but right now it seemed farther away than any time in his life.

Things can go bad real quick, he repeated in his head.

They already have, he responded.

***

The two people headed back to the rover, and one at a time entered the tube decon chamber. After another moment, the door whined shut and the freezing Europa surface and atmosphere was locked out.

Silence returned.

But only for a while as from all around them something was waking up. Something was attracted by the warmth and movement. Something that had already learned about the biped creatures from its hive who had fed on them and become them.

The lifeform's intellect had been trapped on the Europan moon's surface for millions of years, hibernating, waiting. And now something had arrived that heralded food in abundance. And perhaps another life. Another life away from the desolation.

Like a surging tide, the intellect commanded the horde to move toward the rover and its occupants.

PART 05
ARE WE ALONE?

CHAPTER 23

Morgan was last out of the decon chamber and took his helmet off. The group in the rover was quiet, watching him.

Nina's face was drawn and her eyes red-rimmed as she also watched him. Hiro was nervous but looked steady, and Angie smiled brokenly and nodded to him. Eddy just sat down and stared at the floor.

Morgan sunk into the copilot's chair next to Nina and he turned so he could take all his team in.

"There are no survivors. And the Traveler is gone," he said evenly. "No one will be coming to rescue us. Not for years. And we don't have the luxury of that amount of time."

He knew, *they knew*, what that meant. Now that they all realized the weight of the predicament they were in, he needed them to focus on and work toward a solution, as they had just five days before their oxygen and energy ran out. They had food and water for beyond that, but that was useless if they all froze or suffocated.

"What about the spare oxygen tanks in Bruce?" Eddy asked. "We could dig them out and buy us a little more time."

Morgan nodded. "I like your thinking. But we may expend valuable resources of time, energy, and our own oxygen to secure it. Be a high cost low return game for us." He half smiled. "But I'm putting it on the 'maybe' list."

"If we *could* dig down to Bruce, I might be able to rig some sort of hibernation cocktail, plus cryo tanks. We could wait until someone arrived," Hiro said.

"How many could you rig?" Morgan asked, already guessing the answer.

Hiro exhaled. "Maybe two, or three."

Everyone looked away, knowing they weren't ready to draw straws on who lived and who died just yet.

Morgan sat forward. "We have some of the most intelligent people I know sitting here. I want everyone to think laterally. Throw out ideas to me, no matter how wild. How can we survive longer, all of us, or get home?"

He sat back as everyone's vision turned inwards as their minds worked.

Hiro lifted his head. "I can work on the rover's comms. Boost the signal back home."

"Good. That's also a maybe," Morgan said.

He knew getting a message home to tell them they were in trouble was redundant. Because after NASA not hearing from them on their allotted times, they would already guess there was a problem.

"What else have we got?" Morgan sat back.

People continued to stare at nothing as their minds worked.

And then Morgan had a lightning bolt idea. He grinned and sat forward.

Nina glanced at him. "What? What are you grinning at?"

"*Ne vse poteryano.*" He kept grinning.

"All is not lost?" Angie's brows came together.

He got confused stares from everyone.

"What is it?" Eddy asked, becoming buoyed by their demeanor.

"Listen," Morgan said. "The problem we have is that we either need more fuel, a place to shelter, or some way, or something that's going to get us home. Our transport and resources have been destroyed. But there might be another source of all those life-saving resources, right?"

"Oh, oh, oh, no way. You're kidding, right?" Eddy clapped once and rocked back in his chair and then stopped. "You're not."

"*Ya ne.*" Morgan sat back.

"What is it?" Hiro asked.

Eddy gripped Hiro's arm. "That Russian ship that crashed a few years back."

Nina nodded. "We saw it on the way down. And it's within reach."

"Could it still work?" Angie asked. "After sitting here for two years or more?"

"Well, we have a pilot, engineers, scientists, I can understand a little Russian, and Angie can speak and read it fluently," Morgan said. "We know the ship is intact, we just need to see what we've got to work with."

Hiro slumped back in his chair and nodded. "I feel better that we have a plan. Even if it is a wild one."

Morgan turned back to the console. "Hiro, open the sensors in a wide net. Look for a large metallic signature. Nina, let's plot a course. Eddy, do an inventory on what tools we have." He turned to Angie, "And just in case we need to speak Russian, be ready, as mine is a little rusty."

Hiro did as asked, and it didn't take him long. "I found it. Big signature," he said. "Forty-three miles, twenty-five degrees north west. Do we have the fuel to make it?"

Nina nodded. "We sure do. But not there and back. So it's all in on this one."

Morgan knew she was right – it was all in, as there were no more options after this one. He felt good that the team was energized and optimistic. Hope was a great motivator.

But they needed something else: *luck.*

"Nina, plot a course," he said.

She plugged in the coordinates of the Russian ship. And in seconds more, the rover started out.

CHAPTER 24

Morgan flat smiled as he glanced at each of his crew members all engaged in their duties. There was even some light banter between them. Optimism was high and everyone was feeling, if not great, at least better.

No one voiced the risk of what might happen if the Russian craft was a wreck, drained of energy, and its hull so breached it might not even provide adequate shelter. In addition, no one talked about their lost friends and crew mates. There'd be plenty of time for commiserations later.

Until then, he thought he might just clear his mind and also enjoy the ambience of goodwill and hope.

He closed his eyes and meshed his fingers over his belly as Nina piloted the rover. But try as he might, he couldn't forget or even push aside what happened to their ship. He couldn't dislodge the ghosts of his dead team, their faces haunting him. And he further couldn't shake the knowledge that there was a creeping something out there, that might be everywhere or nowhere.

He rubbed his eyers with finger and thumb, and blinked several times. He could do with some real sleep, but that might be far away right now.

"Something on the scanner," Hiro said.

"I see it," Nina replied.

"Too early for it to be the Russian ship," Morgan added.

"Smaller, uniform signature, and basically a composite iron base. Shouldn't be on the surface." Hiro frowned, as he worked to get an exact bearing. "Two miles, ten degrees, north-west."

"Take a look?" Nina asked.

"Sure, it's not far. Might be some space debris. Or a piece of the Russian ship. Worth checking out." Morgan looked over Hiro's shoulder at the pattern on the scanner. "Yeah, looks uniform, and slightly rounded. My money is on space debris like a small asteroid."

"Have to be from space. There's nothing iron based on the surface," Nina remarked.

"Why is it there? Shouldn't it sink after a few centuries or millennia?" Eddy asked.

"Not sure," Morgan replied. "But given the density of the ice, and the fact it's created from below, not from above from falling snow, then it's unlikely to sink or be covered over. It'll only sink now if there is an upwelling from right underneath it. Whatever it is, it might have sat there for countless millions of years."

"Coming up on it now." Eddy peered at his scanner. "Ladies and gentlemen, if you look out your left side portal you will see the object." He looked up from his tiny green glowing screen toward the window and nodded. "There."

The group looked out the portal and saw the rounded lump embedded in the icy surface. It looked to be about fifteen feet high but could have had that much again sunk in the hard ice. Even from where they sat in the rover they could see it looked to have fallen from the sky, impacted, and stayed.

Morgan moved one of the onboard cameras, focused in and amplified the image. The computers cleaned it up to give him a high resolution image. He placed it up on the large screen at the front of the rover.

"I can see a piece has broken away. There's a cavity; might be hollow."

"Wonder what was in it?" Eddy asked.

"Probably nothing but some gas and water vapor that has long since frozen or denuded," Hiro replied.

"Panspermia," Angie said softly.

Eddy turned. "I've heard that word somewhere before; what is it?"

Angie half smiled. "It's one of the theories for the origination of life on Earth. Or on other worlds. It argues that life did not originate on our planet, but instead evolved somewhere else in the universe and arrived by astral object, and so was seeded on Earth. Panspermia suggests that microorganisms could be transported by asteroids and comets through space to places like our planet." She turned to face the dark lump of rock. "And maybe here."

Everyone turned to look at the thing as well.

"It was hollow. Or it is now," Hiro said.

After a moment Morgan sat back.

"Well, any other time, we'd go and investigate. But right now, we make a note, and continue with our prime objective – getting home."

"I second that," Nina said.

Morgan moved the camera a little and was about to stop filming.

"*Wait!*" Angie near shouted.

Everyone turned to her, and she got up from her seat to walk closer to the screen.

"Pan back… just a little," she asked.

Morgan did as asked, and Angie stood looking at the image, her eyes wide. Then she leaned forward to get even closer to the screen. She lifted her hand to point at something.

"See there?"

The group turned to where she was pointing.

"See what? What is it?" Nina asked.

Angie straightened with her hands on her hips and exhaled through her nose. "I can speak dozens of languages. I can read over a hundred, and I've seen ancient proto-language scraps from the Neolithic age. And that..." She pointed again, "…looks like a written language."

Everyone's head whipped back around, and Morgan squinted and enlarged the portion of the image. They then saw that above the hole in the object's side there were some symbols, whorls, and overlapping strokes.

"This is important. I need to go out there and see it." Angie stared at the images as if in a trance.

"Absolutely not," Nina said.

Angie turned. "This is why I am here. If there was contact, any form of contact, with an indigenous lifeform, and it was possible to communicate, I am to attempt it." She pointed. "And something is communicating. Or once did."

"You can read it?" Eddy asked. "Just looks like chicken scratchings to me."

Angie half smiled. "The reading, interpreting, and hopefully understanding of languages is a dynamic field that combines historical, linguistic, archaeological, and technological approaches. I need to fully capture the symbols, and then I can use a language app developed by the great linguist, Matthew Kearns." She turned. "He's the best in the world."

"I said no." Nina shook her head.

"Commander." Angie turned. "I know we are in a dire situation here. And I know we have extreme priorities. But if through God's grace and good luck, we do make it home, this..." She lifted her arm to point. "This is what it's all about."

"No." Nina glared.

Morgan sighed. "Hang on, Nina." His mouth turned down for a moment. "Angie is right."

Nina glared. "She *cannot* go out there. If you had seen what I saw..."

Morgan held up a hand. "She only needs to be out there and up close for ten minutes, tops. Right, Angie?"

"*Hmm...*" Angie bobbed her head from side to side. "Give or take. I just need to capture all the images. I'll break records I'll be so quick." She smiled. "I can be even faster if someone helps me."

"I'll go," Eddy said.

Morgan shook his head. "Sorry Eddy; you're the only engineer we got. We need everyone right now. Except me, I'm expendable."

"What?" Nina leapt from her chair. "Over my..."

Morgan grinned. "You can do my job. But I can't do the job Eddy or Hiro might be called on to do. We need them."

"Then I'm the expendable one," Nina's voice rose.

"But I'm stronger and faster," he replied forcefully. "Angie, get your stuff, we've got fifteen minutes outside time, including there and back. And that's all."

"On it," she said and went to the back of the rover.

***

Morgan and Angie left the rover and walked around the front of the vehicle. Morgan turned slowly – he had his suit's external audio switched on so he could hear the sounds of Europa. But there was nothing save for an eerie background whine, which NASA had told him was just the usual white-noise of space intruding down onto the moon's surface because there was such a thin atmosphere.

He switched the distracting, spooky sound off and turned to the rover. He saw Nina staring down at him with an expression like thunder. On either shoulder was Hiro and Eddy.

He gave them the thumbs up. "You guys are my long range eyes and ears."

Nina's expression remained unchanged. "But if I hear or see anything, you get your assess back in here, pronto, got it?"

"Yes ma'am," Morgan chuckled and saluted.

Angie turned and waved her acknowledgement as well. She then turned to Morgan.

"Let's go. I only need to take some clear photographs and ensure we get the entire script recorded. Plus, I need to see there isn't more writing inside." She began to walk forward over the near polished ice.

Morgan followed. They were only a few hundred feet from the huge, rounded thing and as he got closer he appreciated its size and bulk.

The outside seemed to have been burned black and it was partially sunk into the ice. Its skin was pocked with holes and seemed a little to be made of some sort of igneous rock, but the sensors had indicated a high iron content.

The one thing that screamed at him, was it looked old. Very old. Estimates on the age of Europa was that it was a young moon, less than 200-million years. *Was it that old?* he wondered.

In seconds more they stood about a dozen feet from it, and the huge thing loomed before them. Angie went to the markings and began to film them. He went and crouched before the hole in its front, just at ground level.

He flicked on his flashlight and saw that the object wasn't completely hollow, more like it had a deep cavity inside it. He shone his light around the interior and saw there were things hanging inside like gossamer threads.

For the life of him, it reminded him of some sort of insect or spider's nest. He shivered and stood up.

"How you doing there, Angie?" he asked.

"I'm doing fine." She turned to him with a broad smile. "In my opinion this is definitely writing. And I can see that there are a few recurring symbols."

"Is that good or bad?" he asked.

"That's good, very good." She beamed. "Means it *is* a language, and I have a very good chance of being able to decipher it."

"Wonder what it says?" He stood back a step.

"Yes, I also wonder what it says." She turned to him. "And more importantly, I wonder who wrote it. And when? And why? And where are they now?"

He nodded. "All great questions. Tells me that the surface might not have always been the barren wasteland it is now." He turned about. "I wonder where they are now." He looked up. "Unless this thing dropped from space with the markings already on it."

"I don't think so." Angie stepped closer to the thing. "The writing is too perfectly positioned; whoever carved it wanted it to be read." She reached out to touch the rock. "And I think that the stone is ancient, and though the writing is old, it's not as old as the original stone."

She then looked down and began to kick ice debris aside with her boot. "Notice something missing?" she asked.

He looked down then back up at her face. "No, give me a clue."

"This place is a giant refrigerator. Without a climate, winds, storms, or any sort of weather. There's no erosion, and the things on the surface are only affected by upwellings, space debris, and gravity. Otherwise, objects like this hunk of rock just sit here untouched for millions of years."

"Okay," he asked. "And?"

She traced one of the whorls with a fingertip. "And I think this writing was cut in with something like a laser. Not chiseled as there's no rock debris anywhere, and it's far too perfect."

"Then whoever, or whatever they were, they were advanced," he said and then turned to her. "Think you can decipher it?"

"Yeah, yeah I do." She began to gather her equipment. "And one of the main reasons is that I get the feeling that by the way this message is made so prominent, that whoever left it wanted it to be read."

"Maybe it says, *welcome to Europa*." He checked his gauntlet screen. "Okay, our time is up."

CHAPTER 25

Nina watched as firstly Angie then Morgan reentered the rover. She wouldn't let them out of the decon tube until they had a lengthy decontamination procedure, and in the end Morgan had to yell at her to knock it off.

But she knew they hadn't seen what she'd seen. She had a terrible feeling that perhaps Heather and Benny had, and that was why they tried to take off – they were trying to get away from something – trying to save the ship and themselves. If that was true, then hopefully everything inside the Traveler had died. And with it the threat.

Once the pair had resettled in the rover, Nina set off again toward what they hoped was the downed Russian ship. Though she tried to remain enthusiastic, she had the nagging voice in her head as to why the Russian Earth base had lost contact with their space ship – the same reason NASA would have lost contact with the Traveler.

Behind her, Angie immediately set to work on the translation. Eddy and Hiro used different sensors checking the path ahead, and other proximity equipment.

She turned; beside her Morgan seemed lost in thought, staring out at the icy landscape, but she bet his vision was turned inwards.

"Penny for your thoughts." She watched him from the side of her eye.

He made a soft sound in his throat and turned to her. "Just thinking of home, and Dad, and wondering what my brother, Greg, is thinking."

"You'll see them again," she said, but only half believed it.

"I know, we'll be fine. All of us," he replied, turning back to the Europa surface.

Nina navigated around outcrops and maneuvered between crevices of ice. From time to time they passed by colossal fissures in the ice as if massive tectonic forces had ripped a deep wound in the miles-thick ice.

No one had any idea what caused it, and even though a massive explosive upwelling could punch a hole right through, it wouldn't shatter and crack the ice, more melt a hole through it as the under pressure sea water was so much warmer.

"That one is one-point-eight miles deep – nine thousand, five hundred and four feet all the way down," Eddy said from behind them. "You fall into one of those, you'd be falling a long time."

"Five minutes," Hiro said. "Falling at thirty-two feet per second, it would you take four point nine-five minutes to reach bottom."

"Thank you, Mister Human Calculator," Eddy chuckled.

Nina saw the warning lights on her console. "We've got some large formations coming up. Let's see if we can find a way through or if we need to take a detour."

Morgan checked their fuel levels. "Let's hope if we have to detour, it's not too far."

Looming ahead of them was a line of huge crystal blocks, hundreds of feet high. They seemed to stretch from one end of the horizon to the other, and Nina knew Morgan was right – a detour would cost them way too much fuel. There'd be no climbing over them, and her only hope was to find a path or tunnel through them.

As they got closer they began to see them in more detail.

Morgan sat forward. "Am I crazy, or do some of those blocks look like…?"

"*Structures*," Nina finished. "And if you're crazy then so am I. This is impossible, right?"

"On this place, we're rewriting what is possible every minute." Morgan turned in his seat. "Angie, you wanted to know who carved those words in that meteorite fragment. Well, now we might find out."

Angie lifted her head from her translation program and stared, her eyes narrowing. She stared for a moment. "Could there really be a civilized race living here?"

"Or maybe once was," Hiro added.

Eddy read off more details. "This wall is hundreds of miles wide."

"They built a wall. To keep something out?" Angie raised her eyebrows.

Nina cursed under her breath.

The mountainous barrier was still about half a mile away but as they neared more detail became apparent. Some of the areas just looked like broken ice blocks, each as big as an ocean liner. Others were more uniform, but not in the sense of uniform from a human being's perspective, as their shapes were non-Euclidean, aberrant, and just damned strange. But in amongst them could have been things like doorways and windows, but their size and shape hinted at occupants that were not like humans, but instead much bigger and wider.

Nina stopped. "Anyone see a way through?"

Eddy's hands flew over his console. "Opening scanner. Looking for heat differential."

Though the moon's surface in this zone was a constant two-forty degrees below zero, out of the air, it tended to be a few degrees warmer. And that's what Eddy scanned for.

"Found one," he said and lifted his head for a second to look out the front window, before diving back down to his small screen.

"I read five hundred and twenty feet before the sensor stops reading – twenty-eight degrees north, north-east – yeah, it's big, real big. Could be a deep cave with a bend that stops me seeing the end. Or we could be in luck and have found a way through."

"Checking it out," Nina said and restarted the rover.

They drove along the face of the huge cliffs of ice and then in the distance saw the massive hole. It had to be two hundred feet high and almost that much again wide.

When they were out in front, Nina brought the rover front on to it and allowed the team to use their scanner to delve inside it.

"Can't detect a back wall, but plenty of obstacles. Might be a way through," Eddy said.

Nina turned to Morgan and raised her eyebrows. "Well?" She already knew what he was thinking.

"Best option so far." He nodded. "Let's do it."

"Eyes open, everyone," Nina said.

Morgan, Hiro, and Eddy were either glued to their sensor screens, or straining to see what was coming. At the rear, Angie was still working the translation. Nina switched on the powerful front lights, and the heavily fortified vehicle entered the massive cave.

**

Here we go, Morgan thought.

He prayed there was a way through. There wasn't enough fuel for too many turn backs. And even if they could scale the ice cliffs, he didn't like their chances of traveling for miles on foot with what Nina had told them her team encountered on the open ice.

They entered the utter blackness of the cave and he leaned forward to switch on all the peripheral lights. It made little difference, and he felt they were now like a single candle in a barn at midnight.

"Slow it down," he said, and Nina eased it back to around ten miles per hour; this was due to safety, but it also allowed them to get a good look at where they were.

The walls and ceiling were a deep blue color signifying it was very old ice. There was little debris on the ground meaning the ceiling was solid.

"No ice fall," Nina said. "Good."

"At these temperatures and with little surface geology movement, then the ice should be as hard as steel," Morgan replied. "There's only one thing that might change that..." He turned to her.

"Yep. Us," Nina finished.

The vibrations from the rover and its exhaust might raise the temperature just a few degrees. Might be enough to weaken the ceiling and drop a fifty ton ice boulder on them.

"Still not reading any form of blockage from up ahead," Eddy said. "We might be looking good here."

"No movement. Still air all the way," Hiro added.

Morgan put the binoculars to his eyes and scanned the walls and as far ahead as he could make out. The cavern was big and clean enough, so Nina increased the speed, and they were soon traveling at twenty miles per hour.

After another fifteen minutes Morgan suddenly craned forward. "*Whoa*, go slow."

Nina slowed the rover. "What is it?"

"Something I don't believe." He lowered the glasses and pointed to a place on one of the walls.

Nina swiveled the large overhead spotlight and illuminated a place about a hundred feet up on one of the walls.

"Veer in a little closer," he said, and then, *"All stop."*

Nina brought the rover front-on, and she also turned all the lighting to bear on the ice wall.

"Am I dreaming?" Angie asked.

"Then we all are." Eddy grinned as they all crowded around the front of the rover.

Half way up the sheer ice wall there were structures, buildings, carved right out of and into the ice wall. They didn't conform to any shape humans would recognize as being aesthetically pleasing to the eye or even a home. Some had corners, some rounded, and some looked to have been melted rather than carved. But there were windows, pathways, and in some areas, more of the strange glyphic symbols.

"Angie, more writing," Morgan said.

"I see it. The translation is nearly complete." She looked across at the wall city. "So, where are they?"

"Maybe they don't show up on a visible spectrum," Hiro said. "They're here, but we just can't see them."

Everyone turned back to the buildings and looked along the ice floor as well.

"Great, so we got space ghosts," Eddy scoffed.

Behind them, Angie's console pinged.

"Excellent; translation complete." Angie raced back to read and then reread what the computer was telling her. She slowly straightened with her brows drawn together.

"I don't get it," she said.

"Just read it to us," Morgan requested.

"All are taken," she read. "And there's a word that is repeated over and over. The computer has judged it to be something like, *parasites.*"

No one spoke for several moments.

"I suddenly wish I never heard that," Eddy scoffed.

"Why carve something like that into a rock out in the middle of nowhere?" Morgan asked. "Could the translation be wrong?"

"Sure it could," Angie said.

"Well, when we get back, you tell this Professor Matt Kearns we want our money back," Eddy laughed but just sounded nervous.

"Unless… unless, at one time, it wasn't out in the middle of nowhere," Nina said dismally.

Everyone turned to her.

"I have a theory," she said as she seemed to organize her thoughts. "Those worm things that attacked us are not the intelligent beings that built this structure or carved that message." She nodded as she turned to them. "What if those worm things are the parasite, and they came out of that meteorite fragment."

Morgan nodded slowly. "Go on."

Nina sighed. "The meteorite fragment was the source of the infection. The worms, the parasites, came out of it."

"Then what happened to these guys?" Eddy pointed to the structures.

"*All are taken,*" Angie repeated.

"Like Jake and Ollie were taken." Nina closed her eyes.

"Other than the worms, there doesn't seem to be life, now, on the surface. It's been scoured clean." Morgan turned to his crew. "But we found myriad lifeforms in the oceans. Maybe that's where they went," Morgan suggested.

"They abandoned the surface." Nina half smiled. "They had to flee something that was killing them all. And they couldn't stop it."

"Should we…?" Angie began.

"No, we don't have time for any extraneous explorations." Morgan half turned. "Eddy, get some pictures. It'll be something for the people who come after us to investigate."

"On it." Eddy swiveled the external camera lens and began to take multiple photographs.

"Movement," Hiro said. "Upper wall, coming from the structures."

The group crowded around and stared hard.

"They *are* still alive." Angie craned forward.

"I don't think so," Hiro said. "Whatever it is, it's coming down. Sensors are telling me multiple areas are moving, all across the structure. It's as if, as if, it's coming alive." Hiro concentrated. "Half way down now."

"I can't see anything." Morgan half rose to his feet.

"Maybe like you said, it's invisible." Eddy looked at his own sensors. "Hold it, there's something showing up on the visual now."

He amplified the image and put it on the screen. It showed something like a glutinous liquid coming from the structures and then running down the walls.

"Oh, god no." Nina bared her teeth. "The worms. Millions of them."

"Let's get the hell out of here," Morgan said.

Nina backed up, turned and then accelerated and the rover shot forward.

"Is that the inhabitants of the city?" Eddy asked.

"Yes and no," Nina replied. "That might be the inhabitants now. But I think not originally."

"What does that mean?" Eddy frowned.

"Think about it. Think about the translation," Angie said. "I believe that thousands or millions of years ago the asteroid fragment crashed here, broke open, and whatever came out infected who or whatever was living on the surface. Like it did to Jake and Ollie; it took them over, ingested them, and then somehow swapped itself for them, and became them. I think that's what happened to this race. The worms, the parasites took them over."

"A nightmare," Nina said. "And they obviously couldn't stop them. Even though they seemed an advanced race."

"It probably happened too quickly." Morgan looked in the rear and saw things starting to form up into physical shapes. "What the hell? They're changing."

The horde of worms that had seemed to flow like liquid now coalesced into different shapes and sizes – creatures with horse-like faces began to lift themselves up on multiple legs, or hands, as each seemed to have articulated fingers. Their heads turned towards the rover.

Nina glanced over her shoulder at them. "This is probably what the sentient race looked like, before the parasites took over their physiology." She turned to Morgan, her eyes dead. "They've already done that to some of us too. And they'll do it to all of us if they get the chance."

"They're following," Eddy yelled over the roar of the engine. "And picking up speed."

Up ahead, they were screaming toward a wall, but a small, dark tunnel offered some hope.

"No choice, going in," Nina said. In the next second, they entered the tunnel.

"*Stop!*" Morgan yelled.

Nina slammed on the brakes. "*What, why?*" she yelled back.

"Dump some of our fuel, *now*." Morgan leapt from his seat.

He raced to grab a burner, then put his helmet on and came back to her.

"No fucking way, you are..."

"Listen." He grabbed her arm. "Once I'm out drive forward a hundred feet. We need to slow them down or stop them. Otherwise those things will chase us all the way to the Russian ship."

Nina seemed to think about it for a second or two before nodding. "Okay." She reached up to grab his hand. "Brad, be careful. Please."

"Always." Morgan then stepped into the decon tube. In seconds more, he was outside.

***

Morgan jogged back a few paces to where Nina had dumped the fuel that was still liquid on the ice cavern floor in the mouth of the smaller tunnel. And then Nina accelerated slowly forward until she was about a hundred feet from the fuel spill and slowed.

Morgan watched her until he was satisfied she was far enough away, and then turned to light the small burner.

He looked across the lake of fuel and saw a scene from hell, as dozens of the things were coming at him on segmented, spider legs, and long grasping arms with dozens of claw-like fingers. Their long faces split, revealing glassine teeth. There were also other things that seemed far older and more primordial, with tentacles bursting from their faces, and they moved on a large gastropod-type foot.

But the weirdest thing was they seemed to bristle with fur, and he knew that it wasn't hair but instead millions of the worms all working together.

He was about to throw the burner but stopped – there was something else amongst them. Something different. One of the creatures held something that looked like a soft, yellow bag-like mass in one of its arms.

The thing pulsated obscenely, and he couldn't work out what it was. But he knew what it looked like – *a brain*, his mind screamed.

"Fuck that," he said, and tossed the burner onto the fuel dump. It exploded in a fifty foot wide orange mushroom cloud and the resultant fireball filled the mouth of the tunnel. Morgan felt the heat and force of the pressure wave as a hot shove against his chest.

The suit he was wearing was tough enough to withstand extremes of heat and cold, but he still backed away as the flames filled the mouth of the tunnel – nothing was getting through that. He hoped. After another second or two he jogged back to the rover and reentered.

As soon as Morgan came out of the decon tube he looked once into the rear camera and couldn't see past the flames. For now they still burned strongly, so he was feeling a little safer. Until a huge chunk of ice fell from the ceiling.

"Punch it," he said

"Yep, that's our cue," Nina said and accelerated.

"Dammit," Morgan said as he watched the rear camera.

Behind them the cavern continued to flame strongly, causing the roof to become unstable and more ice to fall down. Much of the softened ice put out the flames but then with the cold returning, it froze quickly, and through the powdery mist that might have partially been steam and ice crystals, he saw glimpses of a new barrier blocking the smaller tunnel.

Morgan smiled. "Okay, good and bad news. The good news is nothing is going to be following us. The bad news is if this tunnel turns out to be a dead end, then this is where we're staying."

"Not a chance," Eddy said. "I'm feeling lucky today."

"That's the spirit." He turned. "Stay on the sensors and let us know if anything is going to cause us a problem."

"You got it," Eddy replied.

Nina still had all the lights on full beam and Morgan had her scale them back. Also to take the speed down a few notches. Though their batteries still had good charge they'd just used up a lot of liquid fuel, and it was time to start rationing.

"How far to Mother Russia?" he asked.

Nina glanced down. "Twenty-two miles. Within reach. If there's no blockage, we can be there within two hours."

Morgan nodded. "We can do it."

"Of course we can." Nina reached across and squeezed his leg.

Behind them Eddy coughed, and Morgan grinned.

They drove at around seven miles per hour through the tunnel, and he began to feel fatigue creeping over him. He needed sleep. They all did.

He turned to the side and his vision turned inward as he thought back to the monstrosities he had seen forming up behind them and remembered Nina saying they were probably the shells, or maybe the ingested memories of the former inhabitants now taken over by the parasites.

If the former inhabitants had been wiped out thousands or perhaps even millions of years ago, did that mean some of his crew, or at least their form, may still be resurrected in eons to come? The thought horrified him that if future humans, or some other beings, arrived on Europa they might be greeted, or attacked by parasites acting as false humans.

He shook his head – *that is not happening to me or any more of my crew*, he thought.

Morgan turned. "Hiro, what else you can tell us about our parasite friends? Anything is going to be helpful right now."

Hiro turned from his microscope and blinked a few times. "They are like nothing I have ever seen before. Like nothing no human being has ever seen before." He exhaled and eased back a little. "They are tiny individual organisms but have the ability to act in unison with their own kind. It's either like some form of hive mind thinking, or they could also be like individual cells of a larger being that are being controlled by something else, or some part else." He shrugged. "I know that doesn't really make sense, but this is not Earth."

Controlled by *some part else*, he had said. Morgan remembered the yellow bag-like thing one of the creatures carried, that to him looked like a brain. Could that be the *some part else*? *Could there be some form of intellect controlling them, storing the information they gathered as individual cells?* he wondered.

Hiro held up the jar with a few of the threads inside. "I have dissected several and I find they are basically a sensory organ and a mouth on a pipe of muscle, that covers a digestive system."

"So they're hungry, smart, and strong," Eddy said.

"They don't just mimic the host once they have consumed it," Hiro replied. "They remember its form, absorb its nutrients, but also they absorb its memories, its mannerisms, its very being, as well. They learn phenomenally quickly."

"How smart can they be?" Angie said. "They're tiny."

"I don't really know. They shouldn't be able to do what they do. But I think they act on instinct and learn. And they absorb brain matter and use it to remake a collective being, a copy, of the thing they've absorbed. All the small parasites working together. Consider that our brains are specialized organs but are made up of individual cells. The parasites are similar in that they perform the same function."

"Those things didn't actually look like Jake or Ollie," Nina said. "They were just human-shaped beings using their suits."

Hiro shrugged. "I'm making some educated guesses here and also theorizing. But I think they would get better at mimicking the more time they spend in their human host, and the more human hosts they absorb."

"That makes me feel sick," Angie grimaced.

"You said they would get better at mimicking," Morgan said. "How much of a mimic could they become? How much better?"

"I don't know." Hiro shook his head slowly. "But I do not think we have seen their final form yet."

Morgan rubbed his forehead for a moment. "You know, when I was out on the ice back there I saw one of the composite things carrying something." He scoffed softly and looked up. "It was soft, yellow, and pulsating...just like a brain."

"An external brain? This is a nightmare; someone wake me." Eddy closed his eyes tight and shook his head.

"Yes." Hiro sprang forward "That makes sense. Maybe not an external brain but a leader caste of creature that does the thinking, stores the information gathered, and directs and controls them."

"This is sounding more fucked up the more I hear." Eddy looked skyward.

The group sat in silence for a few moments thinking through what they had been told until Nina spoke over her shoulder.

"All I want to know right now is one thing – how do we kill the little motherfuckers?"

"Heat," Hiro replied. "They are fantastically adaptable. Much more so than humans. They can tolerate our body temperature, but once inside us, I think they prefer to be outside. Remember when Nina told us Jake wanted to get out because he was hot – the things were making him do that. So, I think if we wanted to slow them down or kill them, then fire, high voltage electricity, even hot water might do it."

Nina's expression was like stone. "That's good for keeping them away from us. But the million dollar question is what do we do if they, ah, get inside us? What do we do if we are infected?"

Hiro looked down for a moment. "From what you told me they fully infected Jake within twenty or so minutes. But then fully infected Ollie within two." He looked up. "They got better at it. More efficient. They learned about our physiology."

"That's right," Nina said.

Hiro bobbed his head from side to side for a moment. "Maybe if they were in an extremity you could try rapid amputation. But I think the best action is to just avoid them getting in or even on your body. Because once they are inside you, and they've ingested you, you, as you, don't exist anymore."

"Yeah." Nina's soft laugh was humorless as she stared straight ahead. "Eddy, distance to Russian ship, and any obstacles?"

"Ten miles, and I can see the ice tunnel is constricting slightly but no end wall." He looked up. "So far so good."

"How're the energy levels?" Morgan asked.

"We'll make it," Nina said and turned to give him a half smile. "Walk in the park."

"Some park." He smiled back.

And then in the next few minutes they were out.

***

They burst from the tunnel out into an area of broken ice. The rover bucked and jumped over the jagged debris.

"Three miles," Eddy said.

"Could be why there is so much broken ice," Morgan said. "Russians might not have come down cleanly."

"Let's hope their ship is still intact and we don't find they crashed and it's scattered over five miles," Nina said.

"Or it sunk. Like ours," Angie added.

"Nope. Single solid object," Eddy said. "I'm thinking they came down just fine."

The rover crested a hill of ice and at the top Nina slowed, and then stopped.

She didn't need to say a word as the group stared down into a valley of massive ice crystals like a redwood forest of white and blue ice.

"And there it is," Morgan said softly.

It was a massive ship. Much bigger than the Traveler had been. The Russian craft was a square design with rounded corners about three hundred feet across and a hundred high, meaning it must have multiple levels internally.

"Thank god, it's intact," Angie said.

"I'll say." Nina flat smiled. "Because one way or another that might be our home for a while, or…"

"Just for a while," Morgan finished. "We're just visiting. We need to see what shape it's in, and what we can salvage."

"And see if there are any Russians in there," Angie said.

"After two years?" Eddy raised his eyebrows. "Would they have supplies for that long?"

"Maybe not for all of them," Hiro said.

"No visible damage. Looking very promising. Let's go and see if anyone is home," Morgan said.

"Yes, sir." Nina powered them ahead, and in ten minutes they were a few hundred yards out and the massive ship towered over them.

"Do a circuit," Morgan said. "We can check it out, and at the same time let them know we're here."

Nina took them around the outside of the vehicle. There were already tracks in the ice, so at one time people had come out in their own vehicles.

"No visible damage," Morgan said. "Anyone see any lights, movement, or activity?"

"I'm getting energy readings emanating from inside, so there's still a power source," Eddy said, and then grinned. "And heat. Ambient atmosphere inside is warm."

"Looking good." Morgan turned. "Looks like some sort of loading bay up ahead. Let's try there."

Nina drove up and entered slowly as it was dark inside save for a few small lights. As they came in sensors must have detected them and illuminated what was probably the loading bay. She stopped at its center and they all saw it was spacious, and there were other vehicles inside.

"Okay, Angie, you and me are up first." Morgan thought about it for a moment. "Forget that. We might as well all go as there's not exactly a plan-B right now."

Everyone kitted up, and in minutes more they were lined up at the exit tube.

Morgan took one last look at the front screen noting where the doorways were. For the hundredth time he wished they had weapons, and all they did have was large flashlights that could serve as a club, and a single burner that they could extend the flame out to a few feet – a pitiful defensive armory.

"Okay, we wait until everyone is out. I want Eddy first, then me, then the rest." He was thinking about having Nina stay behind, which she would have been furious about, to guard the rover, but it was nearly out of fuel so if any Russian decided to take off in it, they'd barely get ten miles before they were out of gas.

"Let's go. Eddy, you're up," Morgan said.

The young man gave a small salute and headed out, just brandishing his flashlight. Morgan went next. Then Angie, Hiro, and finally Nina.

They assembled outside, and he and Nina led them toward what looked like a doorway. Thankfully there were lights on indicating power. Unfortunately, there was no small porthole-type window in it to see what was waiting for them on the other side.

Angie deciphered the writing and pressed one of the buttons. The heavy steel door slid back, displaying a chamber, fifteen feet wide, and fortified. Probably a cargo entrance, and with another door at the end.

Once everyone was inside, Angie shut it, and then went to the opposite door, and pressed a range of buttons.

"Decon and atmospheric equalizing," she said as gases were pumped into the small, claustrophobic chamber, and a blue light blared down on them.

In several more minutes the gases were sucked out and the inner door opened. One after the other they went inside.

CHAPTER 26

The room was chaos.

"This ain't good." Eddy turned slowly.

It was probably meant to be an area where suits were changed out of and racked. There was some equipment and tools, plus even a smaller side room with showers and a toilet.

But everything seemed to be absolutely destroyed – there were several environmental suits that were ripped to shreds, and the helmets pulverized. Equipment looked like someone had taken to it with a sledgehammer, and Eddy picked up a solid wrench that was bent almost double – the force required to do that would have been titanic.

"Could a Russian do that?" he asked.

"Not even a drunk and pissed off one," Morgan replied

"Then Houston, we have a problem." Eddy dropped the wrench that made a heavy clanging noise that echoed away into the ship.

Everyone looked to Morgan, and he knew what question they were asking – go or no-go.

As no-go was a non-option, they needed to proceed. With caution.

"Hiro, enviro stats?" he asked.

The man looked at a small screen on his gantlet, reading off data. "Air is clean, but only a few rooms are heated. Most are cold in there, sixty-five degrees – might just be conserving energy – no need to heat a spaceship this size if nobody is home."

"We don't know that yet," Nina added.

Hiro nodded and continued. "No sign of microorganism contamination." He looked up. "Air is good."

Morgan reached for his helmet. *Here goes*, he thought, and unlatched it and took it off.

***

Morgan felt the chill against his sweaty face and inhaled deeply. He smelled a weird odor, like vinegar and something else slightly rank. It could have just been the smell of unwashed bodies, or something the Russians were using. Or eating.

The group spread out in the large room, looking on bench tops, opening storage compartments, and examining things on the ground.

"Over here," Eddy said.

He stood looking down at something behind a steel bench. Morgan, Nina and the team joined him and looked down where he was facing.

There was a huge patch of blood, dried to a dark chocolate brown, but in it were human tracks made with bare feet. There were also other tracks, but they were weird and unidentifiable.

"That's a man-sized footprint. But what the hell is that other one?" Eddy pointed at the track marks that looked more like pads.

Morgan had an idea what it was.

"Okay, step one before we investigate further. I want us armed with something other than flashlights. Quick check of cabinets and drawers. If I know the Russians they'll have something here."

Angie went to one of the walls where there was a dark screen with a few lit buttons beside it. She tapped the green one and the screen came to life.

"Bingo. Got a working computer here – calling up the craft's schematics."

She accessed a 3D plan of the craft and then drilled down to where they were reading off the names of the departments.

"Okay we're on entry level-1, and down here with us is several large hangar-type rooms and hangar bays. There's a machine shop, decon facilities and spare parts."

She scrolled some more. "Second level is the control and command deck, sleeping pods, galley, washrooms and even a gymnasium."

Morgan joined her. "Anything on the crew?"

"Checking," she said and called up a flight log. "Ah, here we go. Looks like a crew of twelve, including Captain Vladimir Bodin. There's second in command, Tatiana Olgenov…" She scrolled down looking at names and bios. "Yep, engineers, chemists, biologists, physicists, basically a full science team." She snorted softly. "And someone by the name of Valodnin who is a security officer."

"And having a security guy on the crew list tells me there'll be weapons onboard." Morgan straightened. "So, where are they?"

Angie scrolled the list again and noted that some of the names had red dots next to them. She tapped on one and a small box expanded.

"MPD?" Her brows came together.

"It means *missing presumed dead*," Morgan said.

"Oh." Angie tapped on more, and more, until she had found that seven of the crew had gone out and never come back.

"That leaves five still onboard. In here, somewhere." Morgan looked up at the walls and ceiling. "That's why life support is still functioning, I guess." He looked up. "Cameras," he observed. "Can't tell if they're on or not. But we could be being watched." He waved at one. "*Hello*."

Angie explored the schematic a little more. "Got it. There's an armory up on the next deck near the captain's cabin. Also, that's the command deck."

"Good, that's where we are going. Nina, we'll check the command center, Eddy, get the armory open, take Hiro as support. Angie then you're with me as we'll try the captain's cabin. I don't want the Russians thinking we're robbing them."

"Here lies Eddy Bourke, shot on Europa for being a space pirate," he chuckled. "What an awesome tombstone that'd be."

"And you'd only need to travel 390-million miles to read it," Hiro grinned.

They headed to a fortified elevator, and it took them up to the next level. The heavy door slid back, and once again they were assailed by the weird acidic smell.

Morgan held up a hand and the group stopped behind him. He turned slowly, taking in the large room, which looked to be some sort of meeting room with a large table in the center that was littered with papers.

"At least this place isn't demolished," Hiro said.

Morgan nodded. "*Hello, Russian crew,*" he yelled. "Americans. Friends."

He waited. But was greeted by nothing but silence.

"When we get to the command deck we can see if they have motion sensors. I want to find those remaining Russian crew before they find us. I don't want to alarm anyone." He turned to Eddy and Hiro. "Once we're armored up, we can do a full search."

Angie pointed to the left corridor. "To the command deck." Then to a corridor straight ahead. "The captain's cabin and armory."

"Meet back here in twenty minutes. Keep your comms open," Morgan said to Hiro and Eddy. "Stay sharp, everyone. Let's do it."

The groups split, and Morgan headed for the command deck with Nina and Angie. He noticed that the Russian ship was a lot more basic and formidable than the Traveler had been. This seemed more like a flying tank than a space ship. And even though they had lighter gravity on Europa, it would still demand a lot of energy to lift off and head home.

Morgan's priority was to see what their fuel reserves were like. And given they still had life support running after two years, he bet they had been burning it at a low but consistent rate. Even if they weren't fully heating the entire craft.

On their way they went through a large bulkhead hatch and then came onto a fortified door.

"Please don't be coded," he said.

He pressed the button, and the door slid open.

Inside, the command deck was at the corner of the square-shaped craft with the window having an unobstructed view over the Europa moon surface.

There were two chairs at the main desk, and a single larger one behind them that told Morgan that was the captain's chair while the pilot and copilot worked the massive ship. He knew operating the thing would be a challenge, but they needed to learn quickly as they had no choice.

"Okay, Nina, let's check on fuel. And see if they have motion cameras so we can find those missing five Russians."

"You think they're hiding from us?" Angie asked.

"They might be hiding. But maybe not from us." He turned. "These guys have been here for two years. How have they survived? We might have a lot to learn from them."

"One more thing I'd like to ask them." Nina's mouth was pressed into a line for a moment. "If the craft is operational, why are they still here?"

Morgan laughed softly but with little humor. "Good question. And a dispiriting one." He sat down and pressed a button on one of the consoles eliciting a beep of life.

Nina did the same while Angie stood between them offering translation suggestions and advice on navigating the Russian systems.

Morgan found the ship's energy reserves and saw they were as bad as he expected. "There's fuel, enough to lift off, but that's about it. We'd never make it back home."

"Could we send a message and be met in space?" Nina asked.

Morgan shook his head. "The cryo pods need a lot of power to keep us alive for the two and a half years back home. If they ran out of juice, we either wake up and then die as there won't be enough heat, oxygen, and food, in the main ship. Or we'd die in the capsules, never waking up."

"Shit choice," Nina exhaled.

Morgan nodded. "There might be another option. If we don't have enough to lift off and use the cryo tubes, then we just use the tubes."

Nina turned. "What does that mean?"

Morgan folded his arms. "Eventually Earth will send someone. Might take years, but all we need to do is just stay alive until they rescue us."

Nina nodded. "So, we take the tubes, put ourselves into hibernation, and sleep until they arrive. Might work."

"Sure, with the missing Russians, there's enough pods for everyone, even if the five are still somewhere onboard. Until we find them and establish we are friends, I don't want them creeping around, if they think we're enemies."

"Yeah, I don't want to be in a tube, asleep and vulnerable, and have an angry Ruski find me like that." Nina shuddered.

"We need to find them. Or find what happened to them." Morgan had found the comms system and opened the ship-wide communicator.

"Angie, over to you…"

CHAPTER 27

Hiro and Eddy moved cautiously down the dimly lit corridor. Some of the lights were out and in the yellowing beams from the remaining few left they could see dust floating in the air like microscopic snow.

"Creepy as fuck. This ship feels abandoned to me," Eddy whispered.

"There are five people in here somewhere. If they're alive we will find them," Hiro said. "We *must* find them."

Eddy slowed. "I think this is one of the crew cabins. Check it out?"

Hiro grunted his agreement.

Eddy drew in a breath and held his flashlight up at shoulder height. He hit the door button and the steel panel slid back.

He peered around the corner, seeing nothing but a dark room. "Hello Russia. We are Americans. Friends."

Hiro went inside and quickly looked around. There was a cannister of water that had a layer of dust on the top, piles of books in Russian, and a bunk bed in disarray as if someone just rose from it and went out to never come back.

Hiro opened the small door in the wall which he assumed was a closet and found some hanging clothing – men's.

"Nobody home," Eddy said from the doorway. He pointed at the dust layers. "And not for a while. Let's go." Eddy pulled back and looked up and down the corridor. There were more doors to check out.

Hiro joined him. "I suggest we just do a quick scan of the crew's quarters. We can spend more time on them later if we want to."

"Agreed, our priority is to find the captain's cabin and the armory. This way." Eddy headed off.

The pair opened and checked several more rooms and found them the same – all looked to have been abandoned for years but it was as if the occupant was coming back at any moment.

Exploring a little more they came to a triple fork in the corridors, with all three passageways ranging from dim, to dark, to pitch black. Eddy clicked on his flashlight and shone it into the darkest passage.

There was something there, big, and Eddy's mind nearly fragmented as it tried to take the shape in – it seemed man-shaped, but bigger, and wide at the top to accommodate more than two arms and two heads.

Eddy involuntarily screamed and the thing vanished into the darkness.

"What?" Hiro was by his side in an instant.

"*Fuck,*" Eddy said. "Did you see that?"

"You were in front of me so I only just saw something running away." Hiro added his light beam.

"It was a two fucking headed man." Eddy breathed in and out deeply and tried to settle his fear-dizziness.

Hiro put his hand on Eddy's forearm. "Must have been his shadow making him look like that. We need to follow. If it is one of the Russians, we…"

"Bullshit. No way." Eddy spun. "What's down this corridor anyway?"

Hiro checked the schematic on his forearm screen. "The medical center, mess room. Not much more."

"Good, because I'm not going down that one until I have a fucking weapon," Eddy swallowed.

Hiro sighed and checked his screen again. "Then I think we want this way." He pointed to the right side corridor, which still had a few sparse and yellowing lights.

He lowered his arm, looking at his colleague for several moments. "I will lead."

Eddy nodded and allowed the smaller man to go first. His heart still hammered, and he continued to look over his shoulder every now and then. He had only glimpsed the thing, and he knew that was no shadow adding those extra limbs or second head.

They crept along and Hiro raised his hand and slowed. "Careful, there's something on the floor," he whispered.

The pair of men moved ahead slowly until they arrived at what Eddy at first thought was a body, but up closer it turned out to be an enviro suit.

"It's empty," Eddy whispered. "Thank god."

"Strange," Hiro said. "The placement."

Both men looked at the suit that was lying fully intact save for the helmet missing. One arm was up and one leg drawn forward as though it was crawling on the floor.

"It's intact. And closed," Hiro observed.

"Well, no one would be able to get out of a suit through the neck opening, so it means it must have been dropped like that," Eddy said.

"Why leave it here?" Hiro turned. "Enviro suits are your life preserver."

Eddy put his foot on the leg and pressed down. Thankfully there was nothing inside at all.

Hiro went around it. "Captain's cabin is just ahead."

"No, we go to the armory first. Let's get some self-defense. Right now I'm feeling a little exposed and creeped out." Eddy looked over his shoulder.

"Please do not shoot me," Hiro grinned.

"No promises," Eddy grinned back.

They went to go past the captain's cabin but stopped outside when they saw the damage.

"What the hell happened here?" Eddy asked.

The steel doors looked like they had been bent inwards, and there was a baseball-sized hole in their center. It looked like a battering ram had worked on them.

"Torn open," Hiro said. "What could do that?"

"Someone, or some *thing*, wanted in real bad," Eddy said and backed up. I think I want two guns now."

The pair headed fast along the corridor until they came to a room that had a heavily fortified door. Hiro looked at the control plate and noticed there was not just a single button but a key pad.

"This must be it – but it's passcode protected." Hiro stood back.

"Let me try." Eddy had a few tools in a side pouch and levered the plate off of the code pad. He pulled a few wires, broke two of them and stripped the plastic coating. Then he touched them together.

The door shushed open revealing a dark space.

"Well done." Hiro lifted his flashlight to scan the interior.

"Not just a pretty face." Eddy waggled his eyebrows.

"Not even." Hiro grinned.

Both men then peered in. It wasn't exactly the armory that Eddy had hoped for. There were several handguns, a shotgun, and what looked like a small flamethrower. There were also shelves of things they didn't recognize.

"Not exactly everything bar the kitchen sink," Eddy chuckled.

There were spaces for another flamethrower, another gun and shotgun, but they were empty.

Hiro pointed. "That means there might be someone in here with a shotgun."

"Not good." Eddy strode forward. "So we better even the score." He pulled a handgun, ejected the magazine to check it, and handed it to Hiro. He did the same to the other and stuck it in his pocket. He took two more for the captain and Nina.

He looked at the flamethrower and left it, and instead took the shotgun and a box of shells.

Just then overhead, the voice of Angie sounded out, speaking Russian.

Eddy looked up for a moment. "Okay, so now they know we're here." Eddy gripped his flashlight and handgun. "Let's see if Captain Ruski is home."

The two men went back along the corridor fast and came once again to the torn door. This time there was a dim light on inside.

"Was that on before?" Hiro whispered as he flattened himself to the corridor wall near the door.

"Nope." Eddy gripped his gun on the other side of the door. "On three, two, one…"

Both men went in fast, and then stopped dead.

Eddy's mouth dropped open, and he just stared.

***

Angie sat back from the communication console and turned to Morgan. "Again?"

Morgan nodded. "In English as well this time."

Angie sent out the same message and repeated it in both languages three times, and then finally sat back.

"Weird," Nina said.

"What is?" Morgan turned to her.

Nina was checking the crew life-form reader. "When we arrived it said there was five people still on board." She frowned. "But now I'm only reading one."

"Where is it?" he asked.

"Stationary. The captain's cabin according to the ship's schematic," she replied.

Morgan sat thinking about it for a moment but had no idea what that meant. "Faulty tech?" he asked. "After all, this ship has probably sat idle and unserviced for over a year."

"No one has left. No exits were triggered. I guess it has to be." Nina folded her arms, her face troubled.

Morgan tried to raise firstly Hiro, then Eddy on the comms, but got nothing but static.

"Why are we getting interference on our comms?" he asked.

"Could be the shielding," Nina replied. "We'll get Eddy onto it when he gets back."

"Good. You two continue to check out what assets are still in operation for the ship and see if you can get a message home." He stood. "And speaking of Eddy, that life sign is coming from where our guys are going so I think I want to be there too."

Nina turned in her seat. "I should…"

Morgan placed a hand on her shoulder. "I'll be fine. You need to work out what's going on with the rest of the ship. It's now our home whether we and the Russians like it or not. And it might mean the difference between our life and death."

Her lips pressed together for a moment, but then she nodded once. "Be safe," she said softly.

"You too." He turned to Angie. "Both of you."

Morgan then checked the schematic and headed off toward where the captain's cabin was situated. He moved quickly, trying to catch up to his team. So far only Nina had seen the horrifying things that happened to the team, but he had witnessed the strange horde, their amalgamations into single mass creatures, and the weird yellow blob. He knew she was one of the coolest people around, and he knew if anything happened to him, her judgement would keep everyone else safe.

Morgan was at the crew cabins within a few minutes and stopped at the fallen enviro suit in the corridor. He eased past it, and then began to jog.

He checked his gauntlet screen and saw that the captain's cabin was coming up. Then he saw it, and also that the door was open – his team was already inside.

He slowed and when he got to the entrance, he quickly looked back up and down the corridor and then glanced inside – and stopped dead.

Eddy turned to grin at Morgan. "Commander, meet Tatiana. Tatiana Olgenov, meet Commander Brad Morgan."

***

Morgan couldn't help the surprise showing on his face.

There were his two team members standing on either side of a young woman, dark haired and attractive, with extremely pale blue eyes. She wore the inner clothing from an enviro suit that was like an all over body suit and it hugged her slim but athletic figure.

The woman got to her feet and stood about five-nine. She saluted and then held out her hand. "Senior Lieutenant Tatiana Olgenov, Russian Aerospace Forces."

Morgan returned the salute and gripped her hand. "Captain Brad Morgan, United States Airforce, and NASA flight commander of the Traveler Mission."

He saw she assessed him as he did the same to her. He let go of her hand. "Sorry to surprise you aboard your own craft. Ours was destroyed, and we're looking for assistance."

"How many are you?" Tatiana asked.

"Five," he replied. "And where is the rest of your team?"

"All gone." Her mouth turned down. "Just I remain."

Morgan stared back at her. "When we came on board, we detected four other life readings…"

"And I saw someone. I think," Eddy said. "The guy had two heads."

Morgan and Tatiana turned to him.

"Hiro, did you see this…man?" Morgan asked.

"So sorry, I missed it." He looked away.

Tatiana shook her head. "There is no one here but ghosts now." She waved her arm around. "But as you can see, our ship is running down. Glitches in everything."

Morgan looked about. The bed in the corner was still made up, and there was no food packaging so if she was living in here she was the cleanest person he'd ever met.

Maybe she took her meals in the mess, hoping to try and retain some sense of normalcy. He turned back to her.

"Let's go and meet the rest of my team. I'm keen to hear what happened and hope we can work together and perhaps get home."

"Home." She nodded. "That would be good."

Eddy handed Morgan a spare handgun. He checked it, and then slid it into his pocket.

He smiled as he saw her watching him. "Don't be afraid. There's some weird things going on, and we just need to protect ourselves."

"I'm fully aware of the dangers, Captain." Her lips pressed flat for a moment. "I have been marooned here for two years."

Morgan walked beside her as they headed back to the command deck. "Two years by yourself?" he asked.

Tatiana nodded. "The spacecraft Georgy Zhukov was sent on a research and exploration mission five years ago. We came out of cryo as planned and then landed successfully. Big celebration. Then we began our work." She looked up with a fragile smile. "And then as you say, some weird things began to happen."

She faced front as they approached the command deck.

Tatiana's face was grim. "Some of our crew went out to perform their tasks and never came back. We heard them scream over their communication systems. We went out to find them, but there was no sign. They were just gone." She made a small sound of disgust in her throat. "And then some came back. But it was not them. Not on the inside anyway."

Not on the inside, Morgan repeated the words in his head. It was just what Nina had told him.

Finally they might get some answers, he hoped. Or at least a clearer idea of what they were dealing with. If this small woman could survive, then he was confident they could too.

He tried calling Nina on the command deck but still got interference. *We may have to use the ship's comm system*, he thought. He turned to Eddy.

"I want you to look at our comms. See if you can get it back online."

"Will do," Eddy said, while keeping his gaze fixed on Tatiana.

In minutes more they came to the command deck door and Morgan knocked once with a knuckle just to give them the heads up, and then hit the buttons making the door slide back.

"We have a guest." He stood aside as Tatiana came in. "Or rather, we're the guests, and I found one of the owners."

He held an arm out. "I'd like to introduce Senior Lieutenant Tatiana Olgenov, Russian Aerospace Forces."

Nina and Angie stood, introduced themselves and shook her hand rather than saluted. Tatiana was shorter than Nina and the dark skinned woman looked the Russian deep in her face.

"I have a lot of questions. And I really need to know the answers to ensure the safety of our crew. I hope you understand."

"We both have questions," Tatiana replied, her gaze unwavering, and Morgan thought she was refusing to be intimidated by his second in command.

The Russian woman smiled. "You can tell me what happened to your ship. You can tell me about your crew, as I can tell you have also seen things on Europa that have, ah, unsettled you."

"*Unsettled?*" Nina scoffed. "Yeah, I've seen two of my crew turned into a pile of worms. And then they came back together. Them, but not them. And I know we lost two more." She glared. "So yeah, I'm damn unsettled." Nina stepped in even closer.

Tatiana just smiled.

"That's enough, Nina," Morgan said and looked down at the Russian woman. "We should move to the meeting room or mess hall so we have more room, and we can all talk."

Eddy half smiled. "Any coffee left?"

Tatiana smiled and nodded. "Yes, Russian coffee, it is as strong as a Russian black bear."

"Just like me." Eddy grinned but then blushed.

Morgan rolled his eyes.

Tatiana led them down along the corridor until they came to the branch in passageways again. This time they took the middle one. The lights were still out, but she navigated just fine in the darkness.

She half turned as she walked. "I've turned most of the power off to preserve my energy stores. I didn't know how long I would be here before someone came."

"You contacted home?" Hiro asked.

She half turned. "Long ago. But our communications are not working well. Everything breaks down here." She shrugged. "Or gets broken down."

Once in the mess, she made some coffee and Morgan sipped his – she was right, it was like a combination of coffee, tar, and jet fuel. But it was hot and just what he needed.

They sat at a large table, and the Russian woman looked along each of their faces. "It has been nearly a year since I have had someone to talk to. Or even seen another person's face."

"We heard about the Georgy Zhukov and its mission to Europa," Morgan said. "That was around three years ago. Then it all went quiet. I'm guessing that's when things went wrong."

Tatiana nodded. "They began to go strange and wrong before then. Little by little at first. Finally things collapsed and as I mentioned, our communication system was damaged after we got off a single distress call."

"By who or what?" Nina asked. "What damaged it?"

"By the locals." Tatiana half smiled. "They found us, and found us to their liking."

"Who are the locals? All I've seen are the worms," Nina replied.

"And a lot of large creatures below the ice," Eddy added.

Tatiana nodded. "Then they're still down there. I wish we could reach them." After a moment she sighed. "I can tell you what we learned from our time here. When we arrived we began our research, above and below the ice. But all we had was underwater drones. We lost these quickly, but before then, we did make a form of contact. The beings below the ice are the original inhabitants of Europa. I'll call them the true Europans."

"We saw them. I think," Morgan said.

She looked across at Morgan. "Did you communicate?"

"I think they tried to communicate, but we didn't understand them," Angie said. "We need more time."

"More time, yes," Tatiana smiled. "The Europans built cities on the surface, and were the dominant species for twenty million years." She stared at her coffee for a moment. "Until the Wvrm appeared. They crashed here."

"The Wvrm, this is what they are called?" Hiro asked.

Tatiana nodded.

"The meteorite fragment we saw…" Hiro said, "… that was what they came out of?"

"Yes, and the Europans tried to warn everyone by carving their words into it." Tatiana half smiled.

"*All are taken*. And then, *parasites*," Angie said softly. "I knew it was meant to be read – it was a warning."

"Who were the Wvrm?" Nina asked.

"Like they told you – parasites. They're a parasitic race. They are blown around the cosmos stuck to or inside fragments from their destroyed world, crashing onto millions of planets and moons. They are enormously resilient, and all they need is the most basic of climates and landscapes. What is inhospitable to many species is tolerable to them." Her brows went up. "Except salt water. It seems they can't tolerate it."

"And the original Europans?" Hiro asked. "They were overtaken?"

"Yes, bit by bit, cell by cell. There was no stopping the Wvrm. The Europans might have been as advanced as we are. But they still didn't stand a chance."

"How do you know all this?" Angie asked.

"Did you see the cities? Or the remains of them, their ruins?" Tatiana looked up. "They had records. Our linguist Ivan Lebedev was able to decipher much of it. He spent a lot of time in their ruins. We learned they couldn't stop them, but I think the Europans were semiaquatic, so they abandoned the surface to the Wvrm, and live below us in the warm seas now."

"They tried to warn us. Tried to stop us surfacing," Morgan said. "When we were going to rise up they grabbed us."

"In the deep oceans the original inhabitants devolved back into more basic lifeforms and grew big. Semi intelligent whales cruising in a night black sea until the end of time." Tatiana half smiled. "Maybe better for them."

"And then they came for you," Nina said. "The Wvrm."

Tatiana nodded. "Yes, like I said, Ivan spent much time in the Europa ruins by himself. Somehow he woke the Wvrm who had been in hibernation for maybe millions of years. When he came back to the ship, Ivan wasn't Ivan anymore. He was someone else. Some *thing* else," she scoffed. "He was a Trojan horse – you know this meaning?"

"Yeah, we get it," Morgan exhaled.

"I have a question," Hiro said. "How smart are they?"

Tatiana bobbed her head. "I think they are not smart. But when they absorb a being they also absorb its intelligence, memories, and skills. They absorbed the indigenous Europa lifeforms, and became them. Or they looked like them and can act like them, but inside they are still the parasite."

"And your people," Angie said. "They absorbed them, and became them?"

Tatiana nodded.

"Became them. Absorbed their intelligence. And skills. All your crew?" Morgan raised his eyebrows.

"Yes," Tatiana replied.

"So why didn't they use those skills to travel back to Earth? All those human beings to parasite. All that food."

Tatiana half smiled. "Why do you think I am still here? The captain saw what was happening, and one of his last acts was to disable the ship, marooning us. And them."

Morgan laughed bitterly as he sat back. "So much for using the Georgy Zhukov to get home."

"Sorry." Tatiana shrugged. "Maybe we can try and repair it, but the captain anticipated that and permanently damaged the drive core. I have power, but there will never be a working engine without a full workshop with spare parts."

"And he destroyed the communication system," Nina said. "He didn't want anyone else to come. No rescue attempt."

"You said that Ivan came back on board. He was a Trojan horse, and I'm guessing infected your other crew members. So where are they now?" Angie asked.

"My captain, Vladimir Bodin, was the bravest man I have ever known." Her eyes took on a faraway look. "We talked and decided that after he damaged the ship and the comms system, he would draw them all away from us, and out onto the ice. He told me to hide here. And I did. When he got them out, I sealed the ship. No one was allowed to come back in."

"He led them out?" Nina asked.

"You know Pied Piper story?" She shared a broken smile.

They nodded.

"He led them away. They followed. I never saw him again." She stared once again at her coffee. "And so, now I am stuck here."

"All the crew are gone. Save for you?" Angie asked.

Tatiana nodded. "All the crew, all the original Europans, every life form on the surface." She looked up. "There were other creatures here, a living ecology above the ice with a range of biodiversity large and small. But everything was consumed and converted. Everything becomes the Wvrm." Her eyes became hard. "Now you see what is at stake. And why Captain Bodin wanted me to live as a warning to you. And to Earth."

"There's something I do not understand," Hiro said. "You said they became your people. And you couldn't tell them apart. Or at least after a while they got better at playing human. How did you know who was who? Who was the captain. Did you have a test?"

"You can't tell them apart. They absorb the memories as well as the mannerisms. They use them better. Captain Bodin changed all the codes and then led them to believe he was the last one left and only one who knew them. They desperately wanted him. So went after him."

The group sat in silence for a moment. But something was nagging at Morgan. The Wvrm infesting the crew, eating them from the inside out, just like Nina had said. And then reanimating or becoming their bodies. They then had all the memories, and he guessed skills of the people.

Morgan looked up. "So where is the captain? Why didn't he come back? Why didn't they then have all his knowledge of the codes?"

Tatiana stared for a moment. Then her mouth turned down and her eyes glistened. "I told you he was a brave man. He knew he couldn't afford to be taken alive. So he took one of the guns with him." She shrugged. "We found out that they cannot reanimate dead bodies or access their memories for some reason. Once he had them all out, and he was far enough away, his plan was to then kill himself before they got to him."

Nina rubbed her eyes and sat forward. "If I wasn't me, but instead a copy of me, how could you tell me apart? What sort of test is there?"

"Maybe with a microscope." Tatiana shrugged. "They don't eat, don't sleep. They prefer to get you alone but can overwhelm several of you at once if need be." She seemed to think for a moment. "They like when we are sleeping the best as that's when we're most vulnerable."

"Fuck it, that's it. I'm never sleeping again." Eddy shook his head and then seemed to realize what he said. "I mean, I need sleep though." He turned to Morgan. "We need a plan. What's the plan?"

Morgan could tell by the strain in the young man's voice he was on edge. Everyone was.

"We need to look closer at the communication system. See if we can get it working. If we can't fly this tank home, we get Earth to come to us. But we warn them first."

"That'll take…" Eddy began, but Morgan held up a hand.

"I know, years. But we have the cryo bays, and there is enough energy to run them for years. We can sleep until help arrives."

"What?" Eddy's eyes widened. "You just heard her tell us sleeping is when we're most vulnerable. These things will have years to work out how to get in and then we'll all be fucked."

"Then we take shifts, someone stays on duty as security for a month, and we rotate," Morgan said.

He saw the look of panic on their faces. "Before we do that, we seal the ship, change the codes again to ones only we know. And we do a full search, top to bottom, and make sure there's no surprises hiding here." He turned to the Russian woman. "Tatiana, you'll help us there, won't you?"

"Of course," she replied quickly. "I have already checked the ship, as I had the same concerns, but I will help you check it again."

"Okay, Eddy?" Morgan faced the young man, whose eyes were pressed closed.

He nodded once.

Morgan didn't want to split the team up, but they had a lot of ground to cover, and with good reason, he wanted to do it quickly.

Nina spoke up first. "Tatiana is with me."

Morgan snorted. He could tell by the way Nina looked at the Russian woman, she'd be watched like a hawk.

"Okay, you get Eddy as well. That means Angie and Hiro, you're on my team," he said.

The three people nodded, with Eddy still looking a little spooked, Nina angry, and Tatiana seeming resigned to whatever came next.

"Okay, first up, Eddy, I want you to break into the security system and override the passcodes – reset them, giving me full authority."

"To what?" Eddy asked.

Morgan looked around, saw a scrap of paper napkin on the desk, and grabbed it up. He took out a pen and wrote the word 'Wyoming' on it. He showed it to Eddy, who smiled and nodded.

"Got it."

Tatiana snorted disdainfully. "I am not your enemy, Commander Morgan."

"I know." He shrugged, but didn't add anything.

They headed back to the command deck, and Eddy worked quickly on the main console, and in minutes he straightened. "Okay, codes overridden and password changed. We now have full control."

"Good," Morgan said. "We start our check on this level. Then we'll move down to the storage and hangar bays. And finish with checking the upper level. I want it complete. This is going to be our home base and fortress of solitude for some time. Let's ensure it's safe."

"Do you trust her?" Angie asked.

Morgan snorted softly. "Right now, we can't afford to trust her."

Nina, Tatiana, and Eddy took off, and Angie and Hiro turned to him. "First up, I want to recheck the armory and scavenge anything else we can use for defensive work. We'll take anything and everything."

"There were a lot of boxes. In Russian," Hiro confirmed.

"Well, we'll translate that," Morgan replied. "Also I want to have a look at the captain's cabin. There's something missing that must be here. And I want it."

***

The teams headed out for the individual duties, and Tatiana led off with Nina and Eddy following.

Eddy caught up to Tatiana and tilted his head to her. "I have a question; were you staying in the captain's cabin the entire time?"

"No, I heard you in the armory and was going to take a peek when I heard you coming back. I hid there." She smiled. "I mostly hid in the kitchen area. Where the food and water is."

"Smart," Nina said.

"One more question." Eddy raised his eyebrows and Tatiana nodded. "What the hell happened to the captain's cabin door? It looked like it got hit by a charging rhino."

"The Wvrm," Tatiana replied. "When they are in a condensed form, they are very strong. Stronger than us. They wanted to flush the captain out. They did. It was the last time I saw him." Her mouth turned down. "I miss him."

Tatiana led them to the armory, and Eddy and Hiro spent time grabbing up and bagging a lot of spare ammunition. Eddy also picked up a two foot long blade and grinned at Tatiana. "What exactly were you guys expecting on Europa, a jungle?"

Tatiana smiled. "We did not know what we would encounter, so we brought a big ship and everything we would and might need. It works well that way."

"Can't argue with that," Eddy said.

He went to put the machete-type blade back but then held it up to look at it – it was a large Bowie-style blade of polished steel. It was a good one. He pushed it back into its leather sheath and hung it on his belt.

There wasn't much else as the weapons and ammunition had been taken and expended. It didn't fill Eddy with confidence thinking that they were going to be defending themselves with the same type of weaponry that had failed the Russians.

"Now, your supply and machine room, please," Hiro requested.

Tatiana nodded and turned. "This way."

She took them down to the next level and along a more rudimentary corridor. There was little work done on the aesthetics and it was mostly bare steel and girders. A bit like the bowels of an ocean going ship.

Eventually they came to a huge door that was protected with an electronic code lock. She stood aside.

Eddy stepped up and Tatiana put her hand on his arm and squeezed it gently. She smiled up at him. Eddy blushed a little and smiled back, and then inserted the new code. The door unlocked, and he pushed it open.

The store room was basically a warehouse filled with shelves stacked with boxes and crates. There was also an area with significantly larger machine parts.

"This is good," Eddy said.

He and Hiro took off like schoolboys who had found a treasure vault filled with gold. They checked boxes and after a while Eddy located one that simply said: *Laser*.

"A laser?" he asked.

Hiro stopped what he was doing and turned. "You have a laser?"

Eddy nodded and opened the box. Inside was half a dozen of what looked like large pencils. He switched one on and a small red beam shot out that produced a dot on whatever he pointed at.

"*Meh*, just pointers." He turned to Tatiana. "You guys really did bring everything bar the kitchen sink."

"Let me see those." Hiro took one from him and opened it. After a moment he nodded his satisfaction.

"I can adapt these for a stronger, cutting beam." He put the pencil-sized device back in the box with the others and lifted his head. "I must find a carriage for them. Something I can mount them on."

The pair opened more boxes, and Eddy found several useful items and Hiro found a small set of tripods that had motion sensors built in.

"Yes, this will do very well." He tucked both boxes under his arm.

Tatiana pointed. "Through here is another room."

Hiro exhaled. "I have work to do."

Eddy turned from him to Tatiana who smiled at him and held his gaze for several seconds.

"*Ah…*" Eddy continued to look at Tatiana. "Okay Hiro, you go. I'll finish up here with Tatiana."

Hiro frowned and stayed put. "I think…"

"No, you go. I'll be fine. You've got something to work on for our defence; that's the priority."

Hiro moved from foot to foot for a moment.

"It is only a small room." She smiled. "You can have him back in fifteen more minutes."

Hiro grunted. "Fifteen minutes, yes?"

Eddy crossed his heart. "I promise, Mommy."

Eddy watched Hiro go, and then looked at the small attractive Russian woman. "So, what have you got to show *me*?" He smiled back and she came closer.

"Things you wouldn't believe, American boy," she said. "Come in here." She walked backwards, and placed a hand on the door, keeping her pale blue eyes on him. "I haven't seen a big, handsome man like you in nearly two years."

"Well, I'm here now." He drew closer. "We only have fifteen minutes."

"That's all we will need." She kept smiling up at him as she reached forward with her free hand to fondle the front of his pants.

He groaned as his desire became rock hard. He knew he didn't just want her now, he *needed* her now.

"*Tatiana,*" he whispered.

"Yes." She smiled and behind herself she turned the handle and pushed open the door revealing an area inside darker than the vacuum of space. A waft of acrid almond smell blew out and Eddy wrinkled his nose.

The young man baulked a little, but Tatiana had hold of his erection through his pants now and pulled him forward. Her grip was unexpectedly strong, and he looked up, and then over her shoulder.

His eyes went wide and his heart nearly exploded in his chest.

There was an abomination coming at him, the thing he had glimpsed before, big, wide, and on its shoulders were two male heads, and below it had four arms as if two men had been crushed together.

Eddy jerked back, but Tatiana held tight to his wilting penis, and he couldn't budge her as if she weighed several tons. He looked down at her expressionless face and saw the skin begin to ripple and slide and then it broke apart into thousands or millions of tiny, squirming things.

"*Gaa.*" He grabbed her arm and began to jerk hard, but from where he gripped her the strong forearm became as soft as a sock full of sand, and then the worm things began to flow out of her sleeve and onto him.

Eddy reached for the gun, and lifted it but as Tatiana held him, the two-headed monstrosity reached him.

He fired once, twice, but the massive man thing enfolded him, and the shots were as if fired into a pillow. The bullets went straight through it without any damage.

In seconds more Eddy was covered and the Wvrm sought out his ears, mouth, eyes, and any other orifices into his body.

Eddy tried to scream but gagged and choked as they poured into his lungs and stomach. It burned like fire and the pain was excruciating as he felt himself be dissolved from the inside out.

Everything was dark now and Eddy's last thought, as being Eddy, was he wished he could wake up now as this was the worst nightmare he had ever had. And he just wanted to go home.

***

Hiro came back to the command pod where he had left all of his equipment and immediately created a workspace for himself in one of the corners.

He set out to make a prototype model for what he had in mind, and drew forth one of the tripods, the small motion trackers, and also one of the pencil-sized laser pointers.

From his spare parts he had several lenses, and he opened up the last pointer and inserted the thicker lens inside that would magnify the beam of light making it stronger and more intense. When he was done, he would add in a much more powerful battery to increase its power tenfold.

He tried the small laser, and a hair thin red beam shot out, and where it touched on the wall, it left a small dot of melted steel – good – more than enough for what he had in mind.

Hiro then mounted it on the foot tall tripod. He added in the motion sensors with small programmable computer chips.

Hiro checked it over. It looked like a small version of the alien robot walkers from H. G. Wells' War of the Worlds, and he was satisfied with the componentry and look of the prototype.

His last test was to bring out the sample jar of the several captured worm things that Nina had in the rover and set it down on the other side of the command pod.

He then got behind the laser tracker and switched it on. The motion sensor swiveled and the head with the laser pointer moved, searching, and then one of the small worms moved inside the jar. A thin red beam shot out, going through the glass and striking the tiny worm – it was vaporized instantly.

More of the worms began to move in the jar, and the hair-thin deadly beam found them all, and they all went up in wisps of smoke.

Hiro smiled and sat back. "Yes, this will do."

He switched off his prototype and set to creating as many more as his spare parts would allow.

PART 06
THE WHISPERS OF A GHOST

CHAPTER 28

Nina, Angie, and Morgan entered the captain's cabin and stood in its center looking around.

"Captain Vladimir Bodin holed up in here until they dug him out," he said.

Nina exhaled slowly through her nose. "Do you think Vlad really got away? And then acted as the Russian version of the Pied Piper?"

"I want to." Morgan turned. "Because the alternative is he didn't and that means the *Wvrm* are still onboard somewhere."

"I don't want to even think about that scenario." Angie shook her head. "Makes me feel sick."

"Yeah, me too." He stood at the center of the cabin, hands on hips, and turned slowly. "He must have known what was going on, and what was going to happen and left a record." He turned slowly. "And I'm betting his words are in here somewhere."

"What are we looking for?" Nina asked.

"The Russians have similar personal recording tech to us," Morgan answered. "So he would have recorded a Captain's Log. It would record his words and thoughts in a diary-like process."

"So, maybe some sort of portable electronic device, or even a small drive," she replied. "Okay, I'm on it." Nina went to one of the small inbuilt closets. "I'll take this side, you the other. Angie, check the drawers. If it's here, we'll find it."

The trio emptied drawers and looked underneath them, under the mattress and under the bed. On top of furniture, inside it, underneath it. They checked his computer, looked at a writing tablet.

They then checked the small washroom, and as a last test, Morgan put his nails against the side of the mirror over the wash basin and pulled.

It popped open.

"*Hello,*" he whispered.

Nina straightened. "You're kidding." She grinned.

Behind the mirror was an alcove and there was one thing in it – a smooth metallic box. It was no larger than a cigarette pack, and with a clip for his belt.

"An iFLYTEK recorder – top of the Russian line in recording equipment. And still powered up." Morgan pulled it out and looked at the different buttons. He switched it on, and the slow stentorian voice of the captain filled the room.

After a few seconds he struggled with the softly spoken Russian language and turned it off. He checked the buttons again and looked down the list of options on the screen. He found what he was looking for.

"Yes, good, this will help." There was a translation button, and he chose the English option. "Time to hear from a ghost," he said and restarted the recording.

The captain's voice drifted from the device but this time his words were in English.

After a moment Morgan fast forwarded the recording, going past the launch, then the Russian team coming out of stasis, and then the landing, before he found the place where Captain Bodin began to describe the conditions on the frozen moon. There was the jubilation amongst the crew at their success and then the wonder when he described how they found the lost civilization in the ice cave. Morale was high and the Russian home base was delighted with their progress.

But then it turned darker.

The man seemed to be speaking quicker now and his words became less confident and were tinged with a hint of fear. Morgan couldn't imagine the predicament he was facing as he realized the danger he and his crew were in and were finding few ways to deal with it.

Or maybe he could imagine it because right now, he and his team were the Russians. Morgan prayed they learned something that would help them. This was the one time in Morgan's life he hoped that another man really did kill himself.

He placed the device on the table and folded his arms as he, Nina, and Angie stood around it in silence, listening as Captain Bodin's diary revealed the man's terrifying journey.

***

Captain Vladimir Bodin let out a long exhausted sigh. "We went looking for *them*, but they found *us*." he said softly. "They were in the ruins and we woke them up."

There came a sound like the scraping of a chair and then a long sniff before Bodin continued. "They came out of the ice and snow. From the floors, the walls, the ceilings of the buildings. Were they the inhabitants? I don't see how they could have been. Vladimir, Anya, and Yevgeny were overtaken, and Dmitri only just got away. He sounded insane on his speaker, and when he arrived back what he described sounded too incredible to be true, but instead mad ramblings so unbelievable, I put him in quarantine..." and then, "...I should have listened."

Bodin cursed softly. "But I didn't listen. And I was organizing a rescue and recovery mission when my three missing crew showed up on our scanners. They were coming back, walking over the snow and ice. I was overjoyed. Until I saw them. When they came into visual perspective I could see they weren't wearing their helmets – how was this possible in two hundred and fifty degrees below zero atmosphere?"

"When I told Dmitry this he screamed to not let them in. So for caution I decided to just let them in the outer airlock. Only. And then quarantine them in there until I could work out what was going on."

"I organized a security detail, handing out guns just as a precaution, and headed down. Sasha, Nikolai, and Mikhail came with me.

We let them enter the loading bay room, and I closed the outer door. They immediately came to the inner door and stared in at us. I went and looked back at them through the small portal window, and I could see it wasn't them. They didn't look right. When I concentrated on their faces, their skin looked like someone had made a mockery of a human being by using grains of rice stuck together. Even their eyes had no spark of human life. But were alive with something else."

"Then they spoke to me. Or at least Yevgeny did."

Please my captain, he begged. *Let us in. We are hungry and cold.*

"It sounded like Yevgeny. But I knew it wasn't really him anymore. When I said *no*, they became angry. They are strong, very strong, but the steel of the inner airlock was stronger.

They tried everything to break in, and I saw then something that revolted me and scared me deeply – they could disassemble themselves and turn into rivers of small white worm like things that flowed around the edges of the doors seeking the smallest of holes. Then they could form up and make monstrous combination humans. Or they made themselves into other creature shapes that were the things of nightmares, which we believe might have been one of the original Europa inhabitants that were unfortunate enough to also fall prey to these parasitic monstrosities.

I thought for now they could stay where they were. There were nine of us remaining who were not contaminated, so we would all be working on ways to try and fight this horrifying infection. Or find ways to exterminate them.

I called a meeting, and we discussed ideas to eradicate them. We believed we could shock them with high voltage or burn them – we had flamethrowers. And Katerina was able to put together shock sticks.

But testing them was a problem. I couldn't take the chance of opening the inner door. Plus whoever went inside the loading bay room to test them on the creatures might not be coming back out. And it was an awful way to die. Or live if some part of a person's consciousness remained alive while trapped in those living swarms.

It was decided the only safe way to test our defenses was to try and lure them back out of the ship. We used one of the smaller exits for Tatiana to go outside and bang on the outer bay door with a wrench.

When she came back inside, I opened the outer door – it worked, as the three infected crewmembers, Vladimir, Anya, and Yevgeny, all went out to investigate. Once they were out I shut the door again.

We could monitor them from the external cameras, and I was still amazed at how they were unaffected by the murderous atmosphere.

I offered to test the weapons we had devised but Tatiana refused. She then offered herself as a volunteer, but it was loyal Mikhail, who always had eyes for her, to volunteer for the task.

I hugged the man then saluted him. And everyone knew this was probably a suicide mission.

Then through more cat and mouse games we separated the three infected people, and we just drew false Anya back into the main bay area. When the door closed behind her Mikhail was inside and waiting for her.

She held out her arms to him. "Mikhail, I'm cold. Help me."

It sounded so like her that even Mikhail lowered his arms a fraction.

Tatiana opened the channel on his microphone. "Do not fall for it, Mikhail," she said. "Stay strong."

Immediately on hearing Tatiana's voice his spine stiffened.

It was time – I opened his mic. "Mikhail, try the shock stick first."

Anya came toward him, and came fast, not in the shuffling gait we remembered. It seemed they were improving their understanding and use of the human body.

Mikhail held out the stick, moving sideways. When she was close enough, he jabbed it forward and discharged the voltage. The stick had a charge of just two hundred volts. It should have been more than enough to render someone dead or unconscious. And Anya was only five feet four and around eighty pounds, so her light frame should have succumbed easily.

But as Mikhail jabbed the stick forward, striking her, and he pressed the discharge button, the strangest thing occurred – the worms shifted, moving out of the way. In fact, they created a hole in the Anya being.

Mikhail tried again, and again, and could not seem to touch the woman.

"Try swiping at her," Tatiana said into the mic.

Mikhail did as suggested. This time he kept the charge button fully depressed as the sparking rod travelled in one side of the being – this time there was a flash as the shock stick managed to hit some of the body, and some of the worms fell out like sand to the ground either dead or stunned. But in seconds, they gathered themselves and began to crawl over the floor back to Anya to build the body back up.

"Shock it again. Longer," Tatiana yelled.

Mikhail did that, and the same result. The worms were stunned momentarily and he even opened up gaping holes in the woman giving us the strangest sight of a small woman with pieces of her missing. But her face remained untroubled.

It told us several things – the worms could sense an attack coming, and the reaction seemed a whole body defensive mechanism.

"Proves they don't like it," I said.

"But it doesn't kill them," Tatiana replied. "Maybe we need a bigger charge."

The Anya being was quickly back in one piece, now with some black spots on her environmental suit.

Then Anya did something we had seen countless times, but when happening now unnerved the entire crew – she smiled at Mikhail – and it was an Anya smile.

"It looks so much like her." I half turned. "Do you think there could be some of Anya still in there?"

Tatiana's face hardened. "No. It's just using her body like a puppet. It is an abomination that must be destroyed."

I switched to the outside camera, and we all saw the two stranded crew outside. One of them held under its arm a revolting-looking yellow, pulsating sack. "What the hell is that?"

"Probably part of these things." Tatiana made a gagging sound in her throat. "Kill it. Kill every damn bit of it. Burn it to nothing." She spat.

The captain grunted and then opened the mic again. "Mikhail, use the flamethrower."

The man dropped the shock stick and drew the flamethrower from over his shoulder. He ignited the tip and pointed it at Anya.

Mikhail hesitated again.

"*Do it!*" Tatiana screamed.

Mikhail depressed the trigger, and a long gout of liquid flame shot toward the small woman. The effect was instantaneous, as her body just blew apart.

The crew cheered, and even Mikhail turned to give a thumbs up. Tatiana grinned.

The man switched off the flame and the smoke cleared a little. And then we saw what had actually happened. What at first had seemed like a success, had been just the individual worms giving up their collective cohesiveness. But only momentarily.

This time some of the worms began to coalesce, but more began to inch their way towards Mikhail. And just as many were crawling all around the interior of the bay area. They were spreading out. Now it looked like they had another game plan. The previous one of subterfuge and pretense was now changed to one of attack.

Tatiana glared and leaned forward on the control panel, the veins in her neck bulging. "We *do not* want them separating. We would need to check every rivet hole, crack, and crevice in there."

Tatiana leaned over me to the comm system and opened my channel. "Mikhail, burn them all. Every speck."

The man in the chamber nodded and this time sprayed the flames over the remaining lumps of Anya, then the floor, ceiling, and everywhere it touched with the boiling orange tongues of fire the worms were turned to ash.

"Good, good. Keep it up, Mikhail." Tatiana's eyes were wide and unblinking.

Over the microphone we heard a high-pitched squealing that might have just been the gases escaping their tiny bodies as they exploded. Or as we all hoped, it was the tiny monstrosities' death screams.

Black oily smoke filled the chamber, obscuring what was going on.

"We're going to have to vent that," Tatiana said.

"Can't risk opening the outer door just yet," I replied as I kept my eyes on the chamber. I pounded the desk. "Come on, Mikhail, finish them."

***

Inside the chamber Mikhail heard the frantic voices of his captain and Tatiana as they both yelled orders and instructions. He sprayed long rivers of flaming liquid at the squirming horde. They incinerated leaving black smudges, and none of them came back to resurrect themselves afterwards.

"This works," he said, unsure if he was being heard or not over the roar of the flamethrower, and the high-pitched scream from the millions of tiny mouths.

The Anya creature had toppled to the ground and the piles of worms were thinning out. At first he grinned, thinking he had killed the bulk of them. And all that would be needed was a mop-up of the stragglers. But then he saw that the entire floor and walls were moving as if there was sand everywhere that was shifting in a breeze.

"This is not good," he said.

The worm things had spread out in a thin layer and now covered about twenty feet in all directions. He couldn't tell how many there were, as they were too widely spread now.

He tried to track them to try and burn more, but even sweeping long gouts of flame over the floor and walls, he was still only taking a few out as they kept spreading farther apart. And then the most alarming thing occurred – he looked down at his fuel gauge and saw it was going into the red.

He didn't notice exactly when the worms made it to the ceiling until a speck landed on his visor. Then another, and then it was like rain falling. Just on him as they crawled in waves to a position overhead and began to rain down on him.

Mikhail looked up, and saw the ceiling was alive with movement. And something began to form. It was a lump growing amongst the horde. A hole opened in it, and then it turned into a woman's mouth.

"Mikhail, I'm cold. Help me," Anya's voice said.

"*Blya*." He fired the flamethrower upwards, but that only made more shower down on him as they escaped the heat.

He brushed at them, letting go of the nozzle of the flamethrower, and brushed more vigorously. But the tiny things clung to him like they were sticky. In seconds he was covered and when he tried to wipe them hard to crush them, they just flattened and after his hand had passed over them, they continued their peristaltic movement up his body.

It didn't take Mikhail long to see where they were trying to get to – they began to coalesce around the seams of his suit. The ones on the visor stopped their movement, and Mikhail stopped to draw his vision back to concentrate on what they were doing. And when he saw, his level of panic exploded.

They were actually making small holes in the thick visor Perspex.

"Oh no, no, no."

Mikhail knew if they could do that to the toughened visor, then his suit would stand no chance.

"I need to get out!" he screamed.

"Not yet," Tatiana said. "You are covered. Brush them off."

"Help me!" he yelled back.

"We can't until the worms are gone," Captain Bodin said evenly.

The thread-like worms were getting thicker on Mikhail's face plate as more rained down on him. Now he could hear them grinding against his visor as they chewed their way through his helmet's defenses. Mikhail began to panic, and knew there was only one option left.

***

"I can't see what is happening," Tatiana said. "Is Mikhail just standing there?"

"I'm going to send in a retrieval team." Bodin straightened.

"*No, wait,*" Tatiana said. "Look."

They could make out the shape of Mikhail as he danced and slapped at himself for a moment. And then they saw him become still, his shoulders slumped before he lifted the flamethrower nozzle. And turned it around.

"*Don't do this!*" Bodin yelled.

"He must," Tatiana said stonily.

Mikhail pressed the trigger, and the gout of flames exploded out and the liquid fuel covered him completely. He was like a glowing beacon amongst the billowing thick smoke as it filled the room.

From their shielded observation room they saw the man-shaped column of flame writhing and twisting, and all the time screaming. The suit would mostly protect him, for a little while, but he would still be feeling unbearable pain.

That was until the fuel tank on his back exploded and the impact was felt right throughout the steel frame of the ship.

There was silence in the control room and many stood with eyes wide and mouths hanging open as they stared at the chamber that was filled with billowing, greasy, black smoke.

Captain Bodin sat back, his face sagging.

"And that is that," he said miserably.

***

After a few moments the heavy smoke began to settle to the ground and impossibly they saw Mikhail standing there. But just Mikhail.

His suit was tattered and burned, and the helmet he wore was totally blackened from the flamethrower fuel. But his body looked weird, misshapen and it strained the fabric of his scorched clothing.

"He's alive," someone whispered from behind them.

Mikhail reached up to his helmet.

"Please don't," Tatiana sobbed. "I don't want to see what's coming."

The man unlocked his helmet and lifted it. It stuck for a moment as if caught on something, but eventually slid off.

There were gasps of horror.

There was Mikhail's head and face, and jammed in beside it was Anya's face, sort of attached, as if Anya had somehow climbed into the suit with Mikhail as a practical joke.

For a few brief seconds it looked like the Mikhail face was wailing or in great pain, but then his expression changed to one of abject horror as coiling tentacle limbs lifted from somewhere inside his suit to wrap around his neck and gently move up over his face as a dog licks its own limbs. In seconds more, Mikhail's face became more relaxed and calmer. And the thin tentacles or feelers were absorbed into his skin.

Perhaps it was just the greasy smoke still billowing inside obscuring their vision, but Tatiana thought they had just witnessed the metamorphosis from human to whatever the hell those things were.

Bodin turned to his second in charge as she stood stiffly as if every muscle in her neck was tight as piano wire. "He is now one of them," she said sourly and turned away.

"The fire hurt them," Bodin said. "But it was not complete enough."

"Or fast enough," Tatiana said. "Poor Mikhail. What a waste."

"No, it wasn't a waste. We learned some valuable things." Bodin ran both hands up through his sweat soaked, iron grey hair. "We know they can be hurt, and by what. We just need to work out how to use what we know now."

He rubbed a forearm over his forehead that glistened with perspiration. He felt that his entire body was running with sweat. Maybe he was vicariously feeling the heat after watching his crew member be burned.

"We should open the external doors and vent the area," Vladimir said from behind them. "Release that abomination so we can purge and sterilize the chamber."

"No," Tatiana said. "The other two are still outside. They will come in."

"How do we know that?" Vladimir replied.

"Because they don't want to be outside. They want to be in here. Because we're in here and they want us," Tatiana said. "I think that's all they want."

Captain Bodin nodded. "I agree. We need something with a total purging and cleansing effect." He turned to his engineers. "Well?"

"Microwaves," Sasha replied.

"Good." The captain nodded. "Can we rig something to bathe the entire chamber with strong microwaves?"

Sasha looked at the other engineers and they conferred for a moment before she sighed and turned back. "Yes, but we would need to rig the delivery mechanisms inside the chamber. Meaning, we would need to be in there to set it up before we could use it."

"So, suicide then." Tatiana threw her hands up.

The smoke began to settle even more creating a layer of smoke swirling around Mikhail's knees. The second head belonging to Anya had vanished and all that remained of it was a lump on the side of Mikhail's neck.

Captain Bodin zoomed in with the camera on the man's face, and they all saw how perfect a copy it was.

"It looks just like Mikhail," Sasha whispered. "Exactly like Mikhail."

"How can we tell if it is a fake?" Katerina asked. "If they look exactly the same as us, sound the same, and then act the same." She shook her head. "Then how do we tell?"

There was silence amongst the group for a moment.

Katerina's eyes watered and she sniffed. "Many of us went outside. How do we know they weren't all affected? And pretending to be real people."

"Stop that," Captain Bodin said evenly.

"Maybe they're already inside, and we just don't know it," Katerina's voice rose. "Yet."

Bodin banged his fist on the desk top. "Stop it, I said."

"We need some sort of test," Tatiana said softly. Her eyes slid to Mikhail standing calmly in the clearing chamber. "They look the same as us on the outside, but inside, I'm betting they must be different."

"X-rays," Katerina said. "We have a portable X-ray tablet. We look inside everyone."

"Stupid idea," Dmitry scoffed.

"I knew you'd say that." Katerina's eyes narrowed as she glared at the man. "That's why you're going first."

"It's worth a try," Tatiana said. "At least it will give us peace of mind." She half smiled. "So we can sleep at night."

Bodin sighed and raised his hands a little. "Okay, okay. Katerina go and get the X-ray tablet. Everyone is to assemble in the mess room for coffee and we will do our little X-ray test. For peace of mind." He scoffed. "And so Tatiana can sleep at night."

The group took off. Some grumbled, but few spoke, with many casting suspicious glances at their crew mates.

"It is a good idea for morale," Tatiana said. "The crew still inside the ship had to know they were safe. Otherwise distrust and depression might lead to someone shooting their crewmate."

Bodin grunted.

She and Captain Bodin were last and turned to look in through the window at Mikhail and Anya. Or rather just Mikhail now, as what was left of the woman was either hiding inside the man or had been absorbed by him.

"They must be able to compress their cells. Would that make them heavier than us?" she asked. "And if two people are in one body, does that make them as strong as two people?"

Bodin hiked his shoulders. "I have no idea. Let's do this X-ray test and then get back to working on how we can kill them. And then go home." He drew in a deep breath and let it out miserably. "I think our mission is over."

She nodded and looked back inside the hangar bay at the lone figure standing there in the settling smoke. She stared for several moments. "Vladimir," she said softly and the captain turned to her. "You know we can't leave, while that thing is in there. We can't bring it back to Earth."

"I know," he said morosely. "But if we can't flush it out down here, then maybe the vacuum of space will take care of it for us."

The group travelled down to the main mess area and assembled. Tatiana had retrieved two ear-comm pieces and gave one to Captain Bodin.

"No matter what happens, we stay in contact," she said softly as she looked into his eyes.

Bodin looked at the ear piece for a moment, thinking about what she meant, and just nodded, and stuck it over his ear and the plug inside.

The remaining crew members consisted of eight, counting Tatiana and Captain Bodin, plus Katerina getting the X-ray tablet.

They made coffee, some added a shot of vodka, which the captain allowed. But few talked and most just stared at the ground, or off into the distance, lost in their own thoughts.

Maybe they were thinking of home, Tatiana surmised. And if they'd ever see it again.

Katerina returned and held up the two foot wide piece of electronics that looked like one half of a laptop computer. It had a dark screen on one side, and an opaque one on the other.

She switched it on and held it over her own forearm. It showed the outline of the arm's muscles and inside the whiter, more opaque, shadow of bone.

"Works fine," She said.

"Just the arm?" Tatiana asked.

"I'd prefer a skull shot," Katerina replied.

Captain Bodin rolled his eyes. "Just an arm will do for now."

"Do me." Tatiana held out her arm.

Katerina gripped her wrist to position it and then held the X-ray tablet over her arm and froze the image. She held it up, showing a similar image to her own – flesh and bone, all the way through.

"All good," she said. "Everyone else line up." She looked over people's heads until she found Dmitry.

"I said you'd be first. But looks like you're to be second. Come to the front of the line, Dmitry," she said.

"This is stupid," he said. "You're making the crew scared of me."

She looked him dead in the eye. "Then only one way to clear the air, right?" She tapped the tablet. "Step up please."

Dmitry shook his head and cursed under his breath. He came and rolled a sleeve up and stuck out his left arm.

Katerina gripped the wrist and held up the tablet over his arm.

Tatiana was watching more with bored interest and saw the young female medical officer's face go from satisfaction at getting Dmitry to kowtow, to sudden confusion.

Dmitry smiled, and Katerina looked up into his face.

"There's no bones," she said softly. And then louder. "*There's no bones.*"

Things happened quickly then. Katerina went to let go of his wrist, but he had grabbed her hand.

And then it all went mad.

Dmitry's hand melted, or rather dissolved, into a surge of tiny moving worms that swarmed up Katerina's arm.

People yelled, screamed, and jumped at the pair.

Tatiana grabbed Katerina's shoulders and tried to pull her away. Two men grabbed Dmitry and dragged on him. And Nikolai slammed a heavy metal jug into the back of his head.

But then, insanely, Dmitry's face melted away from the front of his head and reappeared on the back. And the serene smile remained. However, the face opened its mouth, and its tongue shot out like a long tentacle that stiffened and then pierced Nikolai's chest. Immediately the spear broke off, softened, and continued on to enter his body through the hole it had made.

Nikolai coughed, went to the ground holding his chest. He screamed and threw his head back.

"Burning," he yelled as his eyes were screwed shut as he clawed at his chest. But then in the next second from inside his throat there came an eruption of the thread-like things as they quickly worked to absorb the man's flesh and blood, his memories, and his soul, and replace them with their own DNA.

Nikolai's face melted and collapsed as the features vanished like they were made of drying sand, and in the next few seconds from the blank head, a face reappeared, this time, looking expressionless.

Nikolai's eyes were blank, white orbs, but slowly they too became filled in with darker pupils, and they swiveled for a moment, before he got to his feet.

That was it, the crew had seen enough and began to panic. And then people just ran in all directions.

The captain pulled his sidearm and fired three shots into Dmitry. They went straight through him.

Tatiana knew the game was already lost – they suddenly had three members of their team infected who were locked outside, four counting Mikhail. And now they had two more who were inside the ship, and they had no way to stop the rapidly spreading infection.

Tatiana knew that if they stayed where they were they were all doomed. They needed time and a place to regroup, to think and plan.

"*Run!*" she shouted and headed for the exit.

As she went through the door, she saw the captain head out another doorway, and more of the crew do the same. But there were more who had been grabbed, and already they were being swarmed and overwhelmed by the revolting horde.

"Going down," she said as Bodin listened in.

Tatiana ran blindly and soon came to the small internal elevator that went down to the machine room on the lower level, and jumped in. Once there, she realized she didn't have a plan, didn't have any idea how she was going to fight the things now inside the ship, and no idea how to gather the crew together. And more depressing was that she had no idea how to get home.

Overhead, she heard the main airlock chamber being opened – it seemed the Mikhail-Anya abomination was being allowed in. She grimaced, remembering an old saying about what happened once the inmates overtook the asylum – then, *the mad would rule.*

She paced for a moment, listening to the sounds reverberating through the steel ship – there were people running, faint screams, and thumps, and gunfire, and men shouted curses.

Tatiana stopped, remembering there was one place she could get that would give her time to think – there was a heavily armored mech suit in the hangar bay. It was expected to be used for dropping a single pilot down under the ice and have him dangle there in the extreme cold and even more extreme depths. It was lockable, had its own power supply, water for drinking, at least enough for a few days, and importantly, it was airtight.

If she climbed into that, then it didn't matter if something that looked like a human, monster, or a million worms came at her, they couldn't get in.

She could call for help. Or at least warn someone.

She sprinted along the bay, punched in her code to the heavy equipment room and went in fast.

The hulking suit stood in the corner, like a seven foot tall robot.

"Now we will see," she said and strode towards it. But when she was just two feet from her goal, Dmitry stepped out from behind it.

"Tatiana, you are so predictable." He smiled.

Oh god. She backed up a step.

Dmitry also took a step.

Tatiana looked to each side. There was nothing. She still had the gun, but knew it was useless against something like this horror.

"What do you want?" she asked.

"I, we, want you. We want your knowledge. We are the Wvrm and have been trapped on this desolate moon for millions of years. We need to consume, and grow, and we can only do that through acquiring more genetic material from species such as yourself. Then, we become the owners of your knowledge." He smiled. "In a way, we keep you alive inside us, long after you would have departed in your death."

"Like hell you will." She pulled the gun anyway.

He smiled sadly. "You know that is no good to you." He kept coming. "Join us, you'll like it. Small parts of your consciousness will remain alive for another million years. Think of the things you'll see and experience."

She shook her head. "Stay back."

Dmitry looked up as though seeing through the decking steel. "It is in now. Our master. What you would think of as a mind."

He nodded as though listening to a voice she couldn't hear. After a moment he dropped his gaze to her. "You will help us." He smiled. "Help us get back to your home world. Earth."

"Fuck off." She lifted the gun and fired off round after round. She didn't wait to see what effect they had but turned to run.

As she did, she opened the mic in her ear to the captain. "Vlad, disable the comms system, the drives, and blow the ship. They want to get back to Earth."

She didn't know if Captain Bodin got the message but as she reached the door, she punched the opening button. She glanced over her shoulder as the door slid back. Dmitry was standing there, his face benign and no sign of any damage from being hit by four bullets.

She was already moving forward fast. And when she had turned back to the front she saw the Mikhail-Anya thing blocking her path. The second head, the Anya half, had formed out of the side of his neck crowding the collar of his enviro-suit. It only had an ear, eye, and half a nose, but both Mikhail and Anya's single eye fixed on her. And they smiled.

She backed up, tears coming to her eyes. Tatiana shook her head. "Please, I just want to go home."

"So do we." Mikhail's voice was expressionless as he approached. "Your home."

He reached for her, his hands already beginning to slide forward as a river of tiny thread-like worms.

***

Captain Vladimir Bodin sprinted into his cabin and hit the security door. His was the only cabin on the craft with reinforced steel doors that slid together with a resounding clunk. At the time he never thought he'd need them.

He still had the small gun but knew that was useless. He paced for a moment, trying to make a plan, but he could think of nothing.

Already the odds had moved against them, and without a way to regroup, and little to fight these parasitic creatures, they would soon be overwhelmed.

Bodin spoke quickly, putting down his words for the ship's log just as he heard the sound of the ship's massive external chamber doors being opened and knew that the worms had done it – the Mikhail-Anya thing and the others from outside were now in – and so their numbers would be increased by even more.

Now his crew was little more than chickens trapped in their own henhouse by a pack of hungry wolves. His ship was lost. But at least he could warn them back home.

Bodin quickly sat at his desk and opened the communication console, composing as detailed a message as he could master within the minutes remaining he knew he had.

He finished just as there came a loud impact at his door that seemed to shake the very structure of the ship. Maybe one of the combined monstrosities was attempting to break in. They had no chance against the heavy steel. Or did they? He had no idea just how strong they really were.

But another more targeted impact came, and depressingly he saw a small lump appear in the steel. The force required to make that would have had to hit like a sledgehammer wielded by a Russian bear. He knew then he didn't have long.

He paced some more, wondering what he could do, how he could get away, when his comm system pinged with a message – it was Tatiana – he listened. She sounded distraught, and her pleas to him were ominous and froze his soul.

Destroy the communication system, she begged. *And destroy the ship.*

And then…

Because the parasites wanted to get to Earth,

Oh shit, he breathed feeling sick from fear. *Of course they did.*

Captain Bodin shut his eyes and exhaled as the impacts rained down on the door and he knew the steel was being weakened now. He had little time left.

Bodin quickly accessed the core logic of the communication system and disabled the software. He then deleted all the engine drive applications and also deleted their backups from storage. Even if they took him over, he wouldn't be able to restart the systems.

It was done. His final message would be the last one they would receive back home. The ship was now disabled and mute. These horrors were not getting off their frozen prison and back to Earth.

There was one thing left to do. He called up the self-destruct mechanism.

It would take a while, as he really needed to circumvent the multi-entry authorization process. He began the code entry, and then prepared to open all the core reactors.

Captain Vladimir Bodin felt tears on his cheeks and his hand hovered. He didn't want to do it. A small part of him was still in disbelief about their predicament, and hoped he could think of another way to defeat the horrifying parasites infecting his ship and crew.

"There has to be a way," he demanded.

The banging on the door became manic and finally a small hole was beaten open between the doors. Enough for him to see movement out there, and when he looked, he saw an eye pressed there, looking in for a moment.

They'll come in through there, he knew – a river of those revolting parasitic worms to overwhelm him, get inside him, eat him, and then remake him as a skin suit carrying an army of invaders trying to get back to his home world.

The banging came again, and he put his hands to his head.

"*Fucking stop!*" he yelled.

And it did.

After several seconds Bodin took his hands away.

Then after another few moments the silence was worse than the banging as it allowed his imagination to run wild about what was happening.

"Vladimir."

Was that Tatiana? He turned.

"Tat? Is it you?" he asked softly.

"Yes, Vladimir," she replied

"Are you okay?" He stood.

"I am now," she whispered. "They've gone. We beat them."

He smiled and got to his feet. Relief washed over him, and he felt dizzy-headed with joy.

"How?" He grinned.

"Come closer. I don't want to shout," she said.

He did as she asked, eager to see his second in command and learn how she escaped. He wondered now how he could get out as the doors wouldn't slide back after all the damage. When he was close to the doors he bent a little.

The eye appeared again. "Vladimir, we need to take off; fly the ship home. Before they come back."

He sighed. "Too late for that. I disabled the drives. Deleted all the reactor codes." He scoffed softly. "You told me to, remember?"

"You can extract the backups for the deleted codes. Restore and reboot the system," she said.

He lowered his head closer. "No. I deleted those too. No one is going home in the ship."

"Is that true? I think it is not. Perhaps we need to look inside you," she said softly.

"What?" Bodin frowned.

The hand punched right through the small opening, shredding its skin, but latching onto his suit top and holding tight.

He looked down and saw the woman's arm had the flesh shredded from the sharp, jagged steel, but there was no blood. And as he stared he saw the wound knit together.

Bodin was scared witless as he gripped the arm, but then became almost frightened into madness to see Tatiana's hand and arm turned into a river of tiny black headed worms that flowed up onto his hands and forearms.

"No, Tatiana." He fought back. "Please, no." He jerked harder, but the arm was like a steel cable and the worms continued to surge up and over his body.

He felt them get to his neck and travel down into his collar. In seconds more they were on his face and he clamped his teeth shut and held his breath. But they sought out his ears, nose, and even with mouth and eyes pressed shut, they found their way in.

Bodin opened his mouth to wail, and the worms surged in. He tasted their oiliness on his tongue and gagged as they poured down his throat like a thick, squirming liquid. And the next sensation was the worst – he went from feeling revolted to illness to suddenly feeling like millions of white hot needles were penetrating his innards as he knew they began to consume him.

Captain Vladimir Bodin's muffled scream was choked off by the swarm as his mouth and throat, and then the rest of his body dissolved back into his suit until he was no more.

But only for a while.

CHAPTER 29

Angie fast forwarded through the recording of Captain Bodin's personal log where it ended at the pounding of the door. She turned the device off. "That's it. No more." She handed it back to Morgan, with a face drained of color. "Now we know."

"They're already inside," Nina said morosely. "In here with us."

"Captain Bodin never got away or died out on the ice somewhere." Morgan frowned as he tried to think through the implications. "Unless he killed himself here in his cabin, and they took his body."

"Come on, Brad, it's obvious." Nina scowled at him. "Tatiana lied. And that means she might not just be Tatiana." Nina suddenly looked up at him. "Oh no, Eddy and Hiro are with her now."

"*Shit*." Morgan turned to run out the captain's door with Nina and Angie right behind him.

He headed fast, firstly to the command deck, and as they neared it, he saw Hiro tinkering with an object he had fixed to the door frame.

"What are you doing here?" Morgan asked.

The man looked a little confused by his commander's tone. "I made some deterrent lasers. They will track and fire on whatever we tell it to. It is computer assisted aiming so will not miss, even if the target is as thin as a hair. They will be good for defense."

"Hiro, where's Eddy?" Morgan pressed.

Hiro then registered the urgency on his commander's face. And came upright.

"He is with Tatiana in the armory. They were going to look at the extra stores." He looked from Morgan to Nina and then Angie. "What is wrong?"

"It's not Tatiana," Morgan said.

"Not Tatiana?" Hiro's creased brow suddenly unlocked as realization struck him. "Oh."

"She wanted one of you alone," Nina said.

"I'm going back," Morgan said.

"You heard what Bodin wrote." Nina bared her teeth. "The chances are about one hundred percent he has been overtaken and assimilated by now."

Morgan nodded wearily. "I know. But I have to check. That's my job as the captain."

"Then I'm coming," Nina announced.

"Me too," Hiro replied.

"No, we'll just get in each other's way." He put a hand on Nina's shoulder. "You hold up here in the command pod. But get to the mess and gather up some supplies, as we may need to seal ourselves in for a while." He turned. "Hiro, finish these deterrents. Anything in our arsenal beside hand guns is a bonus right now."

Hiro nodded but continued to look down at the ground. "I am so sorry," he muttered. "I should not have left Eddy alone."

Morgan gripped his shoulder. "We didn't know about Tatiana. None of us did." He let the man go. "Finish your work. We need it."

"So our job is to hole up until help arrives?" Angie asked. "Whenever that might be."

"Maybe," Morgan said. "Or figure something out." He began to back away. "Our rover is shot, and this is likely the only habitable island on a sea of ice. We need to exist here whether we like it or not." He half smiled, as he began to back away. "And not share it."

"You got fifteen minutes before I come and get you," Nina warned.

"More than enough," Morgan said, about to turn away.

"*Wait!*" she yelled

He froze and turned back. Nina strode forward, grabbed the front of his shirt and pulled him close, kissing him so hard on the lips it hurt.

She let him go but still held on. "You better fucking come back, Commander Brad Morgan." She let him go.

"Count on it." He softly caressed her cheek, finishing by cupping her chin.

Then he turned and shouted over his shoulder, "I'm just scouting. I'll find him. Or find what happened to him."

He turned to run down the corridor.

***

Nina watched him go with a sinking feeling in her gut.

"Idiot," she whispered.

Angie laughed softly beside her. "And if he wasn't here, it's what you'd do, right?"

Nina smiled. "Yep."

She turned to Hiro. "What were you working on? Show me."

"Yes." Hiro stood back and pointed down at the laser on the small mechanism.

The device stood on a tripod that had a motion detector and swivel for movement. On top of that was the pencil-sized laser pointer sticking out front like a tunnel barrel, and behind it a small computer chip to program in targeting specifics. All up it was about two feet high.

"A demonstration." He went to a small screen and brought up the targeting codes. "*Uh…*" He looked around, until he spotted something he could use for targeting – a pen top from a table.

"I tell it what to look for and track movement." He switched the small device on. "Three, two, one…" He tossed the pen top over to the other side of the room.

Almost instantaneously the laser swiveled, found the pen top flying through the air and a small red beam shot out to strike it before it even hit the ground.

"Nice." Angie clapped.

"Well done." Nina nodded.

"I have also programmed it to hit something the size of a worm," he said.

"How many more have you got?" Nina asked.

"I have four. This one works, the other three need to be completed," he replied.

"Then get them working. I want them all fixed around the doorway once Morgan is back," she said. "Then we can switch them on."

"Yes, I can do this," Hiro announced.

"Okay, Angie, we're going on a food run. We need as much water as we can carry as we might not get a second trip."

"Going to be heavy for four people. Plus we need food," she replied.

"I saw some satchels in the mess before. We're just going to have to deal with it. Drag them if we have to." She looked at the smaller woman. "You ready?"

She gave Nina a fragile smile. "Not really. But we have no choice."

"That's all I can ask." Nina turned to Hiro. "Hiro, trust no one but us and Morgan."

Hiro's eyebrows went up. "Eddy?"

"No. I doubt Eddy is Eddy anymore." She nodded at his pile of equipment and pieces of the lasers he was assembling. "Work fast. The madness is happening quickly now."

Nina and Angie jogged toward the mess. Nina tried to keep up on her toes to stay quiet, and passed each doorway with a sense of trepidation that something would launch itself out at them.

Angie, beside her, looked up at the tall, dark woman. "What are our chances?"

"Slim," Nina said, but then regretted it. "But if we can secure the command deck, which is one of the most heavily fortified areas on any craft, then we have a chance."

Angie nodded but looked troubled. "It's just that, the Russians seemed to have tried everything and got overwhelmed."

"And we will learn from their failure. Now we know what not to do." She smiled. "We'll win. I can feel it."

The women got to the mess door and stopped. Nina peered around the frame, and seeing it was empty slid in. The room had every piece of furniture in it splintered or crushed – she remembered the captain's log describing the attack in the mess – it had turned into a massacre.

She drew in a deep breath. "Come on."

She went in fast, and Angie came with her. From a benchtop she pulled a few bags made from some sort of strong plastic material with long handles. She handed one to Angie and she took two.

"Water first, lots of it. Then dried food," Nina said.

The women opened cupboards, refrigerators, and checked shelves. Most of the water seemed to come from the taps and probably a single large storage unit that undoubtedly recycled the fluid. That was no good to them as there were no taps or water supply on the command deck.

But in the refrigerator they found some bottled water – about a dozen large bottles, and they took them all, distributing them evenly in the bags.

It was heavy, probably about fifty pounds apiece. But they needed more.

They ignored perishable things and grabbed dried food, energy bars by the armful and just a few tins that Angie translated – beans, asparagus, sausages, more beans – and the list went on.

The only things discarded were weird sorts of pickled fish that Nina worried would stink or its remains could become toxic in an enclosed area.

In no time their bags were laden and would need to be dragged back along the corridor – the going was as slow as Nina expected and after about fifteen minutes Angie looked up.

"So far so good."

Nina nodded. "Where are they?" she asked. "Why are they letting us do this?"

Angie *hmmd*. "Want to know a theory, and a shit one?"

"Let's hear it," Nina replied.

"They want us to fix the ship and fly them to Earth. They don't know how, but think perhaps we can."

Nina sighed. "Yeah, that is a shit theory." She turned and gave her crewmate a crumbling smile. "But a damn realistic one."

"If we had more time maybe we could come up with some way to fight them or with something that was toxic to them," Angie suggested.

"Yeah," Nina agreed. "Well, we know they are repelled by heat." Nina's mind worked. "Maybe we can work on raising the internal temperature to a hundred degrees. Make them suffer."

"Worth a try," Angie replied.

They dragged the food and water towards the command center's door and Nina saw that there were now four of the mini lasers pointed at them.

"Where's Hiro?" Angie asked.

The command door slid back and Hiro saluted and grinned. "I had you both on the monitor. The lasers tracked you. All are working well."

"Good." Nina straightened and put her hands on the small of her back and stretched. "Now, you can help us get our loot inside and squared away."

She looked at her wristwatch. "Morgan has three more minutes. Then I'm going after him."

CHAPTER 30

"Incoming!" Nina yelled as she watched the monitors in the corridor and saw Morgan sprinting back toward them.

"Oh my God," Angie whispered as she watched from over Nina's shoulder. "Monsters."

Behind their commander came creatures that looked like they were vomited up from hell – there was a massive thing that looked like a combination of spider and centipede, with sharp pincers at front, multiple pointed legs with bristling hairs, and shiny, muscular-looking back. The face wasn't like an insect or arthropod face at all, but had vaguely human features pressed into it.

Coming fast behind it was a man with two heads and four arms, running on elephantine legs without feet, and just behind that abomination was a thing that looked like it had once been a human being, but came on all fours with a long face out front with a mouth full of glassine, near transparent teeth.

"Holy shit," Nina grimaced. "This is what happens when these Wvrm combine our physiology with the previous inhabitants of the planet. Or perhaps combine creatures from many planets they have absorbed in the past. You get these hellish abominations."

Morgan tripped, and Nina held her breath. But he rolled, got to his feet, bounced off a wall, and kept coming.

"Come on, Brad, faster now," Nina urged.

He passed one camera and was picked up again by the next. On this one he turned and fired his gun back down the corridor. Then turned to run some more.

Nina went and picked up the flamethrower.

"You're not going out there, are you?" Angie scowled.

"Just going to ensure he gets back in here. And only *he* gets back in here." She turned to Hiro. "As soon as he's in, arm the lasers, and we shut this place down."

Hiro nodded. "I will be ready." He went to tend to his screen that was the master console for all the laser trackers.

Nina buckled on the flamethrower, went to stand at the door, sucked in three deep breaths and then turned. "*Punch it.*"

Angie opened the hardened steel door, and Nina walked a half dozen paces further out. She guessed from where Morgan was on the cameras, he would be on his way back down the central corridor any second now.

And then he appeared.

"*Run!*" Nina shouted so loud she tasted blood in her throat.

Nina stood to the side as Morgan run-staggered the last hundred feet. As he came abreast of her she saw his breathing was ragged as all hell, and his face flushed from exertion.

"Arm lasers," she shouted as she heard the howls and screeches of hell coming from the darkened corridor behind him.

The thumping of heavy clawed feet came next, and then there they were. Nina stiffened her spine and lifted the nozzle of the flamethrower. Nothing could have really prepared her for the real horrors that met her eyes when she saw the things in the flesh.

These were beyond what she had seen when Jake and Ollie had been taken. These things were an amalgamation of many species, all blended into a single nightmare.

She braced herself, and then fired a long gout of liquid flame at them – the front beasts exploded. The individual worms gave up their cohesiveness to escape the heat of the fire – just as she expected them to.

Nina backed into the room and Angie hit the button for the heavy double layered door that hermetically sealed them in.

Hiro switched on all four lasers. And they began firing.

The hallway was filled with millions of the worms that were trying to reassemble into a single form. But the laser's hair-thin beam picked them out, one by one, and each of the four mounted weapons was destroying hundreds per second.

The laser vaporized the individual worms, never missing, and keeping up a constant stream of deadly accurate destruction.

After just a minute, tens of thousands had been destroyed. So instead of moving forward the worms began to retreat back out of the corridor that led to the command center.

From out of sight and out of reach of the laser, they must have regrouped into a solid mass, as from around the corner, came a trunk-like arm, forty feet long and thick as a light pole. It shot forward and crashed into one of the lasers, destroying it instantly.

"It's thinking through its attack strategy," Nina said. "And where's that brain-blob thing? It has to be organizing them."

"It must be out there somewhere, staying out of sight or away from harm," Morgan said.

Hiro turned. "If we could find and kill it…"

"No one is going out there now," Morgan replied.

From around the corner lumbered a creature straight from the bowels of hell. It was a crab-like being with thick shell and sprouting like toadstools from its top were several human bodies, from the waist up.

The human heads all screamed, some begging, some in pain, and some perhaps calling the names of loved ones they would never see again. Nina could hear English as well as Russian words, and she knew that the Wvrm were doing this on purpose, to taunt the survivors, and demoralize them. As it drew nearer, Nina saw what had happened to their crew mate.

"Eddy," she whispered.

Morgan came and stood beside her.

"Not Eddy anymore," he said. "Here they come."

The thing lumbered forward, and the lasers shot into it, and even though the beams destroyed hundreds per second, the holes the laser made in the beast quickly closed as it fed in more and more worms from all the corners of the Russian spaceship.

In seconds it was close enough to reach out and destroy the lasers one after the other. In several more seconds, Hiro sat back.

"All gone," he said.

Nina picked up the flamethrower as the four people backed away from the reinforced door.

Morgan glanced at her. "You discharge that thing in here, and it'll burn up all the oxygen. And choke us."

Nina never turned. "And if this thing, those *things*, get in here, we'll all be dead, and turned into more of those monstrosities. I am not fucking going to end up another screaming body stuck on top of some monster from hell."

"They can't get in." Morgan shook his head. "They can't."

Nina gripped the flamethrower. "Yeah, Captain Bodin thought the same thing about his reinforced doors. And well, they peeled him out like a sardine from its tin."

Morgan paced as Nina, Angie and Hiro watched the feed from the camera outside the command deck's door. The monstrous creature pulled back and then lunged forward. The titanic impact was felt right through the ship.

Then, like a Titan's battering ram it came again and again. But the doors held.

And then it stopped.

After a few seconds, Angie half turned. "What's happening?"

The small group crowded around the feed from the external cameras. And then they saw – the massive creature was falling apart, the individual worms showering off it, to move like army ants towards the door.

And then they formed lines up around the seams in the doors, trying to find even the tiniest of holes to squirm through.

"Nowhere is safe," Nina said. "It's only a matter of time."

"What do we do?" Angie stammered. "We can't take off, we can't stay here, and we can't even hide anymore."

"Even if we could take off, and opened the ship to the vacuum of space, there's no guarantee that might kil them. If they can survive in an environment as hostile as Europa's then they may just be able to put themselves in hibernation and wait it out," Morgan said.

"Or wait until we get them back to Earth." Nina looked at him. "We need something else."

"Captain Bodin wanted to lead them away from the ship," Angie said softly. "Maybe…"

"You know he never did that," Nina scoffed. "Do you really think he didn't just get assimilated like all the others? Come on, Angie."

Angie went to one of the walls and sat down on the floor and hugged her knees. Nina thought she was shutting down, and probably wouldn't be any more help.

"We can't get a message out to warn anyone even if they did come," Morgan said. "They'd be landing into the same trap." He scratched his chin. "We can't fight them, and eventually they will get in – either eat their way through the door or batter it down as soon as they make themselves into the right creature form with enough power."

"Then we leave," Hiro said.

Nina and Morgan turned to him. Even Angie looked up.

"How? The ship's core drive has been disabled. She wouldn't lift three feet with the power reserve it's got," Morgan asked.

"No, not the ship." Hiro smiled. "But the command pod. It can be used as a life raft."

Morgan scoffed for a moment, but then began to smile.

"There's only two life pods," Nina said. "Plus the life raft command module is only launchable or detachable in space."

"Then we launch from here. We get the ship to throw us into orbit." Morgan grinned now. "The command pod has enough oxygen for all of us, and we certainly don't need what's in the rest of the craft. From here we can flood the ship with oxygen."

"And keep flooding it and keep flooding it," Hiro added.

"Until the pressure is high enough so that when we detach, we'll be like a champagne cork, and get blown into space." Nina clapped.

"This could work." Morgan hiked his shoulders. "Besides, what have we got to lose? Except our humanity and lives."

"And the two life pods?" Angie asked. "Do we take shifts?"

"Yep, we were going to do that in the main ship if we had to bunk down here for several years waiting for rescue. Now, we'll just take shifts – two on two off, or maybe one on duty and three off, for six month stints for the three years back home. It also means we'll be able to make our supplies go further – when we're in cryo, we won't need to eat or drink."

"This could work." Nina grinned. "This could really work."

Just then there was a jarring thud against the door frame.

"Then what are we waiting for?" Morgan asked. "Let's pop the cork and get the hell off this frozen hell."

***

Hiro tapped into the ship's atmospheric systems and isolated the command center from the rest of the craft. He then opened all the air tanks and began pumping, and forcing, it into the entire ship's structure.

Morgan watched from over his shoulder as he tried to blank out the constant battering at the double thickness door. He knew that standard Earth pressure at sea-level was 1013.25 millibars, or 14.7 pounds per square inch.

Already the ship was up to forty pounds per square inch; about the equivalent you would feel if you dove down in the ocean to a depth of one hundred feet.

And Hiro kept feeding it in.

"Okay, everyone, it won't be long until we have enough pressure to blast off," Morgan snorted softly. "Or be blasted off."

Morgan paced again. The atmosphere on Europa was thin, and the gravity much weaker than on Earth. In fact, thinking of it in relation to Earth's moon, both had lower gravity than Earth, with Europa's being even weaker than our own moon's gravity. But they would still need to punch up through it. They needed to attain a height of five hundred feet, at least, with continuing velocity to bust through the tiny blue moon's gravitational pull. And then keep going.

The command pod did have tiny thrusters, so they could adjust their course direction and velocity once they were in motion, and then just let the onboard computer take over to navigate their way home.

Brad Morgan smiled; *things were going to plan, and in fact better than he hoped.*

"One twenty pounds per square inch," Hiro said.

"The Wvrm are being compressed, *look*." Nina stared hard at the feed from just outside their doors.

Morgan and Angie looked at her screen and saw the creatures had coalesced into clumped forms again but now seemed smaller, denser, and they moved slower.

She turned. "Hey, could this kill them?"

"Unlikely," Morgan said. "Maybe if we could crank the pressure up to thousands of pounds, but that'd blow the ship apart. Plus, I think we're reaching maximum pressure right now." He turned to Hiro who nodded.

"One fifty pounds," he said. "Oxygen feed is slowing."

"Okay, give it all we've got," Morgan said. "Everyone get ready. I want us all strapped in. We need to attain escape velocity, and hope we go straight up and not be blown sideways." He snorted. "We'd end up rolling right around the moon."

"Slowing, slowing...*stopped*," Hiro said.

"Well done. Hiro, strap in. Everyone get ready." Morgan and Nina took to the pilot and copilot chairs with Hiro and Angie in the chairs behind. They strapped in and Morgan and Nina navigated the Russian procedures for jettisoning the command pod.

Behind them the door suffered a huge blow that made the entire ship ring like a bell.

"This amount of pressure hasn't affected them as much as I would have liked," Morgan said. "I hope it hasn't just made them denser and stronger."

He shut off all feeds and connections from the main craft so they were running on just the command pod's energy. There was one last thing and he prayed it worked as it was supposed to.

His hand hovered over the release clamp's button and he sucked in a deep breath. "Here we go." His finger rested on the button. "In three, two, one...*blast off*."

He pressed the button.

***

The initial explosive blast of super compressed air punched them straight upwards.

Nina's fingers dug into the straps crisscrossing her chest as she was pushed back into the chair.

"Two hundred feet," Morgan groaned as his head sunk into the soft seat material.

Come on, come on, Nina prayed as they continued to surge upwards.

The front window blast shields had come down, and the inner doors had closed. They were now totally sealed into their command deck pod and were free of the ship. The gravity was weak, but Morgan had said they needed at least a five hundred foot blast off to even have a chance of being free of Europa's gravitational grip.

"Four hundred feet," Morgan counted off.

"Slowing," Hiro added.

Nina felt her heat hammering in her chest. If they didn't break free, they'd fall back to the surface of the moon. And if that happened, then it was only a matter of time before they were peeled out of the pod just like the Russian captain in his sealed cabin.

"Five hundred feet," Morgan announced.

And suddenly they felt their stomachs flip a little as they gained weightlessness.

Hiro leaned forward to examine the rear camera and grunted his displeasure. "The ship is surrounded."

Morgan switched up the feed from Hiro's camera and looked back at where they had just come from. There was the image of a rapidly shrinking Russian spaceship as they left it behind. But around it he could make out thousands of creatures – composites created by the Wvrm, and drawn to the craft, to perhaps enjoy their final meal of human flesh.

He remembered the massive creatures of light below the ice who tried to hold them back. Perhaps it was their way of trying to warn them – stay away from the surface. Don't go back up there.

But we did anyway.

He smiled at the remnant of the thought he was able to retain.

But none of that mattered now. Because he, they, were free.

"Switching on artificial gravity," he said.

Immediately they felt their stomachs settle again and muscles ease back onto their bones.

Morgan sighed and turned his chair around. He unstrapped and leaned forward to read the data coming in from the console.

"Going to adjust our trajectory." He altered some of the spatial characteristics of their drift. They were traveling at an enormous velocity, and barring anything getting in their way, they should be on track to be reentering Earth's atmosphere in good time.

"At this speed, I estimate three years, four months," he said.

Angie groaned out loud.

Nina laughed and leaned her head back. "Yeah, but consider the alternative. We beat them." She looked up. "There could be some remnants stuck on the skin of our pod. Space might not kill them."

Morgan nodded. "You're right. They might just be able to put themselves into hibernation in space." He smiled. "But once we hit reentry, the friction burn will rise to around two thousand six hundred degrees." He turned to her. "And something that loves cold is not going to survive that."

"Works for me. Kill em all," Nina replied.

Hiro was checking the pod's statistics, and he turned in his chair. "Fuel reserves not good. Enough to get home, but if there is need for any significant deviation..." He left it there.

"I get it," Morgan said. "No movement. The less people moving around the less chance of throwing off our trajectory. We have two cryo chambers, I think Angie and Hiro should double up. The pods can take it. Means they'll burn through their own resources quickly, but they have a ten year lifespan, and we only need less than half that."

"The other?" Nina asked.

"We do shifts. Only one of us moving around is less risk to our flight path." He smiled.

She cocked her head. "I know you. You'll let me sleep and you'll stay awake, just because you think it's the chivalrous thing to do."

He pointed at his chest. "Me, my lady, chivalrous? Never." He chuckled.

"I think is good idea," Hiro said. "I've looked at the recovered stores. One of us being awake has enough food and water. Two of us, not so much. Three or four, no chance."

"Then it's settled," Morgan said. "We share a last coffee, and then we bunk down." He smiled at Nina. "I'll take first shift awake." He crossed his chest. "Promise."

"Our mother hen," Nina said and her mouth turned down. "When I see you again, you'll be three and a half years older."

He shook his head. "If anything was going to age me it was that time on Europa in that damned Russian ship. This will be a nice, quiet, and calm holiday. I'll probably just be relaxing the entire time."

Hiro made the coffee, weak and warm, but it was the feeling of happiness and relief amongst the remaining crew that made it delicious.

Morgan raised his cup. "To Heather, Eddy, Jake, Benny, and Ollie. Thank you for your service and sacrifice. You will not be forgotten."

The others raised their cups, their eyes mostly downcast.

They sipped, and all were lost in their own thoughts, until Nina broke the dismal mood.

"First thing I'll do when I get back is go somewhere warm. Hawaii maybe. Or Fiji. Or Australia's Great Barrier Reef. I hear you can ride on the backs of sea turtles down there." She turned. "Hiro, what will you do?"

Hiro smiled and nodded. "I am sick of dried foods. My uncle has a famous Japanese restaurant in Tokyo. Best sashimi, miso ramen soup, and yakatori in the country. That is where you will find me."

"I like the sound of that," Angie said. "But I'm going to gather up all my family. All my in-laws and outlaws and have a big dinner party. I don't care what time of year we get back, I'm going to throw a Thanksgiving party to make up for the ones I've missed."

Morgan laughed out loud and then toasted her. "That's an awesome idea."

"What about you, mother hen?" Nina asked.

He half smiled. "It's a secret," he said.

"Oh come on, what?" Nina asked.

"I don't want to say it out loud just yet." He tilted his head. "But I'll give you a hint...it involves you."

Nina blushed.

Angie drained her coffee and raised the cup. "Okay, looks like the grownups need to have some alone time." She stood carefully. "Hiro, time for bed. And please don't hog the cryochamber."

Hiro and Angie pulled the tube out of the wall at ground level. It was like a long round edged coffin, with just enough room for two people to jam in side by side.

They entered the data of the weight and mass of the occupants, and the small computer would feed in the right amout of atmospheric nutrients, and gases to put them in a hibernating sleep.

They lay down with Nina kneeling beside them. She reached in to squeeze Angie's hand and patted Hiro's shoulder.

"See you both in Earth orbit," she said.

She shut the capsule lid and the pair closed their eyes as the hibernation and nutrient gases were pumped into the tube. It then slid back into the wall.

Nina ejected the second tube that slid out and opened, waiting for her. She sat down, sighed loudly, and faced Morgan.

"Looks like there might be a happy ending after all," she said.

Morgan reached across, placed a hand over hers and squeezed. "Things are working out like we hoped. It was touch and go there for a while. I thought I'd be trapped."

"You and me both." She looked back at the rear screen that captured images of Europa, which was now just a small, blue ball in the blackness of space. "Do you think anyone will go back there? There's a lot to learn, and I guess we'll be better prepared next time."

"No, no one will ever return," he said.

She smiled and her brows came together. "Why do you say that?"

"They won't need to. Or want to," he said as he turned to her. "Because, Europa will have come to them."

"I don't understand that." Her brows came together.

"Because you don't understand me. Or have even really met me," he said soothingly. "But now it's time."

Morgan unzipped the front of his suit, and as she watched, frozen in dread, she saw his chest stopped and where his stomach should have been it looked like someone had inserted a yellow, pulsating bag there.

The revolting thing was alive, and Morgan reached in with one hand and pulled it free of his torso, holding it out to her.

Nina felt her eyes go so wide they could have popped from her head, and she couldn't move a muscle as she stared like a mouse in the gaze of a deadly snake.

Morgan's expression was cold and composed. "This is the collective knowledge of the Wvrm. This is me. This is us. And all of your crew members are in here, as well as the Russians, and a thousand other species. I hold their thoughts and their memories, and they will be alive in me for millions of years."

Nina suddenly felt Morgan's grip on her hand become cold and her head jerked down to look.

She began to cry, and her heart banged so hard in her chest, she felt like she was going to go into shock. Morgan's hand was lengthening, and she saw it was breaking down into the individual thread-like worms. She tried to tug her hand back, but it was like she was caught in some sort of glue.

"Please," she said, breathing hard.

She knew then; Morgan didn't get away. He was the Trojan horse, pushed toward them for them to bring inside the gate. They'd underestimated the Wvrm. The parasites were cunning, and intelligent, and able to plan. And they'd outsmarted them; us brilliant human beings.

Nina looked around as the swarm made its way up her arm, and the most chilling thing was that Morgan sat there as if he was just having a pleasant conversation instead of beginning to absorb and assimilate her.

She needed help and her eyes alighted on the cryo tube that contained Hiro and Angie, and she tried to work out a way to wake them.

"Don't worry about them," Morgan said. "I'll take good care of them." He smiled. "It's a long trip home, and I'll need their bodies to sustain me. Yours too, I'm afraid."

The benign smile never left his face. "It's how we grow, reproduce, and then spread. We have assimilated entire galaxies. Everywhere we touch, we end up ruling. And now you are taking me to Earth, and I thank you." He tilted his head. "We couldn't have done it without you."

Nina felt anger explode within her, and she lunged at him, and threw a punch right into his smug face.

She impacted to his eye, hard. And instead of striking the hard, orbital bone around his eye, her fist sunk in and stuck.

Morgan continued to act like nothing had happened.

"You'll feel better soon. All the fear, all the pain, and anger will go." His good eye swiveled toward her as the tiny thread-like things with their black heads inched up and across her shoulder, to her neck, and then up her face.

Nina moaned.

"This is not the end for you. And don't worry, Nina, you'll see Earth again. Or at least some tiny remnant of your consciousness will perceive it as you join with the horde."

She began to weep, huge raking sobs with heavy tears that ran down her cheeks.

"He loved you, you know. And now, you'll be together forever," he said.

"*Help me!*" she screamed one final time as the river of worms entered her mouth, nose, ears and eyes.

Nina gagged and tried to cough them out, but in seconds more her world turned to a fiery pain as it shrunk to her being just a tiny dot in a black room.

And then that too blinked out.

PART 07
ARRIVAL OF THE BEAST

CHAPTER 31

NASA Administration, Houston – Greg Morgan's Office
Help me, Nina Barker had screamed.

NASA lead scientist Greg Morgan sat back feeling small pops of light go off behind his eyes such was the alarm, confusion, and damned fright he now felt.

The recorders on their individual suits had detailed a monstrous series of events that had killed them all.

Questions swirled in his mind, the first being, what happened to the other mission astronauts Angie Sommers, and Hiroyuki Nakagawa?

He snatched up the phone and called through to the hangar where the Russian command capsule was being broken down and examined.

Marsha Downy, the lead engineer, picked up on the second ring.

"Downy…"

"Marsha, it's Greg Morgan…" Greg heard her begin a brief pleasantry, but he cut straight across it. "Listen. This is important. I need you to check something. The second cryo tube, have you looked inside it yet?"

"Of course," Downy replied. "Must have just been used for storage. Nothing interesting."

"Why do you say that? What was in there?" Greg shut his eyes.

"Two suits, empty. That's all," Marsha replied. "They belonged to…" she sounded like she was reading from a chart.

"Angie Sommers and Hiroyuki Nakagawa," He finished for her.

Marsha chuckled. "Yes, that's right, Greg, just like Nina Barker's suit. How did you know?"

Greg Morgan knew everyone working on the Russian command pod would be wearing the equivalent of a hazmat suit, but there was something else he needed.

"Listen, Marsha, this is important. I want you to take those suits down to the decon chamber and run a full cleanse. All spectrums. Do that now, right now. Can you do that for me?"

"Jesus, Greg, you're scaring me. What is it?" Marsha asked. "Have I got some biohazards here?"

"Just do it. I'll explain soon. I have something else to check, and then I'm on my way." Morgan put the phone down and called the hospital where they were keeping his brother, Brad, in isolation.

There was no answer.

He tried another number, and finally got an answer.

"Martinez," the woman answered

"This is NASA lead scientist Greg Morgan, who am I speaking to?" Morgan said in a rush.

"Angela Martinez." The woman sounded a little out of breath. "Head nurse."

Morgan launched in. "Angela, in your isolation unit, you have one of my people. His name is …"

"He's gone," she said flatly.

"*What?*" Morgan slowly stood with the phone clamped to his ear.

"He's vanished. Didn't check himself out, and no one saw anything. They went into his room to check on him and found his clothing, and that was it," she began. "The hospital is in lockdown and we're searching now. We don't think he's left the building. We'll find him," she finished confidently.

Greg felt a cold prickling perspiration break out on his forehead.

"When?" he asked softly.

"*Um*, probably around twenty-five minutes ago," she said. "Don't worry, like I said, we'll find him. He's in here somewhere and I've been told he hasn't left the building."

Morgan knew that his brother, or whatever he'd become, would probably begin assimilating other people immediately. He needed to get his strength back.

The nurse cleared her throat. "Mr. Morgan, he's basically been unconscious, sleeping, so will be weak. We'll get him back."

"No, he wasn't sleeping," Morgan said dismally. "He was waiting."

He hung up and slowly sunk back into his chair.

He needed to tell people. The police. The military. Cordon off the hospital perimeter and if they could contain him within the hospital, they still had a chance.

But if these things got out into the world…

He just prayed it all wasn't too late.

He yanked the phone back to his ear and started to dial.

CHAPTER 32

Greg Morgan's first briefings were to his senior NASA astrophysicists, Jenny Alvarez, Caroline Jenner, and Eric Chandler.

None of them believed him so he made them listen to portions of the recording while he made some more calls. NASA, his organization, was a civilian agency. But its brother agency was the newly formed Space Force which was the youngest branch of the military. And that's where they overlapped with the other defense force seniority.

Once again he played some of the recordings, and detailed what he thought had happened. He was able to alarm the senior military enough that they set in motion two things – a chopper to pick Greg and his team up, plus bring in enough manpower to throw a security ring around the hospital.

Already they had placed the hospital in an internal quarantine, with no one being allowed to go home – staff or patients. Then when the soldiers arrived they would also make a physical ring around the hospital grounds to further lock it down.

Fire, Greg had told them. And X-rays, to prove who they were. It was all he had for the time being and he hoped the military brought the firepower to contain what he feared – a massive outbreak of the Wvrm.

Fifteen minutes later he was told to come out from his building where the helicopter was landing. His team came with him, and all looked ashen faced, with Jenny Alvarez also looking like she had been crying. The gravity of the situation was sinking in.

"There were no survivors after all. None," Eric said. "They all died up there on Europa."

"As well as the Russians," Caroline added.

"It was too smart for us," Greg replied. "We thought we were going there to look for life. But the life was actually looking for us."

"They were waiting," Eric said. "And might have been waiting for millions of years."

"We were such easy prey." Morgan turned to them as they saw the dot of the helicopter growing larger in the sky. "Our job now," he said, looking them each in the eye, "is to ensure this universal parasite does not break out of the hospital. We cannot let this infection spread."

"It may have already,' Eric said.

"Yes, and by the sound of what happened on Europa, it spreads quietly and quickly. So we need to move even quicker."

"Will the military move as quick? I mean, we've been involved from day one, and we were in disbelief. Until we heard the recordings." Eric looked up as the chopper was descending. "How can we tell them what to look out for when we don't really know ourselves?"

"I think they'll move quickly. They're trained to err on the side of caution here. Perhaps they do not see the problem for all its deadly perspective just yet. But they realize the potential for danger. I think they'll act."

The team crouched a little, holding hands up over their heads and squinting as the helicopter gently touched down.

The military chopper's blade eased back a little, the door slid back, and a man in helmet and goggles waved them over shouting something that was lost in the maelstrom of wind and debris from the massive downdraft.

The four scientists ran toward the chopper, and the man yelled at them until they were in and the door slid shut. "Doctor Greg Morgan?" He still yelled.

Morgan raised a hand, and the man handed him some headphones. Once Greg had them on, the guy gave the thumbs up and turned away as the chopper lifted into the air and quickly veered to the side, banking toward the direction of the downtown hospital.

Suddenly, a new voice spoke to Greg.

"Doctor Morgan, General Alston here." The man was brusque and sounded in a hurry.

"Good to be speaking, General," Morgan replied.

Alston continued. "I have organized for a team of specialists to meet you on site, and everything will be coordinated by Colonel Bowman. He's been instructed to work with you and he has my full authority to act as he sees fit."

"Thank you, sir," Morgan replied. "Any news from the hospital? Have they found my broth… ah, Brad Morgan?"

"No luck there. But we have established an inner and outer perimeter. The inner one is guarding all doors and exits. The outer one has cleared the surrounding apartment blocks. No one goes in or out until we find your man."

"Have you been inside yet?" Morgan asked.

"No, we were waiting on you," Alston replied. "You mentioned something about a parasitic infection? And heat and fire acting as a deterrent?"

"Yes, for now, it's the only thing we know that can stop it," Morgan said.

"Jesus, not ideal. A very blunt instrument to be using inside a hospital. The potential for collateral damage is off the charts. We'll end up burning the place down."

"Let's hope we don't have to destroy the hospital. But if this thing gets out, it could destroy the world," Morgan sighed. "We can't let it get past us under any circumstances. We just can't. There's too much at stake." He spoke softly, even though there was little chance anyone could overhear him in the helicopter. "General, there may be a need for a total site cleanse."

Alston grunted. "I hear you. I hope it doesn't come down to having to do that. But we'll be ready, and we'll cross that bridge when the time comes." Alston sounded like he was reading some notes. "One more thing; says here you want to do X-rays to detect the creature or creatures?"

"That's right," Morgan replied. "We'll be working on other tests, but for now, the Europa team found that the creatures mimic people perfectly to the point of being undetectable. That's how they infiltrated ours and the Russian teams. But that's only on the outside. On the inside they're a whole different physiology."

"Hence the X-rays," Alston answered.

"Yep, apparently they have no bones. Only structures approximating a type of internal scaffolding," Morgan replied.

"Jesus Christ," Alston exhaled. "This is a fucking nightmare."

"Not yet, sir," Morgan replied. "It only becomes a nightmare if this thing, these things, break out of the hospital."

"Roger that, Doctor. You keep me informed, and anything you need, you let Colonel Bowman know. He's my eyes and ears on the ground and is acting with my full authority. He's a good man," Alston said. And then the line disconnected.

Greg sat back, and closed his eyes, feeling the vibration of the aircraft right through his body. It was only a few days ago, he was elated at the fact that one of the mission astronauts was returning from Europa and ecstatic when he learned it was his brother. There was so much they had hoped to learn, he was as excited as a kid at Christmas.

He closed his eyes, remembering.

He still saw his little brother as a friend, buddy, and savior when he was a kid. Brad always stuck up for little nerdy Greg; and even though Brad was younger, he was bigger and tougher.

Greg knew when Brad took the mission the risks were off the chart. But Greg always expected him to come home and the Morgan boys would be together again, talking and laughing about their adventures. And what adventures they would have had to talk about.

And now he was back, and everything was going to shit. And if they didn't find him, then perhaps the whole world would go to shit.

Greg put his thumb and finger into his eyes and rubbed hard.

Fuck it, he thought, remembering he hadn't even told his dad, Clay, that Brad was back. Now what would he tell him? What *could* he tell him?

That it's not him anymore, he had to remember. His brother died on Europa.

"Three minutes," the pilot's voice in his ear was near mechanical it was so devoid of emotion. Greg opened his eyes and turned to look out of the small porthole window beside him. The lights of the city were passing beneath them.

The air traffic had been cleared in the area, and the streets looked empty save for some military vehicles parked across intersections.

Here we go, he thought as the chopper came down in the vacant lawn area out front of the huge square building.

The huge hospital was a five story structure, with several wings. Plus it had an underground car park, research center, morgue, cafeteria, and of course, the isolation center for cases like Commander Brad Morgan.

It could take in five hundred patients and had a range of heavy caliber medical equipment for X-rays, MRIs, ultrasound and CT scanners, plus even some robotic surgical assistants. It was one of the best funded and modern health facilities in the state.

They landed on the lawn, just down from the outside car park. Almost immediately the door was pulled back and they were met with a combination of soldiers and state police.

Morgan jumped down first, and his team was also helped out. He walked a few paces from the vicious downdraft and looked around – there was no one on the streets surrounding the hospital even though it was in quite a built up area.

The ground level temporary car park still had around fifty cars parked out in the open, in a place that could fit two hundred, and he bet they were mostly belonging to the staff, all of whom were trapped inside in lockdown.

A lieutenant lifted an arm and waved him over, and Morgan did the same to his team. They were taken to a tent-like structure which he assumed was the temporary command center, and inside was a short bullnecked man, who turned with his eyes as intense as a pair of diamond drills.

They fixed on Morgan, and he bet that the man never blinked.

"Colonel Bowman?" Morgan guessed.

The man headed toward him and the other military personnel parted like the Red Sea.

"Correct. And you must be Doctor Greg Morgan," he replied.

He didn't salute but stuck out a hand which Greg grabbed. The grip was firm and dry and it felt like holding a piece of iron-bark.

Colonel Bowman led him back to a table that had a large computer screen standing on it, that displayed a 3D image of the hospital schematic.

"You certainly have made a lot of important people nervous, Doctor. You have our attention, so please, briefly now, tell us what we are dealing with, how we can resolve our problem with minimum casualties, minimum damage, and what tools, skills, or strategy we might need."

Greg drew in a deep breath and let it out as a soft laugh. He shook his head. "Let me get this out in the open right now. If we can't control the problem here and now, then my recommendation to the general has been to totally annihilate the hospital." He looked up. "With everyone in it, including us."

A few of the soldiers froze what they were doing and turned. Only Bowman looked unperturbed.

"Let's hope we don't get to that end position, Doctor," Bowman said. "The floor is yours."

"Okay." Greg Morgan organized his thoughts, and then began. "This creature we're dealing with is like an aggressive, transmissible infection, but it's a universal parasite. I can't tell if it started with base intelligence, or has somehow absorbed the human's intelligence. But what I can tell you is that it is strong, smart, cunning, and capable of planning. And is formidable as all hell."

"It came from Europa, right?" one of the soldiers asked.

"Yes and no. That's where it came from to get to Earth. But we don't think it was indigenous to that environment. It probably originated somewhere else in the universe."

"How do we kill it?" a tall solider asked from the back. "Lieutenant Byrne, sir."

"Good question, Lieutenant," Greg replied. "And the first thing I can tell you is the *it*, is really a *them*. It is not a single creature we're dealing with, though it can clump together and act like one when it wants to. But it is a swarm of beings all working together. I don't know enough yet about whether that collection of creatures acts like individual cells in a body, or they work together like a school of fish, or hive of ants. Or even if there's some sort of collective intelligence coordinating them." He snorted softly. "They call themselves the Wvrm."

"They have a name for themselves?" Jennings asked. "Shit, man, they can think?"

"They can think, they can plan, and they can act. Do not underestimate them," Greg pressed.

"But they can be killed." Bowman's eyes bored into him.

Greg nodded. "Individually, they are vulnerable, especially to heat. I'm not sure if any of our Europa team or the Russian team managed to kill a collective. And maybe that's because they were overwhelmed so quickly and completely." He turned slowly. "Remember, if you have read the briefing notes, these things can perfectly mimic another human. So perfectly, they even adopt familiar mannerisms."

"How exactly do they do that?" Bowman asked.

Greg sighed. "This is where it gets nasty. I believe that when they absorb the human brain, they absorb more than the organ and the flesh. They absorb the personality, and maybe the original occupant is somehow retained in some form to help the parasite get close to other people, with an objective to assimilate them as well."

"And it did that to our people?" Jennings asked, looking ashen faced.

"Yes." Greg nodded. "There are plenty of precedents for this. There's a creature called a hairworm, a parasitic animal from the phylum *Nematomorpha*. These worms infect crickets and other land insects and control their bodies. They eat the cricket from the inside out and wrap themselves around the remaining brain. They then get the insect to find a water source and throw itself in, where the hairworm larvae swim free."

'That's fucked up." Jennings' mouth turned down.

"Meals on wheels," another of the soldiers said, but no one laughed.

"I don't understand, Doctor." Jennings frowned. "You said they retain the person inside themselves somewhere. Does that mean there's a chance they can be brought back, cured maybe?"

"No, no chance. Everyone who encountered the Wvrm has been consumed, eaten, and their bodies co-opted. They are just a skin suit, a shell. There is no coming back," Greg Morgan said, looking at each of them in turn. "In Commander Brad Morgan's own words, or rather the thing that became Captain Morgan, the Wvrm were a race of parasites that had existed for millions of years, and have colonized and absorbed many worlds and countless beings. We just happen to be next in line."

"And now they're here," Bowman finished.

"We can't let them win. We can't let them out. In fact, we can't let anyone out, as it might decide that it is finished being Brad Morgan and try and escape as a nurse or another patient, or even a soldier. Once this genie gets out of its bottle, I don't know if we can ever get it back in."

"That's a sobering assessment of our situation, Doctor," Bowman said. "What would you advise?"

Greg turned to look up at the multi-story building. "Frankly, bombing everyone and everything in the building using a high grade thermal device. Everyone in there right now might not be who we think they are."

"I don't think we're there just yet, Doctor," Bowman said. "But that option is on the table."

"There is one sliver of a chance," Morgan replied. "This thing just travelled for several years to get here and may have been weakened. It might need time to gather its strength. And that might mean we are able to trap it. And kill it."

"Then we're going in," Bowman said, and turned to twirl a finger in the air for a second that caused a burst of activity. He turned back. "I'm assuming you'll be accompanying us, Doctor. And your team?"

"Wouldn't miss it for the world. My world." He turned to his three assistants, Jenny Alvarez, Caroline Jenner, and Eric Chandler, who all nodded.

"Colonel, I suggest we break into multiple search area teams as we might be able to track it down quicker that way."

"Good," Bowman said. "You said heat might damage it. So we have flamethrowers, thermal charges, and plasma rounds for the rifles. I think we've got it covered."

"I hope so," Greg replied. "Because right now, we're learning as we go. And we don't have a lot of time to make mistakes."

"No, we do not," the colonel replied.

Over the next few minutes they organized the teams and what their search areas were to be. There would be five teams – each would have a specialist with them, either Greg, or one of his three team members. The final fifth team was the largest, and that was on coordinating and keeping calm the hospital staff that had been told to gather in the downstairs foyer area.

They would be bringing in an X-ray machine so they could screen and clear them all. Any that failed would be incinerated. That ground floor team would also take over the security department of the hospital and the banks of cameras so they could get eyes on the different floors to offer guidance and intel to the search teams.

Bowman knew they needed to move fast and make zero mistakes. He turned to his team.

"Remember, trust no one, and nothing," Bowman said, and then, "Let's do this."

"*HUA!*" came the shouted reply as the hundred soldiers jogged toward the locked doors of the hospital.

Each had an earpiece, and Bowman linked in to each squad's team leader. Each had designated goals – Priority one was to head to the isolation rooms where Brad Morgan had been kept. Then check that entire floor. They would be then taking it floor by floor.

They had already been communicating with the hospital managers, and the floors should be vacated and all the patients and staff gathered in the ground floor area. The portable X-ray machines were set up and ready to go, and as soon as the people were cleared, then they would be released – patients with the greatest need would be screened and let out first to continue their care.

If any infected were encountered, the rules of engagement were simple: don't let them touch you, and burn them to ash. No prisoners.

Greg jogged, trying to keep up with the bigger, younger, and fitter soldiers. Even the women seemed to be more formidable than he was.

All had been given briefings, and he just hoped they all took in the seriousness of their predicament. Right here, right now, was ground zero for the future of the human race.

They were in a war, and the invasion force was already here, and its objective was simple – take over every living thing on the planet. There would be no negotiations, or communication, as this thing, these things, saw humans as just more meat to consume, and more fodder for increasing its own horde.

Bottom line, they either win the day, and eradicate the Wvrm, or the aliens would strike a beachhead, and from here go on to flood the city, then the country, and then the world.

If they did that, then one day the Wvrm may leave. But by then, the human race would just be a memory.

The first soldiers arrived at the ground floor, locked double doors, waited a few seconds as they scanned the inside, and then swiped a card key and the lock disengaged. Two of them held the doors wide, as the Special Force's soldiers entered fast.

The first and largest team going in was to look after the patients and staff. They approached with guns ready, fingers on triggers and pointed loosely at their targets, but their guns were not up and tight in their shoulders so as not to be overtly threatening.

Greg's team herded him toward the elevators and while they waited he watched briefly as the downstairs team organized the X-ray machines and already had the staff and patients lining up.

The technician started the devices, and a soldier stood by watching the results. Also standing ready was half a dozen other soldiers, some with flamethrowers, others with thermal grenades, and more with rifles carrying incendiary rounds.

Greg just hoped they never encountered one of the coalesced things, but a brutal and horrifying thought crossed his mind – what if they were already too late, and every single one of the people milling about was already infected, and they weren't dealing with a single adversary, but hundreds?

He shuddered and said a silent prayer – *something has got to damn well go our way*, he thought.

The first elevator contained Captain Moskovitz who had a direct line to Bowman, as did Greg. They would be heading to level five where the isolation units were, and where Brad was being held. The other elevators contained another team supporting them, and the rest would be going to the top level and working their way down.

Another team would be heading down to the multiple basements level that held an internal car park, generators, and storage areas. He didn't envy them, as this floor, according to the cameras and feedback, was the least well lit. He couldn't image trying to search for shape shifting monsters that want to eat and assimilate you, while doing it in shadowy darkness.

He scoffed. In fact, he didn't think searching anywhere right now for shape shifting monsters that want to eat and assimilate you would be a walk in the park.

The elevator pinged and he exited after several of the soldiers headed out first to check.

"Where to, Doc?" Moskovitz asked.

They all had seen the schematic, but he had been here before. It seemed strangely dumbfounding that it was only two days ago he had followed the gurney down the hallway, as they took his returned astronaut brother to the isolation wing. So much had changed in the short time, it tore at Greg's sanity.

Greg could only indicate the direction as he wasn't allowed to run point. Two large soldiers headed off, moving down each side of the blinding white corridor, hugging each wall, with him at the center of the armed group.

He pointed again and they entered through some double doors, and then came to the locked and hermetically sealed isolation unit.

"In there," Greg said.

Moskovitz nodded, and used the card key. The door's security lights went to green. The big guys at point pushed the doors open and went in with guns up.

To begin with it was empty and Moskovitz used hand signals as the team silently went through several rooms with significant equipment, and just as Morgan was wondering which room was his brother's, they came to one of the largest, and suddenly he didn't need to wonder anymore.

The room had been obliterated. The furniture, both wooden and steel, was broken, splintered, bent and crushed, and the fabric, probably from bedsheets and bandages, was shredded and strewn everywhere.

"Looks like this is where the party started." Moskovitz made more hand motions to his team who entered the room and spread out, checking under, and behind everything.

One of them slipped and nearly fell. The soldier immediately jumped to his feet and looked down.

"Got something on the floor here. Looks like slime," he said.

"Let me see that." Greg rushed over.

"Careful, that stuff is slippery as all hell." The soldier stood back.

Greg went down on one knee and saw the greenish mucous with streaks of red. It was just as Nina had described after they lost Jake and what was inside his brother's suit.

"What is it?" Moskovitz asked.

"Residue," Greg said and felt in his pocket for an ever present sample jar. He used a small wooden spatula to scoop some up. "If I had to guess, this is the byproduct of assimilation. When the Wvrm, the worms, are ingesting and converting a human being, it seems the creatures excrete this."

"So, they're eating us and shitting this greasy stuff out." Moskovitz shook his head. "Nasty."

Greg stood, screwing the lid shut on the sample jar. "This tells me that Brad is no longer alone. There's another of them. And for all we know there might be dozens."

"We expected this," Moskovitz said.

"Damn." Greg frowned and turned.

"What is it?" Moskovitz asked.

"We need a rollcall of who was working here, and line it up with who is downstairs right now. There'll either be people missing. Or we could have an infected lining up who needs to be isolated, and…"

"And fucking burned to ash, ASAP." Moskovitz clicked on his mic and talked rapidly.

***

Down in the main entrance hall area there were people sitting, standing in groups, and all waiting. They were disagreeable and understandably as the military was telling them nothing.

All they knew was that they had to wait and each of them would be getting a full body X-ray before they could go and get a cup of coffee. Or even go and take a damn leak.

Lieutenant Olsen was coordinating the forty men and women in the unit he had under his command, and so far, just through force of will, he was keeping a lid on any pushback, using terse language, the odd flash of humor, and his confident manner.

But the work was slow, each person taking many minutes to get X-rayed, and then the results examined while the rest were made to wait in line. At this rate, Olsen knew they'd be working on the group for at least a few more hours.

Olsen paced. His team were called The Reapers, all of them had combat experience and were prepared to do what it took to keep their country safe. But they were more at home out in some Middle Eastern desert, or swampy jungle than babysitting frustrated hospital patients.

He still couldn't get his head around the idea of their potential adversary being some sort of monster, or monsters, infiltrating the hospital. And he doubted it was real. But he knew Colonel Bowman, and for all the time he had known the man he had never looked worried. Until now. And that made Olsen wary.

He stopped pacing and turned to watch the X-ray team – the setup was like that in an airport, two columns, with people filing in, standing still for several seconds to get zapped, and then the wait for the results.

He watched for a moment and then saw a large woman in some sort of hazmat suit kept stepping out of line to let others go ahead of her. It was unusual as most people wanted to get it over with and head into the cafeteria they had set up to grab a coffee and donut.

Maybe the woman was just nervous about the machine. But if that was the case why the hell would you work in a hospital.

"*You.*" Olsen pointed at her, and she made eye contact with him. "You're next."

The woman didn't acknowledge him but just smiled and stepped up. She walked into the booth, and the technician began to gather the images. Standing behind him was Ellie Rodriguez.

The man frowned, and then craned forward. "What is this?"

Ellie was good. The best. And she reacted quickly.

"*We got one.*" She drew her handgun and gripped it two handed, pointing at the X-ray booth.

The large woman had gone in one side, but what came out the other side was a freaking nightmare.

Olsen had his gun up and sprinted to the X-ray chamber and the emerging monstrosity that looked like a large crab with sharp legs, and as he watched, more arms broke through her hazmat suit.

The biggest abomination was that the woman's head he had made eye contact with was stuck to the front, and still smiling.

People started screaming and running, and Olsen yelled without taking his eyes off the nightmarish creature.

"Get those people back in line." He started moving to Ellie. "And get me some fucking heat over here."

Ellie, being closest, was first to start firing. She was good. The best. But she made a mistake and pulled a gun that didn't have incendiary rounds – any other adversary, and her centering would have meant it went down fast. But she fired four times, each bullet a direct hit. And not one of them slowed it down a fraction.

It was too quick and came at her faster than she could react. It enveloped her, holding her in front of it. She squirmed, but it obviously knew what it was doing – using her as a shield.

Olsen lifted his rifle. He could take a shot but not a safe one. But then, as he watched, Ellie began to gag and cough, and when he concentrated, he saw what looked like tiny thread-like worms bleeding out of the thing and making their way into Ellie's eyes, nose, and mouth.

He remembered the report then – this was how they multiplied. He knew, and so did Ellie, that there was no cure, and no coming back.

The human head on the monstrosity swiveled to look at him, and it held Ellie up a little higher, this time not giving him a clean head or body shot.

"*Take it!*" Ellie screamed, and coughed again.

Olsen and just about every gun on the floor was now trained on the beast, but the thing kept her as a shield while it poured more of the worms into her.

Ellie was a Reaper, and knew what needed to be done. She dropped her weapon, pulled a thermal grenade and looked Olsen in the eye.

He nodded.

She became calm, and didn't hesitate. She pulled the pin, and stuffed it behind her back, up against the thing's revolting bulbous body. And hers. She then shut her eyes.

"*Fire in the hole!*" Olsen yelled and hit the deck.

Everyone threw themselves to the ground, even some of the hospital staff and patients, just as the grenade detonated in a searing orange plume. The thermal grenades weren't big percussion or fragmentation devices, instead they gave off a heat radius of around four thousand degrees, and could melt steel.

When Olsen looked up again, there was a pile of smoldering flesh in a crater on the ground. The creature was gone, and there was also nothing remaining of Ellie Rodriguez.

Olsen got to his feet, feeling weary, and as he turned away he saw one of his men standing nearby with a flamethrower.

He pointed to the pit. "Finish off everything in that pit that isn't charred or melted. Leave nothing."

His comm pinged and he lifted it to see it was an incoming from Captain Moskovitz.

"Sir," he said, his eyes on the gout of flame from the flamethrower bathing the pit.

Olsen nodded wearily as he heard the update that they expected there would be more infected amongst the hospital staff.

"We know, we've just encountered one. We took it out, but lost Rodriguez, sir," he sighed. "The upside is, they were spotted on X-ray just as Doctor Morgan said. And a thermal grenade turned it to molten shit. Not pretty but it works."

Moskovitz acknowledged the outcome and bid him to keep on his A-game as they still had no idea how many were infected, and who they were.

"Count on it, sir," Olsen said and the call disconnected.

He turned back to the assembled people, his anger building. "Everyone else, back in line. I want a ten foot spread between each person. Let's get this over with, *now*."

Suddenly, there were no complaints about seeing who was who. And every soldier there now knew what it was they were fighting.

***

Moskovitz turned to Greg Morgan.

"Something happened?" Greg asked.

"Yeah, they had an encounter, burned it down to shit," Moskovitz exhaled. "But lost a good soldier."

Greg nodded and opened his mouth for another question.

Moskovitz cut across him. "Picked it up on X-ray. Then it changed into some sort of big ugly half human bug thing. Thermal charge melted it. And the soldier who detonated it." He bared his teeth for a moment. "We need better intel."

"That's why we're here. We're the ones gathering it," Greg replied.

"Clear," came the call from one of the soldiers up ahead in the isolation chambers. "Party has gone elsewhere."

"Okay people, we go room by room. Delta team just had an encounter down on ground floor." Moskovitz' eyes were filled with fury. "Ugly was neutralized by heat. But we lost a soldier. I do not like that equation," he said. "Anyone we encounter is to be kept at arm's length until we determine who or what they are. If they try and come at us, we send them to hell. Clear?"

"*HUA!*" came the reply.

They then headed further down the corridor – they had dozens of rooms left to investigate, and many more floors. So far their progress had been good.

And then the lights went out.

"*Fuck!*" Moskovitz seethed. "Could it be that smart?"

"Yes," Greg said. "It or they, know we're looking for them. They're not going to make it easy for us."

"Of course not," Moskovitz scoffed. "Where's the Gen?"

Greg looked at the schematic. "In the basement."

"Where team bravo is," Moskovitz said.

"Call em?" Greg asked.

"No. I'll send an update on Reaper team's encounter, but they'll know by now the lights are out and to get them back on. I also think they shouldn't be distracted right now as if it's down in the basement, and our team is down in the basement, things are about to get nasty down there."

CHAPTER 33

Andrea Bennings lifted a fist in the air, and her team froze, waiting on her as she quickly read the information squirt from Moskovitz. Their helmet beams cut the stygian darkness with pipes of white light but still left far too many shadows.

She had a team of a dozen heavily armed special forces, and all had been in various hot zones over the years. She herself had been one of the first spotter teams dropped into Syria before they targeted the Damascus Air Force base.

"Jesus," she whispered and looked up at her team. "Reapers just had an encounter – one ugly down, and we lost a soldier. Everyone, eyes open."

She turned slowly. Bennings had seen action, as bloody and brutal as it came, and was said to have nerves of steel. But right now, she felt the cold fingers of fear on the back of her neck.

She checked the schematic; place was a fucking rabbit warren, and after they had checked the underground car park, they were now cleaning the sub rooms, pump rooms, and garbage areas. All that was suddenly on hold until they found out what had happened to the generator.

"It's a trap," the hugely muscled Bilson said from beside her.

"No shit," Bennings replied. "And one we got no choice but to walk into face first. We need them fucking lights on." She turned.

Jenny Alvarez, their specialist, turned about. "Plus the X-ray machines don't work, and we know they can detect the Wvrm. We need them."

"Maybe that's why they shut em down." Bennings motioned forward. "Move out. Slow and quiet."

The two lines of soldiers moved forward in a semi crouch with rifles up. At the rear were two men carrying flamethrower packs.

They passed rooms containing hospital bio-waste, and cages that contained overflowing bins full of paper. The humidity with the air con dying was off the charts and the smell alternated from rank shittiness to engine oil.

"Up ahead," Bilson said.

At the end of the concrete corridor their lights found the door to the generator room. Over their heads huge pipes ran back and forth, and Bennings saw that there was another side door just before they got to their main game.

"Secure that," she said, and two men moved forward, as the rest of her bravo squad waited.

The two got to the side door, and on the count of three, pushed it open, shone lights inside, and then went in.

In moments more they returned.

"Spare parts and tool shed," one of the men said.

"Good, we may need them." She motioned forward.

Bennings took one last look up, back, and around, looking for potential ambush points, but it seemed like they had concrete at the backs, overhead, and sides. She didn't like how cramped it was, but that meant at least if something came at them, it came at them head on, and not from multiple sides at once.

"Bilson, Vasquez, take point." She turned to one of the flamethrower guys. "Nomad, you're up."

Jenny Alvarez stepped forward. "I should go as well."

"All in good time," Bennings replied. "Let the bulls clear the room first." She turned to her point team. "Go."

Big Jim Bilson, and Salvi Vasquez went to each side of the door, with Frank 'Nomad' Nomes just behind them.

His flamethrower was one of the new variations, that was smaller, more compact, and didn't need a permanently burning pilot light – it ignited as the special mix of flammable liquids was ejected, and that could be up to forty feet.

Salvi Vasquez turned. "Just don't fucking burn me, man. I got a date this weekend." She grinned as Bilson counted down.

He got to zero, muscled open the door, and went in fast.

***

Bilson went left, Vasquez right, and Nomad went in and waited just inside the doorway covering their asses.

Nomad could tell the room was big by the echo that bounced back at them. From what he could see in their lights it housed two diesel generators; the main one looked like it should be sitting on an old fashioned tractor. And a smaller one to kick in if the primary big one failed. They looked robust, tough, and should be reliable. But he knew that both of them being out was no freak accident.

Light beams swung about, but there were too many hiding places, and after a few minutes, Bilson touched his earpiece.

"No initial contact. No sign of overt damage. Send in the engineers to check the gens over. Out."

"Roger that," came the reply, and immediately more lights joined theirs as two engineers came in fast, with four extra soldiers as support.

Bilson positioned the extra soldiers close to the engineers to give them cover as they worked. He and Vasquez had eyes on the engineers, and the others were facing outwards, covering the basement quadrants. Nomad stood with his back against a wall, watching them all.

"Yep, busted up, but repairable," Quincy, the senior engineer said, who was working on the main generator. He spoke into a mic, telling one of the other soldiers outside what he needed – new cable, and two large socket heads.

Quincy turned to his partner. "Jackson, what've you got?" he asked the man working on the backup generator.

Jackson stopped what he was doing. "Can't see any external damage, but the turbine is refusing to move." He slid out from underneath the backup machine. "Gotta take the casing off."

Quincy thought for a second – it was a bit of work to take the casing off.

And if they got the main gen back up, then the backup was just a nice to have. But if they left it, then of course, they had no backup parachute if the big guy fell over again.

"Do it. Let's see what you got to work with. If it's quickly repairable, we do it. If not, we leave it," he said.

"On it." Jackson immediately began unfastening the casing rivets.

***

Bennings and Alvarez joined them and left two soldiers outside to cover the door. Bennings had been getting updates from the other teams and she was doing the same for them. She already knew about the attack in the entrance area, and the loss of Rodriguez.

Right now, every team was sweating on the generators being up and running as the darkness was increasing every team's risk profiles.

She watched as Quincy spliced in the cable and socket plugs and gave the main generator a final look over – progress was good. She then turned to see Jackson finally getting the shielding plate removed and lifting the large, curved piece of steel.

He looked inside.

"*Jesus Christ,*" he whispered as he backed up a step.

"What's happening, soldier?" Bennings' brows came together.

Quincy joined him and saw what he did. "Got a body here."

Bennings came forward and peered in, feeling a sense of horror when she saw the mangled body in there, squashed in tight and looking like it had done a few rounds with the moving turbines. The broken and splintered bones had jammed up the works.

"Where's all the blood?" Bennings asked.

She also noted that the flesh was a greyish-white and not the red-pink of a normal freshly opened corpse. There was also a strange medicinal smell coming off the body.

"I don't think this person was killed recently," Bilson said.

Captain Bennings came closer and shone her light into the turbine. After a moment she grunted. "Grey meat. This is an old body, and that smell is the antiseptic wash they use on bodies in the morgue." She turned to pace away, thinking for a moment.

"Why would someone jam a corpse in the backup generator?" Alverez asked.

Bennings stopped and turned, noting all her team, their placement, and where they were focused. "Because we're all looking at it." She spun away. "Quincy, fire up the generator and give us some situational lighting."

Quincy switched on the repaired main generator, and as it whined to its full rotational speed, the lights overhead began to blink, softly glow, and then move to full brightness.

And that's when they saw – it had been a trap all along – the walls and ceiling were covered in what looked like a thin layer of small hairs, that rippled and twitched.

And they were all alive, their dot-like heads pointed down as if they were watching and waiting, perhaps for a sign or instruction, because as soon as they knew they were seen, they attacked.

They began to shower down and come down from the walls to create a flood of squirming bodies, all heading for the humans.

Bennings had her team fall back into a defensive ring. And then. *"FTs; light em up!"*

Twin gouts of flame came from the nozzles of the flamethrowers, and thousands, hundreds of thousands of the worms things were incinerated.

Bennings saw that the data they got in the briefings held true – individually the worms were extremely vulnerable and relied more on getting on and then in a human body quickly. If they didn't, they were as good as dead.

"Keep it up," Bennings yelled over the roar of the flames, and the stink of the greasy black smoke. "No weapons firing or thermal grenades; we need that generator in one piece."

The worms began to pull back like a wave, and suddenly they formed up into a massive arthropod thing that had a segmented, armored shell, waving tentacles at front, but also several half-human bodies rising from its top.

"It's clumping," Alvarez yelled.

"Give it a bath," Bennings yelled.

The flamethrowers both focused their streams of liquid fire on the monstrosity, and the massive thing, now with the added collective muscle, used it, and battered down a rear door and dragged its bulk through, splintering the wood and even tearing metal away. And then it was gone.

A few soldiers went after it.

"Hold there!" Bennings yelled.

The senior officer needed to assess her team's status before going after the thing.

"Sound off. Let me know if we have any injuries or infections." She walked amongst them as they checked their clothing and skin.

Two soldiers who had been underneath the falling worms saw that a few of the threads remained on their hazmat-covered bodies. Bennings had them line up and called to her flamethrower guy.

"Nomad, give em a quick wash."

The man grinned as he pointed the nozzle at them. "Sorry boys, but just remember; this hurts me a lot more than it hurts you." He began to laugh as he turned the flame on them.

The flames just briefly ran over their bodies, just enough to vaporize any worms, but not quite enough to burn the men or melt their suits. However, it would have still been painful. Bennings was delighted to see both solders took it without a word.

In seconds it was over.

"Anyone else?" she asked.

When there were no takers she walked back to Jenny Alvarez. "Okay, Ms. Specialist, your assessment of what just happened."

Jenny nodded. "It set a trap for us. Lured us in and kept us occupied."

"I know that. And we got lucky that the main gen could be repaired so quickly. In the dark we couldn't see the little bastards." She turned back. "What else?"

"We confirmed they don't like heat. We can use that," Alverez said.

"Good. How?" Bennings waited.

Alvarez seemed to think for a moment, and then clicked her fingers. "Got it." She folded her arms. "It prefers the cold and doesn't like heat. So, now that the generator is working again we crank up the internal temperature to its maximum. I think that's around a hundred and ten-degrees," Alverez said. "It came from a cold world; it won't like that."

"Yeah, I won't like it either. What else?" Bennings asked.

"We drive it towards somewhere that will remain cool. Even as everywhere else gets hot. Someplace I'm betting it already knows," Jenny smiled.

"It already knows?" Bennings' brows knitted but then began to ease. She half smiled and thumbed at the backup generator. "That body..."

Alverez nodded. "It must have been in the morgue. It's a giant freezer. The only place that will stay cool."

Bennings nodded and smiled. "You ain't bad, kid." She turned. "Quincy, crank the heat up, it's time we gave this monster a sauna bath."

She turned back. "Tell your boss it's about to get real hot and we have a plan. I'll tell mine."

***

Greg Morgan and Captain Moskovitz got the update at the same time. Both glanced at each other, and Moskovitz raised his eyebrows.

"Do you think it'll work?" he asked.

"Good a plan as any. The Wvrm have fully adapted to the Europa environment of between two-twenty to two-fifty degrees below zero. They'll evolve to acclimatize over time on Earth, but for now, they do not like heat."

"Yeah, I get that," Moskovitz replied.

"I think if we can herd them toward the morgue freezer, we have a good chance of trapping them, it, in there. And kill it." Greg looked up. "Or it might try and get out. Better tell your people on the ground floor to be on guard for a possible breakout." He looked up. "You know what? Tell your teams outside to also be ready. This thing might just decide to throw itself out the window. It'd probably survive."

"On it." Moskovitz made some calls, and Greg looked up at one of the air vents. He felt the breeze on his face, and it was turning warm, very warm, in fact it reminded him of when you take a peek in the oven and get a blast of hot dry air in the face.

Moskovitz rang off and turned to his team. "Alright, listen up, people. We have had a second engagement. The first was in the ground floor area after a single lifeform entity was detected by the X-ray machines. The second just now was in the generator room in the basement, where they were ambushed by the lifeform who set a trap and had spread themselves all over the ceilings and walls like butter. They were invisible in the dark."

He shared a brutal smile. "I'm happy to say we suffered no casualties this time, and we beat the monstrosities back using the flamethrowers." He looked along the line of granite tough faces. Moskovitz knew that each and every one of them would go to the mat for what they believed in. And right now this was their fork in the road moment – they won here, or they all lost – the stakes couldn't be higher.

"We have a plan," he said. "We are going to raise the temperature in here, so it gets unpleasant to both us and the Wvrm. Then aim to trap it in the morgue cold room. Then fry it to ash." He smiled flatly. "Questions?"

"Will the lifeform comply?" one of the female soldiers asked.

"We're going to give it a little incentive. The morgue is in the sub-basement. Just up from the car park and generator room. The delta team will be herding it upwards. We are going to put downward pressure on it. We leave it one place and one place only to go – somewhere nice, dark, and cool." He waited a few seconds and then turned to Greg. "Doctor?"

All eyes turned to Greg Morgan. "This can work. We trap it inside the insulated cold room and incinerate it. We finish it here, and we win."

"You heard the man. Time to win." Moskovitz clapped his hands once. "Let's go. Mr. Henrikson, Ms. Jenson, take us out."

The group headed for the stairwell as the elevators had been disengaged as the power went out and hadn't rebooted. There were two sets of stairs on the east and west side, and Moskovitz split his team in two so they could cover both, with both teams leading with a flamethrower.

They had to drop down three floors, and Greg stopped at the first, knowing they'd need to check each one. And he knew that meant a lot of time and risk. Frankly, once they had all their people out, accounted for, and checked, they should seal it off, and incinerate the whole fucking place, he thought.

He was now aware of how cunning the lifeform was, and he also knew that a single worm could infect a human. The only saving grace was the worms needed to band together for safety and strength. Also, they seemed to be almost mindless biological entities when free of a mass clumping, but as a collective they could access the intelligence from the animals they had absorbed and digested. And perhaps from somewhere else. And that bothered him.

"Doctor, a question." Moskovitz walked to the side and Greg Morgan followed.

"We both now know that this thing when massed together can use intelligence. But I don't really get how that works." Moskovitz grimaced. "I just have the feeling we're missing something here."

Greg nodded. "I know, me too. But I have a theory."

Moskovitz scoffed. "Jesus man, let me have it."

"Okay." Greg rubbed at his chin. "You know how some insect colonies have hundreds or thousands of worker and warrior caste? Basically they're mindless drones. But they can and do organize."

"Yeah." Moskovitz turned. "You think these lifeforms are like that?"

"Maybe," Greg replied. "But the thing that is organizing them is a queen, or high ranking lifeform. It's bigger, smarter, and lives longer than all the other caste insects. For all intents and purposes, it is the hive's brain."

"An external hive brain," Moskovitz exhaled. "Then we've definitely got to find where that bastard is."

Greg nodded. "For all I know, we destroy it, and that turns all the other Wvrm back into being just another dumb worm."

"I like the sound of that." Moskovitz turned back to the stairwell. "Let's get this done."

It took them another five minutes to get to the sub-basement doors, and then coordinating with the opposite team, they came in fast.

Moskovitz also had Bennings' team channeled in, and the three groups made their way to the morgue.

By now, each and every man and woman was bathed in perspiration. It wasn't just warm, but searingly hot.

There was a long and wide corridor leading to the morgue and the teams joined up at either end.

"I got nothing," Moskovitz said as he checked motion sensors.

"It can't have got by us," Greg said.

"Unless it climbed into an airduct." Moskovitz turned to one of his team, who quickly read data off a device.

"I've got no movement in there." The soldier shook his head. "This air con system has pressure sensors. Anything climbs in there we'd know about it."

"Besides, I would think the steel inside would be like a frying pan right now. Doubt the Wvrm could take it," Greg replied.

"We've checked every room, closet, every inch, and so far, nothing." He put his hands on his hips and turned slowly.. "Means it can only be in one place…" he stopped cold, "… it's already inside the damn morgue."

The teams joined up on either side of the large white double push doors. Moskovitz made hand signals, and the flamethrower guys came up.

He counted down – Three. Two. One…

They went in fast.

***

The outer room was cooler, but the huge steel door was closed.

Lined up close to each other along one of the walls were gurneys, each carrying a sheeted body.

"These bodies should be in the cool room," Moskovitz said. "Looks like something was making a little more room for itself."

"Maybe," Greg replied.

Moskovitz nodded, and one of his soldiers went and grabbed the handle on the huge steel door.

The team leader counted down on his fingers and then pointed. The man dragged open the door to the cool room with every weapon they had pointed.

At least there was light in there. And once again there were bodies inside, and the draft of cool air could be felt even right through their toughened hazmat suits that had their insides now slick with sweat.

Moskovitz pulled back. "Did we miss it again?"

There were around ten soldiers crowding the morgue room, with the rest remaining outside.

Moskovitz lowered his weapon. "Check those bodies. Check everything."

The soldiers set to working rapidly and expertly, and in a few minutes were satisfied they had nothing but corpses. They looked around, and then a thought snuck into Greg's head – *why were there bodies kept outside of the cool room then?* There was plenty of room inside.

He eased out of the cool room and turned slowly. He saw the row of gurneys hard up against each other, touching, and a strange lumpiness between them. It was almost as if…

"It's here!" Greg yelled and pointed at the gurneys.

The men spun just as the sheets literally blew off the bodies and the thing underneath rose up – it was like a long centipede with multiple human heads on the length of the body, and the ghastly visage of Commander Brad Morgan's at the front.

Before their eyes the lifeform changed and altered, perhaps trying to make a more formidable version of itself. Small waving hairs drew back into it as the skin or carapace hardened. Tentacles slithered out from its sides, each one finishing in a wicked-looking hook or claw.

Men yelled, Moskovitz barked orders, bullets flew, and gouts of flame shot out.

Greg ducked as the flames passed over his head, and in the small room they raised the temperature so much he felt it scalding his skin.

But the Wvrm had tasted the pain of the fire before, and this time it used speed, evasive action, and the men themselves as a barrier between it and the heat of the fire. Its long body quickly encircled the room keeping the soldiers at the center. It also blocked the only door to the outside.

Men were grabbed in claws or long tentacles, and crushed, their bodies being squeezed into paste inside their suits.

The Wvrm creature first went for the flamethrower operators, ducking under the fire, and smashing into them with blows that broke bones and lacerated flesh. Every time an incendiary round struck it, it shed the piece of flesh to allow it to burn freely while not corrupting the rest of the long body. And Moskovitz knew they couldn't use the thermal grenades inside the enclosed space.

For Greg the most horrifying aspect was seeing his brother's face, calmly taking in the death and destruction as if he was simply having a day out at the park.

Moskovitz roared orders, but his men were being worn down, and soon there was just three of them left – Greg, Moskovitz, and Bennings who stood in front of them, rifle up – of the nearly twenty men and women they had brought with them.

They backed up against a wall. The massive creature also paused, and Greg Morgan couldn't tear his eyes away from the sight of his brother's head on top of the thing. It now swiveled to them, its expression still calm. And then chillingly, it smiled.

Greg sighed, knowing the end game was here. He turned to face Moskovitz, keeping his back to the creature.

"When we're inside, shut the door." He then reached forward to grab two of the thermal grenades on his belt and stuffed them in his pockets. "It ends here. It has to."

Moskovitz looked about to say something, but then his mouth snapped shut, and he just nodded, understanding.

He gripped Greg's forearm. "Good luck, and God speed."

Greg then turned back and calmy walked toward the morgue door and went in, standing just inside. He then turned to face the beast. His eyes never wavered as he undid the hazmat suit locks and pushed the helmet back. That was followed by peeling himself out of the entire suit.

Underneath, his clothing was drenched in perspiration, but he felt it cool and dry quickly from the freezing morgue room. The last thing he did was reach down to grab and secrete the thermal grenades in his pocket and then he straightened, and held his arms outstretched.

"I missed you, Brad." He smiled. "I have so much to show you. And tell you."

He began to back into the cool room. "If you want to assimilate me, here I am. My flesh, my mind, and my memories, and all my knowledge. Come and feast. And learn."

The great beast began to unlock its sharp legs from where they had dug into the wall, and it slithered down like a giant centipede. However, it paused and on the hard segments of its back, all the human heads turned to glare back at Bennings and Moskovitz. The huge pincers snapped in the air as a warning.

"I give you my word they won't hurt you," Greg said. "Not while I'm with you."

After another second or two, the thing headed for the freezer door.

Moskovitz didn't move a muscle and just followed it with his eyes. In front of him the muzzle of Bennings' rifle slowly came up.

"Hold your ground, soldier," he whispered to her.

Bennings gripped her rifle so hard, he heard her gloves start to squeak from the pressure. But she did as ordered.

The massive lifeform got its front end inside, but there was another twenty feet of it still sticking out through the heavy steel door. Moskovitz knew unless it went all the way in, their plan would fail. He also tried to work out how to get the man out while keeping the monster in.

But he wasn't sure that was part of Greg's plan. He knew that brave men did things that made them brave men.

The Wvrm took another step forward.

Come on, he whispered. *Just a little more.*

***

Greg saw the huge thing fill the doorway and felt his stomach flip from fear.

How did this happen? he wondered. *How did we get from an exploration voyage of discovery to a frozen moon 390-million miles away, to suddenly standing in a hospital morgue freezer, about to fight a monster for the future of our planet?*

He tried to only focus on the eerie head and face of his brother growing out of the top of the thing.

"Dad still thinks you're a hero, Brad," Greg Morgan said. "I know there is a tiny fragment of you living inside the cells of the Wvrm. They have you trapped in there, forever, a passenger who can only watch as the horrors unfold around you," he said. "Nina is in there too. And Eddy, Heather, and the entire Traveler team." He sighed. "I'm so sorry."

He backed up some more.

The creature followed.

"It's cool in here, isn't it? Allows us to think, and talk," Greg smiled.

"I like this world," Brad Morgan's head said. "So much meat. So much intelligence to absorb."

"Ah, but it's unearned intelligence, isn't it? You never strived for knowledge, you simply eat and absorb it." Greg backed up some more and the thing followed again. "Means you won't know what to do with it."

The massive thing lifted up and its front bloomed open, making a hole in the body. Greg saw that there was something in there; it looked like a yellow sack that pulsated with its own revolting life.

"So, that's who and what you really are," Greg said softly.

"I am the Wvrm." The sack rippled and pulsated as veins ran across it. "I can adapt. And grow. And expand our reach," Brad Morgan's head said. "The previous race that existed on Europa underestimated us as well. But I absorbed them, and now they mostly live inside us."

"Mostly?" Greg looked up.

"Some chose to live in the oceans. A place we have no interest in."

"A place you can't get to." Greg backed up another step.

The massive lifeform closed the hole over the brain thing and dropped down. It followed.

"You've stored all that knowledge. But you're like a library, because you have it, but will never really understand it, and that is the key to everything. Hubris and ego are your fatal flaws," Greg said, feeling his stomach roil in anticipation of what was to come.

Greg stopped and looked up at the thing filling one half of the freezing room. "Brad, I know you can hear me. They're going to tell Dad you died a hero. On a space mission of exploration," he said. "And I died here. But he'll never know we died together."

"But Commander Brad Morgan is not fully dead. He is in here, with us." Brad's face was as dead and cold as a fish. "Would you like to see?"

Immediately Brad Morgan's expression changed. He looked around as though seeing things for the first time. He looked down, and suddenly his eyes went wide and he began to scream.

"Stop it," Greg Morgan said softly.

Brad Morgan heard the voice and focused on him. "Greg, what's happening?"

Brad began to cry. Deep wracking sobs that ripped at Greg's soul.

"You're a fucking abomination. An infection on all worlds," Greg Morgan spoke through gritted teeth. "The universe will be happy to see you gone."

Brad Morgan's expression changed to one of disinterest. "You'll be joining us soon. And there's nothing you can do about it."

Greg Morgan backed up a little more, and the beast followed.

Almost there, he thought.

"There's something you don't understand about human beings," Greg said and touched his chest. "This lifeform loves life, human beings, loves freedom. And will sacrifice itself for the good of others." Greg Morgan started breathing heavily.

He backed up and kept going into the rear of the freezer.

"We also love life. But we love to consume it," the Brad Morgan monstrosity said. "Let it be so." The great creature began to flow forward.

And then it was all the way in. Immediately the heavy steel freezer door clanged shut behind it, and Brad Morgan's head and all the other heads swung around to stare at the door.

"This is where it ends," Greg said softly.

When the multiple disembodied heads swung back, Greg Morgan stood there with a thermal grenade in each hand. The initiators had already been charged.

"Hell is cold. But this won't be."

The massive lifeform roared as the detonation turned the entire freezer into a furnace of boiling plasma, rising to four thousand degrees in a single second.

***

Bennings snatched her hands away from the steel door as it became white hot. Both she and Moskovitz backed up as the heavy frame thumped and swelled but held as the fortified and insulated steel room took the full thermal blast force.

"Thank you, Doctor Morgan," Moskovitz whispered.

He waited several minutes as he and Bennings just stared, watching the door. She had her gun up.

More soldiers joined them after being dispatched from the ground floor team and stood ready to help. They tried to ignore the massacre around them and focused on the heat-discolored morgue door.

Moskovitz turned. "Flamethrowers up." He waited until three men were beside him with the units held ready.

He continued to face the door. "There shouldn't be anything left alive in there, but I want you to incinerate every fucking thing. Every nook and cranny, every stick of furniture, every scrap of potential biological material. Then, and only then, I might be able to sleep tonight."

They needed crowbars to lever the door open, and once done black smoke billowed out. Lights were shone inside, and Moskovitz nodded his satisfaction – the room had been obliterated.

But he wasn't paid to guess. He turned to his flamethrower operators. "Go."

In they went, and in seconds, the room was filled with the bloom of orange flames.

EPILOGUE

Russian Far East, Amur Oblast – Vostochny Cosmodrome Launch Center
Vladimir Volkov paced as the countdown commenced.

After a moment he stopped and turned again to face the launch pad some two miles away; close by normal standards of safety distances.

He marveled again at the massive rocket – The *Svyatogor*, the name of a Russian giant from folklore. The name meant 'sacred mountain', as was this massive ship. It was a giant disc, but had a detachable carriage ringing its perimeter with three huge boosters which would lift it up and away from the grip of Earth's mighty gravitational pull.

The new drives would get the craft and its half dozen astronauts to its objective faster than the previous space mission, this time taking just eight months to their destination – the icy moon of Europa.

The crew would still need to go into hibernation that allowed them to reduce the amount of food and water required. But once there, they were to locate the Georgy Zhukov, the missing craft that landed perfectly, had commenced its mission investigation, but then went dark with some chaotic and rambling return messages.

If there were survivors they would be brought home. And if not, then their bodies would be brought back for hero funerals and to give their families some peace of mind.

Volkov had a personal interest – his son, Mikhail, had been one of the crew aboard the Georgy Zhukov. As a father, he had been explosively proud when telling people his son was on the first mission to the ends of the solar system.

He and his son knew the risks, but he always thought he'd come home.

And then his son and the Georgy Zhukov just vanished from their screens.

nol', startovat' – zero, blastoff!

Volkov lifted his powerful field glasses, drew in a deep breath, and let it out. He watched the massive round ship lift straight up with the assistance of the three powerful boosters. They created a cloud of burning exhaust around the ship, obscuring it for several seconds, before the ship lifted above it.

Volkov knew the captain of the *Svyatogor* personally, Alexi Mironov, a good man, honorable and extremely competent. He and his team would not rest until they found the missing crew and what happened to them.

Volkov folded his arms. "Find my boy, Alexi. Find them all and bring them home."

The End

Checkout other great books by bestselling author

Greig Beck

PRIMORDIA: IN SEARCH OF THE LOST WORLD

Ben Cartwright, former soldier, home to mourn the loss of his father stumbles upon cryptic letters from the past between the author, Arthur Conan Doyle and his great, great grandfather who vanished while exploring the Amazon jungle in 1908. Amazingly, these letters lead Ben to believe that his ancestor's expedition was the basis for Doyle's fantastical tale of a lost world inhabited by long extinct creatures. As Ben digs some more he finds clues to the whereabouts of a lost notebook that might contain a map to a place that is home to creatures that would rewrite everything known about history, biology and evolution. But other parties now know about the notebook, and will do anything to obtain it. For Ben and his friends, it becomes a race against time and against ruthless rivals. In the remotest corners of Venezuela, along winding river trails known only to lost tribes, and through near impenetrable jungle, Ben and his novice team find a forbidden place more terrifying and dangerous than anything they could ever have imagined.

THE FOSSIL

Klaus and Doris have just made the discovery of their lives – a complete Neanderthal skeleton buried in a newly opened sinkhole. But on removing it, something else tumbles free. Something that switches on, and then calls home.Soon the owners are coming back, and nothing will stop their ruthless search for their lost prize. Gruesome corpses begin to pile up, and Detective Ed Heisner of the Berlin Police is assigned to a case like nothing he has ever experienced before in his life. Heisner must stay one step ahead of a group of secretive Special Forces soldiers also tracking the strange device, while trying to find an unearthly group of killers that are torturing, burning, and obliterating their victims all the way across the city.THE FOSSIL is a time jumping detective novella where humans soon find that time can be the greatest weapon of all.* THE FOSSIL first appeared in SNAFU No.1 (2014) as a short story. Due to numerous requests, it has now been expanded and released here in its complete, stand-alone novella form.

Checkout other great books by bestselling author

Greig Beck

TO THE CENTER OF THE EARTH

An old woman locked away in a Russian asylum has a secret—knowledge of a 500-year-old manuscript written by a long-dead alchemist that will show a passage to the mythical center of the Earth.She knows it's real because 50 years ago, she and a team traveled there. And only she made it back. Today, caving specialist Mike Monroe leads a crew into the world's deepest cave in the former Soviet Union. He's following the path of a mad woman, and the words of an ancient Russian alchemist, that were the basis of the fantastical tale by Jules Verne.But what horrifying things he finds will tear at his sanity and change everything we know about evolution and the world, forever.In the tradition of Primordia, Greig Beck delivers another epic retelling of a classic story in an electrifying and terrifying adventure that transcends the imagination."Down there, beyond the deepest caves, below the crust and the mantle, there is another world."

THE SIBERIAN INCIDENT

100,000 years ago the object hit the lake at the deepest point, quickly sinking into its mile-deep stygian darkness. With it came something horrifying that would threaten every living thing on the face of the planetOver the centuries, legends grew of people vanishing, of strange, deformed animals, and of an unexplained luminescence down in the lake depths.When Marcus Stenson won the lucrative contract to create a sturgeon fish farm on the site of disused paper mill on the shore of Lake Baikal, he thought he had hit the jackpot. He refused to listen to the chilling folktales, or even be concerned by the occasional harassment from the local mafia. But then animals were found mutilated in the frozen forest, and people started to go missing. And worse, some came back, changed, horribly.In the depths of the lake, something unearthly that had been waiting 100,000 years was stirring. And mankind will become nothing more than a host.THE SIBERIAN INCIDENT - a tale of invasive Alien Horror from international best selling author, Greig Beck.

www.ingramcontent.com/pod-product-compliance
Lightning Source LLC
Chambersburg PA
CBHW071506170626
46811CB00007B/2747